Praise for *Angel of Death*

3—

"The novel displays the strong narrative and compelling characters that make it Brandon at his best."

—*Houston Chronicle*

"The story line is fast-paced and moving and filled with action that occasionally overwhelms the poignancy of the tale. . . . This novel is one of the subgenre's best books of the year."

—*Midwest Book Review*

"Jay Brandon . . . continues to turn out some of the best legal thrillers in an increasingly popular genre. . . . Once again, Brandon builds his story to a dynamite ending. . . . Surprising to most readers. "

—*Amarillo Globe-News*

"Brandon's taut legal thriller . . . provides vibrant local color and legal detail for both trial sequences. . . . Suspenseful."

—*Publishers Weekly*

"Brandon has crafted an exciting combination of courtroom drama and psycho thriller. . . . Solid. . . . Fresh and always mysterious enough to keep readers turning the pages. Sure to be popular with the legal thriller crowd."

—*Library Journal*

"Politician, polemicist, power-figure Malachi Reese is black, charismatic as they come, and only slightly less scary than Hannibal Lecter. . . . Brandon will have you eagerly turning pages."

—*Kirkus Reviews*

"This is a legal thriller that should strike home. . . . Brandon's courtroom scenes are in top form. . . . Brandon puts San Antonio to good use. . . . Accurately described. . . . Local readers will feel at home. . . . Well portrayed. . . . Brandon's prose flows smoothly and carries the plot's conflicts along. . . . An explosive finish."

—*San Antonio Express-News*

P9-CAL-559

Angel *of* Death

Jay Brandon

FORGE®

A TOM DOHERTY ASSOCIATES BOOK
NEW YORK

ANGEL OF DEATH

A Forge Book
Published by Tom Doherty Associates, LLC
175 Fifth Avenue
New York, NY 10010

Forge® is a registered trademark of Tom Doherty Associates, LLC.

ISBN: 0-812-54043-3
Library of Congress Catalog Card Number: 98-21181

First edition: November 1998
First mass market edition: December 1999

Printed in the United States of America

0 9 8 7 6 5 4 3 2 1

This book is dedicated to my longtime friend
Jake Beasley,
in whose former condo Chris Sinclair lives,
and to Rick Casey,
columnist extraordinaire.

Angel *of* Death

Chapter 1

If the months of the year were put on parade in San Antonio, Texas, and a popular vote taken, April would undoubtedly emerge as the hands-down favorite. April brings both the sweetest weather and the biggest parties of the year. But this April felt more like June in the steadiness of its heat, and on this particular April morning an unusual tension augmented the heat. Strangers in the normally friendly city were less likely to greet one another on the street. Instead there were wary, sidelong glances, and strollers downtown walked to their cars a little faster.

At the center of this uneasiness stood the Bexar County Justice Center, the criminal courthouse on the edge of downtown. There the tension went undisguised. Protestors in front of the building carried signs. Occasionally one shouted angrily. The protestors were dwarfed by the imposing five-story stone building, but employees in the building felt their presence. Guards at the entrance of the Justice Center watched the protestors with hands resting on gun butts.

Inside the building the tension hung in the air like an odor. It emanated from a third-floor courtroom. The courtroom couldn't accommodate everyone who had wanted to watch the trial in progress. Some of the people who had been turned away milled in the hallway, waiting with the television cameramen and sometimes standing on tiptoes to try to get a glimpse through the glass doors of the court.

Inside the courtroom, spectators sat packed shoulder to shoulder. The judge and the armed bailiffs had shushed the crowd more than once, and no one spoke, they strained to hear the witnesses and the lawyers. But the mere breathing of so many people created a low background noise in the courtroom.

At the front of the courtroom the District Attorney of Bexar County, Chris Sinclair, shook his head and said, "No more questions, your Honor." Seconds later the judge's gavel banged down, declaring a long lunch recess.

Chris spoke briefly to his assistant, then stood and turned toward the courtroom's exit. He reached the gate in the railing just as the defendant did. For a moment the two men looked at each other. An alert newspaper photographer brought up his camera and snapped a photo of the two that would soon become famous.

The picture was brilliant in its contrasts: Chris Sinclair the fresh, steady District Attorney who looked too young to have been a trial lawyer for almost fifteen years. He had been elected District Attorney only six months earlier. A newspaper columnist had dubbed the Christian Sinclair campaign "Blond Ambition," and had gone on to say, "His name looks as good on the ballot as his face does on billboards." Chris had come out of nowhere as far as the public was concerned when he had announced his candidacy, but he had surprised himself by being a good campaigner, thoughtful and confidence-inspiring. But first, as many lawyers in San Antonio would ruefully acknowledge, he was a damned good trial lawyer. He had proven that again in one trial since his election, but this current trial was very different. The prosecution of Malachi Reese was being argued throughout the city. Events in the courtroom cast much larger shadows across the city. Major consequences waited to pounce on the outcome of the trial.

The defendant stood close to the District Attorney at the gate in the railing: older, African-American, looking confidently but curiously into his persecutor's eyes. And clearly many saw Malachi Reese as the persecuted, as a black man being unjustly attacked by a white establishment for which Christian Sinclair served as the perfect poster boy.

After that one frozen moment Malachi Reese smiled cordially and held the gate open. Chris went through it and made his way through the crowd. Reese followed more slowly, stopping to receive the encouragement of his supporters and to talk to the many reporters.

Malachi Reese had *not* come out of nowhere to be the center of attention at his own trial. For the average citizen of San Antonio Reese fulfilled the definition of local celebrity: he was well-known for being well-known. People recognized him as having been a part of the fabric of public life for some years, without being able to pin down why or since when. Though active in community groups and responsible for several successful political campaigns, Reese had never run for office himself. Mostly he moved in the background of committees and conferences, but when he did step forward he drew attention. When he served as a spokesman he exhibited the authority and confidence of a leader. People nodded along as he spoke. Even in confrontation, he retained his composure. In the battlefields of emotion, no one wielded logic more forcefully than Malachi Reese.

Reese had brought those same skills to his trial for capital murder. Nearing fifty years old, handsome and well-groomed, he looked distinguished in his dark gray suit. The suit's subtle pattern seemed to compliment his dark brown skin. Old photos showed Reese sporting an Afro of impressive depth, but those days were gone. His black hair was of a medium cut now, more curly than kinky, and going sagely gray around his ears. His small, trim beard made him look Christ-like. An invisible spotlight always seemed to be picking him out of the crowd.

Out in the hallway, Reese stopped to give a group interview to the cluster of reporters. Wearing an expression of sad bafflement, Reese looked like a strong man caught in a Kafkaesque puzzle: confronting lies so outrageous he could barely respond. Malachi Reese's face was his vocation. Even while listening his face communicated. His expression slid from concentration to concern to observation. One never doubted that Reese really *heard* the speaker. He had thoughtful answers to every question, until the questions ceased and his voice flowed on, a river of gold. People listening to that voice not only found it impossible to believe that Reese had committed a brutal double murder, they found it impossible even to hold the accusation in their minds. *Ludicrous,* they thought.

One reporter trailed Chris Sinclair down the hall to ask the question Chris had been asked repeatedly in the last few weeks. The reporter phrased it formally: "Do you really believe Malachi Reese murdered city employee Victor Fuentes as well as a witness at the scene? Do you really think you can convince a jury of that?"

Chris paused and looked back down the Justice Center hallway, half expecting the reporter to add, *because no one else does.* Chris, too, felt the tug of Reese's voice. But he turned to the reporter and said, "Yes and yes. Just wait until you hear this afternoon's testimony."

His voice sounded more certain than Chris felt. His case against Malachi Reese was so solid that he had had no choice but to prosecute; everyone on his staff agreed with that. Soon after Chris's election, as if waiting to pounce on the winner, very believable witnesses had brought him evidence that Reese's respectable public life was a facade. The false front covered a subterranean life of grim depth and reach. Chris had discovered that Reese had been more deeply involved in public life than anyone knew, but in a secret, ruthless way. He hadn't been a background figure at all. Reese had been the pivot on which large stage sets of corruption and fear turned.

But sitting close to Reese every day, watching that marvel of a face convey innocence and bafflement, even the District Attorney entertained doubts about his own case.

Chris Sinclair was losing the image war. And until he called his final and most crucial witness, the trial's outcome remained in heavy doubt as well.

During this recess the trial spectators had flowed out into the hall as well. It was easy to tell which were Malachi Reese's supporters. They were the ones who glared at the District Attorney. The people of all ethnic groups who came to trial every day to support Reese were serious people, many of them well-dressed, most softspoken. Chris had to work his way through the edge of a crowd of them as he proceeded down the hallway. A few made angry eye contact, but they didn't impede Chris's progress.

Outside the Justice Center were demonstrators of a different kind.

The security guard at the outside door said, "I think it would be better if you exit through the sheriff's office entrance and let us bring a car into the bay for you, sir."

Chris followed the guard's gaze to the sidewalks and small parking lot in front of the Justice Center. Twenty or thirty people milled around, watching the Justice Center. A few carried signs, which they shook energetically at the two TV-news vans parked on the asphalt. The two signs Chris could see said "Free Malachi" and "Racist Persecution."

Most of the protestors were black, but not all. They'd been standing in the parking lot now for days, and for two or three hours this morning, waiting. Most looked dispirited. As a group they gave off an air of menace, but when Chris looked at individual protestors he didn't sense danger. People who took the time to make signs weren't too threatening.

"It'll be okay," he said to the security guard, and walked out the doors. He walked briskly but not hurriedly—his habitual pace—toward the street. Sunshine lit his face and blond hair.

"There!" someone yelled, and two or three other voices lifted.

Slowly the crowd converged on Chris, but he'd been right, they weren't physically threatening. Only one man breached the invisible barrier around the District Attorney. A tall black man with a scarred cheek stepped into Chris's path so they almost bumped. The man was around forty, and bore the marks of a hard life. His eyes burned.

"You hate us all so much?" he asked fiercely.

Chris stopped. He stared back. "I don't hate you. Or anyone else here. But I prosecute criminals, yes. Instead of standing out here working yourselves up, why don't you come in and watch the trial? Especially my last witness. Then make up your mind."

They held each other's eyes in a moment that threatened to last forever, until Chris finally said, "All right?" and walked on. No one stopped him.

The April sunlight felt aimed. After the confined mustiness of the courtroom, and the air-conditioned sterility of his car, the sun's rays seemed to seek Chris out. He closed his eyes and tilted his face upward. He was momentarily warmed, then heated as the sunlight clamped onto his dark, navy blue suit.

The judge in Malachi Reese's capital murder trial, Judge Phil Pressman, never one to miss a photo opportunity, had recessed the trial long enough to attend, and incidentally, allow the District Attorney to attend, a civic event of a peculiarly carnival-like righteousness: the razing of a crack house, part of the city's effort to rehabilitate crime-plagued neighborhoods. This residential east side block shrank from the attendant hoopla. The poor neighborhood should have been middle class. When the houses had been built in the fifties they had been pretty two- and three-bedroom wooden cottages, some of them more substantial brick. If the yards had been watered and a little paint applied the street could have been pleasant again. But the spirit of upkeep had been squashed. The discouraged atmosphere of the neighborhood emanated from this hollowed-out shell of a house where men met to buy drugs, fire off occasional gunfire, or take a woman for a six-minute financial exchange. No one would argue that bulldozing the house might not be a worthy project, but the atmosphere put Chris off. The little yellow house needed paint worse than its neighbors did, but otherwise it was like any other house on the block. But this morning the house looked like a surprised jaywalking suspect suddenly surrounded by the SWAT team. The crowd on the front lawn of the house consisted of curious spectators, the mayor of San Antonio, the chief of police, other civic leaders, and news crews. Speeches had to precede the demolition. A good deed was only half done if credit for it went ungrasped.

When Chris had arrived in the mostly black neighborhood, a police officer had approached him quickly and said, "I don't know if you want to be here, sir."

Chris had his doubts too, but only because of the self-glorification of the occasion, not the neighborhood. The stares he received from the small crowd felt more curious than hostile. Rather than take part in the ceremonies the District Attorney stood apart, off to the side, on the cracked sidewalk with a view of an unscreened side window of the marked house. Spray-painted gang graffiti covered the wall, an important verb missing where the housepaint underneath had cracked and fallen away in a large patch. A bitter voice suddenly interrupted the D.A.'s thoughts. "I grew up in that house."

A black woman stood beside him, very young but with a fat-bellied toddler playing around her feet and a baby in her arms. Chris turned toward her apologetically, expecting to see her looking at the house with regretful nostalgia. But her face showed barely suppressed rage. Her eyes glistened. The house stood as a monument to something she wanted desperately to forget.

"Can I throw the first match?" she said.

Chris wanted to put his arm around her. He settled for a hand on her shoulder. She didn't seem to feel it. She continued to stare at the house, her thin face a blend of extreme youth and ancient hurt.

Without glancing at the District Attorney she said, "You're the one trying to kill Mr. Reese, aren't you?"

Chris decided not to argue with her characterization of his job. "Yes."

The young woman shook her head. "Won't help," she said.

Chris found this an interesting response. He wanted to turn his back on the house-bashing ceremonies and listen to her. She seemed the voice of the city embodied. But the woman didn't much want to talk. She walked away, following the little boy as he explored a path that led around the side of the house. Seeing someone beckoning him to take the microphone on the front porch, Chris pretended not to see, and followed the little family. When they turned the corner they were out of sight of the festivities in front of the house.

Yellow police tape strung from sawhorses isolated the house, but the little boy casually walked right under the tape and then spurted ahead, around the back corner and out of sight. "Benjy!" the young mother shouted, shifting the baby awkwardly.

"I'll go," Chris said. He stepped over the tape as easily as Benjy had gone under it, and darted around the corner. He saw the little boy running toward the back stoop, a sagging slab of concrete that had come detached from the house. Chris put on speed, but the boy had almost reached the stoop. Chris called his name, which made the boy run faster and stumble, falling toward the concrete.

A figure in blue appeared from the other corner of the house and caught the boy. Benjy screamed and struggled. He reached for Chris, who suddenly became his friend when the boy was confronted by an even less familiar figure. Chris took him from the uniformed policeman.

The officer had disguised his extreme youth by pulling his

uniform hat down low on his brow. Appearing to recognize the District Attorney, he accounted for himself. "Just about to make a last check before the demolition, sir."

A voice called softly. Chris set Benjy down and watched him run to his mother. When Chris straightened up the young cop was still close in front of him. "Did you hear something, sir?"

They both stepped up onto the tiny porch, which gave the illusion of listing further with their weight. They stood at the rectangular hole from which the back door was missing. There was definitely a sound, but whether it came from inside the house or only carried through from the crowd in front was impossible to say. Chris started to step in, but the young cop stopped him.

"Can't go into a situation like this without backup." He sounded as if he were quoting. He looked the District Attorney over quickly, as if assessing him for the backup role, then said, "Could you just step down from the porch, sir, while I go get another officer?"

Chris complied. The young officer walked away, but stopped to usher the young woman and her children toward the front. She answered back and the officer accompanied her, walking slowly to keep Benjy in sight.

When they were gone Chris stepped back to the house's doorway. He heard the sound again, a human disturbance of the air. It could have been a moan.

Chris looked into the dim interior and couldn't see anything. If the police officer hadn't been there, Benjy could have gone in this doorway. Another child might have gone in, or a befuddled homeless man. Chris stepped through the doorway.

Inside the house felt like another dimension. The sunlight disappeared without a trace, and the tiny sound of boards shifting was louder than the crowd noise from outside. Even when his eyes adjusted to the gloom Chris felt divorced from the outer world. Many of the house's interior walls had been knocked down. Standing in the kitchen, he could see most of the thou-

sand or so square feet of the house's interior. There were a couch
and an armchair in what had been the living room, a kitchen
table and two chairs stood closer at hand, but mostly the house
was furnished with clutter, disintegrating cardboard boxes and
stacks of newspaper. The electricity had been shut off long ago,
stilling the hum of modern life. Chris could have been inside a
cave instead of a onetime home.

The house was so dim inside Chris couldn't see what he was
putting his foot on. It felt like linoleum, with a yielding under-
surface that spoke of termites or fire. He stepped cautiously, calling "Hello?"

A dull boom broke the silence and the whole house shud-
dered. On the front porch the chief of police had just swung a
sledgehammer, bashing a symbolic dent in the house's front wall.
A bulldozer cleared its throat.

Chris decided to go back and wait for the police. But then he
heard a moan and knew for certain he wasn't alone inside the
house.

The sound had been of pain. No longer thinking of danger,
Chris walked toward the dilapidated old couch in the living area.
As he drew closer he saw a figure lying on the couch. In the
gloom it looked like a statue carved out of wood. But then the
man's hand lifted and he coughed.

With a shock Chris recognized the old man's face. He rushed
to him and supported the head the man was trying to lift.

"Mr. Rodriguez," Chris said. "How did you—? My God,
what—?"

He knew the old man from hours spent interviewing him.
Chris had expected to be calling him as a witness an hour
from now.

The old couch was missing most of its cushions. Springs poked
out through its threadbare fabric. It exhaled dust at the slightest
movement, so the old man would have had trouble breathing just
from lying there. Chris got under him and held the old man up.
He felt almost weightless. His cough turned into a mumble, but

when he opened his mouth blood gushed onto his shirt. Mr. Rodriguez's hands had been strong. He had been a carpenter, an artisan. But when he tried to grab Chris his hands skittered on the D.A.'s shirt as if they'd been the hands of the toddler Chris had been holding a few minutes before. Chris stared. Mr. Rodriguez grew very still.

"Hold on," Chris said loudly. "There're people just outside. Hang on, Mr. Rodriguez, they'll have an ambulance here in five minutes."

But he didn't leave the old man. Mr. Rodriguez's lips were moving, and Chris bent close. "Tell me," he whispered.

Dust motes danced. Veins stood out on the backs of the old man's deep brown hands. His hair was thin and white. One eye was cloudy. Chris fought for control of his emotions as he leaned his ear close to Mr. Rodriguez's lips. He held the tendoned hand tightly.

A minute later the front door crashed inward. When police entered they found the District Attorney in tears holding a body, the dead man's blood staining them both.

Chris Sinclair hadn't realized. He'd been told that Malachi Reese had no conscience or qualms—it was what Chris was trying to make the jury believe—but he hadn't believed it himself, not in the visceral way he should have. Now too late he understood: Malachi Reese would win this trial no matter what he had to do.

Chris moved in his own world of shock and disbelief. At the scene, while he still wore Adolfo Rodriguez's blood, a cop asked, "Shall we call the court, sir? I'm sure they'll grant a delay so—" then stopped as he realized neither his touch nor his voice was penetrating the District Attorney's consciousness.

An hour later Chris entered the courtroom wearing a fresh shirt. By then everyone had heard the story of what he had found inside the crack house. Onlookers gave him shocked and curious stares, but the prosecutor didn't notice. He had eyes only for his defendant.

Malachi Reese sat at the defense table with his two lawyers. The judge's bench and the jury box were still empty, so the three figures stood out at the front of the courtroom. From the other table, Chris's assistant, Melissa Fleming, turned to look at him. But Chris saw only Malachi Reese. Reese should have felt the weight of that stare, but it wasn't until Chris passed through the gate in the railing, making the gate creak slightly, that Reese turned.

When Reese looked up he seemed startled. He spoke in a soft voice, but it carried to the many spectators already assembled in the courtroom. "What's wrong?" he said. "What's happened to you?"

His voice conveyed selfless concern. Chris heard a different undertone nonetheless. Nothing gave Reese away, but Chris stared at him as if he saw someone utterly different from the person everyone else in the courtroom watched.

"All rise," said the bailiff, and Judge Pressman hastily settled himself behind the bench. Pressman was a skillful enough politician to have gotten himself elected twice to this criminal district court bench. He needed to be a judge because as a lawyer he'd been useless in a courtroom. He had a long, narrow face, darting eyes, and an unfortunately sudden way of moving his arms and shoulders that tended to draw attention to him even on those rare occasions when he wasn't seeking it. As now, when he stared at the District Attorney with sincere helpfulness. "Mr. Sinclair, do you have a request before we reconvene?"

They were the first spoken words Chris had understood since he'd been delicately escorted out of the crack house. Coming to himself in the courtroom, he realized he didn't know how he'd gotten here, but his gaze moved from the judge back to the defendant and his face changed.

"No, thank you, your Honor," he said distinctly. "The State calls Lou Briones."

Judge Pressman looked sharply at the District Attorney, but then turned to his bailiff with a shrug. The bailiff opened a back door of the courtroom to admit the jurors, who filed quickly into their seats in the jury box. The jurors were not sequestered during this first phase of trial, they'd been allowed to go their separate ways during the long lunch recess. If two or three of them had heard a passing news report of the murder victim in the crack house, they would have no idea how that news related to this trial. But the jurors could sense that something had changed. The District Attorney appeared to have lost touch with the world. He didn't even notice his assistant who touched him lightly and asked a soft question as the D.A. took his seat beside her. He didn't even look at his own witness coming up the aisle of the courtroom.

But the District Attorney's distraction lent heightened anticipation to this witness. The jurors and spectators watched him intently, and there was more than one audible gasp. Everyone knew the name Lou Briones, but they wondered if they were mistaken. Briones was a former city councilman, but much better known as his own TV pitchman for his chain of appliance stores. He was a big, hearty man, with a good laugh and meaty hands that could make a refrigerator dance when he slapped a hand on one to demonstrate its solidness.

But this figure shuffling to his place at the witness stand was the shocking ghost of Lou Briones. Gaunt and pale, his hand trembled slightly as he took the oath. Lou Briones looked half departed from this world.

Chris's assistant Melissa quietly asked whether she should take the witness, but Chris shook his head and said in a clear voice, "Would you please identify yourself?"

The witness raised his head, which made the loose flesh of his neck quiver. He turned toward the jury, knowing they knew him. "My name is Lou Briones."

"Do you know the defendant, Mr. Briones?"

Briones looked at Reese across the narrow space of the front of the courtroom. His gaze offered no greeting, hardly even recognition. His voice went flat. "Malachi, yes. I know him professionally, politically. Personally, too. I guess I know him as well as anybody."

"What about Victor Fuentes?" Chris asked.

"Yes. He was an assistant city manager."

The important word was "was." Victor Fuentes had been the primary victim of the capital murder for which Malachi Reese was being prosecuted.

"What was he like, Mr. Briones?"

"Victor?" Briones sounded surprised to be asked. His voice turned reminiscent. "He was young. That was the main thing about Victor, he had no history. If you'd been off city council for two terms he didn't know you. He was twenty—what? five? six? Had a good degree from someplace, you know. He was ambitious, anybody could see that. It made you think he could be worked with. I think now, though, his ambition ran a different direction."

"Why was Victor Fuentes killed?" Chris asked.

"Because he'd discovered a little corner of Malachi Reese's business. Malachi—"

"Objection!" The slender defense lawyer in his crisp suit made an impressive arrow when he shot to his feet. Initially, for his defense, Malachi Reese had hired Leo Pedraza, who happened to be the District Attorney Chris Sinclair had replaced. But for trial they'd brought in a smooth young trial stud named Jackson Scott who in fact reminded some observers of Chris in his younger days. Leo Pedraza now sat second chair. "This testimony is obviously based on hearsay, your Honor," Scott said.

Judge Pressman turned inquiringly toward the District Attorney. The judge preferred if possible to be helped out rather than rule on an objection. "My next question will answer that," Chris said. Judge Pressman waved him gratefully on.

"May I have a ruling on my objection?" the young defense lawyer said. The formality hiding the contempt in his voice had grown thinner as the trial had progressed. His opinion of the judge was now an audible wedge in everything he said.

"After the next question," the judge said reasonably.

The lawyers sat. Chris asked, "Mr. Briones, how do you know that Victor Fuentes was murdered because he'd learned something about Malachi Reese's business?"

"Because it was my business too," Briones said.

Overruled, Judge Pressman mouthed silently at the defense lawyer, who sulked.

Briones continued. "We were on a team bidding for a city contract. I was part of the group, Malachi was—he was hired as a consultant to the team. It was a big contract, maybe fifty million dollars, to build an expansion to the waste treatment plant. We—"

"Why were you on the team, Mr. Briones? What expertise do you have in waste treatment?"

"I know which way shit runs, son." A few spectators laughed, but that wasn't Lou Briones' object. He was grim. He had hunkered his shoulders high and inward, as if gathering his strength. He wheezed between his sentences. His ears, big and pendulous, hung like burdens on his head. Briones was only sixty, but he looked older, because the flesh on his face sagged. Skin looked superfluous on him, like an old suit he'd pulled out of the back of the closet.

"Here's the way a contract bid works—"

"Objection, your Honor," Jackson Scott said dispiritedly. "Relevance?"

Lou Briones, the former city councilman, not used to being interrupted, turned toward the judge irritatedly. He was obviously about to say, *Can't you shut this kid up?*

"It goes to motive, your Honor," Chris helped out.

"Overruled, overruled. Let's get on with it."

"The way a contract bid works," Briones repeated, glaring at the defense lawyer, "is you put together the best team you can—"

"To get the job done?" Chris asked innocently.

"To get the contract," Briones said acidly. "Job'll get done, everybody knows that. Question is, who's gonna make the money off it? So we had a good team. Me, of course; then a good architecture firm, good contacts. Couple of construction companies that had made significant contributions."

Chris didn't want to play into the act anymore, but he had to ask the clarifying questions. "Political contributions?"

"Yeah, campaign contributions, to city council members. And we had Malachi, of course."

"What was the defendant supposed to bring to the team?" Chris asked, turning to look at him. Reese appeared bemused, as if listening to an elementary civics lesson that had nothing to do with him.

"Who knew exactly?" Briones answered, not coyly. "Sort of the back-room influence. He was owed more favors than anybody in this town. Certainly if you had Malachi on your team you were supposed to be guaranteed the east side councilman's vote. Probably west side, too. And just—grease the process."

"What did this have to do with Victor Fuentes?" Chris asked. He knew the questions, he had rehearsed this testimony. His voice continued, strong and properly inflected, while his mind still dwelt on what he'd seen inside the crack house. He turned wondering eyes on Malachi Reese. Reese never looked back, never even glanced in Chris's direction.

Briones said slowly, "The process has gotten—trickier—"

Less obviously corrupt, Chris translated silently.

"Used to be you had the team you had the contract, no problem. Nowadays it helps a lot if you can get the city staff recommendation too. That meant getting Victor Fuentes on your side. He was in charge of evaluating the bids. I talked to him, kind of—made sure he knew the facts of life. He was—he was almost rude to me." Briones gazed across the room, his voice still sounding shocked. "He not only made fun of our bid offer, he said he was looking into some other stuff, old business. He said he wanted to know where we got off bidding on construction projects anyway. He was looking particularly into a contract that had been awarded when I'd been on the council, that I'd voted for."

"Was Mr. Reese involved in that bid also?"

"Oh yes. And let's just say, we didn't want that one looked into."

Chris had no intention of inquiring into other crimes, not yet. He could feel the defense lawyer getting edgy beside him, ready to spring to his feet. "So what did you do?"

"I talked to Malachi. That's what he was there for. We talked over what we might do and finally Malachi said he'd have a word with Victor Fuentes."

Briones leaned heavily on the last phrase and shifted uncomfortably in his seat. The air was pleasant in the courtroom, but sweat stains were growing under the armpits of Lou Briones' seersucker suit. His breathing was heavier.

"What did that mean to you?" Chris asked quietly.

"May we approach the bench?" Jackson Scott asked, already doing so, buttoning his black suit coat, stiff and straight as righteous indignation. Chris followed him. At the bench the defense lawyer said quietly but forcefully, "I believe this is going to call for testimony implying extraneous offenses. I strongly object to any such testimony, your Honor. It would render this trial completely unfair and reversible." He said the last word sharply, to get Judge Pressman's attention. He succeeded. The judge turned to the prosecutor with obvious concern. "Mr. Sinclair, you're not going to—"

"Your Honor, I will keep the testimony as discreet as possible, but I must establish a pattern to put this witness's testimony in context. Otherwise it will sound like idle speculation."

The judge vaguely understood the word "context" as having a legal meaning. He thought he'd heard it before. "All right," he said authoritatively. "I'll give you some leeway—" He knew he'd heard that word in a legal discussion. He had: it had been on a TV series. "—but not much," he added quickly, to placate the glowering defense lawyer. In that he was unsuccessful. Scott shifted the glare to Chris as they walked back to their places.

Briones had taken the opportunity to rest, staring at the floor. His chest moved as he breathed.

"What did that phrase mean to you, Mr. Briones?"

"It was what Malachi said. It was always the end of a discussion. It meant he'd take care of the problem."

"How?"

"However it took. Whatever had to be done, he'd do it. Whatever it took. I told him—well, I tried to say that we didn't need to do anything drastic, but Malachi looked at me like I was speaking Hungarian. When I read that Victor Fuentes was dead, I knew who had killed him. I remembered Malachi had planned a meeting with him, and I remembered what he'd said. There are some important people in this town, let me tell you, who went cold when Malachi Reese said he was going to have a word with somebody."

Dimly aware of a growing buzz around him, not trying to interpret it, Chris asked, "So other people, elected officials, knew about Mr. Reese's activities?"

"Some knew a little, the way I did, from personal experience. But nobody knew any details. They just knew that things happened. I couldn't believe you found an eyewitness to this one."

"Objection," the defense lawyer snapped. "Hearsay."

"Sustained," Judge Pressman said, and instructed the jury to disregard the witness's statement, knowing how ineffective that instruction would be.

During the interruption Chris looked past the defense lawyer at Malachi Reese. The defendant still wouldn't look at Chris. He stared at the witness Lou Briones, Reese shaking his head slowly, like an innocent man unwilling to sit quietly and listen to lies. But the D.A. was sure Reese knew Chris was watching him. Mention of the eyewitness put a gleam in Reese's eye, but only Chris could see it.

Chris asked a question that put the defense on the alert, because it sounded like cross-examination. "So you don't really know for a fact, Mr. Briones, that Mr. Reese did anything to Victor Fuentes? You're just guessing."

"I know," Briones said thickly. "You had to have known Malachi for a long time, the way I did, know how he got where he was. Malachi wasn't just Johnny-on-the-spot, he was ahead of everybody. While everybody else was just talking, you'd discover that Malachi had already done what some powerful person wanted done—before he was even asked. He would make happen what they most secretly wanted to have happen. So afterward you feel both guilty and afraid, like it sprang out of your own head."

Chris watched Reese, this monster from the id. Reese continued to look sad and perplexed, but Chris thought he saw a flash of pride at hearing himself described.

"If people knew what he had done in some of these cases, Mr. Briones, why didn't they go to the police?"

"Because they weren't sure who'd be arrested. Say you went to the police and say, 'I know who killed X.' 'How do you know?'" they say, and you say, 'Because he did it for me.' And the cops'd go, 'That's right, X was your political rival, wasn't he?' Or business competitor, or whatever. Something bad had happened to the one person you hated and feared the most, and you expected the cops to believe someone else did it, someone who had no motive for it at all?" Briones shook his head. "I don't know anybody who was willing to take that chance."

Emotionlessly, Chris asked, "Do you expect this jury to believe that Mr. Reese murdered so many people?"

"No. Not murder, not very often. But bad things would happen to problem people. A reporter digging too deep, some little official who needed to step aside but wouldn't take a hint, somebody like that. Maybe heroin would be found in the reporter's car. Maybe somebody would break into a house and not take anything. People got the message. There was a cop we really needed to have off the force, but nobody wanted him spouting accusations on his way out. Then one Monday morning he mailed in his resignation and nobody ever saw him again. Nobody knew exactly what happened, they just knew when Malachi said he'd have a word with somebody, the problem went away."

Briones stared across the courtroom at the defendant. He looked tired again. "And then, you know, he'd spend the weekend cleaning up a neighborhood and planting flowers. He brought people out into the sunshine who'd been afraid to leave their houses for years. He did some good things for this town, I don't deny that. But he's the most contradictory man I've ever known. Most people, you know exactly how they'll react before you even say anything to them. But Malachi—sometimes I thought he must be two people."

The defendant remained the master of his face. He looked just the way he should have: distraught, puzzled, painfully innocent, his mouth clenched. In his interviews he hadn't blamed anyone for his predicament. He'd let the writers speculate about his enemies. Reese had only appeared to be trying to figure out why people would have made up such a bizarre fantasy about him. Briones' testimony might not even be that damaging: the more outrageously sinister he painted Malachi Reese, the greater grew the possibility that this was part of a sinister conspiracy *against* Reese.

"I pass the witness," the District Attorney said, which appeared to take people in the courtroom by surprise. It seemed too soon. He had piqued their curiosity. They wanted to hear more of the shadowy world of Malachi Reese. Two or three jurors looked at Chris wondering if he had lost his energy or the thread of his questioning.

But Jackson Scott was ready. Sitting forward even straighter, he said, "Mr. Briones, you've described a pattern of criminal behavior through which you profited, did you not?"

"Yes. Sometimes."

"You and others, public officials, you benefitted in a variety of ways from this great morass of deception and evildoing?"

"Yes. Not on purpose, but—"

Scott would not be interrupted. "But how did Mr. Reese

profit? You say yourself he had no motive. Isn't it fanciful to attribute these misdeeds to Malachi Reese?"

"He did it," Briones insisted.

Speaking as if to a backward child, the defense lawyer said, "To what end, Mr. Briones? People don't do things without a reason, do they? You profited, other people profited, you held onto your public positions. But how could Mr. Reese, who has never shown any political ambition, have benefitted from all this?"

"To what end?" Briones asked with faint mockery. "Power, of course. People owed Malachi, and they were afraid of him besides. He pulled the strings of the people who pulled the strings. That's power, sonny, not being mayor or county commissioner. If you don't understand wanting to control other people, I can't explain it to you." Now out of the game himself, Briones still sounded contemptuous of those who didn't feel that hunger to dominate. "People did what he wanted," he concluded with a cough.

Jackson Scott settled down, as if putting his back into a tug-of-war in which he was certain he could pull the old fool before him right out of the witness box. In an insincere, pleasant tone of voice he said, "You spoke of Mr. Reese's good deeds. Cleaning up neighborhoods and so forth. That was only the smallest part of what Mr. Reese has done, isn't it, Mr. Briones?"

Briones shrugged. "I said he's done some good things."

"But that was an understatement, wasn't it? He has cleaned up neighborhoods in the greater sense, hasn't he? Do you remember his organizing the gang summit that declared safe zones, that lowered the murder rate significantly two years ago?"

"Yes I do. And did you wonder how Malachi could arrange that when nobody else had been able to?"

"Perhaps because he's so widely admired in so many quarters," Scott suggested, and didn't wait for an answer. "He is also responsible for launching an investigation into just the kind of corrupt bidding practice you've described, wasn't he? Involving a school district contract he had no part of, where he didn't stand to profit in any way."

"That's true," Briones said. "And you know the benefit of blowing up a scandal like that? Don't look at the guy who got caught. He's dead, he's out of it. Look at the guy next to him, with the surprised look on his face. He sees what can happen to him the next time if he steps out of line."

Chris Sinclair paid minimal attention to the exchanges, trusting his witness to hold his own with the defense lawyer. Chris thought about what was going to happen next. He didn't know. The points he scored with Lou Briones' testimony were meaningless. Malachi Reese had already won this duel, outside the courtroom. He'd turned the court proceeding into a child's game.

Unperturbed, Jackson Scott said, "You have an answer for everything, don't you, Mr. Briones? You make every public good Malachi Reese has done into a private evil. But only you know, right? Only Lou Briones comes forward with the truth. But you are the one with the motive to lie, aren't you, Mr. Briones? You've been implicated, so you try to shift the blame as spectacularly as possible."

"I've admitted my part," Briones said wearily.

"But you're not being tried for your part, are you? In fact through your testimony you're escaping punishment. What sort of deal do you have with the District Attorney's Office?"

"None. I haven't made a deal."

Scott's voice sharpened. "Look around, Mr. Briones, and tell me if you think everyone you see is an idiot. The jurors, the judge. You expect us all to believe that, after a lifetime of covering up these crimes, you've come forward now just because you've had an attack of conscience?"

"No," Briones said, causing the defense lawyer to smirk triumphantly. "It's because I'm dying."

Even in Chris Sinclair's despair, he closed his eyes in a brief moment of victory. *Thank you, Jackson, for asking the right question.* Chris would have brought out Lou Briones' condition himself on redirect questioning, but it was more effective this way. The defense lawyer sat slack-jawed.

"I've got cancer of the everything," Briones continued. "When I heard about Victor Fuentes, and about the woman who got killed, too, I couldn't forget it. It kept eating at me. Two months after I heard is when I was diagnosed. I think——"

Lou Briones thought he had willed his own death. He had kept the diagnosis to himself, as he had kept so much secret. But he had rediscovered the church, and his conscience. He had gone to the District Attorney almost six months after the murders to say he knew who had killed Victor Fuentes. The story Briones had told seemed fantastic, but Chris had managed to corroborate some of it. Then he'd had to rush the case to trial while he still had the former city councilman, whose cancer was very fast-acting.

Once Briones had named his disease, everyone in the courtroom could see it was true. The weight loss, the trembling, the letting go of this world. Even people who'd never seen Lou Briones before could see he was a man being scoured out from the inside.

The defense lawyer recovered quickly. Rising to his feet, he said solemnly, "Your Honor, as much sympathy as we all feel toward the witness, it is still true that his testimony——the portion that relates to the offense on trial here——is purely speculative. He was not a witness to anything. His testimony has been inadmissible, and very damaging to my client. I'll ask the court to instruct the jury to disregard it. And unless the District Attorney has proof that actually implicates Mr. Reese in the crime on trial, I'll also ask the court to direct a verdict of acquittal, which Mr. Reese richly deserves."

He was right. Even Judge Pressman could see that. Every eye in the courtroom turned toward Chris Sinclair. The one gaze Chris returned was Malachi Reese's. Reese looked like an innocent man puzzled at the District Attorney's reluctance to do the right thing. His expression was patient, waiting like everyone else for the State to call its next witness. But Reese knew better. Chris thought he saw, in the depths of the defendant's eyes, a tiny smile. Reese waited for the District Attorney to rise and acknowledge that he'd been beaten.

Suddenly Chris's perspective changed. There was a shiver through his perception and he felt strangely distant from his surroundings. He looked at the jurors and saw paper figures, rippling in the air currents. As Chris Sinclair's gaze moved he saw only these wafer-thin figures like targets in a pinball game. None of them had the least significance. The judge, the bailiff: no one was real.

Then he looked at Malachi Reese and found the exception. Reese was solid and grim and frightening.

In the next moment Chris returned to reality. He realized that for a moment he had been seeing through Reese's eyes. Life was a game to be won at any cost, and the people who got in the way were insignificant. Reese still watched him, but no longer with a trace of a smile. He stared edgily. Chris believed that Reese saw him as real. Suddenly Reese and Chris were the only two people in the world.

"Mr. Sinclair?" The judge raised his voice to get Chris's attention. Melissa had her hand on Chris's arm as well, whispering. "Do you have another witness?" the judge asked, obviously repeating himself.

Chris saw Reese's shoulders lift with a smooth breath. The defendant regained his confidence. Reese was one of two people in the courtroom who knew with complete certainty that the trial was over.

At least, the normal trial.

Suddenly animated, Chris turned to his assistant and whispered urgently. Melissa whispered back confused questions, but Chris made only one short answer and then rose to his feet. He stood there without a word. Melissa had no choice but to stand too. In a voice she tried to strengthen after she had already started her sentence, she said, "The State calls Chris Sinclair."

Chapter 2

"Objection," defense lawyer Jackson Scott said efficiently, but he said it to the District Attorney's back, because Chris Sinclair was already striding toward the witness stand. "This witness was not listed among the State's witnesses, which the defense is entitled to be informed of pre-trial."

"I'm a surprise witness," Chris said. "I had no idea until two hours ago that I'd be a witness to anything relevant to this trial. Shall I explain how that happened?"

"Objection," Jackson Scott repeated more emphatically. "I object to hearsay, to speculation, to any testimony about extraneous offenses."

"Can we just hear what he has to say?" Judge Pressman asked.

Chris stood just below the judge's bench, in front of the witness stand. The jurors were close behind him. He felt their stares. He was in no-man's-land in the front of the courtroom. He had lost his official position.

"I object to him testifying at all," the defense lawyer said. "How can he be both the prosecutor and his own evidence?"

"Your client shouldn't have made me a witness," Chris snapped.

"Objection, objection, objection!" Scott cried, but while he said it Judge Pressman was giving Chris the witness's oath. "I do," Chris said firmly.

"Please state your name and position," Melissa Fleming said nervously. A tall, slender young woman who looked only a few years out of high school, she was a diligent but uninspired prosecutor, normally at ease in a courtroom, but having her boss at her side for the last five weeks had put a perpetual crease across her forehead. Having Chris as a witness made it worse. Melissa donned large round glasses for disguise.

"Chris Sinclair. I'm the District Attorney of Bexar County."

"And the lead prosecutor in this case?"

"Yes."

"Who were you planning to call as your next witness in this case, Mr. Sinclair?"

"A man named Adolfo Rodriguez."

"Why?"

"Mr. Rodriguez was an eyewitness—"

"Objection," Jackson Scott snapped. "Hearsay."

"Sustained," Judge Pressman agreed.

Chris sat surprisingly at ease in the witness chair. He'd never seen a trial from this perspective before. The lawyers at their individual tables sat nervous as boxers just before the bell, their mouths grimly set, but not looking at each other. Behind them were those dozens of spectators whose presence had grown increasingly larger at Chris's back. Now they could see his face, and he could see theirs. Some few of the trial-watchers looked encouraging. More glared hostilely. But all their eyes were on him. They weren't closed off, they were very curious to hear what the District Attorney had to say.

In the front row were the only happy people in the courtroom: four reporters scribbling furiously in their notepads.

Chris turned his concentration on the jurors. Usually a lawyer could only glance at the jury covertly, trying to gauge their mass reactions. From the witness stand the jurors became individuals. At first glance he saw them as expressions rather than ethnic components. One woman stared at him as if still puzzled at his changed location. A young man smiled surreptitiously, then glanced around to see if anyone had seen.

Finally Chris looked at Malachi Reese. Reese had reassumed a face that didn't acknowledge any link to the District Attorney. He managed still to look puzzled, though suspicion crept through his expression too.

"Are you still planning to call Mr. Rodriguez as a witness?" Melissa Fleming asked.

"No. I can't."

"When did you see him last?"

"About two hours ago," Chris said to the jury. "I was in an old house that the city was demolishing. I found Mr. Rodriguez inside there." As cleanly as he could, trying to keep his voice from cracking, Chris described picking the old man up, bending close to his mouth, and feeling the witness die in his arms before any other help could arrive.

"I'm sure he recognized me. I called him by name. He used up his last strength whispering to me."

"What did Mr. Rodriguez say?"

"Objection. Hearsay." Jackson Scott re-entered the dialogue, intent on breaking the mood if nothing else.

"Did Mr. Rodriguez know he was dying?" Melissa asked.

"Yes," Chris said. "It was obvious. He was cut—so many places. He didn't even have the strength to lift his own head. When I said I'd get help he said, 'No use.' He knew."

"Did he make a last statement to you just before he died?"

"Yes."

"Your Honor," Melissa addressed the judge. "This is admissible as a dying declaration."

Pressman only nodded. Melissa turned back to the District Attorney. "What did Mr. Rodriguez say?"

"He said, 'Malachi Reese did this to me because I saw him kill my wife and that young man.'"

He turned toward the jurors, demonstrating with his arms how he had held his witness. Chris still felt his weightless weight. He saw the gloom of that old house, a house about to die. He was lost for a moment, struggling not with the trial but with trying to hold onto a man who was slipping inescapably out of this world.

An angry voice called him back from that ethereal world where death sat behind his shoulder. In the courtroom, Malachi Reese was on his feet, glaring.

"That is a lie!"

Reese's teeth looked very white, snapping down on his outrage. His neat beard bristled. Chris had this triumph, at least: he had burst the defendant's celebrated composure.

But to the already convinced, Reese looked like an innocent man who could no longer listen passively. "You are a liar!" he shouted again, before his lawyer, looking reed-like beside him, managed to pull him down to his seat. Reese turned to him, whispering. Scott listened in profile, then turned amazed eyes on his client. Leo Pedraza leaned in to join the conference.

Melissa Fleming stared in a moment of panic at her boss. She couldn't think of another question. Chris nodded slightly. "Pass the witness," Melissa said nervously.

Jackson Scott was still frowning in surprise. Before he could gather himself, his trial partner straightened in his chair and said, "Mr. District Attorney."

Leo Pedraza had held that title himself for one term before Chris had defeated him last year. Pedraza had been beloved within the office for his easygoing one-of-the-guys ways, but that had not been a spirit to encourage efficiency, and sloppiness had helped lead to Pedraza's downfall. Carelessness didn't extend to his appearance, though. For trial he wore a white suit with a vest, smooth after a long day. Pedraza was a man nearing sixty who had worked in offices and courtrooms his whole professional life but still bore a field worker's tan and hands. In caricature he was all cheeks and spiky moustache. His small eyes got lost behind this armament.

Jackson Scott frowned at him, but Pedraza stared benignly at his former opponent in the witness stand and said, "Did anyone else hear this dying declaration, Mr. Sinclair?"

"No. No one else was in the house at the time."

Pedraza nodded amusedly. "Did you record this alleged statement in some way?"

"Only in my memory, Mr. Pedraza. I had no idea I was going to find Mr. Rodriguez inside that house. Obviously he was placed there as a message to me."

"Object to that speculation," Pedraza said easily. Sustained, he continued, "Were there reporters at the scene, Mr. Sinclair?"

"Yes."

"Police officers?"

"Yes."

"Did you announce to any of them that your witness had made a statement before he died? If we review the police reports of this incident, will we find that information?"

"No," Chris said. "No. I didn't talk to anyone." Actually he wasn't sure of that. He didn't remember what had happened in the long minutes after Adolfo Rodriguez had been lifted gently away from him. He was pretty sure he hadn't answered any questions, though.

"So the only way this jury can hear about this statement is from your testimony," Pedraza mused. "The testimony of the one person in the world intent on convicting Malachi Reese of capital murder."

Neither of those was a question. Chris didn't reply. He sat in the witness stand watching Reese, who shook his head as if outraged and rolled his eyes.

"Would you repeat the statement?" Leo Pedraza said.

Chris was glad of the opportunity. "He said, 'Malachi Reese did this to me because I saw him kill my wife and that young man.' "

"He spoke amazingly articulately, didn't he, for a man on the brink of death?"

"It was important to him to get it out, I think."

Pedraza's voice strengthened as he dropped his bombshell. "It is even more amazing he was able to say anything to you at all, when his tongue had been severed."

The younger defense lawyer looked shocked again at hearing this news spoken aloud. Pedraza and his client stared at Chris Sinclair flatly, with similar glints of triumph, as crowd sounds broke out around them.

Chris waited for the noise to die down, waited to become the center of attention again, before shaking his head. "It was cut," he said, "not severed. And it's interesting you know that detail, since it wasn't released publicly."

Chris stared straight at Reese. The defendant no longer looked helpless and confused. He stared blackly at the District Attorney.

Leo Pedraza swallowed hard. "It was in the autopsy report," he improvised hastily.

"The autopsy is being conducted right now. There is no report yet." Chris addressed Malachi Reese directly. "Whoever you hired was too rushed to do exactly what you'd told them to do. You should have done the job yourself, like last time."

A minute later the trial judge gave up trying to quiet the courtroom and declared a recess.

The State had no more witnesses. When trial resumed it was the defense's turn, and Jackson Scott was firmly in control again. Leo Pedraza didn't look at anyone. His lips moved, trying out explanations. Jackson Scott started the defense's case slowly, calling a waiter and two other witnesses from the restaurant where Malachi Reese and Victor Fuentes had had their last meeting, shortly before Fuentes' throat was slashed in the parking lot of his apartment building. The witnesses' testimony differed enough to be believable but matched in the essential details:

"Could you hear what Mr. Reese and Mr. Fuentes were discussing, Mr. Johnson?" the defense lawyer asked.

"No. They were quiet," said Herbert Johnson. A tall middle-aged man with large sloping shoulders, he'd been dining in the downtown Mexican restaurant with his wife at the end of a day of shopping and touristing. The Johnsons had driven back from Dallas to be defense witnesses.

"And how far away were you?"

"The next table. Just a few feet."

"So neither of them ever became animated enough to raise his voice, or draw your attention in any other way?"

"No, sir. Looked like a normal dinner conversation."

"Did they leave together?" Scott asked.

"No, sir. The younger one, the Mexican-American man, left first, and this one beside you, Mr. Reese, he stayed at the table and had a cup of coffee."

Reese had also waved over the strolling *mariachis* and listened responsively to a couple of songs, then he'd spoken to at least three people he knew—establishing carefully, if one looked at it that way in retrospect, that he remained in Mi Tierra at least half an hour after his supposed victim had left. Even the prosecution witnesses had placed Reese and Fuentes together only in the restaurant, not later in the apartment house parking lot two miles away. Apparently only two people had seen them together there, Mr. and Mrs. Rodriguez, and neither had survived the consequences of that witnessing.

Chris asked these restaurant defense witnesses only one question: "Did Mr. Reese and Mr. Fuentes shake hands when they said good-bye?" Two of them couldn't remember, but Johnson frowned and paused and said, "No sir, I don't believe they did. Mr. Reese there didn't stand up when the other got up to leave. But I remember they smiled at each other."

"Smiled," Chris repeated.

"Yes sir." Johnson demonstrated, showing nearly all his dentures. He looked carnivorous.

The defense dribbled away the afternoon with these few witnesses that chipped away at the facts of the prosecution's case. All that remained was Lou Briones' testimony to Reese's intention of dealing with the victim, their public meeting shortly before Fuentes' death, and the second victim found in the apartment parking lot: Mrs. Dolores Rodriguez, who had been unlucky enough to be leaving her maid's job just as the murder happened. Her husband, pulling up in his car, had been too late to save his wife but just in time to see the killer. For half a year after that he'd had nothing to do with his knowledge, until Chris Sinclair had shown him a batch of photographs that included one of Malachi Reese.

When Judge Pressman adjourned trial for the day it took Chris by surprise. Chris had no idea what time it was. The Bexar County Justice Center was a new building, designed to discourage envy among judges by making all the courtrooms identical. The courtrooms were all interior rooms. None had any windows, the fluorescent lights would glow the same at 9:00 A.M. or midnight. As the spectators rose to their feet, Chris turned to his assistant, Melissa, to suggest they go upstairs, when he felt a hand on his arm, clamped all the way around his biceps. For an instant the grip was painful. When he turned he was face-to-face with Malachi Reese.

"You want me badly," the defendant said quietly, but with emphasis on the last word, "don't you?"

A chill gripped Chris as he looked into Reese's face. Since

Chris had held Adolfo Rodriguez in his arms everything Lou Briones had said about this man had become real to him. Chris had come to believe that the defendant was a man of relentless amoral will—a villain who, as Briones had said, would do anything to get what he wanted. But it was hard to fit that implacable force behind a human face. And Malachi Reese's face remained a work of art: gentle, expressive, with questioning eyebrows that softened the impact of his adamant eyes. Staring into those eyes, Chris felt a doubt creeping into his resolve.

Then Reese let go and turned away toward another interview.

Chris and Melissa went upstairs to Chris's office, where they were joined by several other prosecutors, some of them jovial, some subdued, but all watching their boss closely. "We have witnesses to talk to?" Melissa asked him.

Chris shook his head. "They'll put Reese on the stand tomorrow. That'll—"

"You sure?" asked Paul Benavides, the first assistant D.A., Chris's hand-picked second in command. Tall, well over six feet, and dark, with a thick crop of black hair giving him an added inch or two, Paul had thick shoulders, long arms, and a little too much gut. But he spoke surprisingly softly and thoughtfully.

Chris only glanced at him in answer. Malachi Reese pass up a chance to address the jury directly? Not likely.

A small crowd had gathered in the D.A.'s office: senior prosecutors, two investigators, a psychiatrist, and an assistant medical examiner who had brought the autopsy report on Adolfo Rodriguez.

"And we don't have any rebuttal witnesses no matter what they bring up," Chris added. "Unless I decide to take the stand again." He smiled faintly.

"That was great," said Mike Martinez, a young prosecutor of

only a few years' experience. Neither his rank nor his duties entitled him to be in this meeting. The only thing that had brought him there was chutzpah: Mike generally went where he wanted and did as he pleased. Normally the grin he habitually wore was infectious, but in this nervous gathering no one joined him. "Seeing you get cross-examined, that was a trip," Mike chortled, unperturbed. There was a general throat-clearing that could have been taken for agreement or contradiction. Paul Benavides broke the silence.

"Did Mr. Rodriguez really say it just that precisely? 'Malachi Reese killed me. . . .'? He must have known. . . ."

Chris didn't answer. The doctor, slapping the pages of the autopsy report lightly on his ample thigh, said, "It's a wonder he could talk at all, the shape his tongue was in."

Chris turned from his study of his office wall to find them all glancing sidelong at him or looking carefully away. "Maybe it was his ghost who spoke to me," he said.

That broke up the meeting. They all filed out. The psychiatrist, Anne Greenwald, came last. In her thirties, Dr. Greenwald's obvious professional authority contrasted with her youthful energy. Her dark gray eyes—flecked with green, Chris noticed for the first time—studied him. Anne Greenwald was slender and she had to look up a few inches at Chris, but she carried a forceful presence.

"You want me to tell you about Malachi Reese?" she asked.

Chris had obtained a court order allowing Anne Greenwald to examine Reese, in preparation for the punishment phase of trial. But punishment looked a long way away tonight.

"I know him," Chris assured her, at the same time feeling that Malachi Reese was a stranger to everyone on earth.

Anne Greenwald kept watching him. She put a hand on his arm, where Reese had gripped it. Her grip was surprisingly strong too. Chris looked more closely into her pale face, close to his own. Anne Greenwald looked at him in a very personal way.

"You want to talk about what happened today?" she asked, concern obvious in her voice.

Chris shook his head. "Thanks. I've got some important staring into space to do."

"All right." She let him go. "Call me if you change your mind. Midnight if you want. I'll be up." She turned and walked away. Her pace was briskly professional, but her light brown hair swung playfully at her shoulders. Chris found himself waiting to see if she would turn back to give him a departing glance, but the psychiatrist never looked back.

Later, in the north side condo where he'd lived for three years and that he was going to get around to decorating one of these days, Chris took a break from rehearsing his final argument to watch the news. He didn't have to wait long to see his adversary. The top of the newscast was another interview with Malachi Reese, taped right at the end of the trial day. "Like a lot of people, I was very glad to hear that the District Attorney had uncovered the source of all of San Antonio's problems. But imagine my surprise when I heard it was me."

The microphone picked up the sound of laughter, and the camera cut to a shot of the TV reporter joining in. Then Reese stopped and grew solemn, facing the camera. "It isn't that simple. It never is. I hope when this is over Christian Sinclair will join me in the search for the real truth."

The camera held on Reese's face, and the image lingered in Chris's memory long after he snapped off the TV.

Chapter 3

Chris Sinclair arrived at the Justice Center earlier than the protestors took up their posts. As the trial neared its conclusion the area in front of the building grew more congested with demonstrators. But inside the courtroom, where Malachi Reese's most ardent supporters sat packed shoulder to shoulder, the tension of the outside world took another form. Outside, the anger of the protestors grew steadily, fueled by speculation about what was going on inside the building. In the courtroom, the spectators listened intently, some literally perched on the edges of their seats.

Reese himself seemed relaxed, confident of vindication. Reese, never having been convicted of anything and a prominent citizen, was free on one hundred thousand dollars' bond during his trial. Like the District Attorney, he strode up the steps of the Justice Center every morning. During breaks in the trial he stood among his supporters in the courtroom as reporters jostled for his attention. Malachi Reese was not only a free man, he was at center stage. He would shrug off a false accusation such as this.

When Reese took the witness stand the morning after the District Attorney's testimony, he wore an impeccable navy blue suit, crisp white shirt, and muted crimson tie. His long-fingered hands rested relaxed on his crossed legs. He looked too fastidious ever to have dirtied his hands with crime. Wisely, he had dropped the amusement from the night before. That had been aimed at the reporters; once you've laughed with a man, it's hard to believe him evil. For the jurors Reese looked terribly sad at the accumulation of deception he saw all around him.

His attorney Jackson Scott asked him, "Were you surprised by your indictment in this case?"

"I knew I had made enemies, of course. Anyone does who chooses to be active in public life. But I never dreamed anyone hated me to this extent."

Chris Sinclair, sitting at the State's table, shook his head. He didn't hate Malachi Reese. He respected Reese so much he felt kinship with him. Chris hadn't shaken off the feeling that he and Reese were the only warm-blooded people in the courtroom. When Reese glanced at Chris the defendant had regained his secret smile. Its intimacy made the D.A. want to shudder.

"You have an example of an enemy you've made?" Jackson Scott asked.

"Yes. Officer—"

"Objection," Chris said. "Relevance?"

"This is relevant," Scott said. Judge Pressman let him continue.

"A couple of years ago," Malachi Reese said to the jury, "I represented three citizens in filing a complaint with the police department's internal affairs division against Officer Ray Heinz."

"Why did they need you?"

"Because they were afraid to do it on their own. Afraid of retaliation. I offered to be the figurehead for the complaint, to take the heat."

"Why did you do that?"

"Someone had to," Reese said simply. "Officer Heinz had demonstrated a pattern of brutality that couldn't be allowed to continue. And I had a higher public profile than the victims. I was less vulnerable to retaliation—I thought."

"What was the outcome of that complaint?"

"Officer Heinz received a one-week suspension without pay." Reese did not look triumphant.

"Did you consider that adequate?"

"No. But there were other consequences. Officer Heinz was knocked to the bottom of the promotion list. He was transferred to what he considered a less desirable assignment. He was furious."

"How do you know that?"

"He confronted me," Reese said. He told his story to the jury, not looking away from them. Jurors watched him attentively. "He called me names. He promised me he would get back at me."

Anticipating the District Attorney's cross-examination, Scott asked, "Were there any other witnesses to this confrontation?"

"A police officer doesn't make a threat like that in front of witnesses," Reese answered. At least two jurors, from their expressions, agreed. "He doesn't carry it out in front of witnesses, either."

"Now to the present," Scott said. "Was Officer Heinz involved in this charge against you?"

Chris knew the answer. He had a copy of the offense report in his hand. Reese said with dramatic significance, "He was one of two officers who first interviewed Mr. Adolfo Rodriguez when he reported his wife's murder."

This announcement sent a stir through the courtroom. Chris watched the jurors. Most of them kept straight faces. Chris couldn't tell if they accepted Reese's claim, but if none of the jurors had ever heard of or encountered a brutal cop, then the lawyers had managed to choose an amazingly uninformed jury. Reese's testimony played on every fear of authority the jury might harbor. He expanded on the theme.

"Councilman Briones seemed to understand your business well," Reese's lawyer prompted him.

"He understood how some business is done, let's put it that way," Reese said, losing some of his sadness in anger. This was going to be a mistake, Chris thought, attacking the dying Lou Briones, who had looked almost saintly in his last moments on the witness stand, asking a city's forgiveness. "Yes, we were on the same bidding team. But I had a very specific assignment, and that was to present our proposal to Sharon Wallace, my council representative. Sharon and I went way back together, people thought I might have some influence with her." He shrugged. If this was a sin, he confessed it. "But that was all I was to do."

"Then why did you meet with Victor Fuentes?" the defense lawyer asked.

"He called me. He'd uncovered some—"

"Objection. Hearsay," Chris said, on his feet.

"Sustained."

Before Chris could sit again, before Jackson Scott could ask another question, Reese said to Chris, in a conversational tone that carried across the courtroom, "You can put words in a dead man's mouth but I can't?"

Chris didn't answer or make a futile objection. Reese returned his attention to his own lawyer.

"What did you and Mr. Fuentes discuss in your meeting at Mi Tierra?" Scott asked.

"The bidding procedure on the waste treatment addition. Whether there'd been any irregularities."

"Did Mr. Fuentes suspect someone of any wrongdoing?"

"Y—"

"Objection," Chris said more firmly. "To anything that Mr. Fuentes may have said, or anything coming from that source, which Mr. Fuentes is no longer here to deny."

"Sustained."

The lawyers struggled tensely with nothing but legal terms as weapons, because the outcome mattered greatly to the trial. Reese could make up any subject for that restaurant conversation. He looked like an easy liar to Chris, but Reese sat sincere and straight-faced. The defense lawyer would win this duel, though, because he had one striking advantage over Chris: his client was alive.

"What did you say to Mr. Fuentes in the restaurant?" Scott asked. Without waiting for an objection, he turned to the judge.

"Your Honor, I'm not asking for hearsay, I'm asking the witness what he said himself. Furthermore, I'm not offering it as the truth, only to show he said it."

Chris answered, "It's back-door hearsay, Your Honor. Obviously whatever the defendant said was in response to something he's claiming Victor Fuentes said to him, and his answer will imply that inadmissible statement."

Judge Pressman had a way of looking thoughtfully in control, while those who knew him suspected that behind his thoughtful-looking countenance chaos reigned. After a moment he said, "How can I decide that until I hear the answer? Go ahead," he said to the defense lawyer.

Triumphantly, Jackson Scott handed the floor over to his client. "What did you say, Mr. Reese?"

"I told him I was sure Lou Briones hadn't done anything wrong, but that I didn't really know personally because I hadn't been with him."

A ripple of murmurs circulated through the courtroom.

"So it wasn't you Mr. Fuentes suspected?"

"Objection, objection," Chris said, sure of winning, but the defense lawyer answered quickly:

"Your Honor, I'm not asking the witness to assert that anything Mr. Fuentes told him was true. I'm only asking whether it was said. This goes to my client's state of mind, Your Honor. This goes to motive. The prosecution claims Mr. Reese killed Victor Fuentes because he was afraid of Mr. Fuentes' uncovering illegal activity. I am allowed to refute that claim by showing Mr. Reese had no reason to think Victor Fuentes was investigating him."

Scott looked passionate. He waved his hand and his hair became disarrayed. By the time he had finished speaking it didn't matter how Judge Pressman ruled on the hearsay objection. The defense lawyer had already presented his case to the jury. It was just the cherry on the sundae when the judge mulled it over and said, "Overruled."

"That's right," Malachi Reese said quickly. "Victor Fuentes told me he suspected Councilman Briones, not me."

This was news, withheld from the public until now. The fact that its truth was suspect only made it more newsworthy. Conversations erupted in the courtroom. One reporter got up and walked quickly out.

Reese maintained his calm demeanor. His gaze passed from his lawyer to the jurors, only resting on the District Attorney for a moment, but that one glance struck deep. To Chris it seemed they locked eyes for a long moment, and in his mind he distinctly heard Malachi Reese's voice: *Two can play at using the dead, Mr. Prosecutor.*

"Order," Judge Pressman called. "Order." Something else he had heard on TV.

Reese wasn't content with the speculation he'd thrown into the trial stew. He knew the power of the Big Lie. Go for it all. In response to his lawyer's next question he shook his head and said, "I don't believe Lou Briones does have cancer. I haven't seen any independent confirmation of that claim. He's suffering, yes, anyone can see that. He's suffering from a bad conscience. Murder is a very nasty business, it weighs on a man. That's what's eating at Lou Briones. I'm sure his guilt has called up—"

"I object to this speculation," Chris said angrily.

Reese went relentlessly on, bearing down, "As Mr. Briones *testified,* he's sorry for the way he's conducted his professional life. Like weak men do, he's looked for someone else to blame, and found me. Apparently I have a great many sins to atone for." He smiled sadly at the jury. "But they are not my sins."

Scott began his wrap-up. "Mr. Reese, did you kill Victor Fuentes?"

"No. I did not."

"Did you kill Dolores Rodriguez?"

"No. No. I have never seen the lady."

"What about Adolfo Rodriguez, whom the District Attorney says accused you of murder?"

"Yes, you phrased that exactly correctly," Reese answered, turning to look at Chris Sinclair. "The District Attorney says. Mr. Sinclair is an elected official. He owes favors, too. For some reason this case is so important to him that when it fails because there's no evidence against me, he'll take the burden on himself and make the case with only his own testimony."

"Are you accusing the District Attorney of lying?" Jackson Scott asked, with slight awe in his voice. They were stepping onto perilous but thrilling ground.

But Malachi Reese softened. "It may not be that way. Perhaps Mr. Rodriguez did say what Mr. Sinclair says he heard. It may be Mr. Rodriguez himself who was deceived. I have never seen the man. He never saw me. For long months after the murders he didn't accuse me. Not until, supposedly, he picked out my photograph, after a long time when he could have been coached, when he could have been told over and over, 'This is the man who killed your dear wife.' Until Mr. Rodriguez believed it himself. I know how these things are done. Ray Heinz is not the only police officer who's sworn to get back at me.

"I did not kill anybody," he concluded emphatically, and turned his face to the jury for inspection.

Offered cross-examination, Chris remained lost in admiration. He sat there, just staring at Reese, allowing the silence to interrupt the mesmerizing flow of Malachi Reese's testimony, until even Reese glanced inquiringly at the District Attorney.

"Mr. Reese, you are impressive," Chris finally said. "I'm surprised you've never been elected to anything."

"I never had any ambition in that direction, Mr. District Attorney."

They smiled at each other ever so slightly, just a softening of the eyes.

"Your theory that Officer Heinz influenced Mr. Rodriguez is

interesting," Chris said. "But like all the rest of your testimony, it can't be corroborated. Do you have any evidence of this improper influence?"

Reese shrugged sadly. "Now that Mr. Rodriguez is gone, he can't be asked."

"No," Chris said ironically. "But in fact it wasn't Ray Heinz who developed you as a suspect, was it?"

"Not officially, no."

"Do you happen to know who it was who showed Mr. Rodriguez the photo spread from which he picked your picture?"

"I believe that was you, Mr. Sinclair."

Chris nodded, testifying from where he sat. They were outside the bounds of the rules of evidence. "Yes," Chris said. "That's right. So I would have to be lying in order to convict you. Do you know any reason why *I* would have such animosity against you?"

"As I said, I'm willing to grant you the benefit of the doubt, Mr. Sinclair." Reese held his palms up, clearly asking, *Why won't you give me the same?*

Chris wouldn't be drawn into that exchange. "But your real enemies will go to terrible lengths to get you, according to you, Mr. Reese. Rather than just see you discredited, or charged with some variety of theft or fraud, they want you falsely convicted of capital murder. This is a rather amazing conspiracy against you, isn't it?"

"Not as amazing as what you and Lou Briones accuse me of being. This sort of master of the night, stealthy spectre of the nightmares of the rich and powerful." To Chris Reese sounded as though he enjoyed describing himself this way. But to the jury he shrugged, looking modest and flabbergasted.

Chris changed tacks, hoping to use Reese's elegant appearance against him. "How do you make a living, Mr. Reese?"

"I have a small consulting business. I advise business and political leaders."

"And you continued to make a good living at that in spite of the number of influential people who hated you so much they would frame you for capital murder?"

"I have my *compadres*," Reese said feelingly, with a perfect Spanish accent. "It has been a long struggle to achieve what we have. Some people don't forget."

His smoothness remained unshakable. Chris gave up trying to get Reese mad. But he had one more question to confront Reese with. For Chris the question was more personal than legal: "How did you know Mr. Rodriguez's tongue had been cut?" he asked icily.

Reese answered as quietly and quickly as he'd answered every other question. "My attorney asked that question. You'd have to ask him."

"I'm asking you, Mr. Reese. You're the one who told your lawyers that detail. What did you say to Mr. Pedraza?"

Jackson Scott stood quickly to make his first objection. It was as if until now his client had instructed him to back off and leave him to battle the prosecutor alone. But now Scott stepped in to rescue Reese. "Objection, your Honor. This is prying into a privileged attorney-client communication."

"That privilege belongs to the client, not the lawyer," Chris snapped. He ignored the defense lawyer. "How about it, Mr. Reese? Do you assert that privilege?"

Please do, he was thinking. Refuse to answer. Take the Fifth. Look guilty.

"No." Reese shook his head. "I don't assert it. I have nothing to hide because I don't know anything. I didn't tell Mr. Pedraza about Mr. Rodriguez's injury. He told me."

Everyone's attention turned to the mostly silent senior defense lawyer. Momentarily startled, Pedraza then frowned knowledgeably. He even nodded.

"How did he know?" Chris asked.

"I imagine—" Reese said slowly, and Jackson Scott jumped in. "Object to speculation."

"I believe that should be my objection," Chris said. "And I don't object. Go ahead, Mr. Reese."

"Your Honor?" the defense lawyer appealed.

Judge Pressman hadn't been called on to rule in many minutes. Though he had been following the exchanges closely, he looked surprised to be drawn into them.

"You said—" He turned to Chris. "You don't object? Then what—? I guess there's no objection. Overruled."

"I was only going to say," Malachi Reese said, still sounding like the most reasonable person in the room, "that this building is rife with news and rumors. I'm sure any number of people knew about the victim's condition."

"I don't think so," Chris said harshly. "Let's get to the bottom of it. Call Leo Pedraza to the stand."

"Your Honor," Scott beseeched. "I believe the defense can present its own case?"

"Fine," Chris said. "Then I'll call him in rebuttal—if you want to give him more time to think up an answer."

"Objection! Would you please stop grandstanding to the jury?"

"When you stop trying to hide things from them," Chris snapped back. He felt childish quarreling with the defense lawyer, but he was flushed with genuine anger. He clenched his fist so tightly that his forearm began to cramp.

Jackson Scott acquiesced theatrically, trying to match his client's resigned composure. "Fine, let's call Mr. Pedraza. But outside the jury's presence, your Honor? To determine whether anything he has to say is even admissible?"

The jury was taken out, looking back as jurors always do, hungry to know what was going to happen in their absence. Malachi Reese looked down sadly. Two of the jurors were African-American, five Hispanic. Reese let them see him as a prisoner, his arms resting on his legs as if dragged down by chains. He didn't raise his eyes until the last juror had filed out.

Leo Pedraza made a much less imposing figure on the stand. He lifted his chin as if for an official portrait, but his eyes sought refuge. His client had instructed him from the witness stand exactly what to say, but Pedraza hadn't had time to rehearse. When Chris asked him abruptly, "How did you know that Adolfo Rodriguez's tongue had been cut?" Pedraza cleared his throat and stammered.

"Well, of course, everyone knew about the event. There had been news crews there, after all. And word gets around—you know this place, Mr. Sinclair, news travels—"

"Through whom?" Chris demanded.

Pedraza frowned. "I heard police officers talking in the hall, I believe. Then I made a few calls to confirm—"

"To whom?" Chris insisted. "Who told you? I didn't tell anyone, and until the medical examiner concluded his autopsy, I don't think anyone else knew. How did you?"

Pedraza sat thinking. What would happen next was obvious: when he named a name that person would be called to the witness stand. Even if he or she backed up Pedraza's claim, the witness's source of information would be questioned. The District Attorney's face made it clear he was going to stay on this trail until it was revealed as a lie.

"I'm not sure," Leo Pedraza finally said. "I don't remember exactly."

"That's your answer?" Chris asked incredulously. "You don't remember?"

"I wish I could," Pedraza said helpfully. "But I talk to so many people in a day . . ."

He tried to look both knowledgeable and ignorant at the same time, and managed to look shifty. His eyes moved everywhere except to his client. At the defense table Malachi Reese sat stiffly, arms crossed. With the jury gone and his back to the spectators, he let his strict control of his face slip. He almost glowed with suppressed rage.

———

When the jurors returned Reese looked completely different. He was back on the witness stand in his sad, shaken posture. The jurors looked around suspiciously. Nothing seemed to have changed. What had happened to the other witness? They were not to know. The judge had ruled Pedraza's claim of ignorance inadmissible.

"I have another question for you, Mr. Reese," Chris said. He, too, sounded weary, but his voice lifted as he talked. "Let us say you're telling the truth when you deny knowing the details of Mr. Rodriguez's murder. Nevertheless, that murder was a lucky break for you, wasn't it? Now the prime witness against you can't be here. That's quite a coincidence, isn't it?"

Reese didn't hesitate. "It's no coincidence. The people who planned this didn't want that witness questioned in court. They didn't want this jury to hear his real story, or to see how unsure he was of what you wanted him to say."

Again Chris marvelled. It was impossible to take Malachi Reese by surprise. Chris shook his head admiringly. Then, as if he'd just thought of it, he asked, "One more question. How did Victor Fuentes get to Mi Tierra?"

"I gave him a ride from City Hall."

"But you didn't give him a ride home, did you?"

"No," Reese said. "He said he wanted to walk off the meal. Victor was a big walker, everybody knew that about him. He liked to roam the streets. If only—"

Reese left the thought hanging, scoring a last point. But Chris had the satisfaction of seeing his antagonist look momentarily puzzled. What had the question meant?

Late in the morning, in rebuttal, the prosecution called Lou Briones' doctor, hastily summoned to testify that Briones did indeed have cancer. Malachi Reese dismissively looked away during the testimony. Chris thought it a necessary but probably futile offering to present the doctor's confirmation of Briones' illness. Once a conspiracy theory is offered, anyone who denies it becomes part of the conspiracy. Calling a dozen doctors would have only made the conspiracy against Reese appear more massive, if any of the jurors already believed in the plot.

Testimony ended. The judge's instructions to the jury were prepared. The lawyers had a brief break to prepare for argument. Chris and Melissa rushed upstairs to the D.A.'s offices. Along the way they were joined by Anne Greenwald. The psychiatrist hadn't been in the courtroom, because she was scheduled to testify in the punishment phase, but she was obviously following the trial closely.

"Do the facts," Chris instructed Melissa once they were in his office. "The reason for the murder, the timetable. You can explain the walking. Ten minutes, twelve minutes tops. I'll handle the rest. Okay?"

Melissa walked out to prepare. Chris's office, which was seldom empty, still held a few prosecutors. Paul Benavides leaned on the desk and tried to look encouraging. Outside the door Mike Martinez, the young assistant, peeked in. Standing close to him was his friend Lynn Ransom, the highest-ranking African-American in the D.A.'s office. Chris's eye caught on Lynn for a moment.

A gloomy silence hung in the office. Only Anne Greenwald spoke up. The psychiatrist had her arms folded and looked concerned. She seemed small in that posture, condensed to her essential strength. Her eyes held Chris's.

"Can I give you one piece of advice? I heard about how your questioning went this morning. You need to change that dynamic in your argument. *Don't* pit yourself against him. If you ask the jurors to vote in a personal contest between you and Malachi Reese, you will never get all their votes."

Chris nodded, but to Dr. Greenwald he didn't seem to be paying attention. "Am I the only one who can see into his eyes?" he asked. "If you could have seen what I—"

"I am the one person you don't have to convince," Anne said

passionately. "He scared me to death. He's completely fluid, he has no hard beliefs except that Malachi Reese must win."

Chris looked at her in surprise. He'd never heard the psychiatrist sound this convinced. She emphasized what she was saying with a slashing gesture of her hand. Her eyes shone.

"You got all that from examining him?" Chris asked.

Anne only shrugged. "You must be very good," Chris said. The psychiatrist almost smiled.

Melissa Fleming was nervous, but she carried the lightest burden. She only had to lead off the arguments, she didn't have to be the most convincing lawyer in court. She stood tall and her voice was steady. She tried to make the prosecution theory sound scientific in its accuracy.

"Two people were killed with the same knife. The medical examiner told us that from his examination of the wounds. Victor Fuentes in the parking lot of his apartment building, Mrs. Dolores Rodriguez some seventy feet away, around a corner. Mrs. Rodriguez was sprawled facedown. Her first wounds, Dr. Garcia told us, were to her back. She was chased down and murdered. She fought with her attacker.

"But Victor Fuentes didn't. His throat was slashed from the front. His hands were free, but he didn't use them. There were no defensive wounds on his hands. Why? You can tell me the answer. He didn't defend himself because he didn't know until too late that he had to. He knew the man walking toward him with the knife hidden until the last second. Victor Fuentes looked up in surprise, because he had just left this man forty-five minutes earlier in a restaurant."

Melissa demonstrated, looking up, which exposed her long, slender neck. Rapidly she drew a hand across it. "And he was murdered, that fast. Victor had one more wound to the chest, just to make sure, but his murder happened very quickly and should have been over."

Melissa Fleming had the common habit of assuming a first-name basis with people she knew only from autopsy reports. It made Chris wince, but the jurors didn't seem to mind.

She went on to describe how the murderer had realized he was being watched, how he chased down and murdered Mrs. Rodriguez. Melissa was walking slowly backwards, and by the end of her recitation she was no longer saying "the murderer." She was saying "he," and she was pointing at Malachi Reese. Reese watched her attentively, occasionally shaking his head.

"But Mr. Reese had remained behind in Mi Tierra," Melissa said. "People remembered him there, for half an hour after Victor had left the restaurant. Mr. Reese made sure of that, didn't he? Because he didn't have to be in any hurry. He knew where his victim was going and he knew how he was going to get there. Walking. You heard him say it. Victor Fuentes was known as a man who liked to walk. And Malachi Reese knew where Victor was going, more than two miles away. Reese bided his time, he waited, and then he drove away and arrived at that parking lot just about the time his victim did.

"Why?" Melissa remembered for the jury Lou Briones' testimony. "Malachi Reese was afraid not just that this crooked deal was going to be ruined, but that his whole secret, nefarious life was going to be exposed. Victor Fuentes was his mortal enemy."

She did her best with this explanation, but there was an element of conviction missing from Melissa's voice. She was a straightforward young woman, weaving a lurid secret life was foreign to her. But she raised her voice and forced it to be emphatic as she concluded: "This man. This man. He has gotten away with so much in his life. Victor Fuentes couldn't stop him. Mr. Rodriguez couldn't stop him. There are only twelve people who can stop him."

She saluted the jurors with a significant stare.

Jackson Scott took a unique approach in his defensive argument. He didn't deny anything. In fact, he admitted the possibility the prosecution's case was true.

"Did Malachi Reese kill Victor Fuentes? Maybe. We can't absolutely prove otherwise. We have Malachi leaving the restaurant long after Mr. Fuentes left, then arriving at a party a few minutes later. The District Attorney will tell you those witnesses were lying or mistaken about the time, and that's possible. So maybe Malachi had time to stop off at that parking lot and murder two people. Possibly."

The defense lawyer had a thoughtful, professorial gaze. He moved to another possibility. "Why would Malachi have done such a thing? Councilman Briones told you it was because Victor Fuentes meant to uncover some sort of nebulous wrongdoings of Malachi's. We don't know exactly what, but it was bad, very bad. Bad enough to drive a man to murder.

"Mr. Briones has his own skeletons in the closet. You heard from Malachi that it was Lou Briones Mr. Fuentes actually suspected of something criminal. Lou Briones is the one who has the motive to lie, who has reason to throw blame on someone else. We always see this finger-pointing after a crime, don't we? And we just have to guess who's telling the truth and who's lying. So again, maybe the State's case is right. Maybe Lou Briones, a lifelong politician, a man who admits to his own shady deals, maybe he was the one telling you the truth. Maybe Malachi was lying.

"Maybe he lied about Mr. Adolfo Rodriguez, too. That is a horrible tragedy." The defense lawyer grew very sober. "Never in my experience, or the judge's experience, or the District Attorney's experience, has something like that happened during a trial—because of the trial. It's frightening. You might ask, why wasn't Mr. Rodriguez better protected, if he was such a crucial witness for the prosecution? I don't know. Ask Mr. Sinclair that.

But if, as Malachi said, it was someone on the police force who wanted Mr. Rodriguez dead, someone in authority, it would have been impossible to protect him.

"Did Malachi Reese kill Mr. Rodriguez? No. He was here in the Justice Center at the time. But, Mr. Sinclair implied, Malachi had the murder committed. He ordered it. He has those kinds of contacts in the criminal underworld. There are people loyal to him who would do that kind of thing. You haven't seen any evidence of that, but maybe it's so. Maybe the District Attorney will even investigate that crime and uncover some evidence against Malachi. Because that would be capital murder, too, paying to have someone killed. Maybe the prosecutor can find proof of that crime.

"Proof!" Scott suddenly found his passion. He bobbed his head, he glared. But he stayed in control. "Because he hasn't brought you any so far, has he? The District Attorney has offered you theories, he's raised possibilities. But has he proven anything—beyond a reasonable doubt?"

He went and stood close to his client, trusting Reese to have his face composed, and he was not disappointed. Reese gazed at the jurors with determination, trusting them.

"Maybe this man was at the heart of a terrible conspiracy," Scott said contemptuously. *"Maybe* he murdered Victor Fuentes. Maybe he murdered Mrs. Rodriguez, too, and Mr. Rodriguez. Maybe Malachi Reese is responsible for every unsolved murder in San Antonio history. Maybe!"

He walked closer to the jury, which brought him close to Chris Sinclair. Scott stopped and pointed at the prosecutor. "He is asking you to convict Malachi Reese of capital murder. The worst crime on the books. And all he's offered you is conjecture, theory, one man's word against another. We can't positively place Malachi somewhere else at the time of the murder, but he can't place him at the scene of the crime at all! No blood, no fingerprints, no torn cloth, no witness who saw a license plate number.

"But maybe he did it, they say. Yes, maybe! Life is full of possibilities. But in this courtroom, maybe isn't good enough. To convict this man of capital murder, to take his life? No. Please tell the prosecution, don't bring us a maybe case. Make a better case next time. Maybe? You tell them, maybe not."

Chris sighed. He felt the truth of the defense lawyer's argument. The prosecution's case appeared to be nothing. He wanted to refute the defense argument point by point. But then he remembered what Anne Greenwald had said. Don't make it a personal contest. And he remembered his strength.

"They didn't shake hands," he said. "Victor Fuentes and Malachi Reese, at the end of their meal and their long discussion. They said good-bye but they didn't shake hands.

"A handshake is such a casual thing." Chris strolled to the jury box. He extended his hand and one of the male jurors reached for it automatically. "We do it without thinking. It doesn't mean much anymore. We do it when we meet strangers. Men in business do it as a matter of course. But Victor Fuentes and Malachi Reese refrained. If they'd had the discussion Mr. Reese says they had, if they'd just made an alliance to investigate Lou Briones, they would have shaken hands to seal the deal.

"But they didn't. Victor Fuentes stood and they looked at each other, and they smiled.

"Strange," Chris said, inviting the jurors to join him in analysis. Give them a small puzzle, you get them used to turning to you for answers. "They wouldn't shake hands, but they smiled at each other."

He turned toward Reese. "I'm sure you all heard Mr. Reese ask me, 'Why can you put words in a dead man's mouth but I can't?' The difference is, my witness knew he was about to die. Victor Fuentes didn't. He hadn't made a pact with Malachi Reese. They had only agreed to disagree. To be opponents. They were men who enjoyed a good fight, and they had just announced one. Malachi Reese smiled to put his enemy at ease. Victor Fuentes smiled to show his confidence. He thought he understood the battlefield. But he was wrong. Dead wrong. He didn't understand the man he was dealing with. A man who decided a long time ago that people who play by the rules are fools. A man who will do anything—anything—to take care of a problem."

For a moment Chris felt himself slipping back into that otherworldly mind. To win a conviction he had to convince the jurors that Malachi Reese was utterly different from what he appeared; that such rage and ruthlessness filled him that he would murder a man rather than risk exposure, then also murder an old woman who happened to see him. Chris felt certain he had been inside Malachi Reese's cunning, implacable mind in court the day before. In that moment of awful clarity he'd become convinced of Reese's guilt. But could the jury see it?

"Mr. Scott was right. This is very thin evidence for a capital murder trial. Malachi Reese made sure of that. There was only one witness against him. I won't ever forgive myself for Adolfo Rodriguez's death. I didn't understand, you see. I didn't realize how ruthless Malachi Reese is. I was playing by the rules, like everyone else. It took death to make Victor Fuentes understand. And Mr. Rodriguez understood. He lifted his head and he said to me, 'Malachi Reese killed me because of what I saw.' "

Unconsciously Chris held out his arms. He spoke to the phantom in them. "He gathered his life's last strength to say that. Because Mr. Rodriguez knew that his death was all that mattered.

"Not his children. Not his wife. Not his seventy years of blameless life. He knew that none of that had anything to do with why he was dying. He was dying because of the terrible accident of witnessing a murder.

"He might have wanted to leave words of comfort to his family. He might have wanted to sum up his life the way people do on their deathbeds. But Mr. Rodriguez knew he didn't have that luxury. His last words had to be spent on an accusation. Because his life didn't count. His death was all that mattered—to this man."

He turned and pointed at Malachi Reese. Reese wasn't surprised, he had his face composed into a sad and innocent mask. But the quick glance he shot at the District Attorney didn't match.

"And you think Mr. Rodriguez spent his last breath on a lie? No. He knew. People in their graves know the truth about Malachi Reese. Mr. Rodriguez tried his most desperate best to reach you with that truth. He knew he would never get to this courtroom, but he spent everything he had to see that you had the truth before you.

"Please don't tell me he failed."

An attentive silence covered the courtroom, but Chris had no more to say. He was dead tired. It wasn't until he sat down that he felt the wetness on his cheeks.

"I think crying works," Mike Martinez said. Even in the grim atmosphere of waiting for a verdict in Chris's office, the assistant D.A. remained jaunty and irrepressible. Martinez was a thin young man sometimes known as El Rojo because though he was Mexican-American, his hair glowed red in sunlight. He felt the stares on him and said, "Hey, I don't mean you were being phony, Big Guy. I mean if you don't feel it, how can you expect the jury to? It worked for me, that's all I mean. I was listening to you and I swear I could hear that old man." He gave a little shudder.

There was a shocked silence in Chris's crowded office, until the District Attorney laughed. El Rojo always had that effect on him.

A few assistants chuckled along. Chris felt suddenly how little he knew any of them. They were here with him on this deathwatch, but he had no friends in the room. His friends he had left behind among the ranks of defense lawyers who were now on the other side. Of his nearly two hundred assistants, there were many who still didn't trust him because of Chris's own defense background, others who resented him because he'd fired friends of theirs when he'd first taken office and tried to clean house of incompetents.

It was after six o'clock, the jury had been out for five hours. There'd been no notes from the jury room, no hints. Judge Pressman was getting ready to call them out and ask if they wanted to keep deliberating or call it a day. When Chris's desk phone buzzed, Chris figured that was the reason. He walked out of his office in silence.

But as he came down the stairs to the third-floor courtroom he felt a stir in the building. People were in the hallway. When he stepped into it he felt the tension. He knew even before one of his assistants came running toward him.

"Verdict," the young man almost shouted. "They have a verdict!"

Chris didn't hear anything else in the hall. A white noise that blanked out human speech filled his ears. What was he going to do? Knowing what he knew, he couldn't let Malachi Reese just walk out of this courtroom and resume his life. How could Chris bring him to justice once the jury freed him?

He was at the counsel table and the jurors were filing in. He turned toward the defendant, but Malachi Reese was concentrating on the jurors. Finally Reese looked slightly nervous.

The jurors filed in slowly, many ducking their heads from the attention of the half-filled courtroom. Some few of them looked at Chris, and they looked frightened. What were they scared of—what he might do to them if they announced "not guilty"?

"Mr. Foreman, we understand you have a verdict," Judge Pressman said. The judge had re-donned his robe hastily, one shoulder rode a little higher than the other.

"Yes, your Honor." The foreman was a thin Hispanic man in his forties wearing a white shirt with the sleeves rolled up his forearms. He had the long pages of the court's charge flipped to the last page, the verdict form.

Judge Pressman enjoyed informality at such moments. "Let us hear it," he said.

The foreman cleared his throat nervously. He read from the paper. "We find the defendant guilty of capital murder."

A woman screamed. Not the shrill shriek of a teenager but the full-throated scream of a mature woman whose heart had just broken. It was the signal for a melee in the courtroom, with the screaming woman at its focus. Chris ignored her. He may have been the only person in the courtroom who turned and took a long look at the defendant, Malachi Reese. Reese sat utterly still, as if still waiting for word from the jury. His mouth slightly open, his eyes glazed, Reese's consciousness had fled inward.

Chris understood now why the jury had looked toward him. They were afraid of what the D.A. had made them believe. They hadn't been able to choose between Christian Sinclair and Malachi Reese, so they'd believed instead in Chris's portrait of the dying Adolfo Rodriguez. It was Mr. Rodriguez's guilty verdict.

It was two hours later when Chris made his slow way down through the Justice Center, the last person in the building except for a nervous security guard at the front door, looking out at the protestors milling in front of the building. Outside the front doors of the Justice Center was a small parking lot for officials' cars, empty now. Chris had parked across the street in the five-story parking garage.

"I'd go around if I were you, sir," said the guard. "Or I can call for a police escort if you'd like."

Chris looked out at the parking lot that now served as a huge stage, eerily lit by tall, bright halogen lights that gave a parody of daylight. There were more than thirty people in the parking lot, mostly black, but there was no organization. People wandered from group to group, looking mournful. One man stood giving a speech in the center of the parking lot, but no one else paid him much attention. The prevailing mood seemed to be sad puzzlement rather than rage.

"I think it'll be okay," Chris said, remembering how easily he'd passed through this same crowd two days earlier. "Thanks."

His suit felt baggy on him as he stepped out. The April air held only a little coolness. Chris felt the bulk of the building behind him, a trickle of concern as he left its protection. Unconsciously, he searched through the crowd for the face that had become so recognizable to him: Malachi Reese could have stirred this crowd. But not Reese as Chris had last seen him, in the courtroom, looking stricken, a man abandoned by his best ally, his reason.

People looked at Chris, faces lifting with hope of a message, then changing as they recognized the District Attorney. Two or three started toward him, the most menacing-looking a tall black woman in her fifties.

"Hey!" shouted the speaker in the middle of the parking lot. "Hey, man, I wanta ask you a question!"

Keep moving, Chris thought. The crowd didn't have enough energy to pursue him, but before he reached the street the rage parade arrived.

The protests had begun on the city's east side, where the African-American population of San Antonio was most concentrated. People had come out of their houses to ask one another if they'd heard the Reese verdict. In a few homes and beer joints and vacant lots groups gathered. In the groups that had stayed together for the two hours since the verdict, rage had blossomed. It had been slow and isolated at first, but began to feed on itself.

Self-appointed messengers drove from one neighborhood to another, and soon a small line of cars formed. Men talked, drank, got mad, distorted what they'd heard, kicked at stones and bar stool legs, and trickled outside. By the time they organized into a caravan, some of them decided they needed to go to the Justice Center to vent their anger.

The looseness of these protestors' organization allowed them to elude police. They didn't honk or scream or otherwise draw attention to themselves, and it wasn't until they parked at the Justice Center itself that their anger found a focus. They didn't become a mob until they stepped out of their cars. Unfortunately, Chris Sinclair crossed the small parking lot in front of the Justice Center at just that moment.

Suddenly the angry men had a target. They began to run. The lone TV cameraman still there to film the protestors bravely kept his camera working. The new protestors, a different breed from the quiet crowd milling in the parking lot, nevertheless flowed around the cameraman, tolerating him for his function, wanting their images spread as far as possible.

The men from the cars weren't all black, nor all young, but those qualities predominated. Someone threw a bottle that glinted high in the arc lights then shattered loudly on the pavement. Chris backed slowly away, trying for invisibility, unconsciously holding his briefcase as a shield. But his face stood out against the black asphalt, and the new arrivals quickly spotted him.

"There!" shouted one man, with a shiny dark face and his shirt unbuttoned to the night. Sweat striped his body. His teeth seemed to grow as he bared them. He ran toward Chris, brandishing a makeshift club.

Chris faced him, lifting his briefcase slightly. The man stopped and screamed at him, inarticulate with fury. When the scream ended he found words. "Racist bastard!" He lifted the club, the wooden handle of some garden tool.

"No," Chris said, shaking his head, but his voice was lost even to his own ears. Other protestors came running. One grabbed the first man's club. Several shouted at Chris, others tried to turn the rage to something productive, but those few were quickly drowned out. Angry people jostled Chris on all sides, pushing him, thrusting their faces at him. He still held his briefcase. His face lost what color it had. He felt as if he couldn't breathe. In moments he would be crushed.

The only other non–African-American in the crowd was a Hispanic man who looked as angry as everyone else, but nevertheless found himself pushed aside. The tall angry woman pushed his shoulder and someone else elbowed him out of the way. Then the tall woman turned toward Chris, and the crowd deferred to her rage. Her eyes shone furiously.

"You know what you've done?" she screamed. But this was no discussion group. Yells lifted in answer. "Stop it!" Chris shouted, but no one heard. Someone reached out and grabbed his briefcase. As Chris struggled to retain it a fist struck him in the side of the head. It was a glancing blow, but made him lose his grip and stagger backward.

He willed himself to keep his feet. Blood trickled down his temple, and for a moment it held the crowd at bay, shocked at what they were about to do. But the blood stirred them, too. They moved toward Chris again, and he turned to run, but when he heard the squeal of more tires he knew he was doomed.

The scene flashed bloodred, then white, then blue. The new arrivals were squad cars. They'd come quickly in response to the security guard's call, from the police station only three blocks away.

Chris ran toward them and when his blue suit mingled with the blue uniforms he felt a huge relief such as cops had never inspired in him before. The young uniformed officers swarmed past him, toward the crowd. Screams and shouts renewed.

Chris found a Hispanic sergeant leaning on one squad car, hand holding a radio. "Stop them!" Chris yelled. "They haven't done anything!"

He meant the protestors, but his voice sounded panicked even to himself. The sergeant gave him a contemptuous look. Chris looked back at the tumult. The cops were vastly outnumbered, ten against fifty, but had the advantage of training and momentum. The protestors gave way before them. But everywhere Chris looked he saw struggle and rage. He had never seen a confrontation like this before in San Antonio. It was like a scene transported from another, angrier city.

Chris turned and fled.

His way home took him naturally east. A few angry-looking people walked the streets, but downtown, usually festive with tourists and conventioneers, had now mostly emptied of people. Chris hoped visitors down on the Riverwalk were safe. When he reached the expressway that divided downtown from the beginning of east San Antonio he turned up an entrance ramp to the expressway, heading for the safety of the north side. His windows were rolled up and his doors locked. Streetlights shimmered down his windshield. High on the expressway, he looked to the right. Police cars streamed out East Commerce. At every intersection on their route a crisis drew attention: a crowd, a stranded car, a fight. Streetlights were broken all over the quadrant of town Chris could see, but here and there fires took up the missing lights' task. The fires seized Chris's attention. They looked like signal fires, like flares around a terrible highway wreck.

The image of the fires seemed to pursue him.

Chapter 4

Deep in the heart of the District Attorney's office, on the fifth floor of the Justice Center, where outsiders couldn't come without permission and an escort, only a few steps from Chris Sinclair's own office, was a conference room. It was a white rectangle of a room, furnished with a long oak table. The walls were minimally decorated with prints of scenes meant to be reassuring to witnesses or angry citizens: a forest glade, the ocean. The hotel-room art went ignored this morning. At 8:00 A.M. the morning after the guilty verdict and the ensuing public violence, eight or ten of the senior staff of the District Attorney's Office had gathered at the table. They included First Assistant District Attorney Paul Benavides; Alice Wellback, the chief of the felony section; Melissa Fleming, the capital crimes chief; chief investigator Jack Fine; and Lynn Ransom. Lynn's minimal seniority in the office wouldn't ordinarily have admitted her to such a high-level strategy session. She had only been in the D.A.'s office three years. But Lynn had been included because she was the highest-ranking black prosecutor in the office. She knew it and so did everyone else; they were all determined not to refer to the fact.

Mike Martinez also lurked in one corner of the room, lying low because no one had invited him to the conference.

The District Attorney's wound drew everyone's initial attention. Chris had tried to downplay it with a small bandage on his temple. But his face was whiter than usual this morning; the bandage's "flesh" tone was several shades darker than Chris's. "I'm okay," he'd had to say more than once. They had all seen him, either last night or on this morning's early news, being attacked by the crowd of protestors in the parking lot. It added deference to their voices, but it didn't stop them from speaking their minds.

Paul Benavides led off. The first assistant was tall and broad-shouldered, but with a scholarly appearance in his dark-framed glasses. He knew Malachi Reese personally; they had been active in several of the same civil rights organizations. Benavides was the voice of political considerations within the office. He had opposed the Reese prosecution as a public-relations mistake, while deferring to Chris's decision that the prosecution's case had to be pursued. Now, though, Paul Benavides felt justified in his original opinion.

"Last night was just the beginning," he said, glancing at the D.A.'s bandage. "You really want to see this city burn, you go ahead with seeking the death penalty."

"So we let protestors in the streets dictate our policies?" asked Alice Wellback, the felony chief. She and Paul Benavides stared at each other, ready to make the argument personal. Alice was a career prosecutor, and had made no secret of the fact that she didn't like having politicians for bosses.

"Should we instead be blind to everything outside this building?" Paul shot back. "Already on the national news we're being reported as a backwater that somehow escaped the last forty years of progress. You know the reputation Dallas had after Kennedy was murdered there? Memphis after Martin Luther King? That's how we'll look. Redneckville."

"But you know that's not true," Chris said mildly. In fact San Antonio was a city where integration and other civil rights gains had been achieved with a minimum of physical confrontations; where an Hispanic had been elected mayor in citywide elections a quarter of a century ago. Hardly anyone in the room was old enough to remember a time of real racial tension in San Antonio. Chris seemed to have conjured up the spectre of racial antagonism out of an ugly alternative past.

"It wasn't true a week ago," Paul Benavides retorted. "Have you looked outside this morning?"

Protestors had appeared outside the Justice Center again this morning. They raised angry voices but were under the watchful eyes of police reinforcing Justice Center security. What was more disturbing was that this morning the protestors against the Reese guilty verdict had opponents in the Justice Center parking lot. These counter-protestors, nearly all white, were equally angry. Some of the signs they carried were nakedly racist. As Chris had made his hasty way through them this morning, they had raised a cheer at his appearance. Their happiness had chilled him. The people who hated Chris didn't scare him; his own supporters did.

Chris hadn't ignored his first assistant's dire predictions about the consequences of prosecuting Malachi Reese for capital murder: he had gone ahead in spite of the warnings. Chris had concentrated on the technical problems of the trial itself. He had overcome those only to find his victory turned into disaster.

Alice Wellback insisted, "May I point out that the jury that convicted Malachi Reese of capital murder has an Anglo minority? Two blacks and five Hispanics found him guilty. Can't we point to that and say—"

"And let the jurors take the heat, like always?" Lynn Ransom said suddenly.

"The heat will be short-term for them," Paul Benavides said. "It'll be a daily fact of life for us."

Once Lynn had spoken up, everyone watched her less obliquely. Lynn had clear brown eyes that matched her skin, and an expressive face that this morning showed the strain of her position. Her broad cheeks were flat planes, her eyes dark above them.

"Lynn?" Chris asked quietly.

She gave him a long, simmering stare. "You want my position as a prosecutor? Or am I just here to represent the African-American community?"

Everyone looked shocked except Chris, whose open, questioning expression didn't change. "Give me your gut reaction," he said.

"Gut?" Lynn lowered her eyes a moment, then looked up again more sad than angry. "I know it's going to be awfully tough to ever talk to a group of black students again. What kind of a fool am I going to feel like when I tell them that instead of doing something stupid like shooting a store clerk they should work hard and make something of themselves and make the world a better place? When I know they'll be thinking, What difference does it make, I'll end up the same place no matter what?"

Chris sighed. He tried to remember a moment of triumph in this very difficult case and couldn't recall one. He had won in the courtroom, but Malachi Reese seemed to own the rest of the world.

"May I say something?" Mike Martinez asked. A few people glanced at him in surprise, because El Rojo had no business being in on this conference. Martinez was flamboyant and a little reckless, but he was also sharp as hell, and a very good trial prosecutor—something respected by everyone in the room.

Chris nodded.

Mike Martinez looked uncharacteristically serious. He stared around the circle of mostly white faces and said, "You won the first phase of trial and now you're thinking of quitting? You're going to go in there and let Reese off the hook after proving that he murdered three people?" His stare focused on Chris. "Three *Mexicanos*," he added. "If it was three white people he'd killed, would you think of waiving the death penalty?"

Chris looked at his first assistant, and saw Paul Benavides stricken by the question. Chris raised his eyebrows around the table, asking an answerless question. *Is there a good way to go in this case?* No one spoke up. Paul Benavides sighed and shook his head.

Chris stood. His color looked a little better. "Mike has a good question. He murdered three people. What do all of you think I should do?"

It was a rhetorical question. Lynn Ransom watched Chris closely. Before he turned away he said to her, "You tell them there aren't any shortcuts. Tell them crime never goes unpunished no matter what else you do. Okay?"

When Chris emerged from the conference room he almost bumped into Anne Greenwald, the psychiatrist, hardly recognizing her at first. Dr. Greenwald had appeared to do her part in the punishment phase of trial. She was dressed very professionally, in a discreetly checked suit and a white blouse pleated down the front. She looked different from the woman Chris remembered, but he couldn't say how. Her lips were fuller, he decided. Certainly her eyes were brighter. Dr. Greenwald projected the sense of responsibility and urgency he felt. As soon as she saw him she started talking.

"In punishment you have to reassure the jury," Anne said. "They've done a very frightening thing, convicting a man of capital murder. This isn't just about punishment now, you have to reassure them they did the right thing in voting guilty. You have to make him look even more monstrous. Don't worry, I'll help with that."

His assistants filed past, some of them nodding to Anne, who was well-known in the office as a witness. Chris waited until they had all passed and he and the psychiatrist were alone again. Then he said, "I've decided not to call you as a witness."

"What? I'm the one who knows him, Mr. Sinclair. I can tell the jury—"

"You know what happened last night," Chris interrupted. "I don't want to start a race war. I hadn't thought enough about the racial aspect, it's been too personal between Reese and me."

"What can you do to stop it?" she asked, genuinely curious.

"I can not call you as a witness."

Sarcasm was a natural urge in Anne Greenwald, and sometimes she didn't resist it. "What, a Jewish woman can't read a black man's mind?"

"I don't want to put you on the witness stand to say you can. It would alienate too many people to say you know what it's like inside his skin."

"Skin!" Anne said harshly. "Skin, skin. I'm sick of hearing about skin."

That was too bad, because Chris found himself thinking about hers, thinking he'd like to soothe the angry red skin of her temples. The thought took him by surprise.

Dr. Greenwald's eyes slashed a path across his face, then returned more curiously. The moment changed. This fight was too personal, Chris had said. It was dangerous, too. She suddenly felt his concern; not just for the community, for her. He didn't want to put anyone else in the path of Malachi Reese's rage.

As a psychiatrist she was prone to these fits of insight, she had to fight the feeling that she understood everyone. But this time she was sure she was right.

She touched the tiny bandage on his forehead, so lightly the touch soothed him like cool water. Concern returned to her voice. "You might not get the death sentence without psychiatric testimony."

"I'd rather lose it than drive that kind of wedge into the community."

He didn't sound heroic. He made a shrug of the eyes and turned away.

"Chris—I don't think you can get to him. He's a boulder that's been in the stream a long time, there are no rough edges left. The best you can do is smash other people against him."

He gave her an odd look, surprised to find a collaborator, and went out without answering. Anne was left pushing her hair back from her forehead and resolutely not chewing on a fingernail.

Judge Phil Pressman would have liked to postpone the punishment phase of trial, or better yet get it out of his courtroom altogether, but he couldn't think of a good judicial-sounding reason to do so. So trial resumed about 9:30 that morning, just as if it weren't the center of the city's attention.

There were five extra bailiffs in the courtroom. Three of them prowled the aisle in the audience section, where the seats were jam-packed. Ethnic groups at their edges sat shoulder to shoulder, but otherwise didn't mix. Those who'd carried signs had been relieved of them. A constant murmur rose from the spectators, but no raised voices. The bailiffs had already ejected five people. The others were here to watch. Chris, entering the courtroom from a door at the front, returned their stares for a moment, then took his seat. He continued to feel the spectators' stares like heat on his back.

The extra bailiffs were also for Malachi Reese, who was now a convicted double murderer. Judge Pressman had wanted the defendant handcuffed, but Chris had convinced the judge of the badness of that idea.

The tension heightened several notches when Reese appeared, coming in through a side door and escorted by a bailiff. But Reese was very subdued, and didn't look into the audience. He had spent the night in jail, his bail revoked after the guilty verdict. Either the night in jail or the shock of the verdict itself had changed him appreciably. He wore the same suit from the day before, the first time he had repeated himself in clothing, and his tie was not as crisply tied as usual. But the real change was in Reese himself. He looked as if he'd had no sleep, or only of the unrefreshing variety. His eyes blinked too often, his hands rubbed each other. His movements were jerky; he seemed afraid to look at people.

Chris thought how perfect Reese's stunned appearance was. The best thing a defendant could do in the punishment phase was make the jury think they'd been wrong to convict him, so they would go as light as possible in sentencing. Reese had that look down perfectly: the stunned look of an innocent man.

But Chris's cynicism couldn't hold up. Unwillingly, he felt his sympathy for Malachi Reese rise. How would a genuinely innocent man look any different?

It was not just the jury Chris had to convince on punishment.

"The State calls Lou Briones."

The former city councilman was aware of the increased curiosity of the stares that fell on him. Some of them were hostile, but Briones no longer had to be concerned about the electorate. He walked as briskly as he could up the aisle, head held high. He sat straight in the witness stand, bristling with some of his old energy. The contrast between that energy and his appearance was frightening.

"Dress for a funeral," was the only advice Chris had given his witness. Briones had—for his own. He wore a black suit, fashionable but badly in need of re-tailoring for the smaller man Lou Briones had become. The shoulder seams fell to his biceps. The yards of dark cloth obscured his body, so his head seemed to emerge from a void. Briones' elegant black suit encased a ghost.

Chris spoke carefully. "Mr. Briones, during the first phase of trial you hinted at other crimes Malachi Reese had committed. Can you give us an example?"

"One," Briones nodded. "The cruelest one I ever heard. Jack Pearson—"

"I re-urge my objection," Jackson Scott interrupted. " 'Heard' is the key word. It tells us all this testimony is going to be hearsay."

"But admissible anyway," Chris answered, "as a statement against interest."

If a person admits something that would subject him to prosecution or public distaste, that statement is thought to be so reliable that someone else can relay it in court. Judge Pressman had held a hearing on this issue in a hearing weeks earlier, as part of the many pre-trial maneuverings. Luckily he now remembered that he had already ruled in favor of the State. He nodded for Chris to continue.

"Jack Pearson was divorcing his wife," Briones said heavily. "It was . . . ugly. Myra was very bitter because Jack was leaving her for a younger woman. Myra wanted the kids, she wanted every penny Jack had, and she wanted to ruin him, too. She claimed she knew some dirty secrets, and she started talking. He couldn't appease her with settlement offers, Myra had family money of her own. It was one of those deals where everybody was going to be wrecked. Jack went around all day in a panic.

"That's when Malachi offered to have a word with her. I was there when he said it, in Jack's office in City Hall, and as soon as I heard it I walked out. But I knew Jack said yes. He told me later he hadn't realized what he was saying, but I knew better than that. Jack was going to be the next mayor, if he could deal with the Myra problem. When Malachi offered to take care of her, Jack said yes."

Briones was directing his story at Reese himself. The defendant didn't look up. He sat slowly shaking his head. But gradually, as the story progressed, Reese sat up straighter and stared back at Briones, as if trying to figure out why his old friend would say these things.

"What happened next?" Chris asked.

Briones shifted in his seat. His suit didn't. "The next time I saw Jack he was in his car, just sitting on the side of the road. I took him home and poured him a drink and he poured himself two more much stronger ones before he'd say a word, and the first thing he said was, 'Myra's dead.' "

"Did you know that already?"

"Nobody did. Her body wasn't found until the next day."

"So Mr. Pearson knew his wife was dead before her death was discovered?"

"Yes. I said he must be mistaken, but he said he had proof. Then he took a videotape out of his pocket and turned it over and over. It didn't have a case or any markings on it, it was just a black plastic videotape. Jack said, 'This is Myra's death, in my hands.' "

"Who had given him the tape?" Chris asked.

"Malachi," the witness said, saying the name as if he were greeting the man across from him. Malachi Reese didn't respond. "Malachi Reese gave him the tape."

"Why on earth would Mr. Reese implicate himself in a murder and give the victim's husband proof of it?"

"He didn't confess. Malachi said he had learned what had happened to Myra, and that the killers had videotaped her death. But here's the thing: Jack said no one could be identified on the tape except Myra herself. And a voice telling her the last words she ever heard. 'Your husband says good-bye.' "

Briones had started out sounding a little forced and overrehearsed, but by this time his eyes had grown round and he was leaning forward. His mouth opened dryly. Anyone who didn't believe Lou Briones was suffering, and from more than cancer, must have thought him the finest actor San Antonio had ever produced.

"Councilman Pearson had seen this on the tape?" Chris asked.

Briones shook his head. "Malachi had described it to him. Jack sat there in my house saying, 'It can't be true.' But he didn't have the nerve to watch it. I said, 'Jesus, Jack, throw that thing in the trash.' But he couldn't do that either."

Chris sat staring at his witness, letting the jury imagine the subtle cruelty, to put a thing like that tape in a man's hands. He turned toward Malachi Reese and saw him roll his eyes, but thought he also saw a tiny hint of the pride he'd seen before in the defendant's eye.

"After Myra Pearson's murder was discovered, why didn't Mr. Pearson turn the tape over to the police?"

Briones stared at the young District Attorney. "Give the cops a tape of some faceless guy saying, 'Your husband says good-bye' and then slitting your wife's throat. Right." He turned back to the jury. "See, it was a perfect Malachi deal. Let somebody know you've done him a big favor, and scare the shit out of him at the same time. It worked big time with Jack Pearson, but not the way Malachi'd planned. Jack never went to another city council meeting, and when his term was up he didn't run for mayor or anything else. Malachi had to go looking somewhere else for a mayor to own."

Chris hoped most people on the jury remembered that this part of Briones' story was irrefutably true. Jack Pearson, a bank president, had been the shining political star of a few seasons back. But after his wife's never-solved murder he had died a political death, never showing his face in public again. Chris hoped the jurors appreciated hearing the private explanation of this public mystery.

When trial had resumed the spectators' murmurings had quieted, and now they had ceased altogether. Chris didn't turn to look at them, but he wondered at the crowd's absorption in his evidence.

"Jack had an alibi," Briones continued explaining, "but it wasn't a good one. It was the new girlfriend. What was that worth? So the cops never charged him, but they never forgot him, either. Malachi would've had him forever. Jack only got away by bailing out completely."

To Chris's surprise, when he passed the witness Jackson Scott said, "No questions." Scott said it in a firm voice with a clear-

eyed stare at Briones. Whatever had happened to his client, the
defense lawyer hadn't lost heart. There was another explanation
for this gambit.

The State called three more punishment witnesses, but none
with the drama of Lou Briones' testimony. Cops had investigated Malachi Reese, they could cast some suspicion on him, but
there was no one who really knew his secret life who would
come forward as the dying Briones had done. And Reese had
already managed to cast suspicion on any police testimony
against him.

When it was the defense's turn, Jackson Scott's reason for not
questioning Lou Briones became clear. "The defense calls Jack
Pearson," he announced.

Everyone turned to look. The former city councilman and
leading citizen was already coming up the aisle, as if to take the
witness stand by stealth. But Jack Pearson looked nothing like the
stricken figure Lou Briones had described. He was little changed
from his public appearances a few years earlier. In his late fifties,
Pearson was a shorter than average man whose posture denied his
shortness. He had thin gray hair and the forehead of a Roman
emperor, though his face narrowed rapidly from there down to
a small mouth and a pointy chin. Seated in the witness stand, he
looked at Jackson Scott and at no one else, until it was time to
turn to the jury.

The defense lawyer began formally. "Please state your name
and occupation."

"John Pearson. I'm in private investments."

"And you're a former San Antonio city council member?"
Scott asked respectfully.

"Yes." Said without pride or irony.

"Mr. Pearson, I'm sorry to remind you of such a tragedy, but
the prosecution forces me to ask. Your wife died a few years ago?"

"Yes." Pearson spoke clearly.

"How?"

"She was murdered. It happened at her parents' house. They were on vacation at the time and Myra was staying at their house. Apparently she surprised a burglar. Some things were stolen, and he—or they, I believe police thought there was more than one—tried to set fire to the bedroom."

Pearson spoke distinctly, as if he'd written out this explanation ahead of time, but when he finished speaking he swallowed hard, visible to everyone in the courtroom.

"I'm sorry, Mr. Councilman," Jackson Scott said sincerely. "Was anyone ever arrested?"

"No. Just a burglary, you know. The kind of stupid, senseless crime somebody gets away with out of dumb luck."

"Mr. Pearson, do you have any reason to believe Malachi Reese was involved in your wife's murder?"

"Malachi?" Pearson feigned surprise. "No. None at all."

"Did Mr. Reese offer to do something about your wife?"

"No."

"Did he come to you before her death was discovered and give you a videotape that allegedly depicted her death?"

Pearson began to look incredulous. "No."

"Mr. Pearson, you know Lou Briones? He was a colleague of yours on city council?"

"Yes, of course," the witness said with brisk authority.

"Was there an evening the night before your wife's body was discovered when you went to Mr. Briones' house and told him the story I've just relayed to you, that Malachi Reese had arranged your wife's murder and provided you evidence of it?"

Pearson was shaking his head before the question was half over. To the jury he said emphatically, "No. Nothing like that ever happened. It's ridiculous."

"Why would Mr. Briones say it did?"

Pearson shook his head sympathetically. "Lou hasn't been right for some time. Right in the head. He had a breakdown some months ago—"

"Objection," Chris stood quickly to interject. "This man isn't qualified—"

"He's delusional, everyone knows that!" Pearson overrode the District Attorney's objection loudly and with his strongest sign of passion. "This ridiculous story—I ask you, would a rational man say that?" Chris subsided, looking thoughtfully at the witness, and Pearson finished to the jury, "Lou Briones is sick, he may be dying, and there are some old scores he wants to pay off before he goes. Whatever is wrong with him, it's affected his mind. He'll say anything."

He ended sounding sympathetic again, shaking his head sadly over his old friend's decline. "I pass the witness," Jackson Scott said, unable to keep smugness out of his voice.

Chris sat regarding the witness a moment longer. Pearson was still holding eye contact with the jurors when Chris said, "Mr. Pearson, you were on the city council when your wife was murdered, weren't you?"

"Yes. I left at the end of that term."

"In that position, you had some authority over the police department, didn't you?"

"I had a vote, on their budget and so forth," Pearson said deprecatingly.

"You had direct contact with the chief of police, who serves at the pleasure of the city council, and with other top management at the police department, yes?"

"Yes."

"You were in a position to do them favors, you probably had favors you could call in, you could apply all the pressure you wanted."

"I was just a citizen," the former almost-mayor said, which sounded silly, so Chris was satisfied with it.

"Yet police never solved your wife's murder," Chris concluded.

"No," Pearson said sadly. "Sometimes an investigation just doesn't get the breaks."

"So a couple of what you called stupid burglars got away with an enormously high-profile murder, police couldn't find any informants, couldn't turn up any significant leads, in spite of all the pressure you could bring to bear on them?"

The question didn't need an answer. Pearson stared flatly at the young District Attorney, re-evaluating him.

"Mr. Pearson," Chris said gently. "Did you ever look at the videotape of your wife's murder?"

"No," Pearson said quickly, in a small voice. Then he recovered and said, "There was no such thing." But his eyes had changed. He was no longer wholly present in the courtroom. After a pause Chris asked:

"Would you do one thing please, Mr. Pearson?"

"All right," Jack Pearson said with some surprise at the soft, matter-of-fact tone in which this favor was asked.

"Will you look at the defendant, please? You haven't since you walked into the courtroom."

Chris felt the indecision at the defense table as Scott almost rose to his feet to object. But his witness had seemed so candid, the defense lawyer didn't want to appear to be shielding him. He decided to leave Pearson on his own to carry out the simple request.

"Of course," Pearson said. He slid his eyes quickly along the defense table, not stopping, then looked down again. He cleared his throat. He returned his gaze to the District Attorney, raising a hand to shield his small mouth.

"That wasn't much of a greeting," Chris said gently. "Mr. Pearson? Could you just look at Malachi Reese and tell us again that you know he had nothing to do with your wife's murder?"

"He didn't," Pearson said in a strangled voice. "I didn't. I swear." The jurors stared at Pearson's battle with himself as he finally glanced at Malachi Reese's face, held there a moment as Pearson's face changed, then slid his gaze away again. The widower's eyes moistened.

"Pass," Chris said simply.

It took Jackson Scott a long ten seconds to think of a question, while everyone watched his witness try to master himself. "Mr. Pearson? It hurts to see an old friend in this position, doesn't it?"

"Yes," the witness said, making his voice stronger. He looked straight at the defense lawyer. "It's very painful."

"And to be reminded of the tragedy of your wife's death."

"Yes," Pearson said to the jurors. He had regained control. But when he left the witness stand he walked straight out between the tables, never glancing at his old friend the defendant.

Chris turned as if to watch Pearson depart, but mostly he wanted to get a look at that quiet audience. They were still jammed together, more than a hundred people in the few rows of spectator seats. Their racial characteristics seemed less significant now, because their faces were so similar in expression. Most studied the exciting Pearson, their faces mixing disbelief with wonderment. Others stared at the back of Malachi Reese's head with the same blended expressions. Hostility had departed, replaced by intense curiosity. The spectators were no longer racially conflicted strangers. Instead they were now witnesses to a horrifying mystery. What was this man before them? Like Chris, the spectators seemed to have put aside the question of Reese's race. Other things about him were much more important.

If Chris could have brought the entire population of San Antonio into this small courtroom, he thought, he could defuse the racial tension outside. Instead he could only convert people into believers a hundred or so at a time.

The defense called a string of character witnesses, some prominent, some common, of every color and stripe, to testify to

Malachi Reese's good deeds, his service on boards and to the community, his dedication to the principles of activism. Chris questioned these witnesses minimally, except the politicians among them. He tried to turn these prominent witnesses against the defense, as evidence of Reese's secret influence, but couldn't tell what the jurors thought.

That consumed the first day of the punishment phase. It was the next morning, after another bad night for Chris and apparently a better one for the defendant, when Leo Pedraza announced, "Malachi Reese, your Honor."

Reese took the stand and turned his attention to the jurors, nodding to them like acquaintances, sad but refraining from recrimination. He looked much better this morning than he had the first day of the punishment phase. He had regained his sense of himself. Even after a second night on a thin-mattressed jail-house bunk, he was crisply dressed and straight-backed.

It was the older defense lawyer, Leo Pedraza, who questioned him: "Mr. Reese, will you please tell us something about your early life?"

"I was born here in San Antonio," Reese began simply.

"Your parents?"

"My father was never in the picture. I was told who he was, but he wasn't a factor in my life. My mother . . . was not a very stable person. We moved a lot. Sometimes my mother would forget and leave one of us behind, and we'd have to wait at the old house until somebody remembered to come get us."

Chris knew about Reese's terrible childhood. He grew up not knowing when he'd come home to find his family evicted from the latest shack or filthy apartment, or to what man might be living with his mother. He took to the streets at an early age. The street had been dangerous, but less frightening than home.

"Yet you managed to finish high school and go on to college?" Pedraza prompted.

"Yes. I was on my own by then, so it took me longer than the customary four years, but I did get a degree in political science from St. Mary's."

"Were you already involved in public life by then?"

Reese smiled modestly. "That's how we'd put it now. I didn't know it was public life. I just saw some things that needed changing and did my best to help change them. Housing, that sort of thing. Discrimination. Just . . . unfairness. I hated to see hopeless people. I tried to tell them there were things they could do, people who would listen if they could only be reached." He shrugged.

"So you made a smooth transition to your current position of eminence of which you heard so much testimony yesterday?"

Reese laughed. He had grown relaxed, and the atmosphere of the courtroom had relaxed with him. The jurors watched him closely, but looked less tense than when Reese had first taken the stand. Chris remembered what Dr. Greenwald had said. Without her testimony about the state of Reese's mind, he didn't have much hope of convincing the jurors that Reese was so dangerous he deserved to die.

"Not smoothly at all," Reese said. "You see this ironic eyebrow?" He lifted his left eyebrow in demonstration. It peaked in the middle, giving him a wry, knowing expression. "That was split by a policeman's riot baton. I was only addressing some of my fellow students, but he didn't like what I was saying. There were other incidents like that. People who didn't like what I had to say grew more subtle, but I have always felt that opposition. Ending here."

Pedraza let the phrase echo. A few seconds later he explained why there were a television and a VCR on a stand against the wall. Pushing the equipment forward, he said, "Mr. Reese, we want to show the jury an example of your civic involvement. The tape is silent, so could you explain what's happening on it?"

"Of course."

The screen flickered into snowy life and buzzed while the defense lawyer sought the controls of the tape player. Someone turned off the courtroom lights. In the eerie darkness, blacker in its suddenness, Chris felt the illusion of Malachi Reese close behind his shoulder, whispering to him alone. As the screen cleared Reese spoke clearly from the witness stand.

"I had testified in a public hearing that the police department's hiring practices were unfair, why more black and Mexican-American officers should be hired, and why those officers should be assigned to areas like the public-housing projects."

"Some of those policies have since been adopted by the police department, haven't they?"

"Yes. But what we didn't know at the time was that some protestors had gathered outside the hearing."

On the television screen placed a few feet in front of the jurors, unedited newstape began to run, longer than what had aired on the TV news. The word Reese had used, "protestors," was a kind euphemism for the angry rabble on the city sidewalk, waving flags and mean-spirited signs and shouting angrily. They looked in fact like the people Chris had seen in front of the Justice Center this morning: his people. His supporters. There may have been only a dozen of them, but the camera was focused tightly enough that they filled the screen, looking extremely menacing. With a chill, Chris remembered his own encounter with an angry crowd, two nights ago.

Reese continued calmly, "I think they'd been misinformed about my position, and I know they hadn't been inside to hear what I'd said. They thought I'd been somehow attacking the police, and they were there to show their support."

The taped scene cut to a small group emerging from City Hall and starting down the steps. It was a Malachi Reese younger than the one in the witness stand, tall in the middle of a very small group: a black minister Chris recognized and three other people, two of them women. The group stopped on the stairs, spoke briefly to one another, then turned back—all except Malachi Reese.

"What did your friends say?" Pedraza asked.

"They said let's wait inside, let the police break them up, no use making a confrontation, they might have guns."

On the screen, Reese started down the steps, unhurriedly, with a slight smile. Of all the people in the courtroom, no one had more admiration for the figure on the TV screen than the District Attorney. Chris, who had just survived a similar encounter by running away, knew exactly how much physical courage it took to walk into the midst of a screaming mob.

Leo Pedraza asked his client, "Why didn't you take your friends' advice to wait out the situation?"

"Crazy, I guess. I've always had this crazy idea I could talk to people."

That's what the screen showed: Malachi Reese slowly approaching the crowd, which grew more frenzied as he neared. Some of the men were grinning, an ugly sight. The biggest one, wearing jeans and a vest that freed his hairy paunch, waved a large Confederate battle flag, the famous stars and bars. The flag-waver had a red bandanna around his forehead and his face was blood-filled.

"What was he shouting?" Leo Pedraza asked.

"You know what he was shouting," Reese said. "And telling me to go home. As if I had some other home."

As the Reese on the screen approached, the big protestor held out his flag so that it draped over Malachi Reese's face. It was an incendiary moment. Chris heard sucked-in breaths as people in the courtroom waited for violence to erupt.

Then on the screen the young Reese grabbed the flagpole. He didn't struggle over it, he only turned it, pushing the banner high, so that for a moment Reese and the protestor seemed to be re-enacting the Iwo Jima flag-raising. They were face-to-face, and the protestor looked shocked. Reese's face shone with earnestness. His mouth began to move.

"What did you say?" Leo Pedraza asked softly.

"I said hold it high," Reese said fervently. " 'It's the flag of a defeated nation that never gave up, that never lost honor. I know something about that.' "

On-screen Reese took the Confederate flag without a struggle. He held it high, moving it so the banner spread wide over his head and the heads of the protestors. He was talking more loudly, gesturing. The two or three other people in the crowd holding smaller flags waved them along with Reese. The ones holding signs looked embarrassed. A few seconds later they were all cheering as Reese handed the giant battle flag back to its owner, carefully as if they were members of a color guard, both their hands entwined for a moment around the flagpole.

"I won't let people be what they insist on being in their worst thoughts," Malachi Reese said. "I wouldn't let these people say, 'I am the only true southerner.' I'm one, too."

The scene flickered out, Pedraza scrambled to turn off the TV set, the lights in the courtroom came back on to find Malachi Reese sitting tall in the witness stand, his face a mix of pride and sadness.

Seeing that face, Pedraza had the good sense to pass the witness.

Mentally, Chris sighed. You won't be able to break him, Anne Greenwald had warned. Looking at Reese, Chris felt sure she had been right. Reese already sat posed for a statue of the martyr he had become.

Chris crossed to the TV set that still stood between him and the defendant. As he pushed it slowly back, he said, "Do you know if he's still alive, Mr. Reese?"

"What?"

"The man with the flag," Chris explained. "Is he still among us?"

"I have no idea," Reese said calmly. His small smile was for the D.A.'s silliness.

Chris walked to the railing and looked out at the crowd of

spectators. "You seemed to have made a convert of him that day. It seems like his curiosity would have been piqued enough to come and see your trial." The spectators were looking at one another. The jurors swept their eyes over the audience too. "But I haven't seen him," Chris said. "Have you?"

"No. We didn't stay in touch."

Chris walked slowly toward the defendant. "You won your public duel with him, so you didn't have to do anything to him privately, did you?"

"No, I didn't. I didn't have to and I wouldn't have."

Still approaching, Chris said, "You had to take a lot of crap in your early life, didn't you?"

After a pause Reese said, "I didn't think of it that way."

"Of course you did. Anyone would. You never had anyone on your side, did you? You never had a protector. Everything you've ever gotten you've had to fight for, haven't you?"

"Not fight," Reese said slowly. "I had to struggle, that's true. I think I did it the right way. Not lawlessly, like some of my contemporaries."

"And you don't have to take any crap from anybody anymore, do you?"

Chris put his hands on the front of the witness stand. He had purposely come to stand face-to-face with Reese, hoping to provoke a response. But the shock of how intimidated he felt as he stood there surprised him. Reese could reach him in half a heartbeat. Reese was a thin man, but he emanated power. Up close he looked coiled. Energy crackled from him. Chris wished he could have each juror stand where he stood.

"You have no idea what my life is like," Reese said with an edge of bitterness. "It'll never end. The blatant discrimination. The waiters who ignore you. The clerks who grit their teeth when they put your change on the counter instead of into your hand. The petty contempt from people who aren't fit—"

His lips closed then, clamping off the next word. For an instant

Reese glared at Chris. Then he took a deep breath, thinning his aquiline nose. "Yes, Mr. District Attorney, I have to take crap every day of my life. You learn to live with it. I think these people understand that." He turned an empathetic gaze on the jurors.

"These people have decided that you committed two murders, Mr. Reese, and implicitly a third. What would you tell them is the appropriate punishment for those crimes? How many good deeds does it take to be awarded one free pass for murder? How many to get three?"

"Hardly a free pass," Reese said. "The best thing that's going to happen to me now is a life sentence with no parole for as long as I can be expected to live."

He looked at the jurors earnestly. "But I wouldn't tell them that. I'd tell them that if they truly believe that a man did the things you've accused me of, they should kill him. If they think a man's life doesn't have any redeeming value, if he should just be thrown away the way so many people like me get thrown away every day, then they should vote for death. Death."

Reese studied each juror individually. His voice came soft but his eyes were passionate. Chris stepped back from him in awe.

Texas jurors do not vote for or against death. It's not that naked a decision. At the punishment phase of a capital murder trial the jurors are asked to answer two questions: is the defendant a continuing threat to society, and does any mitigating evidence regarding the defendant's life warrant a life sentence rather than death?

Those were the questions the defense and the prosecution argued about to the jury when the evidence ended and it was time for the final presentations. The defense, of course, focused on the second question: does any mitigating evidence merit saving the defendant's life?

"Yes," Jackson Scott argued. "You know it does. You have seen this man at work. You've heard about the many, many beneficial changes he's helped bring about. This man isn't a dealer in death, he's a builder of bridges. He can continue to build bridges from prison, where he will never be a danger to anyone. Maybe he can some day prove himself to you. I beg you to give him that chance. Don't throw away all the good this man has done and can still do."

When Chris stood up he had an urge to say, "The State waives the death penalty." He still felt off-balance from standing next to Malachi Reese as the defendant had instructed the jury to sentence him to death. Reese's defense team had put on the proper evidence, but Chris remained convinced that having lost the most important phase of trial, Reese himself wanted to die—or at least, to be sentenced to death. Chris felt complicit in some scheme as he stood to argue.

But he did his part in the adversarial system. He made the case for death. "I won't deny that Malachi Reese has an instinct for good. And he has done some good things for this community. But does that good make up for one murder? You have decided that Malachi Reese killed three people, utterly remorselessly. In this phase you've heard about a fourth murder. How many good deeds does it take to excuse those crimes?

"Incidentally, while doing those good deeds, he's made a nice life and a very good living for himself. He's profited through the system. Malachi Reese has spent his life learning the ways of power. And on his own he discovered a secret power greater than anyone else's: that a man could advance himself much more efficiently if he's willing to wipe out of existence anyone who gets in his way. A man with no scruple against murder can make himself the most powerful man in this city. That's what Malachi Reese believes."

Chris walked slowly along the front of the jury box. He didn't raise his voice. He was talking to the jurors alone. He made eye contact with each juror, and paused when he came to the African-American jurors. During jury selection Chris had deliberately refrained from striking all the black candidates for the jury. One way to defuse the racial aspect of the prosecution was to make sure the jury reflected the racial makeup of the city. He remembered this woman and this man. They had worked hard all their lives, been responsible voting citizens, and had given thoughtful answers to questions. The death penalty was a terrible punishment, but sometimes deserved, they had said. For their honesty they had been punished by serving on this jury. They were a woman and a man, both past middle age, sitting one behind the other. They couldn't help but feel the pressure on them, emanating from the audience and the city. Chris wanted to help them if he could. He stood there and said, "If you say that anything in Malachi Reese's life mitigates against the maximum punishment, you're telling the children of this city that he's right, that it's okay to kill people who disagree with you.

"I wish there were some way we could save the good in Malachi Reese and only do away with the evil half of his character. But that's not possible. He killed two people in one night. The third one, Mr. Rodriguez, he stalked and planned. He had him murdered *during this trial*. Do you need any better proof of what he'll do even when he's in custody?"

Chris stepped back, taking in all the jurors. He still felt a chill from his near-contact with Reese, and hoped the jurors felt it too. He sounded more sad than angry.

"Yes, he had a horrible early life. A life we wouldn't want inflicted on any child. But he's not a child any more. And that life did something to him. You saw it, didn't you? That rage compressed inside him. He won't accept any slight from anyone ever again, real or imagined. He won't let any other life interfere with his."

He turned toward the defense table. The jurors were glancing that way, and Chris wanted to guide their study.

"You will never see a more dangerous man than this innocent-looking figure before you. A man who knows how to manipulate the truth and is willing to do anything to remove someone who stands in his way. None of us is real to Malachi Reese. None of us is safe from him."

Reese maintained his innocent expression, but from the mild, careful study he gave the District Attorney, Chris knew his last sentence was true. The stare Reese directed at Chris struck Chris as very personal, but detached: the way a man looks at a stain on a favorite shirt, wondering if it can be removed or if the shirt has to be thrown away.

Before he sat Chris looked out at the spectators. The ethnically mixed audience looked as if they, too, had begun deliberating. There were some true believers the District Attorney would never reach: they glared at him, ready to spring forward and embrace Malachi Reese as soon as the trial recessed. But many others, black, brown, and white, sat staring into space, or curiously across the courtroom at the man they had once admired unquestioningly.

"I don't envy you your job," Chris concluded to the jury. "But it's not a difficult decision. Malachi Reese has proven again and again that he's dangerous as long as he lives. That answers both the questions you have to answer."

Again the jury was out until dusk. Even in the bowels of the windowless jury room inside the Justice Center, the threat of nightfall seemed to weary the jurors. Chris waited wearily as well.

Life would seem to be the compromise verdict. Convict Reese of the worst crime there is, but spare him the ultimate penalty. It was hard to imagine how such an ethnically mixed jury could reach a common opinion of such a complex man. Chris thought of another way the jurors could compromise, though, and when they were all assembled in the courtroom again he thought he heard them thinking it.

The reporters and spectators didn't feel it, they were relaxed in their expectation, but Malachi Reese did. He sat contempla- tively at the defense table with a tiny smile, like a man who knows he's about to be surprised with a party.

"Will you please read your answers to the punishment ques- tions?" Judge Pressman asked, more formal than usual. "Will the defendant please rise?"

The jury foreman, looking even thinner, referred to the paper this time. " 'Is there a probability that the defendant will commit criminal acts of violence that would constitute a continuing threat to society?' Yes.

" 'Do you find, taking into consideration all of the evidence, including the circumstances of the offense, the defendant's char- acter and background, and the personal moral culpability of the defendant, there is a sufficient mitigating circumstance to warrant that a sentence of life imprisonment rather than a death sen- tence be imposed?' " The foreman looked up at the judge. "No, we don't."

Yes and no: the formula for death. Not the expected life sen- tence. Chris in his seat turned immediately toward the defense table. Jackson Scott's face was bloodless; he looked about to faint. Leo Pedraza lowered his head. Malachi Reese loomed tall be- tween them. He gazed straight at the jury foreman, solemnly but without anger, then ran his eyes along the other jurors. He might have been memorizing their faces.

Reese's expression softened, and he nodded.

The reaction from the dozens in the audience was more muted than it had been for the guilty verdict. There were sharp gasps but no screams or shouts. Chris turned and saw faces look- ing stunned. But more of the spectators had inward-turning eyes. They had heard the evidence. How would they have voted? These people had been changed by what they had heard.

Out in the streets, things would be different.

Chris was one of the few people in the courtroom not shocked by the jury's decision. He understood what five of them would say at their press conference the next day. Hopelessly tangled in the evidence of good deeds and evil ambition, they had thrown up their hands and let someone else decide. They had let Malachi Reese make the decision himself. "He told us to do it," two of the jurors would say in interviews the next day.

Yes. Malachi Reese had asked for his own death sentence. His face placid in the courtroom, Reese looked satisfied.

The formal sentencing took place quickly, the jurors dismissed, the defendant taken away by a small army of sheriff's deputies. Chris made his escape to his office. Along the way, through the maze of hallways to the District Attorney's office on the top floor of the Justice Center, prosecutors stepped out of their tiny offices to pat him on the back or put their hands together in faint applause. Among prosecutors there is a presumption that whatever a defendant is charged with is only a tiny portion of what he's gotten away with, so only the maximum sentence can be satisfactory. In the outside world Malachi Reese may have been an ambiguous figure; within the beige walls of the D.A.'s office he was a mass murderer who'd finally gotten what he deserved. One young assistant raised a hand for the boss to high-five, but Chris ignored it, so the younger prosecutor used it to clap him on the back.

Chris went out onto the tiny balcony that gave a view of the parking lot four stories down. He saw small bands of protestors, their faces from this height blending with the asphalt at their feet. The protestors had received word of the death sentence. Police were prepared this time; they were in force in the parking lot. Nothing would be allowed to get out of hand.

But out in the city the police wouldn't be able to contain the reaction to the verdict. Among these protestors were people who had actually heard some of the evidence at trial. Their reactions were muted compared to those of citizens who would take the death sentence only as a sign that a black man had raised himself too high and so had been slapped down hard by the establishment. People who barely knew what Malachi Reese had done would know very well what had been done to him. There was no way to stop Reese—or Chris—from becoming a symbol of something larger, that the District Attorney had never intended.

Chris spent another hour in the office, watching the protestors slowly disperse, listening to police reports. It would have been a good night to rob someone on the north side of San Antonio, because all the police were concentrated on the east and south sides. A few demonstrations broke out, but police kept things under control. What they needed to worry about, Chris thought, were the bars and churches and living rooms where people were talking and thinking and a long, slow rage was developing that wouldn't be vented in one night. There weren't enough police in the world to quell that change.

Chris left the Justice Center through a tunnel under the street, then out the side door of the old courthouse next door, neatly eluding the few demonstrators left in front of the Justice Center. Darkness had fallen. Chris stood indecisive, not wanting to go home, not having any other destination in mind. As a warm wind picked up, a car glided to a stop beside him.

"Way to go, Big Guy," shouted a happy voice. Mike Martinez, El Rojo, clambered up from behind the wheel of a convertible to sit on its door, posing. Chris ran a hand over the car's gleaming skin. The classic red Mustang looked like perpetual youth, and the kid sitting on it embodied that spirit too. Martinez wore jeans and boots and had been celebrating.

"Be careful, Rojo. Nice car. Where'd you get it?"

"Auction." El Rojo grinned. "I made a preemptive bid."

Martinez offered a ride, but Chris declined. Mike slid down behind the wheel again and rolled slowly out of sight. *"El Rojo en el coche rojo,"* Chris muttered. The Red One in his bright red car. Somehow it looked like the fun part of Chris's own life disappearing down the dark street.

Chapter 5

Anne Greenwald and Chris Sinclair bumped into each other at Night in Old San Antonio, literally. Anne had been looking forward to Fiesta. Chris had forgotten it was coming. Fiesta: ten days in April, smaller than Mardi Gras but no lower-key, drawing party-lovers from all over San Antonio and much farther. The heart of Fiesta is Night in Old San Antonio, a party that goes on over four weeknights in the old village of La Villita, preserved in the heart of downtown. The small stone and log buildings put up as shops and homes by early settlers look like stage sets to provide a historical theme for the twenty-five-thousand-plus people who pack the narrow streets each night to drink beer, eat food on sticks, drink beer, crack *cascarones* on one another's heads, drink beer, listen to music that varies in everything except volume, and stand in line for the portable toilets.

A week had passed since the trial of Malachi Reese. Chris had not been reclaimed by routine. The verdict and death sentence received national press coverage. Its tone was about as Paul Benavides had predicted. Protests over what had been done to Reese continued. His name became a symbol of oppression. "Remember Malachi," people who had never met the man would say, and they could have been saying Martin or Malcolm. *Newsweek* did a story whose headline asked, "America's latest political prisoner?"

Even without the constant reminders, Chris couldn't have put aside thoughts of the trial and its implications. He brooded. He began to feel that he would be linked to Malachi Reese for the rest of his life, as if they marched handcuffed together. Even people who knew him regarded him differently. He felt their sidelong stares of reappraisal. While he'd been convincing the jury and himself of Malachi Reese's ruthlessness, Chris had inadvertently given himself the same reputation. People who'd known him for years thought for the first time that it might be dangerous to cross the District Attorney.

Sundown would catch him by surprise, still in the building. This evening in the middle of April he took his now-traditional dodge through the tunnel and the old courthouse, and when he came out on the side street, instead of circling the building toward the parking garage he headed toward the river. At first his steps were aimless, then he became caught in a flow. Walking the darkening downtown streets, Chris thought at first he heard the sound of an enormous riot, but then realized there was musical accompaniment, and remembered Fiesta. Night in Old San Antonio wouldn't be shut down or even slowed by tragedies elsewhere in town. Half the partiers probably hadn't even heard of Malachi Reese, or of Christian Sinclair. Chris followed the sounds to La Villita, put money in somebody's hand, and passed through the gates into the crowded outdoor party of NIOSA. It was not the distraction he would have chosen, but being in a crowd of people seemed immensely preferable to going home to sit in his condo. Chris hadn't been to NIOSA in years, this would be his first time since becoming the minor public figure the District Attorney is, recognizable to students of the newspaper and the TV news, but anonymous to the great majority of the populace. That was what he wanted tonight. People grinned at him. Only a very few watched him curiously, and if a face or two here and there twisted into anger at the sight of Chris, the crowd immediately swept him into safer, anonymous territory.

He had a beer, and soon another. The food smells held no appeal. La Villita was divided into sections representing past faces of San Antonio: the frontier, Spanish colonial, French and German and Chinatowns. The Great Depression wasn't represented, nor any war, so Chris didn't feel at home in any section, and kept moving. He had wanted to be where people were, but Night in Old San Antonio so perfectly filled that bill that his desire quickly died. He walked through the press of strangers trying to think of whom he could call, where he could go.

His strongest desire was to talk over the trial with its honoree, Malachi Reese. Oddly, the defendant had been the only person in the courtroom with whom Chris had felt a real personal connection. He wondered if Reese thought so too. Only the two of them had operated on all the layers and byways of the trial's action.

Each section of the Night came with its own ethnic food and particular music. "Loud" was inadequate to describe the omnipresence of sound, of music and clapping and twenty thousand people talking and laughing. Noise became a physical presence. Between the sections smells blended, fried dill pickles into refried beans, and there were odd betrayals and insights of music, Tejano infiltrating R&B, jazz turning symphonic. After nine o'clock true night descended, above and outside the dome of lights. Partiers grew more frenzied, searching for friends, for particular music, for celebration's perfect pitch. In the narrow lanes between the sections the crush of people was so dense it was impossible to move against the flow, and smaller people could be lifted off their feet. Chris found himself caught in one of those whitewaters of people, his plastic beer cup crushed between his chest and the bare back of the woman in front of him, feet barely moving, noise oppressing him as much as the pressure of the crowd, just looking for a place to be spewed out, when he saw a familiar face passing. Her face was painted, a bright red clown dot on one cheek, a star on the other, eyebrows painted into a leering question, but in the flash of her passing he recognized Anne Greenwald. She was going the other direction, caught high in the crowd, her mouth open in what could have been a scream or a laugh. Her eyes caught on him for an instant.

Chris tried to cross the crowd, a good way to break a leg. He'd been carried far past by the time he managed to turn and follow Anne's path. When he got back to the spot where he'd seen Anne he'd lost hope of finding her. At NIOSA one could meet people only by accident, not intentionally. Their moment had been lost. He managed to escape the tightest press of the crowd, stumbling when his feet found themselves responsible for movement again, and he walked on, looking for one more beer or an exit.

He had spotted a beer stand surrounded by people, and headed halfheartedly in that direction, when a woman hurrying across his path stopped and turned, and he found Dr. Greenwald in his arms. A small ripple in the crowd held them against each other for a long moment while she gasped and apologized and then recognized him. He saw these things on her face; he couldn't hear a sound she made. He couldn't hear a sound *he* made. They briefly carried on a conversation that had to be clichéd and obvious, because neither could hear it, until they moved away from a loudspeaker and found a zone of what passed for auditory normality. People were still close at hand, but they ignored Chris and Anne, so it was possible—no, imperative—to hold an intimate conversation at the top of one's lungs.

"You look like fun!" Chris shouted. When he'd seen her pass smiling in the crowd Anne had looked as young and full of plans as he'd felt when he first took office.

She shrugged ruefully. The paint on her face exaggerated her expressions. "I promised some people months ago I'd come with them tonight!" she said close to his ear. "Of course I had no idea—"

"So you've got a long-standing date?" Chris was surprised at how much that news diminished the happiness he'd felt at seeing her.

Anne saw his reaction, struggled with a small question of confidentiality, and said, "The promise was we'd all come together if they were still alive."

Oh. Chris knew she counseled at all kinds of clinics and special interest hospices and in schools. She could have been talking about AIDS patients or gang kids or battered women. Chris felt like the Masque of the Red Death, a spectre at the fiesta. Death followed him.

"Are you all right?" Anne called from the narrow distance. She put a hand on him and he let his eyes linger on her face. He saw through the face paint to her concern. "You did the right thing," she said.

He nodded vaguely. He didn't want to discuss it and he didn't want to let the subject drop.

Anne's brown hair was high on her head with a few wavy tendrils falling alongside her face. Bits of confetti fell too. The most popular Fiesta activity aside from drinking beer was attacking people with *cascarones,* confetti-filled eggshells that cracked satisfyingly on friends' heads and left the victim marked for the rest of the evening. If you had friends you had confetti in your hair. It made Anne look more festive, even as her expression remained sober. Chris wasn't wearing any confetti.

Someone passing in the crowd apparently noticed that and tried to remedy the deficiency. But it was a poor hit, or perhaps a toss from too far for accuracy. It may have been only random *cascaron* violence. A confetti egg suddenly brushed Chris's hair, bounced intact from his shoulder, and fell to the pavement between Anne and Chris, where it cracked and bled its contents. When Chris lifted his eyes from the sight, Anne saw a tear.

"I think I saw all the king's horses in the French section," she shouted, trying for lightness. "And all the king's men are drunk somewhere—"

Chris smiled appreciatively, but he might not have heard. He took her hand with more pressure than he'd intended. "Can we get out of here?" he asked.

Their hands hovered over coffee cups. Anne's hand was stamped, a smudge of ink that would let her back into Night in Old San Antonio to reunite with her friends. She and Chris sat only a few blocks from NIOSA at a table along the Riverwalk behind the Hilton Palacio del Rio, close enough to hear the noise of the street party.

Chris looked at Anne's rather pale hand, with tendons visible but not prominent. Her nails were red, almost the color of the one bright dot of paper confetti that floated in her coffee cup, fallen from Anne's hair. She hadn't noticed.

"Did you know there are factions in this town?" Chris asked seriously. "I don't mean political factions, I mean factions of people. People from different parts of town are different. They read the same news story and have completely different reactions. They hear about something that happened—a, a crime, or jobs being lost—and their sympathies go in completely different directions. Did you know that?"

Anne looked at him sympathetically but with amusement. "I know," Chris acknowledged. "But I didn't know it here—" He touched his stomach. "—until I started campaigning all over the city. I was the mall-world candidate for D.A. When the votes were counted it turned out I was the darling of the suburbs." That had been no surprise. He had sprung from the suburbs. But now, half a year into his term, he had realized he was supposed to be the suburban delegate to the ugly world of the courts. The Justice Center stood as the fortress that held crime on the south and west and east sides of town, away from the nice neighborhoods.

"So Malachi Reese and I really do have constituencies, and they're both frightened and angry."

"This is news to you?" Anne said.

Anne sat at ease across the table from him. She was still made up for Fiesta, but somehow he could see her face more clearly now. She wore a simple dress and sandals. At the end of a long day, she didn't look tired. "You didn't really think voters were voting for you personally, did you?" she asked. "Voters don't know the candidates, just the image."

"So what was my image? Why did you vote for me?"

"Who says I did? I like Leo Pedraza. He's easy to get along with, he'd listen to people. He has a good working ego, just the right size."

"Gee, I'm sorry—"

"But you can be ten times the D.A. he was—"

Silenced by the sincerity of her voice, Chris watched her. "—or a complete disaster," Anne concluded.

They smiled at each other. "What I need is guidance, I suppose," Chris said.

Regarding him carefully, but with a little smile, Anne said, "I watched you during the trial. I was around a lot, backstage in your office, remember? I saw you worry over everything. Over whether you were doing the right thing. I expected you just to be concerned with winning, or with how you looked in the media. But I saw you agonize—"

"That was just a show when there was a civilian in the room. After you left—"

Anne brushed aside his attempt at humor. "I'm not easy to fool." Chris looked again at her hand. It looked strong but soft, he thought, wanting to reach out and find out whether he was right. Maybe you're not simple enough for this job," Anne continued. "Maybe it needs someone who just worries about image and winning."

Anne appeared both relaxed and concerned, as if she understood something unspoken and nothing could shock her. He could see why her patients confided in her. Her gray-green eyes held on him, seeming to see the urge he felt to take her hand. She put her hand on his arm and, returning to the real subject of their conversation, said, "Don't worry about Malachi. Time will take care of him. He can't keep rage like his under wraps forever."

"How is it you know so much about him? Just from that one court-ordered interview?"

Anne leaned back. She glanced at a tourist couple passing on the Riverwalk, following the music. "Are you consulting me professionally?" she asked.

Chris finally reached for her hand on the table. He ran one finger along the back of it. He'd been right about its texture. "I certainly hope not," he said.

Anne leaned toward him again. Her mouth opened eagerly, then closed as she frowned at herself, looking down, hesitating, then she looked up at Chris and laughed lightly at both herself and him. She shrugged and asked very seriously, as if giving him a diagnosis, "Would you like to go to a dance?"

Meetings consumed most of the District Attorney's days. If Chris found himself alone during the day, something had gone wrong. After less than six months in office, the schedule no longer even seemed odd to Chris: breakfast meeting, nine o'clock meeting, 9:20, ten o'clock at City Hall. Chris arrived right on time, but the mayor kept him waiting for five minutes, a little more, then suddenly came lunging out of his office as if he'd just been informed of the District Attorney's presence.

Raeburn Foley, the mayor of San Antonio, was halfway

through his first term in office, and the nation's most stringent term-limit law would allow him only one more two-year term, but he acted as if he had accepted the office of mayor as a hereditary right and would hold it as long as he pleased. Foley's age, somewhere past forty, seemed to change from moment to moment. When he frowned, the streaks of gray in his dark, thick hair became more prominent and he looked like an elder statesman. When he grinned he looked about twenty-five.

Foley grinned as he stretched his arm to take Chris's hand, saying, "Ray Foley. Good to see you again, Chris."

They had met briefly at a couple of luncheons and civic affairs, but had never had a conversation. Chris represented county government, the mayor city, normally their jurisdictions didn't intersect. But Foley drew Chris into the inner sanctum of his office as if they were old, intimate, non-political friends.

Inside the office a third man stood, back against the plaster wall on the far side of the room as if he had just materialized through the wall.

"I asked Councilman Phillips to be with us, too." Mayor Foley's voice became more deferential as he gestured across his office. Winston Phillips, who carried the inevitable political nickname "Win," leaned against the wall beside the broad window, arms folded, staring at Chris and making no move toward him. The councilman and the District Attorney had never before been in the same room together, though they had certainly been in each other's thoughts. Phillips represented the east side district of San Antonio, the most heavily black part of town. But even in that carefully-drawn district African-Americans were not a majority of voters; it had taken some smooth political skill for a black man still in his twenties—Win Phillips—to get elected to City Council from that district.

Phillips had publicly denounced the prosecution of Malachi Reese before, during, and after the trial. In press conferences he had said the charges needed more investigation before such serious allegations were brought to trial. In gatherings of his own constituents Phillips had said more emphatically that a white man in Reese's place would never have faced prosecution.

Phillips hadn't led any riots after the trial and death sentence, but he hadn't done anything to quell any, either. Now in the mayor's office he stared at the District Attorney with silent intensity. Chris nodded cordially to the slim young councilman and got nothing in return.

The three public officials were meeting in the mayor's office in City Hall, natural enough since Win Phillips had an office in the same building and Chris had had to walk only a couple of blocks from the Justice Center. But if Chris had been sensitive to lines of power he would have realized he had lost an unspoken power struggle because the meeting wasn't held in his own office. The mayor sat on a corner of his big desk. Foley's pinstriped gray suit maintained its classic lines, as if it had been designed for desk-sitting.

"A nice explosive present you handed us," Foley said to Chris. "Getting the death sentence on Mr. Reese made things a little tough on city support services. Luckily the chief of police and I had some idea what might happen, so we were prepared."

Chris's frown deepened. Seeing it, Foley added smoothly, "Not that I'm criticizing. I know you think you did what you had to do. Absolutely. Just the prep work could have been a little better, on the raising the public consciousness side. We're still feeling repercussions."

"Repercussions?" Win Phillips said loudly, coming off his perch beside the window. "In my district we call them burned-out businesses. Kids afraid to walk to school. And cops exercising presumptions of guilt on anybody who doesn't need to use sunblock in the summer."

"Now listen to the contradictions there, Win," Mayor Foley said reasonably. "You want those businesses and kids protected, but you don't want any arrests. I believe the police are being very restrained. Although if you know of any contrary examples, I want to know about it immediately."

Not waiting for an answer, the mayor turned quickly back to Chris. "If we're going to get through this summer, we'll need the help of community leaders like Win pouring oil on the troubled waters. We'd just like to know nothing might happen on your end that would jeopardize that."

"I'm not planning any prosecutions of Sharon Wallace or Horace Greer," Chris said, naming two black politicians.

Foley laughed sincerely but efficiently, then grew quickly sober again and said, "We'd just like you to come to us if anything . . . sensitive is looming on the horizon." He raised his hand. "Not going to interfere, promise you that. I've told the chief of police the same thing. Just like to all be in the same loop if you have any more investigations that might have . . . political consequences."

Chris stared at the mayor. Raeburn Foley was both smooth and fluffy—the cashmere man—but underneath his habitual stroking and glad-handing he had a hard core. You don't get to be mayor in your early forties without long, deep involvement in local politics and business, and success at both.

"Sure," Chris said easily, but he had hesitated too long. Foley continued to watch him. And Win Phillips had been quiet long enough.

"Look, I know why I'm here," he said harshly, coming toward Chris as if he might take a punch at him. Phillips had rather delicate features but a street fighter's glare when he chose to use it. "You want some reassurance that African-American citizens are going to quiet down and go back into their holes. So men like this can pick us off one at a time."

"I'm not after anybody," Chris insisted, knowing as he said it how defensive his denial sounded. No one who hadn't been at the trial could understand, they had to have stood closely enough to Malachi Reese to feel his rage purring softly. They had to have exchanged those secret glances with him. The trial had been very personal to Reese and Chris. Race had had nothing to do with it.

Phillips stood very close to Chris. "Was Malachi a symbol to you? Is that how you intended his prosecution to be: an announcement of what your administration will be like?"

"You don't know him," Chris said. "You don't—"

Genuine shock widened Win Phillips' eyes. "*I* don't? Mister, I worked with Malachi. He's a role model for me—and hundreds more like me. Maybe thousands. You think *you* know the real man just because you heard something bad about him? You think that's what it means to really get inside one of us, don't you? That you'll find some festering—"

"Now, now," Foley said calmingly. "We brought you men together to have a meeting of the minds, not to snipe at each other. Chris was only doing his job, Win. Like he said, what was he supposed to do with evidence like that? And Councilman Phillips, Chris, has constituents to represent. He's the public voice of people who—"

Phillips wheeled on the mayor. "You think I take a position just for the sake of votes? Is that what you believe? Or do you believe anything?"

"I most certainly—"

Chris said over the mayor's protests, "That's not what I meant. If you'd just—"

Phillips cocked his head in an exaggerated listening pose. "Neither of you boys is very good at expressing yourself, are you? You keep failing to make yourself clear. Go ahead, I'm listening."

He demonstrated his attentiveness by exaggeratedly closing his mouth. Chris said carefully, "You didn't come to the trial. You didn't hear the evidence, or all the other evidence I heard. I will lay it all out for you and anyone else you care to bring, in a private demonstration."

"I've heard your evidence. Nothing will make me believe it, not about Malachi."

"I can't help that he was a role model. He was also a murderer."

"Oh, he's still a role model," Phillips said. "But now he's the role model you made. The example of what happens if you step on too many pale toes."

Chris just shook his head. Mayor Foley didn't intervene. Phillips, no longer shouting, said close to Chris's face, "Why don't you come after me next? Come on. I'll be ready."

When Chris didn't take up the challenge, Phillips cocked one eyebrow and his tone softened. "You know, I had hopes for you. I'd heard good things about you. I guess reputations aren't what they used to be."

He turned sharply and walked out of the office without a backward glance. Foley gently scratched his ear, as if it were burning. "Well, that could've gone better. He'll calm down, though. We've worked together before and we will again. But it would be nice, Chris, if you could refrain from doing anything to make the situation worse."

Chris returned the mayor's regard, and suddenly said, "You must've worked with Malachi Reese. Did you know him well?"

Foley smiled. "You mean did he ever offer to have a word with anybody on my behalf?" He shook his head.

"But you knew about that phrase? You heard stories?"

"Only from reading about the trial." Foley gave a mock shudder. "Amazing what went on around here. No, all that was before our time, Chris." He gave enough of a smile to make himself the District Attorney's contemporary.

Then he grew serious again. "That's the dead past. You've put it behind all of us now. Let's let it lie there, okay?"

Foley stood, drawing Chris close and clapping a hand on his shoulder. "We're behind you a thousand percent," the mayor said solemnly. "Had to be done. What happened to Victor was horrifying. I did know Victor Fuentes. Damned good staffer. Good man. Might've been mayor himself some day if not for . . ."

Foley's voice broke with utmost sincerity. Chris looked at Foley's earnest profile, feeling a chill where the mayor's hand touched his arm.

Chris said to his chief investigator, "Victor Fuentes was a pain in the ass, that's what he was. No respect for his elders, didn't take anything at face value. You know the type."

Jack Fine didn't acknowledge the gentle dig from his boss. Jack knew the type intimately. He saw one in the mirror every morning. The D.A.'s chief investigator was a thin man of slightly less than average height. He had a sharp nose, very alert eyes he tried to disguise with drooping eyelids, and a face that at its happiest looked skeptical. He had been a twenty-five-year veteran of the San Antonio Police Department who had blown open a minor scandal about police handling of a charity fund and been "rewarded" by being made head of Internal Affairs, a position from which he could do nothing but make more enemies within the department. "The funny thing about those whistle-blowers who get commended by the administration," Jack once said, "is that they never become *part* of the administration."

When Chris had taken office he had known Jack only from cross-examining him and by reputation. He had been slightly surprised when Jack had accepted his offer to retire from the police force and become the District Attorney's chief investigator. There hadn't been much by that time to tie Jack's loyalties to the S.A.P.D.

He had turned out to be a formidable investigator, and the first person Chris had thought of when wondering where the Malachi Reese investigation should go next. Chris had gone straight from his meeting with the mayor to Jack Fine's small office on the fifth floor of the Justice Center.

"We've left one very important thing undone," Chris said.

Jack nodded. "Who killed Adolfo Rodriguez?"

Chris added, "And why wasn't he better protected? Who knew how to get to him? And also knew I'd be in that crack house that morning?"

"You know we don't put witnesses in protective custody," Jack said. "And I think whoever did it just wanted the body found in a very public place, lot of public officials around, so it'd be sure to break open Malachi's trial. He just got lucky having you be the one who found him. Although not so lucky for Malachi, as it turned out." He, too, gave Chris one of those looks of reappraisal. Chris hardly noticed anymore.

"But I've already started looking into it," Jack said with feeling. "Who owed Malachi Reese such a big favor he'd kill for him? I'll see what the cops have turned up—assuming they'll cooperate with me. You've, uh, smoothed the way for me, right? In that little way you have. When the mayor told you to cool it, don't you think maybe he meant this investigation too?"

"Maybe he did," Chris said. "He damned sure meant for me not to pursue any more of Malachi's connections. And when he told me all that Malachi business was before his time, that was strictly bullshit. They're practically contemporaries. Foley must know—"

"Oh, well, a politician lied to you," Jack said. "Time to put the staff on alert, all right."

"It's not just politicians," Chris said quietly. "There's still somebody out there who'll kill for Malachi Reese. What I told the jury wasn't a lie, was it, Jack? He's still dangerous, isn't he?"

"Yeah," Jack Fine said dismissively. "Look, Chris," he continued in a quieter, more thoughtful tone, staring at his boss. "I know that expression you're wearing. Believe me, I know it. That feeling ruins a lot of nights, and sometimes other parts of your

life too. At some point you just have to let it——" He stopped himself from saying "die," and changed it to, "——let it go."

"Hey, I'm not obsessed," Chris said quickly. "I'm lighthearted,
I'm easy." He cracked his first small smile of the day. "I'm going
to a dance."

Anne Greenwald insisted on picking Chris up Friday night. "It's
my obligation, not yours." After her initial outburst of enthusiasm at the table on the Riverwalk, when she'd smiled at him
questioningly when inviting him to a dance, looking bold and
shy and about sixteen years old, she kept saying things like the
"obligation" remark, making the occasion sound like an in-
escapable bore she was grateful to Chris for helping her out with,
rather than like, oh, say, a date.

They were attending a charity gala. On the phone Anne said
apologetically, "It's black tie."

Since Chris was doing her a favor by agreeing to escort her—
that's how Anne kept treating the engagement—she insisted on
doing all the work, including driving. Which sounded nice but
left Chris waiting for her to pick him up, sitting on the couch in
his tuxedo, at her mercy inside his own condo, doing his best not
to feel like a sixteen-year-old girl himself.

Mercifully, Anne didn't keep him waiting. In fact she had arrived in his parking lot ten minutes early and taken a very slow
walk around the swimming pool, then paced outside his second
floor door. A casually dressed couple on their way out had smiled
at her finery, embarrassing her. That slight blush still colored her
cheeks and the evening breeze had disarrayed her hair a little
when Chris opened the door.

"My," he said. Anne gave a slight shrug and lifted her hands in
a gesture that said, *Yes, this is as good as it gets.*

She looked the way a woman should when dressed for a ball:

striking and rueful. Anne wore conservative black, an evening dress that encased her tightly from her chest to her hips, but then opened up to let her walk. The filmier material covering her legs seemed to float about her. The dress left her arms and shoulders bare, but a cream-colored drape collar softened the gown's edges, covering her shoulders.

She had confined her brown hair mostly to the top of her head, though feathers of hair escaped around her face. Her eyes held a familiar satirical Anne-edge, but at the same time asked shyly for approval. Chris gave it silently, standing and admiring her.

Finally he said, "Dr. Greenwald, you've been—"

"I know, I know, you didn't realize what a knockout I am in those rags I usually wear."

"I was going to say, your lipstick's a little crooked." He corrected it for her with his finger. Her lips opened speculatively.

He stood aside for her and she laid a hand softly on his chest as she passed. "I knew you'd look good in a tux," she said.

"Would you like a glass of wine?"

"Please."

The door to Chris's small kitchen opened on his right just inside the condo's front door. Anne moved past, into the dining-living area, a very long, rather wide rectangle ending at patio doors onto a balcony. When he joined her Anne was frankly studying the room, passing the chrome and glass dining table into the living area. She stood before the one painting, on the wall above the white couch. The large watercolor depicted an old house in the country, pillared front porch predominant, done mostly in pastels, except in the upper left corner, back in the tangle of the woods, where the gray suggestion of an older house crumbled into ruins. Anne studied the painting for a minute, thinking it must have significance since it was the only thing on the long walls. She turned and looked at him across the room.

"I lived like this," she said, "one year in college. Then my parents let me move out of the dorm."

He smiled, but didn't apologize or explain.

"This is why I wanted to come, you know, to see your secret lair. But you don't give much away, do you?"

"It's not that I'm deep or anything."

She walked suddenly through the door in the long wall and the light came on in his bedroom. He was glad he had made the bed. He found Anne looking at it with a frown. "You don't live like a bachelor, do you? Or a carefree college boy. Where's the basketball? Where're the sweaty gym shorts?"

"Shorts over in the bathroom. Basketball up on the shelf," Chris said. He sipped his wine, wanting the game to continue, silently urging Anne not to give up. He wondered about her secret lair, wanting to see her in her own setting. Anne still looked gorgeous in her finery, but her teasing had turned her back into the Anne he knew.

Closet doors covered the wall closest to her. She slid one open, found shirts and shoes that didn't interest her, tried the next door. "Ah, here we are. Your secret identities."

She had found his suits. They filled one long closet rod, more than a dozen of them, in shades of blue and gray, one wild and frivolous brown toward the back, and at the very far end of the rod, pressed up against the dividing wall, the one completely uncharacteristic suit Anne pulled out with a small cry of triumph. He had thought when he bought it it was cream-colored, but in fact he'd been informed by now that the suit was a pale lime green. It seemed to crackle in Anne's hands.

"The first suit I ever bought for myself," Chris said. "With the first credit card a department store gave me."

Anne opened the jacket to look at the pants. "Bell bottoms!" she exclaimed delightedly. Then she looked from the electric suit in her hands to the thin gray line in the closet, then back at Chris, and didn't ask, or have to, "What happened?"

She followed him into the small kitchen to put their wine glasses in the sink. When he turned they were close, almost as close as they'd been in the throng at Night in Old San Antonio. Chris hesitated, then reached past her and opened the refrigerator. Surprised, Anne looked inside.

"Oh, no," she said, putting her hands on her cheeks.

"Yes," Chris admitted.

Almost alone on a cold shelf sat an orchid corsage in its clear plastic box.

"I figured I could get one and feel like a dork or not get anything and feel like a clod," Chris said.

He pinned it on without much fumbling. "Thank god for this collar," he said. "Otherwise I'd have had to staple it to your dress."

Anne bent her head to sniff. "Probably smells like ketchup," Chris said. Anne still hadn't spoken. She sniffed again when she raised her face, and touched his check.

Then her eyes brightened. "I've got one for you." She retrieved her tiny black purse from the dining table and from it drew a small symbolic blue ribbon. She pinned it on his lapel rather ceremoniously, smoothing the fabric of his tuxedo jacket.

"Of what is this demonstrating my awareness?"

"This is you taking a bold stand against domestic violence," Anne answered. "That's not too controversial a position for the District Attorney, is it?"

In her car he sat a little awkwardly in the passenger seat, not used to wondering what to do with his hands in a car, and thinking Anne was smiling inwardly at his small dilemma. The skirt of her dress had expanded inside the car. He wondered how her feet could find the pedals. Once she put her hand close beside his leg, and he covered it with his own hand.

"Don't you have a regular escort on tap for things like this?" he asked.

She smiled out at the evening through the windshield. "No, you give up your history first. You shouldn't be available. The next time the Sunday supplement does one of those lists of the ten most eligible men in town you'll be at least number three. You're too good-looking, but you're not gay, I hope."

He liked her hope. "No. Although of course—"

"Yes, yes, some of my best friends. But I have enough best friends." Chris liked that declaration too. "Which means you're divorced," Anne concluded. "Only once, I hope."

"Yes, just once." That accounted for the bareness of his condo. When he'd moved out of his home he had found there wasn't much he wanted to take with him, and in the three years since he'd been too busy with work to do much more than sleep in the condo.

He tried to recite his history without thinking about it. "We met in law school, got married as soon as we graduated, I went into the D.A.'s office, she went to work for a big civil firm. She worked eighty hours a week, I played basketball and tennis on the weekends when she was at the office. When she'd win a big case she'd celebrate with the people in her office. I did the same when I won one. Then she made partner but nothing changed. . . ."

"I feel your pain," Anne said, touching him to add sympathy to the remark. "But the story itself—"

"I know, just a tiny bit common." Chris kept his voice light, too.

"Children?" Anne asked, congratulating herself on the neutrality of her tone.

"We talked about it that last year, and even started . . . trying when there was time. But gradually I realized that the baby was supposed to bring us together, and it didn't seem fair to have a child who would be born with a job description. For a month after I moved out I was so scared . . ."

"But you got away clean."

"Yeah." He looked away. They were driving into the country, to the Hyatt Hill Country Resort just outside town. When Anne exited the expressway night grew broad around them, softening the edges of the scrubby live oaks of the countryside, from there spreading to cover the world.

"So how many exes do you have lurking around?" Chris asked.

"None. But I've been affianced more than once. One was to please my parents, or being a slave to convention, but there were one or two others that had the potential of pleasing my own self. But there's something in me that resists. Or that drives men away."

"Really," Chris said thoughtfully. "Would that be your schedule or your attitude or your manner?"

"Hard to imagine, isn't it?"

"The possibilities are endless. And yet . . ."

She stopped for a stop sign and sat there, though there was no traffic. They gave each other half-smiles. Slowly he leaned toward her, and when he was halfway there she leaned too. They kissed softly, then drew apart an inch and breathed each other. He heard her smile.

The hotel was new but made of sand-colored stone that blended into the dry landscape and simulated the look of an old Spanish mission. Light stabbed out the windows of the hotel's ballroom. As Chris gazed at it Anne returned the lipstick favor, dabbing at his lip with a tissue. He took her hand as they walked up the path. Just outside the open glass doors, where a printed sign announced the evening's function, he stopped and frowned at her.

"Anne," he said reprovingly.

"What?"

"Why didn't you tell me?" Because the sign announced that the guest of honor for the evening in support of the Battered Women's Shelter was Dr. Anne Greenwald.

"What would you have done if you'd known? Dressed better?"

They gave each other that look again, the half-smiles that looked as if they'd just had the same thought. Inside they separated, each knowing many people in the crowd, having half-professional, half-social conversations, but every few minutes their eyes would find each other to exchange that look.

Nearly two hundred well-dressed people filled the anteroom, a few victims, many contributors, and of course a few public officials. Across the way Chris spotted the mayor, resplendent in black tie. Foley smiled and waved. Chris pretended to be caught up in conversation. He watched the mayor obliquely. A few minutes later Anne joined Foley for a photograph. Just before it was snapped Foley turned and kissed her forehead. Anne rolled her eyes but smiled.

Anne didn't break away as soon as the photographer withdrew, she stayed to talk to the mayor. He listened with an earnest expression but gazed across the room. She was still talking with Foley when the crowd began to filter into the banquet room and Chris came to take her hand. "Soliciting funds?" he asked softly.

"Always."

Chris and Anne greeted the eight other people at their table and chatted politely, but kept leaning toward each other. They were widely observed. Anne's and Chris's was a natural alliance, the counselor of the abused and the prosecutor of abusers, but people who thought them what Anne had tried to make of it, a professional obligation, glanced at them together and then took a second look.

Anne made a short and gracious speech that made her audience applaud themselves and also made them blink back sudden tears. "Breaking out of an abusive relationship isn't a job for cowards. Yes, they have to bring their own strength to the process. But they have to have somewhere *to* bring it."

She drew a standing ovation.

Anne was so obviously admired in the crowd that Chris felt self-conscious dancing with her, but when she put her mouth close to his ear to whisper some passing, self-deprecating observation, he forgot the crowd.

———

Awkwardness re-entered the relationship toward the end of the drive home. Their thoughts turned forward and silences interrupted the conversation. When Anne pulled into a parking space in his condominium complex she didn't turn off the engine. "Thanks. I mean it."

"Don't thank me. Can you come up? I've got brandy and some fancy coffee or herbal tea or bottled water if you're real health-conscious."

Anne shook her head. "Not this time."

Chris's disappointment showed, but her refusal sounded tentative. He climbed out of the car, then walked around and leaned in her open window to kiss her. This time they pressed each other longer, but the kiss wasn't quite as good as the first one; too much speculation crept into it, there in the parking lot beneath his condo. Their first kiss had been a statement. This one was a question. When they broke apart Anne leaned her forehead on his shoulder for a moment, then brushed her hand on his jacket again. "You look too elegant to undo," she said.

"Next time burgers and jeans, then."

She smiled. "It's a d—eal."

He heard the word she had almost said instead. "Let's make it a date then. Next Friday."

She nodded. "Call me."

"I don't have your number."

She smiled again. "Let's hold onto that illusion a while longer."

She put the car in gear and he stood and watched her white hand, lifted in the night air as the car disappeared around a corner.

Chapter 6

A man asleep in his near-west-side apartment heard his car alarm going off in the middle of the night. When he went sleepily to turn it off three would-be burglars beat the car-owner so severely that he had to be hospitalized. What should have been a commonplace property crime became attempted capital murder, with no suspects under arrest. The Hispanic victim could remember nothing about his attackers except that they had been black.

A tourist couple were pushed off a Riverwalk bridge into the San Antonio River. The couple escaped with minor injuries, but the story spread and grew. Word of mouth emphasized the racial aspect of the confrontation. The downtown streets became less safe for everyone. Even on the expressways gunfire flared between cars.

All such crime reports reached the Justice Center and the District Attorney. Chris Sinclair took each one personally. One of these incidents was going to end in murder, and Chris Sinclair would be held—and would feel—responsible. There had always been burglaries and assaults, but there had never before been such smoldering racial hostility that every exchange of words threatened to erupt into riot. The city waited for it to happen. Chris felt it as soon as he stepped out of his car inside the parking garage. Was that sound a footfall? What gang waited for him around the corner?

He looked over his shoulder as he walked. Chris felt the city's tension. It was his own.

City Councilman Win Phillips grew in prominence, filling a vacancy no one explicitly acknowledged. Phillips used his new-found prominence subtly, appearing to try to calm the hostility, but actually funneling it in the direction he wanted.

One morning on the steps of the Justice Center, where a small crowd that included reporters had gathered, Phillips asked in a heartfelt tone, "Can't we all just get along?"

His answer acknowledged the irony of his question. "I wish I could tell we can. But getting along requires the desire to get along. To embrace all of us. Some things can never be achieved as long as some people wield too much power in the wrong ways."

Phillips looked straight at the District Attorney. He didn't glare, he didn't overtly accuse, in fact his stare was rather warm. It took Chris by surprise. Momentarily he felt joined with Phillips in a common enterprise, as if they had their assigned roles to play, and memorized cues to feed each other.

But Chris didn't want to play his part. He started up the steps to the Justice Center doors, head down. Win Phillips intercepted him with a hand on his arm. In a sincere, even brotherly voice, the councilman asked, "Prove me wrong, Mr. Sinclair."

They met each other's eyes. After a moment Chris said, in a voice too low for speechifying, "I'm just doing the job, the same way every day."

"Really? Nothing's changed?"

Chris went on into the building, where his investigator, Jack Fine, caught up to him. And, as if they were already in mid-conversation, Jack said, "You know, a cynical person would say that one thing Mr. Phillips is doing is insulating himself from prosecution. Didn't he tell you to come after him next? The way things are now, you couldn't."

Chris closed his eyes briefly. "Jack, don't go there."

"You mean for the time being prominent African-Americans

in San Antonio have a free pass for whatever crimes they want to commit? How long does the moratorium last? Maybe you should hold your own press conference to announce it."

They walked up the broad stairs to the second floor. "You know that's not what I mean." Chris almost laughed, suddenly surprised by humor. "I just mean if any of them are, please God don't let it be discovered on my watch."

But Chris still had his work to do. In the sparsely furnished conference room a few steps from Chris's office, sitting in the midst of a small group of people wearing suits and looking weary of the meeting, Chris's capital crimes chief Ed Grimes said, "Not much punishment evidence. The kind of juvenile arrests they all have. Another robbery pending, but no convictions. Eighteen years old." He turned a hand over, a small gesture of resignation.

"Yes, his first juvenile arrest was when he was fourteen," Chris said. "Later than average, but from there it only took him four years to work his way up to capital murder."

"Is there a jury in the room?" Lynn Ransom asked. She was the only person in the room, probably the only one on his staff, with the balls to make fun of the boss to his face. Lynn wasn't bored; she carried her own amusement behind her lively brown eyes. Chris answered her without heat.

"I always feel them watching over my shoulder. What would you do, Lynn? This'd be your case if it goes to trial."

"We go after everybody, don't we?" she said quietly. Chris locked eyes with her for a moment but didn't return the volley.

He said over his shoulder, "Paul? What's the justification? Why should I offer this one life instead of death?"

Paul Benavides, the first assistant, gave what he knew was a bureaucrat's answer, unpopular but necessary: "The justification is that that court has five capital cases pending in it. If we try them all that uses up most of the year, while a thousand regular felonies pile up on the docket. And even if we do try them all, by the end of the year there'll be five more to take their place. We have to choose our battles, Chris, and this one's nothing special."

As usual, Chris had heard only the facts of the crime. He hadn't looked at the name or ethnic identity of the defendant or his victim. The capital murder had been a painfully common convenience-store robbery in which the clerk had reached under the counter and gotten shot in the face, then twice more in the back as he lay bleeding on the linoleum floor. Chris looked only at the facts—horrible but, as his capital chief had said, far from unique.

But he knew Paul Benavides would have familiarized himself with the political repercussions. Paul had served briefly as a misdemeanor prosecutor then, years before, switched to a personal injury practice, when Chris had asked him to serve as first assistant. Paul had also been active in political and civil rights organizations. He was a very efficient administrator who kept at bay his natural suspicion of cops and, for that matter, of prosecutors. "You complain about the system, get back into it," Chris had invited him, and Paul Benavides had taken him up on it.

In discussions of the kind they were having now, Chris suspected Paul kept a secret tally of how many death penalties the office had gone after and how many had been dealt away, categorized by skin shade and side of town, keeping a careful eye on the balance. Chris didn't keep that tally, and wouldn't have let anyone bring it up to him, but Paul got a vote like the others. Except that in the end, only the District Attorney's vote counted.

"All right," Chris said. "Make the deal. *After* you tell the victim's family."

The capital crimes chief grimaced but nodded. The meeting broke up. Chris rubbed his eyes and tried to remember what day of the week it was. His staff filed out of the conference room, but when he looked up Lynn stood over him. She didn't look angry, only deeply curious. "Just like that?" she said.

Chris winced. All his major decisions were being second-guessed all over town now. He supposed it was just as well one of the questioners was so close at hand. He looked at her very seriously and said, "Sometimes."

Lynn didn't move, and Chris didn't do anything to escape her scrutiny for a long minute.

Luckily Anne Greenwald's house had a porch, and luckier still there were chairs on it. Not comfortable chairs—they were wrought iron, with canvas seats, but after Chris squirmed around for a while he found a position that afforded a semblance of relaxation. In fact, with his feet up on the low railing, looking cool in his short sleeves and sunglasses and sipping a beer, he looked the picture of contentment when Anne first caught sight of him, as she hurried across the yard from her car. She stopped flat, surprised. Chris saluted her with the beer can.

"We had a date, remember?" he called.

Anne looked more tailored than usual, wearing a navy blue dress with tiny white dots and a short yellow vest over it. Stockings and high heels made her look more severe than usual, which heightened the effect when she put one fist on her hip and stared at him. "But you were supposed to call."

"I did," Chris said easily. "I called the clinic and your office and in a wild, crazy waste of time I even called here. But you were always a step ahead of me."

He stood as Anne came up the three steps, taking off her shoes as she did. That gave her a lot to carry. Chris took from her the stack of folders and books and set them down in the chair, where they were probably more comfortable than he had been.

Anne's shoulders slumped, she lost the severe look. In fact she looked in need of help of some kind. Chris put his arm around her and she leaned on him for a moment.

"Sorry," she said. "I haven't picked up my messages in a—"

"Days," he said, but he wasn't angry. Instead he felt surprised by how energized and happy he felt at the sight of her.

"Well, when I call in for messages I ask for just the important ones," Anne explained. "And the staff knows that means anything to do with patients. I guess you didn't make the cut."

"Monday morning you can go in and reorder their priorities." Chris opened and held out to her the tiny ice chest he'd brought, just big enough to hold two cans, and now holding the one Tecate he'd saved for her. Anne took it out and rolled the can along her forehead. Then she glanced at the nutritional information printed on the can, grimaced slightly, and instead reached for Chris's opened can and took a sip. She made a face at its warmth.

"You've been here for a while. How did you find my address, anyway?"

"I have a staff of highly trained investigators. One of them even offered to come by and open the door for me, but I told him I'd rather wait to be invited."

Anne hesitated. She put her hand on her doorknob, then turned. "I wanted to get the place ready before you came. You know, straighten up, make myself look presentable. . . ."

"You look great," Chris said. She did. Anne looked like the end of a long day, but she was reviving before his eyes. He hoped his unexpected appearance accounted for the sparkle returning to her eyes. The corners of her mouth began to twitch. He reached for her cheek, and when she rested her head intimately on his hand he stepped closer, she raised her face, he bent to her, and they shared the best kiss yet, tender but with a slight sense of growing urgency. It didn't convey a statement or a question, just a communication of lips. They embraced for a long moment before he stepped back. As soon as he did, the urge to touch her again grew very strong.

"I meant the house," Anne said. "I don't want you thinking I'm some—"

"My God, what are you hiding in there?" he asked playfully. "I think you've dated too many psychiatrists, Dr. Greenwald. I'm not looking for clues to your twisted personality. Although you are making me curious—"

Anne was searching through her purse for her keys. "I don't date psychiatrists," she said with some distaste.

"I feel the same way about lawyers. What's this escapist literature you're reading?"

He'd picked up her papers again. The book on top looked like a textbook, but had a provocative title: *Friday by the Phone: Teenage Suicide and the Failure to* . . . something or other.

"It's a study of teenage anxiety, especially with dating and relationships."

"Isn't it nice to be past all that," Chris said, and Anne laughed as she opened the door for him.

The outside of the little frame house had given him an idea of what the interior would be like. The front door opened directly into a large living room. In its far wall an archway opened into the dining room. The kitchen would be back at the far end. There were only two bedrooms, one behind the other, separated by a bathroom, on the right hand side as Chris entered the house.

The sixty-year-old house could have been in any state of repair but to Chris it appeared to be in good shape. The plaster walls were freshly painted a pale coral color. The hardwood floor shone. To his left a small fireplace with a tile hearth displayed an interior blackened by use. When Anne closed the front door Chris saw to his right two large old bookcases, at right angles to each other in the corner of the room, their shelves full to the point of spilling out. A door on that side of the room opened into the front bedroom, which he could see had been made into an office. He saw a computer monitor and a filing cabinet.

Anne took the books and papers from him, waved at the room as she turned away, and said lightly, "So what do you know now, Sigmund?"

She carried her work papers into the office and closed the door behind her after she came back out.

Chris knew a lot. He knew Anne's profession could have made her very well off but hadn't. He could guess without seeing her tax returns that she gave away a large chunk of her income; and much of her time was given to charity patients. He also knew, from the way most things in the room seemed scattered but were probably in their places, that home was important to her, she needed a refuge and probably didn't invite people here often.

What he chose to say was, "Now I realize I knew you in college. You were one of those serious hippies. You acted real carefree and loose in the world but secretly you went home and studied. And even bought art like a grown-up." He indicated the wall behind her, filled with paintings and framed photographs.

She smiled. "Most of those are inherited."

"But you picked them out." There were a lot of faces on that wall, faces of animals and people, faces composed for the artist or just turning toward or away from capture. The wall was a little eerie. He didn't approach it. Anne came toward him and took his arm as if she'd give him a tour, but she just stood close to him. She studied Chris's face intently enough to make him wonder about his expression, and want to start conversation again.

"The deal was jeans and burgers," he said. "You can see I kept up my end of the clothes bargain. You probably don't own any jeans, though."

She laughed. "Everybody owns jeans, cowboy. Mine fit me better than yours do you, too."

"I'd like to see that."

Anne still held his arm. She let her hand slide down its length to his hand. She looked lost in thought, her face a little troubled.

"What's the matter?"

Looking up at him seriously, she said, "I'd really like to take a shower first."

In the same tone Chris answered, "Mmm, that's a problem, all right. I've got a lot of demands on my time. If I allot you some extra shower time, it throws off my whole schedule."

Her expression lightened, she shook her head. "No, I get the whole evening."

His hand was still in hers. They kissed again. He put his other arm around her back. Anne's lips were moist and tender and firm. He seemed to hear a murmur in her breathing.

"That's right," he said.

She didn't give him any coy backward glances as she walked out carrying her shoes and beginning to unbutton the navy blue dress. Anne went through the archway and the dining room into the back bedroom. There were a few minutes of doors and drawers opening and closing before Chris heard the sound of running water.

He'd lied when he said he wasn't looking for clues in her house. Anne had seen what she called his lair, he'd wanted to see hers. He stood in her living room, a blend that produced a sort of homey elegance, and felt he knew her much better. The furniture featured a lot of blond wood and not much cushioning, so it gave an ascetic effect. The couch was only about five feet long, not a comfortable place to spend the night. Anne had lived alone for a long time, she didn't have to compromise her taste with anyone else's. Everything here was hers. He glanced through the arch and saw a scarred old mahogany table set with six place settings, fringed thick burgundy fabric placemats, thin flowered plates and slender wine glasses, all lightly patterned with dust. Anne would do her eating in the kitchen or on the run.

He still heard water running, pictured her in the shower, her face lifted to the water. The late May weather was too warm for a hot shower. The water would be cool, turning warm only as it coursed down her skin. It would revive her even more. Anne would turn her head, listening, wondering what he was doing.

The door into her bedroom stood half-open. Chris slipped off his loafers and approached it. The water continued to run. Was she waiting, expecting him? He walked into the bedroom and saw the bathroom door ajar. He glimpsed a shower curtain.

The small bedroom had four windows, barely adorned with almost transparent curtains that would blow in the slightest breeze. A four-poster bed, rather high off the ground, featured wood the same dark color of the dining room table. The bed had been "made" just by pulling its thin coverlet up over the pillows, without any effort at tucking in. Chris smiled: a pair of jeans was already laid out on the bed. One back pocket had a small hole. Tossed beside the jeans were a bra and panties. The panties were white with little blue flowers, a girl's panties. Chris approached but resisted touching her underwear.

Stepping into the shower with her might be the beginning of a lovely fantasy, one Anne might be imagining at that moment, but it might also be a bad mistake that would ruin everything. Waiting might also be a mistake, but a less bad one; it could be corrected later. Chris hesitated, listening, so that when the water shut off with a clunk he was startled by the sudden absence of sound. The shower curtain rustled. With the door ajar between them they were practically in the same room. Chris stepped softly backward, glad he had left his shoes in the other room.

Then he heard her voice. She didn't raise it, but spoke distinctly, so that he knew she knew he was there.

"Yes," she said.

She waited for an answer. Chris finally cleared his throat and said, "Yes what?"

The bathroom door opened and Anne stuck her head out. She looked younger and softer. Her shoulders were bare. Her hair was wet at the ends, stabbing down to her shoulders. Droplets decorated her neck and upper arms. "Yes, I was half-expecting you to come in," she said.

Chris nodded, acknowledging his stupidity. "And would that have been okay?"

Anne smiled. "We'll never know now, will we, barefoot boy?"

She stretched out a slender arm. She was wrapped in a big white towel. "Could you toss me my clothes while you're here?" She watched him. "Or bring them to me?"

Her face had become elfin—challenging, questioning, drawing him in while withholding something. The something was herself; even as she held back, her eyes asked him to seek her.

Without picking up her clothes as an excuse he went to her, took her outstretched hand, and drew her out into the room. She wore a very large towel, it covered her from her chest almost to her knees. It clogged the space between them. Chris put his hands on her cheeks, then moved his fingers through her damp hair. He and Anne seemed to be gliding, or the room to be turning around them. Anne looked very serious. She watched him intently. They stood holding hands and looked at each other. Changes of expression were only in their eyes.

Then Anne caught the collar of his shirt and pulled him to her. One of them laughed; probably both. He held the back of her neck, she reached inside his shirt. She pulled his shirttail out of his jeans and he took the shirt off over his head. Her towel seemed very intrusive. Chris reached inside it, ran his hands along her sides, and the towel fell away.

Anne would never have made a magazine model. Her bones didn't show. Her breasts, white, cinnamon-tipped, rose over a white abdomen that protruded slightly with interesting musculature. Chris ran his hands over it, then around to her back. Anne stood on tiptoes to press her lips against his neck, then busied her hands with the fastenings of his jeans.

They touched each other wonderingly, examining. Anne ran a hand over his shoulder, then kissed it, then bit it lightly. Chris meanwhile traced the line of her hip. They kissed very gently, then less so. She pressed against him, her arms circled his neck. He held her around the waist, fingers stretching to cover as much of her skin as he could.

Anne drew back a bit and smiled. Her bed seemed taller behind her. Chris asked, "Do you need a boost onto this bed, or do you take a running start?"

"It's easy," Anne said. She bounced, turned in the air, and was sitting on the bed in front of him, at a nice height. She put her hands in his hair while he leaned to kiss her chest. His lips moved along her body. "You don't get much sun, do you?" he said, marvelling at her skin.

"Not there I don't," she said primly. "What about you, where's your tan line?"

It was on his legs, at the tops of his thighs, from occasionally playing tennis outdoors. Chris climbed up into bed with her and Anne ran her finger along the line, bringing the short crinkly hairs of his legs to attention.

They took their time, exploring, in no hurry. At one point Anne turned, and he took her leg, the muscle of her calf. He frowned. "You're a jogger," he said accusingly.

"No, I'm a treadmaster," she said. "I don't have time for any exercise unless I can read while I'm doing it."

"Oh, really?"

"I can't think of an exception," she said, then laughed as he caught her under the backs of her knees and lifted, sliding her toward him.

Later she lay full length atop him. They watched each other's faces, barely moving. Their breaths deepened in unison. Anne closed her eyes and sucked in air. He held her tighter. She lay her head on his chest and he gradually loosened his hold, until he was only stroking her sides and they were murmuring wordlessly.

Light still shone from the bathroom, the only light in the house, which had grown very dark but also familiar. Chris felt he could hear the air moving through all the rooms of her house. He had no idea what time it was and no inclination to find out.

Anne stirred. Her fingers touched his face lightly, as if she would sculpt him. The air held that tremulous expectancy that one of them was about to say something, and that it might be something significant. Things had changed between them, but Chris didn't want to hear either of them say how.

Luckily, Anne spoke first. "I'd love to lie here all night—"

"Don't tell me you've been lying."

"I hope you weren't, about the burgers. Or am I not worth a hamburger now?"

Chris leaned over her and looking devotedly into her eyes said, "You are worth—onion rings."

She feigned swooning. Slowly, stopping to touch or kiss again, they climbed down from the high bed and sorted through clothes. Chris continued to watch Anne. The slanted light from the bathroom was perfect, it made her body mysterious and alluring. He stepped on his underwear, pulled them on, then found jeans. Anne walked to the closet, put on a shirt, then stopped buttoning it to watch him. Her gaze made him self-conscious as he pulled up the pants. The jeans caught on his thighs and seemed tight around his calves.

"Uh—"

Anne looked at him with quietly amused speculation, as if seeing him in a new light. He reached down for a better grip on the jeans and his finger went into a hole in the back pocket.

"Now you can honestly say you've gotten into my pants," Anne observed. "And if you can button them I'm really going to be pissed."

The best and closest place for hamburgers was Chris Madrid's, and the time had grown late enough that the happy-hour crowd of lawyers had probably flowed away. They decided to risk it, and the occasion rewarded them with an evening cool enough to sit out on the patio. In a corner, at the end of a picnic table, they found a semblance of isolation from the festivities. Of course, they had to sit very close in order to hear each other.

"You can whisper little endearments to me," Anne said, "but don't start taking bites of my food in public, okay?"

A breeze blew her brown hair back, and her scent to Chris. Inside a white shirt, her skin even looked as if it had some color. Knowing what she looked like didn't remove the intrigue from the curve of her breast as it disappeared inside her shirt. He touched his paper napkin to the corner of her mouth. Anne frowned inquiringly.

"Your ketchup's a little crooked," he explained.

Anne looked at him fondly, but in spite of the easy banter her eyes were slightly troubled. He felt sure that making any declarations would only increase her anxiety. He let the conversation slide toward work.

"I have to be in court next week," Anne said. "Maybe I'll see you."

"Sure. What court is it? Maybe I'll—"

She shook her head. "Don't interfere in it. It's just a case."

He thought he understood her nervousness. Let's not get too involved in each other's lives too quickly. Let's save some room on the edges. They shouldn't be all-encompassing to each other, they might use up too quickly whatever was happening.

"Let's try not to work together anymore, okay?" Anne said, as if she were asking for a commitment.

"That's a deal," Chris said emphatically.

Monday Chris went by Jack Fine's office. It sat empty. Tuesday Chris left a note on his chief investigator's desk. Wednesday he saw no sign Jack had been back to the office. Thursday Chris stood frowning in the empty office and, as he turned to go out, a body bumped into him.

"Jack! How nice. It's convenient that we work in the same building, that way we can run into each other once in a while."

"You're the one gave me the assignment," Jack said grumpily. He sat and rummaged in one of his desk drawers.

"And?"

"And I'll let you know when I know something."

Chris didn't move. Staring down at his investigator, he said, "You know something now, Jack."

Jack sighed. He sat up in his chair and looked at his boss. Jack looked wearier and at the same time more sharp-eyed than usual. He got up and closed his office door casually, as if he felt a draft. Then he stood close to Chris and said, "No, I don't. What I've mainly been checking on so far is how much cooperation I'm going to get. The answer is turning out to be not much. Cops're investigating the Rodriguez murder, of course, it's an open file, but they've got, like, tunnel vision. Somebody's told them not to go looking up any side streets."

"This was a very public murder," Chris said. He stepped away from his investigator, wanting to pace, but feeling claustrophobic in the small office. Jack's office had boxes of papers and files taking up most of the floor space. Two big filing cabinets were like guards holding Chris in place. "Are you saying they don't want—?"

"It's not like that," Jack said, anticipating the question. "Look, here's how you investigate this kind of murder. You look at the scene itself. That hasn't given 'em anything. Mr. Rodriguez was alone that morning, his usual routine, going from a coffee shop where he usually had breakfast, to a barber shop, a fix-it place where he hung out. Somewhere along the route he disappeared. The next place anybody knows he was was inside the crack house."

"That took some doing," Chris said. "Getting in there and out without being seen, with cops checking out the place."

"Yeah, probably more than one guy to carry him," Jack said. "But other than that not too tough. They had to get there early, but it wasn't like the President was going to be speaking there later. Everybody knew that house would be rubble in a couple of hours. They didn't think they had to post a guard on it."

Chris pictured the interior of the house again, remembering moving through it, the air dim while the crowd outside waited to cheer the demolition. Chris had probably been the next person inside, after the murderers had left. How long had Mr. Rodriguez lain there waiting for him?

"So you go to the other end next," Jack said, interrupting Chris's thoughts. "They know who was ultimately behind it, Malachi Reese, so they start looking from him to his associates. Where was the connection? Chris, they've been doing that for years. I can tell you from when I was in the department, we were always trying to make a case against Malachi Reese. We had leads, but they went nowhere. He had that very public life. He had a million friends. But his personal life? That was a mystery. Never got married. Went out with some women, sure, but whether he was serious about any of 'em or whether he had others in the background, who knew? Interviewing the women we know about is like talking to yourself."

Chris waited for more, then realized there was no more, not yet. "Don't you have anything?"

Jack pulled a battered black briefcase up onto his desk and opened it. He took out a slim manila folder that turned out to be full of photographs. "The press took a lot of pictures," he said. "The crowd around the crack house. There's the chief of police, there's the mayor. Judge Pressman. Look over their shoulders."

There had been a small crowd of spectators, maybe thirty or forty people. Jack arranged the photographs into a kind of mosaic that captured most of the crowd. The faces blurred together. The photographer in most cases hadn't been out to capture these people, they just happened to be in the background. The people's expressions were hard to read. The crowd featured a variety of colors and ages, that was about all that could be seen.

"Recognize anybody?" Jack asked—not a serious question. Still, Chris pored over the faces. No, he couldn't make anyone out, except in one photo he saw himself standing apart from the crowd with the young black woman he'd met there.

"I'm thinking the killer was probably proud of his work. Probably wanted to see the excitement when they found the body." Jack's voice was listless. The pictures hadn't told him anything yet. "I'm getting outtakes from the TV news crew footage, too."

Chris continued to look at the faces. Did one have a gleam of eagerness? After a few minutes the faces began to break down into the dots that composed them.

Chris looked up at his investigator. Jack answered with a shrug Chris's unasked question: *We're down to this?*

"There's one other thing," Chris said. "We're looking for connections. What about the murder weapon? The knife that killed Victor Fuentes and Mrs. Rodriguez that night. Do their wounds match *Mr.* Rodriguez's?"

"I don't think Malachi would've been that stupid," Jack said.

"Who knows what he might think? We didn't recover either murder weapon, did we? Maybe he would've *wanted* to leave his signature on my witness."

Jack just nodded, acknowledging the order from his boss. Chris had to be satisfied with that. He went back to work, wondering if he had any other allies anywhere.

Chapter 7

Chris Sinclair strode through the halls of the D.A.'s office, looking very purposeful, but with his mind elsewhere. Someone who
would kill for Malachi Reese was still out there, but that no
longer seemed important. Where Reese was now, murder
couldn't help him. He would turn to other tools, the political
skills that had served him so well in the past.

Reese's personal life was a mystery, Jack Fine had said. It had
been for years. And now Chris knew how much that personal life
had encompassed. When Reese hadn't been on the public stage
he had virtually disappeared. Hadn't any of his associates noticed
that, hadn't that triggered suspicions? No. They hadn't wanted to
know. Reese's political associates had probably thought it appropriate that Reese keep his private life to himself.

But they must have had some inkling. Chris felt again the
touch of the mayor's hand on his arm. *Let us know if you find out
anything significant,* the mayor had asked. A reasonable request
among friends.

But it would be his political connections Reese was working
now. Calling in the many dark favors owed him. Had that been
Reese's touch on Chris's arm?

Lynn Ransom stood in the doorway of an office, watching her
boss as he approached her. The dark brown planes of her face

didn't betray her thoughts. Unlike most of Chris's assistants, Lynn didn't slink back to her desk and pretend to be working as he passed.

"What's up, Lynn?"

"I was working on this great case," she said immediately. "Then it got snatched away from me and handed to a special prosecutor."

Chris knew at once what she meant. His past as a defense lawyer still lingered. When one of his former clients got charged with a new crime, a special prosecutor was appointed, so there'd be no appearance of conflict. In fact, Chris couldn't offhand think of any of his former clients for whom he'd want to do a favor such as reducing the sentence for a new offense. "Which of my boys was it?" he asked idly.

Lynn said a name that was little more than a name to Chris. He listened while she recited the details of his former client's new crime, but Chris wasn't paying much attention. Compared to Malachi Reese, other criminals seemed so unimaginative and relatively harmless. Very few of Chris's former clients could stir Chris's interest again.

Very few. But . . . Chris walked on to his own office. As he passed his secretary's desk she handed him a stack of letters. Irma Garcia had been with Chris for eight years, since his days of private practice. She knew how to order the mail in importance. When she handed him the short stack of envelopes, Chris looked down at the return address of the one on top and sighed, and stopped being the District Attorney.

Prison officials like to keep good working relationships with elected prosecutors all across Texas. In Huntsville, some two hundred miles east of San Antonio, they granted Chris an unusual privilege, though he was there not as a prosecutor but as a one-time defense lawyer seeing a former client: They let him walk down Death Row itself, to the cell he sought, instead of meeting his client in the semi-public large bullpen with thick wire mesh and bulletproof plastic between them.

Chris had removed his suit jacket and rolled up his shirtsleeves, and didn't carry a briefcase or anything else. A guard captain accompanied him through two thickly barred gates onto the Row proper. The central corridor was wide and clean and surprisingly like any other prison in Texas. Death Row is now a misnomer. No single row could hold the more than four hundred and fifty men awaiting execution in the Ellis Unit. The wide central corridor was like a high school hallway. Branching off it to the left at regular intervals were the cell units, with individual entrances guarded by guard rooms that looked like large cages.

"Here," said the guard captain, Ben Stillwell, consulting some mental map. He turned to one of the guard cages, waved casually at the three guards inside, and the barred gate slid open for him. He motioned Chris inside with him.

Claustophobia would start here, if one were subject to that fear. Chris's hands swung free and his shoulders tingled as he walked down this aisle. This was the real Row. It seemed old-fashioned: iron bars and concrete floors, the same security equipment the unit had featured at its opening, decades ago. Televisions hung on the walls outside the cells, one TV for every three cells. Otherwise Death Row was surprisingly low-tech. No surveillance cameras, no eavesdropping microphones. Prisoners awaiting execution had a minimum of privacy, but they did have that much.

The cells were stacked three tiers high. Large fans mounted on the walls turned lazily, the only comfort provided these prisoners; no Texas prison is air-conditioned. Chris walked by the cells, glancing in surreptitiously. Some of these inmates had only recently arrived from a courtroom. Most were nearer the opposite end of the string of years between their crimes and their punishment. Chris felt their eyes. Many of them, though, didn't look up. They never raised their heads, as if they could blot out their surroundings by not acknowledging them.

Chris came to a cell more than halfway down the row and stopped. "Hello, John," he said softly.

John Tinnamon looked up eagerly. The whites of his eyes were very white, and shown all around as he jumped up and strode to the bars. "Chris," he said fondly. His long fingers reached through the bars like the twigs of tree branches reaching for the sun. Chris's accompanying guide looked on unmoved as Tinnamon's hands clasped Chris's shoulders, close to his throat.

"You sure?" the burly captain of guards said.

Chris nodded. "Back," Captain Stillwell said, not unkindly, and John Tinnamon backed up, though still leaning forward eagerly. The guard unlocked the heavy bars, Chris went inside the cell and managed not to flinch when the door closed at his back. The guard walked away without assuring Chris that he'd remain within earshot.

John Tinnamon swarmed over him. "Oh, man," he said happily. "Man, I knew you'd come."

"Good to see you, John." Chris hugged back, briefly. The prisoner finally stepped back. John Tinnamon had been a very big man—probably one of the factors that had prompted a jury to sentence him to death—but now he'd lost his bulk and grown thin. He was a milk-chocolate–colored man, gone very bald on top with a thick fringe of crinkled hair, almost all gray. Chris calculated. John couldn't yet be forty, but he looked older, except in the bright shining light of his eyes.

John Tinnamon had been on Death Row for seven years. His next execution date would probably be the real one. He'd already bounced off the ceiling of the U.S. Supreme Court twice. When a Death Row inmate nears the end of the legal process they say his appeals are exhausted. John Tinnamon didn't look exhausted. He looked like a man eagerly starting a new career.

"What do your lawyers say, John?"

Tinnamon shrugged with a smile. "I don't talk to them. Volunteer lawyers, you know, man. Belong to Amnesty International. They think they doing a good deed by keeping me alive. I told 'em but they don't understand. I'm ready, Chris. I want to meet the Man."

Chris nodded uncomfortably. He'd heard occasional reports of John Tinnamon's career on Death Row. He seemed to be a rarity, a man who had really been rehabilitated while awaiting execution. He tried to convert his fellow condemned. His warden believed in him. Chris didn't doubt Tinnamon's sincerity. His sanity, maybe, but not his sincerity.

"I've come awake here, Chris," Tinnamon said quietly. "For the first time in my life. Wakin' up from a bad dream. I can remember everything I did, and why I did 'em, but my reasons don't make sense to me anymore. Like as if somebody showed you a picture of a place where you lived for years and you see for the first time that the place had no windows. You think, 'How could I have lived like that?' "

Tinnamon's face shone with wonder again. Chris asked, "Is there anything I can do for you, John?"

Tinnamon put his hand on Chris's shoulder again. The prisoner had a formidable physical presence, but his touch was light and trembly. "Maybe—talk to her family. After, you know. I know they wouldn't want to hear anything from me. But tell 'em how sorry I am." Chris tried to remember the name of Tinnamon's victim in the robbery-murder, but had only a vague recollection of her family. Tinnamon's memory obviously retained much more.

"It wasn't until the trial that I thought about her having people who loved her, who'd miss her. That night I didn't think of nothing like that. It was just her and me in that crummy little store. She kept looking at me. That's why I cut her throat, to stop her looking at me." Tinnamon hugged himself as if cold. His serenity had fled. His voice barely emerged, soft and scared. "Now she's always looking at me. Only Jesus can get between me and her stare. I'm going to see her, too, Chris, to tell *her* how sorry I am. I know she'll believe me."

Chris felt a little trembly himself. "I'll tell them, John. I'll be here when—the time comes."

John Tinnamon smiled again. His smile covered his whole face, up over the top of his head. He patted his former attorney. Tinnamon hungered for contact, even as he claimed to look forward to giving up the flesh. He raised one long finger, and his face grew more sober. *Uh oh,* Chris thought.

"That's not why I asked you to come, though. I've got to warn you, Chris."

Chris sighed inwardly. He really didn't want to discuss the condition of his soul with a giant doomed man in a tiny prison cell.

"You got to watch your step, man. They after you."

Chris nodded, thinking his old client was talking about demons. But Tinnamon remained sharper than Chris realized. He saw that Chris didn't take his warning to heart. He stepped closer and, in a no-bullshit grumble Chris remembered from years before his conversion, said, "I'm serious, Chris. People out to get you, and you not gonna know where it comes from."

Chris listened more carefully. "Who, John? Friends of yours?"

Tinnamon snorted softly. "Nobody cares that much about me. They don't even remember I'm still alive somewhere."

"But you hear things, John?"

Tinnamon nodded sagely. "I don't know much yet. I'll find out and I'll tell you. You didn't tell anybody you was coming to see me, did you? You kept it secret like I told you in the letter?"

Chris nodded, a lie. Of course he had told his secretary where he would be today, and he'd told Paul Benavides, in case he needed to reach Chris quickly. And he hadn't been anonymous with the prison officials. Chris's visit to John Tinnamon was hardly cloaked in secrecy.

Tinnamon looked intently into his face. "Don't trust anybody," he instructed Chris solemnly.

The air in the little cell had grown very close. Chris could feel Tinnamon's breath, the way Tinnamon's victim must have felt it ten years ago as the convict had leaned over her and stabbed upward. Tinnamon's concern was too sincere. Chris stepped away, as far as he could, and looked around the cell, its cinderblock walls undecorated, a short metal shelf holding no book except a Bible.

"Is there anything I can get you, John?"

"Listen," Tinnamon said, and a voice interrupted, "Done?"

"Yes," Chris said too quickly, to the guard staring curiously through the bars. "I think we are, aren't we? Unless there's some other message you want me to take to anyone, John?"

Tinnamon shook his head. He ignored the guard, but his eyes fastened on Chris were no longer joyful. Nor did they shine with religious fervor.

After the door opened and Chris stepped out, Tinnamon reached through the bars again. His fingers were skeletal on Chris's shoulder. "Remember," he said.

"I will, John. Thanks. And I'll see you again."

Chris stepped quickly away, as if he had to keep up with the guard, turning back to wave while thinking, Nine years in the isolation of Death Row. No wonder John Tinnamon had changed from the typical truculent, unfeeling defendant Chris remembered from his trial. Nine years on the shelf in this steel warehouse waiting to be put to death. John Tinnamon had found refuge in various obsessions. He had been stretched like Silly Putty, out of recognizable human shape.

Chris and the guard captain walked past several cells, Chris barely glancing into any of them. The guard was glancing askance at him. Chris felt obligated to speak to the only other free man in sight.

"Strange," he said. "John knows perfectly well I'm on the other side now, it's part of my job to put people here, but he somehow still trusts me. He—" In the much less confined air of the walkway beside the cells, Chris spoke lightly. "He asked me here because he wanted to help me."

The guard registered no surprise. Captain Stillwell was a little shorter than Chris, built like a weightlifter who'd been inflated then had a little of the air leaked out of him. His arms were thick inside the short sleeves of his uniform shirt. He had an extra chin and the beginning of jowls. "Tried to warn you, did he?" he asked in a folksy drawl.

"You heard?"

The guard shook his head. "I was down the corridor. But John warns everybody. He always has secret information. He must get it from the Man upstairs, though, 'cause nobody else talks to him." The guard stopped and looked at Chris squarely. "He hasn't had a visitor in a year. The only mail he gets is from Publishers Clearing House telling him he may already be a winner."

Now Chris's visit to Death Row seemed like a fool's errand. He felt how long a trip it had been and how short a visit he'd had with John Tinnamon. Chris stopped walking and looked around, soaking in the reality of the place. He looked up at the three tiers of cells. Vague human shapes were recessed in the shadows of some. Out of others faces and hands pressed as far as they could. Some of the men stared curiously or sullenly at Chris. His chest swelled with an ugly, secret joy. Everyone here had been condemned to die. Standing outside their enclosures, Chris indulged himself in the illusion that he had not.

Captain Stillwell waited patiently. Suddenly Chris's thrill in being alive dwindled. He searched the cells across from him more carefully. When he resumed walking beside the guard he listened as well as looked. When they returned to the gate that opened into the much larger corridor Chris said, "Can you do me another favor?"

A few minutes later they were walking down another row. This time Chris had to go up a ladder. The air turned warmer. Chris felt he was following a path he knew. Next to him a hopeless pale face stared out.

Ahead of him down the short row somebody was chanting. "Watch out," the guard said, catching up. "Sometimes that one throws things." He went ahead of Chris.

They came to the cell from which the chanting issued. Inside it a short, very thick black man hung his head and steadily shouted a stream of obscenities and random words, vile in their juxtapositions. "Shut up!" the guard said, banging his stick against the bars. The prisoner ignored him, except to add the word "kill" to his vicious monologue.

Chris walked on. Just beyond the chanting man, he stopped and looked into a cell that seemed a little brighter than the others. Then Chris knew why he had come to Huntsville.

The cell looked very orderly. On the neatly made bunk papers were spread in neat stacks, a thick book open in their midst. Leaning over a small portable stand, Malachi Reese sat typing on an old manual typewriter. He had a pencil between his teeth and had paused in thought, fingers still poised over the keys.

Though Chris had been looking for him, he was shocked to see Malachi Reese. He seemed so out of place. Next door the inmate continued to babble his murderous drool. From other cells music clashed and fought. Somewhere a toilet flushed. But inside Malachi Reese's tidy office of a cell none of that penetrated. Reese wore his gray uniform like a suit. He still carried his old elegance—not in his clothes—in his manner: the way his lips pursed as he pursued a thought, the way he obviously felt his visitor's presence but turned only slowly. From where Reese sat on a short stool, he smiled.

"Well, here we both are," he said. "Did they get you too?"

Seeing Reese in this place stirred a guilty feeling in Chris. He could forget Reese's crimes. Chris remembered Reese as a cunning adversary. It seemed somehow unfair that their lives had taken such drastically different turns as a result of Chris's winning the trial. It could have so easily gone the other way.

He said, "I came to see someone else. I just—" Chris trailed off. ". . . stopped by" sounded so inappropriate, like greeting someone on his front porch on a lazy Sunday afternoon.

Reese knew why he'd come. He spread his arms, displaying himself and his setting. This Reese seemed like a new creature, divorced from the things Chris had proven about him at trial. Chris peered closely at him, but felt none of the intimacy he'd felt at trial. This Reese had become a quiet, self-contained man in a ludicrously awful place.

"Working on the appeal?" Chris asked, nodding at the typewriter.

Reese shook his head dismissively. "Little piece of my own." He stood up. "Tell me, my man, did you get a lot of calls of congratulations after the verdict?"

Chris shook his head.

"Any special one that surprised you?" Reese continued, concern in his voice. He came closer to the bars. "No? You got anyone you can trust to watch your back, son? Because once they're done with you, you'd better watch out."

Now Chris had received a second warning from a second dead man. Where, from where they were, did they find concern for anyone else? "No one pulled my strings," Chris said. "I made the decisions."

"They did," Reese said quietly. "They played you so carefully you didn't even see it coming. I think you were playing it straight, Chris, I do. But you were fed that case, piece by piece. They set me up."

He had come close enough now for Chris to see his eyes.

Sometimes, Chris remembered, Reese's pupils grew so big they consumed his eyes. The pupils were hungry voids, contained by the earthwork bulwarks of his brown irises. A war fought in his eyes, between a gentle, intelligent concern and a black rage. Reese's voice remained mild.

"You don't think it's over, do you?"

Chris felt a strong urge to ask Reese about his connections. What politician still in power in San Antonio might do him favors. Maybe Reese would be willing to talk—but Chris had nothing to offer him in exchange. "It looks over to me," he said.

Reese understood the reference to his Death Row cell. He shrugged it away. "It was always a race with me. I was always headed either to this place or the White House. Not the big chair in the Oval Office, you know, but somewhere off to the side, on staff. It could've happened. But the hounds caught me first. I'd always known they were there at my heels. Maybe I got complacent because I'd beat them so many times. Or maybe they got themselves a faster hound."

He smiled at Chris. "I don't blame you. You were just the lead dog. Not the master of the hounds. You'll see."

Chris decided not to answer. Not drawing a response, Reese changed tacks. He ran his eyes down Chris's white shirt, collar open and sleeves rolled up. "A shame they made you take off your nice suit to come in here. It's a dreary place. But it'll be okay for you by tonight. You can go home from it at night. Change your suit, go out to a nice restaurant. Fondle your lady friend's leg under the table. Your nights are pleasant, aren't they? You can forget it all for a while."

"You've been seen in some nice restaurants," Chris said.

"But always working. Or at least always on guard. I had to be."

Reese looked at Chris as if gauging his trustworthiness, which struck Chris as funny under the circumstances. Chris glanced down the walkway and saw that his guard waited thirty yards away, pacing patiently up and down, glancing into other cells.

"Let me tell you something," Reese said. "On the east side and the west side we know something you north-side boys don't know. You think you've got separate work lives and personal lives. But we know better. We know when you get into the game you put everything in play. Your future, your children. Their futures. Everything you have or ever will have is up for grabs." Reese sighed. "I guess they'd gotten subtle the last few years. Made me forget that."

"The only reason anyone was after you was because of your crimes," Chris said firmly. He sounded too staunch to be real. He was reminding himself that the evidence he had presented at trial must have been real. He had investigated the case himself. He had believed his witnesses.

"Crimes," Reese said bitterly, lowering his head. Then his eye gleamed in the shadow. "Subtlety didn't used to be part of their repertoire. They thought they could get me with the old, old tricks. I mean fifteen, twenty years ago. Listen to this 'crime.' One time I was trying to raise a stink about some bad cops. Racist sadists—they wouldn't be tolerated today. But back then . . ." He shrugged. "Anyway, I knew they'd come for me. I rested up all day, then I—"

"How did you know when it would happen?" Chris asked. He didn't accept on faith anything Reese said, but the story engaged his curiosity.

"They always come at night, Chris. You could take a nap on your front porch when it's light out, you're okay. But better snap to when that sun goes down.

"So night fell and this car comes gliding to a stop down the block from my house. Two cops in suits get out and walk slowly up the street. I had a fence around my front yard, and the grass was a little high. But they saw lights inside the house and heard music from the stereo, and they looked at each other and nodded, and they opened the gate quiet as they could and slipped inside. They had pistols on their hips, of course, and one of 'em was carrying the riot gun, but loose, not expecting trouble 'til they got to the house. They hadn't counted on the dogs."

Now Chris vaguely remembered the incident. Reese saw memory awaken in Chris's eyes. He leaned toward him. "You know the expression 'white dog,' white boy?"

Chris did. Dogs trained to hate blacks, to attack any on sight. A strange, sick notion: racist dogs.

"Well, these were black dogs," Reese explained. "Somebody loaned them to me for the duration. Man, those were amazing dogs. Reacted to white skin just like some of the brothers I knew. Better not gleam palely when you came across my yard, boy. Those old Dobermans were trained not to bark, just to strike." His hand shot out. Chris managed not to flinch. "Go for the wrist, the throat, the back of the knee. Ripped those cops new assholes, boy."

"One of them almost bled to death."

"Almost," Reese acknowledged, a touch wistfully. His eyes held Chris's. "Bled heroin all over my yard, too, from the packet in his pocket that got ripped open. The baggie he was going to plant under my sofa cushion. Or in my pocket. Ever seen 'em do it?" He studied the District Attorney. "No. Silly question. Sometimes they do it like a magic trick. 'Nothing up my sleeve, nothing in my hand.' Other times, if they really hate you, they just throw it down at your feet. Say, 'What'd you drop, nigger?' Then you know you're fucked, no matter what you do."

Reese's nostrils had flared, his shoulders had expanded. Then he closed his eyes and willed composure back into his posture. When he opened his eyes again detachment had returned. He watched the prosecutor, waiting for him to say, you could tell your story in court. But Chris wasn't that naive. Reese nodded approvingly at the D.A.'s silence.

"One thing they didn't have in their pocket was a warrant," Reese said cheerfully. "So they were just trespassers in my yard. They tried to say the shit in the yard was stuff I'd spilled during all the wild dope parties I'd had there in the front yard. But one of them still had traces of the stuff in his pocket when they cut his pants off in the ambulance. He got fired, after he got out of the hospital." Reese smiled. It was a good memory. Then his smile faded.

"But they learned," he said. "I've had cops on my ass ever since. It's something you learn to live with. I thought I could handle them, but this time . . ." He didn't have to look around his surroundings to finish his message. Reese came as close to Chris as he could, wrapping his hands around the bars. His face emerged, inches from Chris's.

"They don't give up," Reese whispered.

Chris stood very close, staring into Reese's face, under the common illusion that if he stared hard enough he could determine the man's truthfulness.

"I'm not a murderer," Reese said, helping him out. He was trying with even greater intensity to stare into the District Attorney's soul. "You're having doubts, aren't you, Chris? I don't think you're part of it. You can't live with this, can you? That's why you're here."

The two men stared at each other, surrounded by the dimness and noise of Death Row. Reese hesitated, then reached out. "All my hopes are on you," he said.

Chris repressed a shudder.

Chris didn't slide easily back into his life after his one-day trip to the Row. He'd gone to Huntsville as a former defense lawyer, then been recast as a prosecutor by seeing Malachi Reese, but Reese had spoken to him past the role, human to human. His voice stayed in Chris's mind—not just the words that kept sounding in Chris's ears, but the concern with which Reese had insisted that they both remained in danger. It was easy to shrug that off as a lie: Chris did it a dozen times a day.

In prison he'd felt none of the hateful intimacy with which he'd thought he'd seen into Reese's mind during trial. Chris's sense of insight had faded, that illusion of understanding. Reese should have hated Chris, he should have lunged for him through the bars. Instead he had tried hard to make him understand. The intensity of Reese's desire to connect was impossible to dismiss.

Once again Chris found he had no one with whom to talk about what had happened. Anne was too busy, he felt intrusive if he called her during the week. It was like a mirage when he emerged from the District Attorney's offices, headed for a courtroom, and saw her standing there in the Justice Center hallway.

His face lit up. Anne Greenwald's smile widened a secret fraction. He restrained his impulse to kiss her, but put his arm around her and led her away from the receptionist's window, toward the relative privacy at the top of the stairs.

"You look great. What're you doing here? Are you testifying somewhere?"

"No, I'm being a victim," she said disgustedly. "I just came from the police station. Somebody broke into my office over the weekend. Probably some damned stupid juvenile delinquent was afraid I'd taped his session, or thought I was dumb enough to leave money or drugs in the office."

Chris grinned at hearing her speak of her patients so derisively, since he knew the opinion was both true and beside the point for Anne. "Good," he said, "then you can give the cops a list of suspects."

She just gave him a look. Of course she would keep her patients confidential, even after they had violated her trust. Chris looked at her fondly. Her eyes were relaxed, smiling back at him. Anne didn't look as harried as she usually did on a work day. Her lips moved as if deciding whether to hold onto a secret. She looked the way he'd seen her the few times they'd been alone.

"So it shouldn't be a total waste to come down here, I was coming to see if you were free for lunch," she said.

"Boy, a man's got to talk fast to beat you to an invitation."

"It's a control thing," she explained. "I don't want you getting the idea you're in charge."

"But didn't your mother ever explain about playing hard to get?"

"She did, but I looked at what she got and thought there must be a better strategy."

"So you hated Dad," Chris said in his best Freudian tone. "Poor child, come and tell me all about it."

He took her arm and led her down the stairs. The stairways in both the Bexar County Courthouse and the Justice Center are largely uninhabited. Chris found it amazing the number of people who will take an elevator up or down one floor, leaving the stairs relatively free of traffic.

When they reached the landing between the fifth and fourth floors Anne and Chris were struck by their isolation. Anne experienced the expansive feeling of being in charge of an unfamiliar public place. Chris enjoyed discovering an unknown niche in a well-known world. They stopped, she leaned into him, his arm circled her, and they kissed deeply, forgetting their surroundings. Anne's hand moved inside his jacket, resting on his chest. Her teeth caught his lower lip lightly, held it for her tongue to soothe. He brought his hand to her neck.

Then the treasured intimacy was broken. In his ear Chris distinctly heard Malachi Reese's voice: "*. . . fondle your lady friend's leg under the table . . .*"

He looked up quickly. Footsteps passed in the hallway of the floor below, but no one stood nearby.

"What's the matter?"

Chris took a step, poised to go up or down. He took a deep breath. "Nothing. Sorry. I just suddenly . . ."

Anne came down the stairs, bringing him along. "Afraid discipline would break down if some member of your enormous staff saw us necking in the halls?"

"Actually," Chris said, touching her, "I seldom think about my enormous staff."

Anne laughed. She took his hand and led him out of the building. It felt like skipping out on school.

But for a moment there on the stairs Chris had been transported to a tiny dark cell.

Anne lifted the day out of the commonplace. Sitting in the cramped little Mexican restaurant—appropriately called Little House—across the street from the Justice Center, leaning toward each other across a metal and Formica kitchen table, Chris marvelled at seeing Anne, at the way she gave him another life just by being there.

But what he said was, "Suppose Malachi's right?"

"It's not a question of right or wrong," Anne replied, "like he's a scientist who's made a discovery. He knows. It's whether he's telling the truth or lying. And why on earth would you think he wouldn't be lying to you?"

"What's his incentive? Why keep lying to *me?* He knows I'm not going to do anything for him."

"You're not?" Anne said. Chris looked down at the scratched tabletop. Any number of paths could be traced through its crevices. Anne continued, "With some people it's not even a question of volition. They lie like they breathe. But when Malachi Reese does it he's got a reason. He's working you, Chris. Don't think you're the first."

"All right. I know that." He remembered standing in the dead men's warehouse with Malachi Reese's eyes reaching for him, his firm whisper coming sincere as a lover's endearment. "But put Reese aside and think about the implications. If he committed the murders it's okay, he's done. But if he's telling the truth then I've put an innocent man on Death Row and that means there are very guilty someone elses walking around free and like he said, keeping a very close eye on me."

"All right," Anne said mildly. "Say he's telling you the truth when he denies killing anyone. Then he knows a lot more than he's told you. Whatever else, you know Malachi was deeply involved in whatever wrongdoing he's talking about. Otherwise he wouldn't know about it. He could give you lots more information. Not just a warning. He could give you names, where to look. He'd be willing to do that, wouldn't he, if he were innocent?"

Chris nodded thoughtfully. "Are you always so sure of your opinions?" he asked.

When Anne's mouth set in an appraising line, a small knot of muscle appeared at the hinge of her jaw, near her ear. Only on one side, the left side of her face. She only clenched her teeth on one side. She was left-mouthed. Every time Chris looked at her he saw something new. Letting his train of thought travel on without him, Chris turned her hand over in his. Anne had a long lifeline, but it was interrupted at the highest point of the mound of her palm. He lightly stroked her hand from wrist to fingertips. She laughed a small throaty laugh and pulled her hand away with a mock shudder.

Chris felt observed, turned and saw a busboy—an inappropriate term for a black man who looked to be nearing fifty—holding a push broom and staring at him. The man dropped his eyes. Chris pushed his plate aside.

He and Anne sat over refills of tea. Anne didn't feel Chris's constant tension that he was about to be the center of a confrontation. She surveyed the crowd.

"So this is what keeps you going during the day?"

"I used to have lunch at my desk a lot, but it's nicer to get out of the office for a while."

Anne's gaze took in the human tableau inside the narrow confines of Little House. Posters of long-gone musical and sporting events sparsely decorated the restaurant walls, along with hand-lettered signs announcing plates that had been the daily special for as long as human memory ran. The two rooms had the atmosphere of the busy kitchen in a poor family's home. Every table was taken, by cops, lawyers, and judges wolfing down serious Mexican food while emphasizing their conversational points with their forks. At the next table a defense lawyer bragged, around a mouthful of chili-enriched tamales, about having won a motion to suppress evidence in a DWI. Across the room the patrol cop who'd made the arrest glared at him. Close at hand, a district court judge was droning on, imitating a civil lawyer's droning final argument. The three lawyers at the table with the judge had fixed smiles on their faces and fingers poised to grab the check when it came.

Anne took it all in. "You call this getting out of the office?" she asked.

"Someday you'll have to take me to the secret club where the psychiatrists lunch together," Chris suggested.

Anne shook her head. "Very boring. Total silence prevails. Everyone's afraid to speak for fear of what they'll be giving away."

"Everyone analyzing what each other ordered?"

Anne nodded.

"We could go and give 'em a thrill," Chris said.

Anne had a way of raising her eyes slowly, up his shirt to his face, seeming to glance askance at him while looking directly into his eyes, that made Chris think he'd heard her reply. They chuckled.

Chris had thought about taking her some place nice for lunch. Instead he wanted to immerse her in his world. Every time he came to Little House from now on he would remember Anne here, plucking a thin paper napkin from a dispenser to wrap around her iced tea glass, absorbing the droplets that had condensed on its outside.

"Well," she said regretfully, nodding toward the door. "Souls to save."

———

When they emerged from the restaurant they were in the shadow of the Justice Center across the street. Normally Chris would have jaywalked back to work, but he wanted to prolong the time with Anne. He asked about her car, she pointed a direction, and they turned right. Flores was a narrow, busy street, the curb lined with cars crowded up to parking meters the way cowboys used to tether their horses when Flores had been a dirt thoroughfare, a hundred years ago when the courthouse had been newly built. The buildings Anne and Chris passed seemed almost that old, dark storefronts housing law offices, bail bondsmen, and tiny businesses, standing shoulder-to-shoulder with no gaps between the buildings.

A few people sat hunched on the sidewalk, leaning back against the walls, either at their daily posts or resting from having no place to go. Pedestrians jostled. Chris walked close to Anne on the wide sidewalk. He had to lean toward her to hear what she said. The street seemed more crowded and noisier than usual. Out on the street someone was having loud car trouble. People on the sidewalk shouted advice. A walker brushed quickly by, making Chris think to check his wallet.

The car with the trouble backfired loudly, Chris thought, twice, three times, a long series, more times than he'd ever heard a car backfire.

The noise level increased dramatically. Some people began running. The runners lived in very different neighborhoods from Anne's and Chris's, they were quicker to recognize the sound of gunfire.

A man running frantically burst between Chris and Anne, jarring them apart, spinning Chris halfway around so that he saw the car in the street, an old model American hardtop—Pontiac, probably, Chris thought fleetingly—paint rusted off in streaks, no shine to the chrome anymore. The car moved slowly, in the lane closest to the curb, twenty feet behind Chris and Anne. But the hand sticking out of the passenger window pointed a pistol straight at them.

Instinctively Chris ducked, but he still didn't believe it, until the sound of glass shattering behind him convinced him. He turned and covered Anne, hunching over. For a moment he pulled up short at the sight of the disintegrated store window in front of him. One large slab of glass hung poised like the blade of a guillotine. He glanced at Anne's face. She had turned so white she seemed to have lost all her blood at once.

Chris ran, grabbing her, pushing her in front of him. They ran awkwardly, ducking to keep the line of parked cars between them and the pursuing car. It worked briefly. A kid shooting a machine pistol is usually more interested in noise and terror than in aiming. But the line of gunfire pursued them. They could hear the shots distinctly now, not only the small explosions of the gun firing, but the bullets hitting the parked cars, the storefronts beside them, the sidewalk. A ricochet zinged across their path. They ran.

Chris was trying to carry Anne with him. He could almost do it. She seemed to have grown abruptly smaller. The street filled with shouts, but he couldn't hear.

Damn it, where were the gunmen on their side? Where were the cops, the court bailiffs with guns on their hips? The area should have been full of them. The restaurant had been. Why wasn't anyone shooting back at the car?

Chris took a quick glance back at the scene. The crowds had diminished abruptly, but there were still many people in sight. Some cowered in doorways. Across the street, people coming from the Justice Center didn't know what was going on. They pointed, faces questioning. Others began to cross the street, oblivious. Back down Flores, a bicycle patrol officer, in short pants and a helmet, had fallen over in the street—maybe shot, maybe knocked over by a fleeing pedestrian. The officer struggled to push his bike off himself.

Even if the cop got up in the next second, or another were

aware of what was happening, they couldn't fire. Police regulations wouldn't allow them to return fire to the car on this crowded street. They would be as dangerous as the drive-by shooters themselves.

The Pontiac remained thirty yards away. But then it sped up, coming closer to the line of parked cars. The occupants seemed aware that Chris had seen them. Gunfire resumed with a joyful bravado. The car seemed to grow rapidly.

Chris turned and ran again, but Anne stumbled. She almost dragged him down until he righted her. Chris tried to pull her to her feet, cover her, and run all at the same time. When Anne tripped and they almost went down, Chris's instinct for flight suddenly turned to one for fight. Sudden rage consumed him so powerfully that he felt momentarily invulnerable. He wanted to stop, pick up the car beside him, and hurl it at the shooters. The kind of unreasoning fury that gripped Chris makes a man sacrifice himself without knowing it.

He glanced again at the shooters' car. He saw more than one face, but no details. The car's dark interior seemed to glare at him.

The noise was deafening. Every sound of the street seemed to have amplified, to compete with the noise of the shots. Someone inside the car shouted. Chris screamed back, without being aware of it.

He turned to run again, but saw that just ahead a large empty space loomed between the parked cars, a no-parking zone next to a fire hydrant. In a few seconds Chris and Anne would reach that spot and no longer be shielded by parked cars. The gunmen would have clear shots at them.

The driver of the pursuing car must have seen the space too. The engine revved. It would catch them at the open space. The car angled even closer to the sidewalk.

Chris had a terrible idea, and acted on it at once. He grabbed Anne's hand and almost yanked her arm from the socket. She tried to pull away, because Chris seemed to have gone crazy. He was trying to turn her back toward the shooters' car.

"Come on!" Chris shouted. There was no time to explain. He had seen that they would be killed if they kept running ahead. But he had suddenly realized that if they ran *back,* toward the shooters, there would be only one point where their paths would intersect. It would be a point of terrible risk, but preferable to running in the same direction as the car, which could easily catch up to them. By reversing direction, if Chris and Anne got past the car, behind it, they would be safer.

At the point where they would pass the car, if he timed it right, were a metal mailbox and a newspaper rack for cover, as well as a parked car. Chris ran for it, dragging Anne and trying to stay between her and the gunfire. Either she saw what he planned or regained her confidence in him, because she ran too.

Their sudden reversal seemed to disconcert the shooters. The gunfire slackened for a moment. Chris and Anne reached the mailbox, a blessedly heavy old metal box. He ducked behind it, dragging Anne down beside him. The rusty Pontiac glided past, a few feet away. In a moment, when the car was past, Chris and Anne could run back toward Little House, which seemed like home. If they reached the restaurant they'd be safe, surrounded by various armed cops. The drive-by shooters would have to drive on. Maybe someone had even called for backup already. Maybe squad cars were on their way. The police station was only a few blocks away.

Chris pulled Anne close to him behind the mailbox. There was still no time or silence for explanation. He hoped she saw his plan. Anne's eyes stared widely as she gulped air. She'd been cut by something. An inch-long gash on her cheek had opened to emit a single ooze of blood, like a teardrop. Chris drew a ragged breath.

And then the shooters' car did a terrible thing. It stopped. In Chris's panic he'd forgotten a car could do that. The car had barely passed their hiding place, maybe fifteen feet away. At least two arms thrust out the windows. Gunfire poured from the car. All the windows in the parked car beside the mailbox exploded at once. Colorless rainbows of glass seemed to hang in the air as bullets continued to course through the empty gaping eyesockets of the parked car's window frames.

A car's doors could open, too, Chris suddenly remembered. Nothing confined the shooters to their car. In a moment they could emerge, stroll to where Chris and Anne cowered, and casually riddle them with every bullet the shooters had left. As if the Pontiac's driver had had just that idea, the car began backing up, to let its passengers step out almost next to Chris and Anne.

Chris screamed, as if noise were a weapon. Bullets flew all around them, they couldn't run in either direction now. But he saw another option. Only a quick dash across the sidewalk behind him would bring them to the nearest building. Chris picked Anne up, stooping so the mailbox still protected them, and rushed Anne and himself across the sidewalk, through the doorway behind them. Anne gave him no resistance. She lay strangely limp, dead weight in his arms.

They fell to the floor of the little room behind the door, both gasping at the impact. But the quiet sounded like safety. Chris rose to his knees to look for a back way out, then stopped. Their refuge was a shoeshine stand, barely eight feet across and a dozen feet deep. The proprietor pressed himself as flat as he could against the back wall, thin arms covering his head. If there'd been another way out the shoeshine man would have taken it, but there wasn't. The room's only door was the one Chris had come through from the street. He had chosen a barrel as a hiding place, as in "shooting fish in a barrel."

He left Anne where she had fallen and stood up. If he left her there and darted back outside, the shooters would follow him. He gave two seconds' thought to which way to run. If he took the safer course, back toward Little House, the shooters would run past this spot in pursuit. One of them might spare a few seconds of chase to step in here and briskly shoot the witnesses. Chris wouldn't expose Anne to that. It would be much riskier to run

back in his original direction, past the shooters' car, with no
known refuge down that way, but Chris preferred that risk.

In the next moment he decided instead he would run straight
out into the street, between the parked cars, toward the Justice
Center. Maybe an armed bailiff had come across the street by
now, or the bicycle cop had righted himself.

Chris stepped out the door of the shoeshine shop.

Out on the street the drive-by car kept backing up. Everyone
inside must have been staring at the doorway through which
their target had disappeared. Certainly the Pontiac's driver didn't
care about traffic. But Flores was a perpetually busy street. The
gunfire had lasted less than a minute so far, though it had seemed
like hours. Some cars had tried to turn and speed away. Others
were trapped, or their drivers had frozen.

Behind the shooters' car, one such car had stopped. The Pontiac's driver didn't look in his rear-view mirror, he just backed
toward Chris as fast as he could. As Chris watched, looking
for his best chance to run, the Pontiac backed into the car behind it.

The driver of the stopped car might have been deaf. He might
have had his windows rolled up and the radio playing loudly. Or
he might just not have been very bright. But when the shooters'
car backed into his, he went nuts. The man screamed in rage. He
honked. And then, splendid man, he won Chris's heart forever by
producing a pistol of his own and shooting at the Pontiac.

Chris stepped out onto the sidewalk. Now he had a chance to
run. But the street was full of motion by now. Chris looked to
his left and saw two uniformed cops and a court bailiff running
toward him, guns drawn. The bicycle patrolman peddled furiously down the middle of the street, also with a gun. The pro-
tectors had finally appeared.

Receiving return fire wasn't on the agenda for the Pontiac's
driver. The car's tires squealed and it roared forward. The arms of
the shooters, still sticking out the windows, were whipped back-

ward by the car's momentum. Last shots were fired wildly. A brick chip zipped by Chris, nicking his ear.

He stepped out toward the street, watching the car flash away. The Pontiac picked up speed, screamed through the red light at the intersection amid a blare of horns, and sped on up Flores out of sight. Chris heard a methodical voice and turned to see a police officer talking into a radio microphone. In the near distance Chris heard a siren. He hoped the shooters kept driving in a way designed to call attention to themselves.

The street came alive with sounds, as if waking up first thing in the morning. The driver whose car had been backed into got out and raised the hood. The bicycle patrolman approached the driver to confiscate his pistol. Argument ensued, sounding like the happy voices of children on a playground.

People came out of doors, pointing, asking questions, witnesses already turning the event into a narrative. Human sounds prevailed again on Flores.

The skin of Chris's face stretched to the point of pain. He had no idea that his face was smiling maniacally. He turned, expecting to see Anne in the doorway of the shoeshine shop. But the shop's doorway yawned empty. Many people on Flores weren't yet ready to come out from cover.

Chris pushed the door wider and said, "It's all—" then almost stumbled over her leg.

Sudden weakness made it easy to drop to the floor of the shoeshine shop beside her. Anne lay facedown. She had lost one shoe. She didn't move, even when he said her name.

Chris turned her over onto her back and looked into her blank, staring eyes. "Anne!" He checked her dress front for blood, didn't find any. He put both hands on her cheeks. Her skin felt cold. He warmed it with gentle rubbing. She moaned. It didn't sound human, it was air escaping from a squeezed bag.

"Anne! Hey! In here!" he shouted out the doorway, but he didn't move. Her eyes blinked. Chris gasped with joy. He supported her head, rubbing the back of her neck.

Anne's chest rose once. Gently Chris pressed her cheeks so her mouth opened. He bent toward her lips. As he breathed into her mouth he held her hand. He wouldn't let go. He held her hand more and more firmly, until Anne's hand returned his grip.

Chapter 8

Chris Sinclair paced the narrow confines of the police detective's office. The walls were white, so white they glared. Sergeant Esparza must have chosen the non-regulation color himself. He had unusual taste. The white walls gave a disconcerting effect that must have been helpful to interrogation, except that the detective would normally conduct interrogations in an interrogation room. He had brought the District Attorney to his own office as a courtesy. Chris wanted sunglasses. How could the man work here?

Chris put his hand on the doorknob. "That's enough. Let's go."

"I need a few more details first, sir." Sergeant Esparza looked about fifty, and had the lines in his dark brown face to show for it. They were a few deep lines, notably on his forehead and down from his nose, rather than a network of finer ones. The detective spoke very patiently, with no apparent effort, which was a surprise because he looked more like a shouter or a hitter. He had a thick neck and shoulders to match. The pen he held disappeared in his hand.

"I'll give you all the details you want as soon as I see Anne," Chris said, glaring.

Sergeant Esparza shook his head. "You know that's not the way it works, sir. I have to get a complete statement before I let the witnesses get together and compare stories. We want this to hold up in court, don't we?"

"I don't want to collaborate with her, I just want to make sure she's all right! I don't give a damn about court—"

"That's how people often feel in the immediate aftermath of the event, but they change their minds later. I expected a little more professionalism from you, sir." Sergeant Esparza's voice sharpened. He stood up, his knuckles on his desktop. "We didn't make up these rules, you know. You guys did."

Chris took a deep breath. His hand fell from the doorknob. "All right. Ask."

But he didn't hear the question the first time the detective asked it. Chris pictured Anne as he'd last seen her. He'd been stepping into the ambulance where she lay on a stretcher when one of the uniformed officers had pulled him back. "Sir, we need a description."

"Later," Chris had mumbled, shrugging off the patrolman's hand. That cop's voice had grown more insistent too. "Sir, we're still after these guys. We can get them if you help."

So Chris had acquiesced. He had called Anne's name as the ambulance's rear doors slammed shut. He had seen her head lift, as if she were looking for him.

Now, thinking back, he wondered if Anne had really raised her head, or if it had just limply shifted as the ambulance started moving. He couldn't remember whether her eyes had been open.

"What?"

"The driver, sir. What did he look like?" Sergeant Esparza repeated.

"Young," Chris said. "Maybe only a teenager. Dark complexion, black hair."

"Hispanic?" asked Sergeant Esparza.

Chris thought about it. The Pontiac itself superseded all other images of the drive-by shooting. His glimpses of its interior had been so brief and panicked. "I'm not sure. Medium complexion. You know, dark eyes. He wore a bandanna. . . ."

Esparza made notes with exaggerated patience. Chris knew how he sounded. So far his description had narrowed the investigation to roughly two-hundred-thousand suspects, assuming the driver was from San Antonio rather than an out-of-towner.

"I hate being a victim," Chris said. He hated discovering he did it no better than dozens of dim-witted witnesses he had railed about over the years.

"Sucks, doesn't it?" Esparza said mildly. "What color was the bandanna?"

Chris scratched irritably at his memory. "Red, I think."

"Sure?"

Chris walked to the sergeant's desk and turned off the shirt-pocket–sized tape recorder that was turning there. "You tell me," he said.

The detective gave him a mildly exasperated look. Chris continued insistently, "You already have these guys in custody, don't you? You tell me what they looked like. I'll say it right. You said I make the rules? Well, they're off now."

Esparza looked flatly at him, calculating. When the detective said nothing, Chris knew the decision he'd arrived at. Yes, this case engaged Chris's emotions. And the District Attorney and the cops were on the same side. But the vagaries of elective fate being what they were, Chris would likely not be D.A. forever, which meant he'd become, again, a criminal defense lawyer, one who remembered that Sergeant Esparza had been willing to break the rules. They were teammates now, but the cop looked at Chris and saw only a lawyer. There was nothing permanent about their partnership.

"Look," Chris said, quietly but with underlying force. "Somebody tried to take me out and that makes it personal enough. But they tried it when I was with her. They could have killed her without giving a damn. Maybe they did kill her for all I can find out from you. That means . . ." There was nothing strong enough he could say about that. He kept going. "I'm going to get whoever's behind this. I don't mean just the punks in the car, I mean the men who gave them the orders. And the ones behind them. And if anybody's told you to go slow with this investigation, I'm going to get them too. And you."

Esparza sat at his desk unimpressed. "You're the one delaying the investigation, sir. Not me." He gave a little. "We found the car. Nobody in it. For all we know the driver and his passengers could've been a mile away or they could've been some of the people standing on the sidewalk staring at the uniformed cops who found the car. Assuming we got the right car—"

"I can identify the car. Positive."

"That's good, sir, but we already have the car in custody. What we need help with is the shooters."

The men gave each other long looks.

"It was purple," Chris said. "The bandanna. And one of the shooters had one the same color wrapped around his wrist."

Esparza nodded with slight satisfaction and made another note. "Helps a little. Come on, I'll take you to her. She's just over at Santa Rosa."

Sergeant Esparza opened a drawer and took out a crowded key ring. What he'd said didn't make sense to Chris. Santa Rosa Hospital was downtown, only a few blocks away. Had the emergency medical technicians thought Anne needed to be rushed to the nearest emergency room?

"Why not BAMC or Wilford Hall?" Chris asked as they went out the door. The two military hospitals in town had contracts with the city to provide emergency service, so military doctors could get experience working on gunshot wounds.

Chris was looking back, already three steps ahead, as Esparza came stolidly down the linoleumed hall of the police station.

"Apparently she sat up and insisted the EMS take her to Santa Rosa," the detective said. "She said Santa Rosa could use the cash, and she might get an employee discount."

For the first time since lunch, Chris smiled.

In the emergency room, he found Anne by the sound of her voice.

"I'm all right, Eddie!" she called. "I'm getting out of here. Stop trying on my clothes and bring them to me, Eddie!"

Chris made his way through the curtained-off cubicles, ignoring people who told him he couldn't go back there. He pulled back one curtain.

"About damn time! What've you—"

Anne was lying on a narrow table, staring up at the ceiling. Chris had to step into her line of vision before she sat up. Her face changed. Annoyance drained out of it as her blood had at the first sound of gunfire. She looked surprised, even frightened.

"Are you all right?" She reached for him.

He went quickly to her. "Are you?" His hands hovered close, but he was afraid to touch her. A vertical bandage on her cheek drew his attention. He reached for it. Anne grabbed his hand and held on tightly.

"I thought there might still be shooting going on when they took me away," she said throatily.

Chris shook his head. "It was all over. They got away for now."

Anne didn't care about the men who had tried to kill them. "Are you all right?" she asked again.

"I'm fine. Just irritated to discover I'm no good at being a victim."

"I thought you were," Anne said.

He smiled. But then he looked down the front of her hospital gown and his concerned look returned.

"Did you get—? Are you—?"

Anne grimaced. "I fainted," she said with thorough disgust. "That's all, I fainted. Like a Victorian heroine."

"Victorian heroines never got shot at with automatic weapons."

Anne ignored his attempt at comfort. "But you," she said accusingly. "You were like some kind of hero. You acted like this kind of thing happens to you once a week."

Chris nodded thoughtfully. He could barely remember what he had done while the bullets had been flying around them. "And you know the funny part? In law school, I made a *C* in dodging gunfire. And barely passed it on the bar exam."

Anne sat up abruptly and swung her legs over the side of the table. Before Chris could move she had bounced past him and gone to the curtain, where she raised her voice again. "Eddie Guzman! Do I have to walk out of here naked?"

She was not, in fact, naked, though she might have felt that way. The hospital gown that draped her was tied so loosely in the back that it afforded Chris a long glimpse from the middle of her back down to her bare heels. Anne was lifted up slightly on her toes, as if to make her voice carry farther. He looked at the twin parallel lines up the backs of her knees, where the muscles looked so strong and so vulnerable. Her legs rose smoothly to where her white panties, barely paler than her skin, tightly encased the flare of her buttocks. Her back was indented along her backbone, where the muscles pulled away strongly but the spine looked only thinly protected. Chris went and put his hands around her waist, inside the gown. Anne didn't turn or gasp; he hadn't surprised her.

He was right, her waist felt strong and solid. He held her tightly, his fingers imprinting her skin.

Anne turned her head, laying her cheek on his shoulder. Chris kissed her neck.

"This is a common reaction," Anne said. "I've seen it dozens of times."

"Keep talking," Chris murmured. "I love to hear you talk."

"But this is the first time I've ever felt it," Anne said. She turned and put her arms around his neck so tightly she cut off his breath. She pulled their bodies hard together as she kissed him, as if she were trying to crawl inside his shirt.

"Ah," said a voice behind Anne. "Survivor's horniness. Isn't it great? Someone should open a shooting range where people can go walk through the gunfire on first dates. It's a wonderful way to break the ice."

Anne seemed inclined to ignore the voice, but Chris looked up and saw, inside the cubicle, a young, thin Hispanic man of in-determinate sexuality—he might have been gay, he might have only had a stylish attitude. He looked at them indulgently, patiently holding, like a butler with a tray, a small stack of clothes.

Anne took a deep breath and had regained her professional, ir-ritable tone when she spoke. "Thanks, Eddie. About time. I hope they were too tight for you."

As she took the clothes the young attendant said, "Put those on and you'll still be naked. But we won't mind, will we?"

Anne held up the blouse she'd been wearing. There was a long, neat, surgical slash all the way up the front. She sighed.

The attendant in his green scrubs said, "They were looking for wounds, sweetie. You can always buy new clothes. How many times have you said that yourself?"

Anne dropped the ruined clothes on the stretcher table. "What about my shoes? I'm not walking barefoot across hot asphalt just so you can add to your collection."

Eddie produced a pair of low-heeled brown loafers from be-hind his back. "Honey, these aren't fashionable enough to steal." Relieved of the shoes, the young attendant held out his hand to Chris. "Hi. You're the District Attorney, aren't you? Nice to meet you. Hope we don't again."

Anne had stepped into her shoes. She raised her head, shak-ing back her hair. "I'm leaving," she announced.

"I told them you'd say that," Eddie said. "Just sign the release and you're a free woman."

"They've got my signature on enough papers around this damned place. Let 'em forge it."

"Funny, I told them you'd say that, too." Eddie put his hands on Anne's shoulders and looked at her. She let herself be in-

spected. He pinched her undamaged cheek and produced a little color. "You look gorgeous, honey. Knock 'em dead. Eat some
soup, okay? And when you need to cry on somebody—" He
lowered his voice. "Will he do?"

Anne nodded. "Thanks, Eddie."

"One more thing—"

The young attendant's voice was so solemn Chris's attention
sharpened. Even Anne looked at him nervously. "Your mother
called," Eddie said. "She asked me to make sure you've got on
clean underwear."

"Get out of my way."

Eddie grinned. "Let me see you sashay out of here now."

Anne took Chris's hand, pulling him along in her wake. "Stay
close behind me," she said.

"Yes, ma'am."

Later, after Anne had found a change of clothes in her office in
another part of the hospital, after a different police detective had
questioned her for forty-five minutes while Chris waited impa-
tiently in the hall, after they'd gotten into Chris's car and realized
they didn't know where to go, after by unspoken agreement they
had chosen Anne's house, after they'd walked into the dark house
and not turned on any lights, after, after, after, they lay atop Anne's
bed breathing in rhythm. They were holding hands. Chris stroked
her shoulder with one finger. His hearing had turned dual. He
listened not only to Anne's breathing but to the silence of the
house, to the street outside. He hoped whoever had tried to have
him killed didn't know about Anne. Her house had seemed safer
than his. He'd thought about going to a hotel for the night, but
how long would they have to do that? The question of home had
to be faced some time.

Anne was thinking the same thoughts. "Is there a patrol car out
front?"

"I didn't tell them where we'd be," Chris said.

She turned and looked questioningly at him. "I don't know who to tell anything," he went on. "Malachi warned me. He said they'd come after me—"

"And you believed him?"

"I don't know what to believe. But it's an amazing coincidence, isn't it?"

Christian Sinclair's little suburban childhood hadn't prepared him for this. *If you get lost, find a nice policeman.* Malachi Reese and thousands of others had grown up with a wholly different view of authorities. Chris had seen enough to know they weren't always wrong. Chris had served his purpose, Malachi had said. He would only be a potential liability now, if he started questioning. If instead the District Attorney were killed in a drive-by shooting, who would be surprised?

Even after five years as a defense attorney, hearing stories of brutal police methods and knowing for a fact that cops sometimes lied on the witness stand to make the facts fit the law, Chris resisted the way he was thinking now. A conspiracy as vast as Reese had hinted at couldn't have held together for years, a secret shared by too many ambitious people. But, that a few influential men held by mutual necessity a few dirty secrets—he found that entirely believable.

Also believable was the possibility that he and Anne had been the near-victims of the inherent hostility that lived in San Antonio's air constantly now. Could it have become impossible for a white man to walk down the street safely? Chris couldn't stand the thought that he'd turned his city into such a place.

"What can you do?" Anne asked.

"Keep investigating. What else?"

Anne didn't answer. Chris heard what he'd said hanging in the air and knew Anne had no counter-argument. The alternative would be not knowing. Spending the rest of his nights staring into darkness like this. He would have to be very careful. He didn't know whom to trust. Today had proven that he was still at war, but he didn't know with whom. So he would have to choose his allies very carefully.

"Maybe it was just random violence," Anne suggested. "Maybe kids just taken by an impulse. They might not even have known who you were. It happens to people every week, Chris."

"Maybe." But it had never before happened in glaring sunlight within spitting distance of the Justice Center.

He pulled Anne close and waited for her breathing to deepen. His eyes didn't close. He waited a long time.

The next morning Chris took a walk with his chief investigator, Jack Fine. They walked out of the Justice Center and watchfully along the streets, heading only three or four blocks to Hemisfair Park, site of the 1968 World's Fair that had become a collection of restaurants, city offices, a playground, and pleasant walkways from which a pedestrian could see a long way in any direction.

Jack appeared much jumpier than Chris, making sure he stayed on the street side of his boss, his hand going inside his jacket when a car approached. The traffic had grown very sparse at ten o'clock on a Wednesday morning, everyone due inside the courts buildings had already gone inside.

"I don't much like walking with you, if you want to know the truth," Jack said. "You sure you want to be outside?"

Jack relaxed once they went inside the park, where they were the only people on foot in sight. "It looks like we were wrong about Malachi Reese's killer," Jack began. "We thought he'd lie low after killing Mr. Rodriguez, but—"

"You think it was him who shot at me?" Chris asked.

"Who else?"

"It doesn't make sense, Jack. Killing Mr. Rodriguez, that was a precision operation, with a very good reason for it. He was going to testify against Reese, he had to be stopped. But killing me? What sense does that make?"

"Stop you from talking," Jack answered. "Stop you from investigating."

"Why would Reese want that? He's trying to make me question the case I made against him. He'll want to see if that's paid off, he wouldn't want to take me out now."

"Maybe his communication's not that good with the outside world. Maybe his boy just decided on his own to kill you, for revenge."

They stopped at a large fountain to watch its droplets tinkling into the sunlit, shallow water. A pump worked underground, recycling the water. In drought-prone south Texas, water couldn't be wasted on display. By the same token, public water had a certain fascination. Chris sat on the edge of the fountain, Jack Fine put one foot up on it. Jack's eyes remained bright, even when just peering into the fountain.

"What about the knife wounds?" Chris asked.

Jack shook his head, diminishing the impact of what he said. "Inconclusive. The medical examiner said the wounds to Victor Fuentes, Mrs. Rodriguez, and Mr. Rodriguez were made by very similar knives. But he can't say they were the same."

"We never found a knife of Malachi's," Chris pointed out.

"Sounds like he'd passed it on to his killer."

"I don't know." Chris looked off at the office buildings of downtown San Antonio, sunlight beating down on them. "A knife is a very personal weapon, isn't it, Jack? Would Malachi give his away? Maybe the murders were committed by the same person, but it was someone else."

"You're just taking a position," Jack said. "You're just testing your adversarial abilities. Don't you believe in the case you made?"

Chris's answer came only after a lengthy silence. He stood, put his hands on his hips, and turned in a slow circle, feeling watched. "I'm just trying to reconstruct how the case came to me. A piece at a time, Malachi said. First Lou Briones, then . . . Were they framing Malachi Reese, oh so slowly so he didn't even notice at first?"

"But they didn't, did they, Chris? Cops didn't manufacture a case against Reese. It wasn't until months later when Lou Briones came to you that anybody made the case against him. If they'd wanted to lay the blame for Victor Fuentes' murder on Malachi, why'd they wait so long?"

That might have been the smartest way to do it, Chris thought. Let the District Attorney think he was uncovering facts for himself, so he'd believe them inherently, while behind the scenes someone fed his case to him piece by piece. *They got more subtle,* Reese had said.

"Don't you believe your own witness anymore?" Jack asked. "You were the one who testified that Mr. Rodriguez told you Malachi had him killed."

That was one of the things over which Chris had been wracking his conscience. *Had* he heard that? It had only been a soft mumble. The man's tongue had been cut, and he'd been dying. Had Chris heard what he'd wanted to hear? Had the dying man been asking a question instead of making a statement?

"Don't let this guy get to you, Chris." Jack was almost pleading with him to keep quiet. Jack still had a cop's mentality. It was all right to cover up as long as you knew you were right. The explanation Jack gave next underscored that mind-set.

"Chris. You think cops targeted Reese just because they didn't like his politics? No. I was there, remember? We weren't after him for no reason. We've known about Malachi Reese for years. Cops remember these unsolved murders. We remember how many times Malachi was on the fringe of an investigation. He was an addict."

"What?" Now his investigator had baffled Chris.

"You can get addicted to other things than drugs," Jack said. "We suspected Malachi Reese a long time ago, when I was just a patrolman. I'm positive he killed a guy. It was a low-level thug, bully, undoubtedly thought he could push Malachi around. And Malachi killed him. Maybe it was an accident, or self-defense. No witnesses, nobody thought the victim was much of a loss to the world. Case of littering. The investigation wasn't real intense. So Malachi got away with one."

"And that was enough?" Chris asked, a little shocked by the story but not buying the larger implications Jack was trying to give it.

"How old were you when you saw your first corpse?" Jack asked. "One the undertaker hadn't gotten to yet."

"When I first joined the D.A.'s office, some of us took a tour of the Medical Examiner's Office, saw an autopsy——"

Jack shook his head. "I mean a body still on the floor, still looking like he could have a conversation with you if you could just get his attention. It changes your perspective, man. Especially if you saw it happen. One second somebody's just like you, has the same possibilities of going to a movie that night, the next it's all over, he's just a disposal problem.

"You look at people different for the next few days. You think, why are you here and not so-and-so? And if somebody's in your way at work, giving you a problem, or just too many people in front of you in the cafeteria line, you look at 'em and think, what gives you the right to take up space? It would only take that little second. . . . Didn't you ever think that?"

He leaned toward Chris, holding his thumb and forefinger almost touching, indicating a tiny fraction of time, or the small difference between being alive and being dead.

Chris slowly shook his head. Jack's gaze at him flattened. He spoke more objectively. "Well, that comes from a shortage of corpses in your life. But I've often thought, if a guy was careful, and smarter than the average half-wit that commits murder, he could go far if, when somebody really got in his way, he was willing to take them out. That's what I mean by addicted. Once Malachi got away with one . . ."

"They say power's addictive too," Chris interrupted. "Imagine being a man who'd been in charge of things for a long time, and then somebody like Malachi Reese starts causing you problems. By your same theory, wouldn't you be willing to do anything it took to get him?"

Jack shrugged. "So, who? Lou Briones? I can't see it. And if he's fronting for somebody, what did they bribe him with? A miracle cure?"

Chris had already thought about and abandoned that line of investigation. He started walking out of the park. Jack fell into step beside him. "Let's go back to the beginning," Chris said. "Somebody wanted Victor Fuentes silenced and Malachi Reese, too, according to Malachi. Those somebodies are still around. Let's keep looking. Maybe Victor Fuentes kept notes somewhere, a diary in a computer, something. Get a subpoena to search his home, maybe his parents' house. And like you said, we don't have to be secretive about it. Let's get people nervous and see what happens."

"Spoken like a true nut case, considering what happened to you yesterday." Having reminded himself of the drive-by shooting attempt, the investigator gave his boss a studious look. "How do you feel? Still shaky?"

Chris took a deep breath and scanned the area around him again. "How long's it been since somebody shot at you, Jack?"

"Four years." A little silence. "Four years and almost three months."

"How long does it take before you get over this feeling that you want to choke anybody who looks at you cross-eyed?"

"I'll let you know." Jack glanced askance at his boss. "You carrying?"

Chris shifted his shoulders, and smiled. "I've got you for protection, Jack."

"Yeah, but I don't wanta go to lunch with you. Let's order in from now on, okay?" Jack looked around. The streets were empty enough to calm him, but his voice had a nervous tone as he continued. "Uh, Chris? It's kind of lonely out here."

"Aren't you used to that, Jack?"

"I mean, don't we trust anybody else? Paul Benavides, anybody? How about the President, can I cross him off my list of suspects?"

"After you check on his whereabouts the night Victor Fuentes was killed. Jack, I had to think a long time before I decided I could trust you."

"Thanks, I'm flattered."

They gave each other sidelong glances.

They were back in the vicinity of the Justice Center. Jack looked around. Normally calm to the point of drowsiness, he seemed to have caught a worse case of paranoia than Chris had. As they walked in front of the old red stone courthouse they heard a squeal of brakes. Jack's hand shot out, pushing Chris aside, then going inside his jacket to his hip as a car swerved in close beside them. It was a big, new car, a silver Continental. Jack spread his legs, bracing, as the car screeched to a stop. This time Chris stood stunned, not believing that he could no longer go outside safely.

The driver's door opened and a huffing lawyer, his navy suit rumpled, hurried out of the car. He carried an old brown leather briefcase with a strap and a lock. Jack glared at him. The middle-aged lawyer, not noticing, brushed past them with a mutter, almost drawing a gunshot in the leg. Jack's hand came empty out of his jacket. He put his hands on his hips and yelled, "Hey. Hey!"

The lawyer turned around, but continued backing up toward the courthouse. He was a busy man, he didn't like being accosted. But when someone calls a lawyer there might be future money involved, so the busy man gave them two seconds of his attention, raising his eyebrows.

Jack pointed his thumb at the blue handicapped parking sign standing prominently beside the Continental. "Hey, pal, moral handicaps don't count."

The lawyer held out a hand, exempting himself. "I'll only be a minute. Just got to get a judge to sign an order. Won't take a second."

And he turned and hurried into the courthouse. Jack stood glaring ineffectually. By this time Chris, suffused with relief, found his chief investigator's exasperation amusing. Jack looked around the idle streets. "Never a cop," he said.

Jack turned and walked briskly to the illegally parked silver Continental. His hand went into his front pocket. Quickly he opened a pocketknife and bent beside the rear of the car. The expensive, steel-belted tire resisted him, but Jack was very determined. He stabbed deeply through the white sidewall, then wiggled his knife in the cut. From where Chris stood ten feet away he could hear the hiss of air.

Jack looked up, outrage still reddening his face. "Now his car qualifies. It's handicapped."

Chris refrained from laughing at him. He, too, felt a rush of satisfaction as the rear of the Continental gently sank. But he said, "If I let you get away with this, you'll probably turn into a serial tire slasher."

Jack held up the knife. "Want a turn?"

Chris hesitated, then shook his head. Jack stood up, contemplated the front tire as well, then closed his knife. He had lost a little heat, felt slightly foolish, and a need to justify himself. "I suppose you don't know anybody in a wheelchair, either."

Chris put his arm around his investigator's shoulders and led him away from the scene of the crime. "I do, Jack. I do." He looked carefully both ways before crossing the street toward the Justice Center.

"This is why I knew I could trust you," he said to Jack Fine. "Your fine-tuned sense of justice."

Winston Phillips, the city councilman, had formed a Courts Watch group that did just that, watched the courts. His monitors roamed the hallways, observing trials and particularly guilty pleas and sentences handed down by judges. They looked for disparity in treatment of defendants based on race. Courts Watch could have compiled these statistics from the district clerk's records, but that would have meant trusting someone else's observations. And it would have made them less visible and newsworthy.

Mostly volunteers performed these observations, but regularly Phillips himself appeared. A few days after the drive-by shooting attempt, the city councilman emerged from a courtroom in the Justice Center just as Chris passed. The men stopped and faced each other. Neither offered a handshake, but otherwise they treated each other cordially.

"Councilman. Always nice to see you. Busy observing?"

"Got to make sure this building lives up to its name," Phillips said with an ironic smile. "What a discovery this is: imagine, the source from which all justice emanates. Ponce de Leon should have sought this." He sounded as if he were building a speech, but abruptly changed tacks. His expressive features exuded sympathy as he studied Chris, head and shoulders. "Are you all right?"

"I'm fine," Chris said, thrown off stride. He tried to respond with humor. "They barely nicked me."

"I know this feeling," Phillips said, still watching Chris closely. People had drifted closer to watch the confrontation between the councilman and the D.A., and now they moved closer still, to catch Win Phillips' soft voice. "This combination of vulnerability and rage. You want to do something but there's nothing *to* do. It turns you to jelly inside, then the jelly hardens into concrete. You can't get it out of your guts." He nodded knowingly.

Chris couldn't help nodding along.

Then Phillips changed again. His voice grew stern. "And now *you* know how some people in this town live every day of their lives. Looking over their shoulders, cringing at any sharp sound. You know why teenagers feel they have to pack guns."

Phillips' manner had grown confrontational. Chris tried to resist answering in the same tone, but he did say the first thing on his mind. "And what am I supposed to do with this newfound knowledge? Stop prosecuting—"

"Do? You're not supposed to *do* anything. You're supposed to *become*. Grow some empathy, man. Develop some compassion for all your constituents."

I do have, Chris started to say, then realized the mockery Win Phillips would make of that. So he said nothing, and as usual the councilman had the last word. Phillips realized he'd won the encounter. Was that a tiny smile of sympathy he gave Chris just before he turned away, to the congratulations of his supporters and the silent applause of the television reporter who happened to be standing nearby?

Chris woke at four o'clock in the morning. The king-sized bed seemed very big. It seemed to encompass the condominium. Chris heard only the sigh of air-conditioning. He felt oddly safe in his second floor condo nestled inside the complex, with a slow-moving security guard making occasional rounds. His home made a very poor target for a drive-by shooting, and if a burglar came through the doors or windows an alarm would shrill through the place. The tension Chris felt wasn't for his own safety. The time of night concerned him. Four o'clock. Four hours since he had talked to Anne. They hadn't met today, and they had gone to their separate homes after work. Chris should stay away from her, probably. That had been the theory. But in the darkness of 4:00 A.M. theory evaporated. He pictured Anne's small house with its many windows. He saw the tall bed, like a platform, offering her. He imagined the street in front of her house. Chris had made a call to the commander of the nearest police substation, alerting him to Anne's address and that she had been the near-victim of a shooting recently. The commander had promised to send a car by the house frequently. But even "frequently" would leave long gaps.

His digital clock flipped to 4:03. The last time he had looked at the clock before falling asleep it had been 12:27. A long time.

He would have heard something if there'd been trouble. He should have, anyway.

He lay on his side watching the clock and the phone beside it. That way sleeplessness lies. He turned over, but it didn't help. The digital clock didn't make a sound, but in his mind the digits were still turning, faster than in reality. Energy built in Chris's torso, spreading to his arms, finally his legs.

There were a few cars on the expressway. Chris wondered if their drivers were crazy too. He had passed only a handful of human beings getting to the expressway, and they had looked very out of place working or jogging through a landscape as dark as the middle of the night. The city belonged to paperboys and the obsessed.

Moisture filled the air. It glowed in diaphanous spheres around the streetlights, making the nightscape eerie. Chris glided off Anne's exit and slowly through the streets, rolling down his window. The humid air of July crowded into his car, not remotely cool. He turned off his lights early and stopped a couple of houses before Anne's. He hadn't seen a police car. Anne's car sat in the driveway.

Oddly, Chris didn't feel foolish standing watching Anne's house, wearing basketball shorts and the tennis shoes he'd slipped into, the pistol he'd had to search for on his closet shelf now dragging down the pocket of his light nylon jacket. It was a heavy weapon, a silver-plated .38 semi-automatic. Years ago, defending a client on a murder case, Chris had held the gun in court and become strangely attached to it. The pistol had felt so right in his hand. After the conviction and the appeal, when the gun was confiscated, Chris had bought it from the cops. That had been years ago. He had never fired the gun except on a practice range. Chris had never killed, but his gun had. Carrying it felt like having a friend along.

He felt sharply alert, as if he could hear and see for miles. His ephemeral 4:45 self-satisfaction was fueled by the thought of all the unconscious people around him. He felt himself the master of the night.

Anything can become an addiction: Night. Ownership. Chris felt on the verge of an insight, but it didn't come. He walked around the house, through her easy-to-unlatch back yard gate—get a dog, he thought—to make sure Anne's back door was secure, too. He tried not to rattle the doorknob, in case Anne inside lay awake in the darkness too. He decided to make sure. Moving very slowly, grass brushing his ankles, he made it to the window of her bedroom.

She slept on her back. The sheet had worked its way down to her waist. She wore a white T-shirt with some kind of slogan on the front. Chris watched her through his own reflection. After a minute Anne turned onto her side, toward him. She nestled comfortably into the bed, hands under her face. Finally, Chris felt sleepy. He had to get out of the back yard again, quietly.

He took one last look at Anne. He couldn't see her eyes. She could have been watching him. She looked very contented. Suddenly she smiled. Chris watched her soberly.

Chapter 9

Two deaths erased Chris Sinclair's doubts. Both were long expected, but one death shocked him nevertheless.

Lou Briones sent out a call to what would obviously be his last
press conference. A few representatives of the news media came
straggling in response to the former city councilman's summons.
Chris joined them, a little puzzled by his own invitation. Did
Briones want to make the occasion more official-seeming, or
just appear to have the support of the District Attorney? None
of Briones' past political colleagues would come. They were all
men of a certain age by now, and they might have seen Briones
as tainted by death. Or perhaps none of the old politicos wanted
to appear before a deathbed whose occupant had been stricken
by truth-telling.

The press conference was at Briones' home, to which he had
insistently retired from the cancer-center hospital. Briones had
lived for decades in the Monte Vista neighborhood on a street
that had prospered and declined and ironically had come into
vogue now at the end of the old businessman's life. The
house stood on one of those lots that lifted high off the street,
with a yard that ran straight then sloped abruptly downward to
the sidewalk, so the front yard ended almost at head level for a
passerby. The tall, old, wooden frame house, painted white with

yellow trim, featured a gracious front porch. One had to look high to take in all of the Briones home.

Only two of the five or six television news operations in town had sent crews, but even two satellite vans camped in front of the house gave the quiet, narrow street the look of a disaster scene. There were also one metro reporter and one columnist from the *Express-News,* and a couple of radio reporters. It must have been a slow news day. Or maybe the shadow of Malachi Reese made the event potentially newsworthy. Chris spotted the stringer from *Time* slipping in the front door.

On the front lawn, heedless of the dying grass, a TV reporter rehearsed an intro with the house as background. Onscreen he'd look formally professional, but below his suit coat and tie he wore shorts and running shoes. He gave the District Attorney a wink as Chris walked by, feeling overly formal himself in his blue suit.

"Hello, Mrs. Briones," Chris said to the iron-haired lady who opened the screen door for him. He had met Stella Briones several times, always in trying circumstances, and had never seen the careful whorls of her gray hair move an iota. Her face was plump enough to be relatively unlined, and Mrs. Briones exuded a perpetual air of neglecting some urgent domestic task long enough to be gracious to her guest. She seemed full of energy, but her eyes looked tired. Her eyes awaited the release of true mourning, when she wouldn't be distracted by the chores of caring for a dying man.

"Oh, thank you," she said, clasping Chris's hand. "He'll be glad to see you."

The living room was large but crowded. Bulky furniture had been pushed back against the walls to make space for a hospital bed that dominated the room. With the folding chairs set up around it and the cameras and microphones, it looked as if the Briones household had been hastily remade to put on a theatrical production. The reporters didn't comprise the make-believe, carefully selected audience of a TV show, though. They were all white. Chris noticed that these days.

He hung back, letting the host retain center stage. Chris needed to get his first recent look at Briones from a distance, so he could prepare a face for greeting his former witness.

Lou Briones' appearance made the way he'd looked at trial seem a happy memory. He weighed maybe a hundred and thirty pounds. His yellow and mottled skin hung on him. Only Briones' eyes still lived. His weary flesh looked as if it would fall to the floor, leaving only those welling eyes. The sight of Briones made even reporters usually adept at professional insensitivity look away. The nearness of his death seemed pornographic; he *should* be confined at home, kept out of public view.

Someone had cranked up the hospital bed so that Briones sat almost upright. Bedclothes covered his legs, but above the waist he wore a white shirt and a yellow tie. His few strands of still-dark hair had been combed neatly across the dome of his head. Briones drew a deep breath and smiled, drawing strength from the bustle of attention. Scanning the small crowd, he spotted Chris and lifted his hand. Chris managed to smile and wave back.

But when Briones began speaking he looked very solemn. He spoke as if reading a prepared statement, though he didn't glance at the few sheets of paper in his lap.

"I've asked all of you here because this will probably be my last chance. I want to do what I can to make people believe, and to support my friend the District Attorney." He gestured. Chris nodded, tight-lipped. "Soon he will be all alone," Briones intoned. "And I know there are people who still don't believe the evidence we put on at trial. The evidence about Malachi Reese.

"So I have been sitting here these last weeks, looking through my files and just trying to remember. I want to give you these leads, so you investigators can follow up. I know the truth, and I know how hard it is to prove, but it's your job to dig for it. Isn't it?"

Briones donned half-glasses with black frames and lifted the first page from his lap. "These are the names of people who died under unusual circumstances, after getting in Malachi's way." He read a brief list of four names, none of which meant anything to Chris. Looking around the room, even while reporters wrote notes on their narrow pads, he saw nothing but blank looks. Only the *Express* columnist, who was the only person in the audience older than Chris, looked more alert at the sound of one of the names.

With no further explanation, Briones lifted another sheet of paper and said, "These are people who disappeared, or left town for not very good reasons." He read half a dozen more names. Chris recognized one because the man's name ended in "Junior." He was the son of a San Antonio mayor from ten years back.

Lou Briones looked up sharply. "If you could find one of these," he said intently, "you'd be on to something."

Well, maybe, Chris thought, not seeing eagerness light any face around him. But there are lots of reasons for leaving any city. The mayor's grown son, for example, might have been tired of living in his father's shadow. There'd been no bombshell so far.

There wouldn't be. Next Briones read a list of successful contract bids, stretching back almost twenty years, in which Malachi Reese had been associated with the winning team or, according to Briones, assisting in the deep background. The reporters' expressions of skepticism faded to boredom. Malachi Reese didn't even need a representative in the room. Chris could make the counter-argument for him, and so could everyone else. Patterns are as false as statistics. With effort someone could put together the same pattern showing Briones himself as the manipulator, or several other contractors, architects, businessmen, or lawyers in town. Why, after all, did companies hire Malachi Reese, except for his pattern of success? How many teams had he been part of that *didn't* win a contract? After twenty years in hard-fought, fiercely competitive public life, how many people had gotten in Malachi Reese's way but were still living happy, prosperous lives?

Dig, Lou Briones had instructed these investigative reporters. But looking around, Chris didn't see anyone ready to rush out to his car for a shovel.

The silence that followed Briones' reading of his lists had a quality both embarrassed and startled: *That's it?* A TV journalist in a dark suit and bright eyes cleared her throat and stood to say, "Mr., uh, Councilman, if I may ask—why this vendetta against one man, Malachi Reese? If you want to give us all the political secrets you know before you—while you still can—why not give it all? Why implicate only this one man? Surely you have leads you can give us to investigate other local political figures too. What did Malachi Reese do to you to set you so against him?"

Lou Briones' expression hardly changed as he listened to the TV reporter's long sequence of questions. As he watched her a gentle smile grew, as if he appreciated her phrasing, or the graceful way her thin, athletic neck rose out of her well-cut jacket. Under his gaze, the reporter ended her question sounding more embarrassed than emphatic.

In the short silence Briones said, "He killed people, Miss." He added weight to the sentence by pausing. Then his smile faded and he continued, "You know, they say a guy like me knows where the bodies are buried. But that's just a figure of speech—except in this one case. Sure, I could maybe point you toward some bribes, some kickbacks. Some gentlemen's agreements you folks might not think were too gentlemenly. But *Malachi Reese killed people.* He ruined lives. That makes the thieving and lying I know about seem pretty petty."

The former councilman looked around the room. He had begun to tremble, unused to sitting up for this length of time. Briones wasn't rousing the mob. The reporters wrote dutifully in their notepads.

"The law agrees with me," Briones said. "What's the statute of limitations on theft, Mr. District Attorney? Three years?"

Chris half-nodded, half-shrugged, unwilling to offer a legal opinion on the spot.

"But there's no statute of limitations on murder," Briones said. "See, the law thinks murder is different too. Most of the things I know couldn't even be prosecuted. They're not worth ruining people's reputations now. But murder . . ."

He coughed. The reporters waited respectfully, then continued to wait. No one asked another question, so Briones continued to answer the one.

"I don't have a vendetta against Malachi. But I'm afraid of him. I'm afraid because I know we didn't convince enough people. I'm afraid he'll talk his way out of this. He'll get out again. And if he does, God help all of you."

Briones had paled. He seemed to have lost even more weight during the short press conference. He sank back against his white pillows, and the pillows looked more substantial than he did. It seemed cruel to question him further, even if anyone had been so inclined. The TV camera lights were turned off. The room seemed dim in the suddenly unassisted daylight. Reporters put their notepads in their pockets. "This won't air," the woman TV reporter muttered. "Page six, Metro," the newspaper reporter answered. "If that."

Chris put his hands in his pockets and watched the floor as it gradually cleared of feet. Someone asked him a perfunctory question and he shook his head.

When he looked up again only the *Express-News* columnist remained. He had shed his brown suit coat, revealing a striped short-sleeved shirt. The columnist had covered politics and celebrity in San Antonio for close to thirty years. He knew Lou Briones better than Chris did, but with a professional wall between them. Now the wall seemed to have grown as thin as Briones himself. The columnist stood beside the old politician's bed, talked softly to him for another minute, listened, then clasped Briones' left hand at right angles, like an old-fashioned student power handshake.

Turning away, the columnist gathered up his jacket and gave Chris a level look, with not a wink or a smile, just a sad, ironic gaze, as if to say, *Meet you here some day*. Chris nodded. As the columnist exited Briones gestured feebly. Chris walked to him. The room still seemed crowded somehow as Chris made his way through the folding chairs.

Mrs. Briones bustled in. She turned a valve on a green metal tank beside the head of the hospital bed and held a clear plastic mask to her husband's face, but Briones shook his head and waved her away. "Minute," he asked.

Mrs. Briones held the mask to his face anyway, and the old man wasn't strong enough to push it away. Over the mask he rolled his eyes at Chris. After a few breaths the oxygen seemed to help. Mrs. Briones took the mask away and turned off the oxygen flow, but stood close. Her husband ignored her. He took Chris's hand and said, "Thanks," simply.

It was hard to think of an answer. Chris settled on, "You did great, Lou."

Briones shook his head. In his mind Chris heard Briones' old rumbly voice saying, *Don't try to kid a kidder.*

"Maybe some of 'em'll keep lookin'. It's already old news to them. Kids. They don't have any memories. Half of 'em probably have agents looking for jobs for 'em in Houston or Los Angeles. I'm sorry. I did what I could for you, Chris."

"It was more than I could have asked, Lou."

Briones shook his head again, barely moving it. "It's you I'm worried about. Pretty soon it'll be just you, Chris. If he manages to get a reversal you couldn't even convict him again without me, could you?"

"That won't come up, Lou. It was a good clean case." Chris kept his new doubts to himself. There was no sense adding worry to Lou Briones' last few days.

Briones watched him intently, seeming to listen to something other than what Chris said. "I swear it's true," Briones said suddenly. "Don't *you* start having doubts."

Chris wondered if Briones knew that he had seen Malachi Reese since the trial. Briones seemed to be acting on some information, but Chris had only confided his doubts to Anne. Briones stared at him as if he could see the District Attorney's thoughts.

"I know, Chris," the old man said. "He has the gift of persuasion. I've heard him, I know. But he's guilty as hell. Don't let him convince you."

Briones gripped Chris's hand with surprising strength, pulling him close. The old councilman's sincerity was palpable. Looking at him, Chris found Briones very convincing. He couldn't believe a man would die with a lie on his lips.

But doubt didn't disappear. It crept back in immediately. Lou Briones believed, but he could have been deceived himself, as Reese had said of Adolfo Rodriguez. What an opportunity for some shadowy old politicians, to use the dying Briones as a sort of father confessor, convincing him of the good he could do before he passed on—by telling the world that Malachi Reese was responsible for all their sins. Chris had never seen any sign of gullibility in Lou Briones, but Briones had never been as vulnerable as he was now.

The dying man had used up the last of his strength in gripping Chris's hand. His eyelids drooped. Mrs. Briones stepped in. She loosened her husband's carefully knotted tie, unbuttoned his collar button—not that the hanging collar had constricted Briones' thin, quivery neck—and put the oxygen mask in place over his mouth and nose again. Briones' chest moved shallowly. That seemed good enough for Mrs. Briones, who took a deep breath herself as her husband's eyes closed. She cranked his bed down so he lay flat.

Over Chris's protests that he could see himself out, she led Chris to the wide archway out of the room. They both looked back at Briones, who had fallen asleep, his energy exhausted. With the chairs grouped around the formally dressed man lying with eyes closed, the room appeared eerily like a funeral parlor. Stella Briones gave her husband a long look from the short distance. Her voice came surprisingly strong.

"This is another one you can lay to Malachi Reese's account," she said, the statement touched with bitterness but mostly flat, reporting a fact. "Lou'd be alive today if he hadn't had Malachi on his conscience."

She didn't seem to have heard what she'd said. Chris had no response, and knew that whatever he said he'd have to repeat to her in a few days or weeks. He knew that the next time he saw Stella Briones she'd be in black, with her children and old friends around her. He shouldn't be the one given this preview. It wasn't right that Chris had such a personal place in the last days of Lou Briones' life. Circumstances had put him in a role he had no right to play. Even Stella seemed to think of him as a close family friend, but only death had given him that status.

He hugged her. She accepted it as she would from an old friend, putting her head on his shoulder and letting her poise drop. They stood there for a long minute. When he left Chris wished there were someone standing by to take his place, but Stella Briones remained alone in the doorway.

Chris and Anne Greenwald stood on the sidewalk three blocks from the Justice Center, on their way to lunch. Oddly, they could still do that, though they took precautions, walking against the flow of traffic on a one-way street, so they could watch the cars approaching. They'd gotten out of the Justice Center in Chris's now-habitual way, through the underground tunnel and out a side door of the old courthouse across the street, and the farther they got from the courts complex the safer they felt.

"It's not fair," Chris said, and Anne let it pass as if the sentence had any meaning at all. "I can't disbelieve him, but that's only because he's dying. If Briones were a normal witness I'd pick apart every word he said. I might never have brought the case against Reese. At least I wouldn't have rushed it the way I did."

Anne said patiently, "If Lou Briones weren't dying you might not have believed him, but if he weren't dying he probably never would have come to you at all."

Chris stared at her. He followed what Anne was saying, but didn't arrive anywhere. "So?" he finally said.

Anne shrugged. "I'm making as much sense as you are," she said defensively. "I mean, except for the accident of cancer the story might never have come to light, life would've gone on as always. Would that have been preferable?"

It was too hard a question. Chris just kept staring at her. "Yes, it would have been," Anne answered herself, "because then it wouldn't have fallen into your lap. You wouldn't have had to make the tough decisions. Right?"

"Right," Chris said. They both laughed, false, bright laughter rising up to the cloudless sky, bouncing off the bank building beside them.

During his workdays Chris was efficient and sharp, watching the people around him intently rather than showing them any cracks in his own demeanor. But as soon as he saw Anne, at night or during the day, his uncertainty came pouring out.

She put her arm around him and he reciprocated. Their lunch destination was off the beaten track for the courthouse crowd: the Garden Cafe in the Marriott, a bright restaurant with sheltered nooks, where tourists ate in patterned shirts, mismatched shorts and wingtips with black socks, along with a few business people in suits. They could all watch bustling people pass through the Marriott lobby. There'd be a buffet or they could order off the menu, blackened trout perhaps, with a crisp salad first. Anne and Chris wouldn't see anybody either of them knew, and if they had a quiet corner table and he were taken by a sudden impulse Chris could even fondle Anne's leg under the table.

"I shouldn't dump all this on you every time I see you," Chris said with a sudden change in perspective. "This must be a pretty gloomy relationship for you."

"I like gloomy men," Anne said. "They give an impression of being deeper than guys who smile all the time. Usually it's not true, but I fall for it anyway."

She smiled and watched him closely. She took his hand, the pads of her fingertips tracing a pattern on the back of Chris's hand. In spite of the joke, Anne wasn't trying to change the tone of their conversation. "Dump all you want," she said. "I'm the one who has no doubts, remember? I know you did the right thing."

"Because you read his mind, right?"

Anne tapped Chris's forehead lightly with her finger. "Something for you to bear in mind," she said.

It took John Tinnamon's murder to put an end to Chris's doubts.

There was no reason to notify Chris, he had no official status in John's case anymore. But the captain of the guards who'd given Chris the short tour of the row remembered, and called him before the story appeared in the newspaper.

"I'm sorry, Mr. Sinclair. You seemed like you were friendly with him."

"Yes," Chris said softly into the phone, making a strangely true claim on Tinnamon. Some time over the last ten years, mostly while apart, Chris and his former client had become friends.

"He wasn't a bad guy," Captain Stillwell said. "Little nutsy for Jesus, but that's okay. Of course I didn't know him before. But John was one of those guys that you thought, if he could start his life now, already past all the craziness, he'd be all right."

Chris stood up behind his desk. In a knowing voice, he said, "Who killed him?"

"Guy named Morris. Pres Morris. Not from down your way. Houston, I think. You know him?"

"No," Chris said, thinking he'd been wrong.

"John hardly did, that's the funny thing. We don't let any of 'em spend much time together. But this was one time too much, I guess."

"I'll be there this afternoon," Chris said.

"No need of that, sir. John had a sister. She's taking—"

"I'll be there."

Again Chris caught a short flight to Houston and rented a car for the hour's drive to Huntsville. The trip gave him more than enough time to think. Why would anyone kill a man already on Death Row? How much longer had John Tinnamon had to live? Two months? Six? Who was Pres Morris?

Chris wore a suit, both because that's what he'd been wearing when the call had come and because he wanted to look formal for the prison officials, to ease them into letting him back onto Death Row, when Chris had no official reason to be there. He didn't have any problem. Ben Stillwell, the guard captain who'd called Chris, did look at him a little strangely. "The D.A.'s office here in Montgomery County'll decide whether to prosecute Pres Morris," he said slowly.

"I understand."

" 'Course, what's the point? Even if they try, he'll be found incompetent to stand trial. Guaranteed."

"How can you be sure?" Chris asked. "The legal standard—"

"Because he's already been found too crazy to be executed."

They stood before the gate onto Death Row. Stillwell locked his sidearm away in a small locker; the guards on the row were unarmed, except for large locked cabinets inside the guard cages labelled "riot gear." Chris doffed his suit coat and tie, unbuttoned the collar of his shirt, and rolled up his shirtsleeves. He looked like a politician making a quick transformation into a man of the people. Stillwell and the guards were watching him sidelong, glancing at each other.

As they walked slowly, the only free men on the row, Stillwell reverted to the earlier subject. "That's one of the sad, funny parts," he mused. "Pres Morris shouldn't even be alive. He should've gone a year ago, but his lawyer had him shrunk and the psychiatrist said he was too far gone to know what they were doing to him."

One of the many grim ironies to which Death Row has given rise is that only the sane may be executed. The law holds that the death penalty is not merely state-sponsored revenge, it is to be instructive. So a man so far removed from reality that he can't understand why he's being executed is to be spared until such time as he recovers his sanity.

"*That's* what's crazy," Ben Stillwell said as they walked. "Suppose he does wake up sane one morning, and we tell him, 'Good to have you back, Pres. Now we're gonna put the needle in you'? Wouldn't that drive a sane man crazy? Pres may be here into the next century. Bad luck for John Tinnamon. Killed by a dead man."

They were taking the same path along the wide main corridor they'd taken before. Captain Stillwell led Chris to a guard cage Chris remembered. When the guards inside opened the door onto the side row, the real Death Row, Chris remembered this as the way to Malachi Reese's cell—and he suddenly knew who Pres Morris was.

In the late afternoon on Death Row, most of the men had already had their daily hour in the exercise yard; some had had one of their twice-weekly showers. Now most of the inmates were back in their cells for the long haul to morning. Not many of the inmates took advantage of this time for study or recreational reading. Most lay listlessly on their bunks. Some stood at the bars and stared out at the TVs mounted on the wall. Again Chris noticed the absence of surveillance. Things were still done the old-fashioned way on Death Row: guards assigned to cell blocks, expected to make rounds every few minutes. It wouldn't be surprising if in the late stretches of the evening those rounds became less and less frequent. There had never been a successful escape from Death Row. These inmates weren't going anywhere.

Chris stopped at the ladder to the second tier. "Where'd it happen?" he asked.

"The exercise yard. We've got so many we have to let 'em take exercise together, maybe a dozen at a time. They're watched, but if somebody's quick enough—" Ben Stillwell lowered his voice. "It happens more often than people think. I mean, these are four hundred boyos that've proven pretty definitively that they don't work and play well with others. Throw 'em together and . . ." He shrugged. "Does anybody on the outside care? Save the state a few dollars in food and chemicals. They're all supposed to be dead once they're here anyway."

Chris absorbed this information with an unmoved expression, but the guard captain glanced at him and quickly added, "I mean, we do what we can. We certainly don't encourage murder. But we've got to let 'em have exercise and showers, that's policy, so they've got to spend a little time together. We rotate 'em around, mix up the groups, don't let anybody spend too much time together. Like this time, nobody knew John and Pres had anything against each other. They'd hardly even talked."

Chris nodded and climbed the ladder. Without being directed, he got off on the second tier and walked to the fourth cell on that level. He was in front of the cell that held the short, very muscular black man who'd been babbling murderously during Chris's last visit. Now the man sat quietly on the floor of his cell, absorbedly studying his own hands as they held each other, cupped as if the inmate were cuddling a small animal. His hands were empty.

"That's him, all right," Stillwell said. "How'd you know? The Press Man. Killed a woman and her little girl. Think he even remembers?"

Chris did, now that the guard captain had used the key phrase. By the time of Pres Morris' trial in Houston a dozen years earlier both his parents had been dead and no one in his family remembered if Morris' first name was short for anything. One guessed Prescott, another Preston. But a reporter had dubbed him the Press Man because that was how Morris had killed, pressing his victims to the ground with the weight of his body, choking them with the pressure of his thumbs in their necks. Seldom had a jury, even in Houston, taken a shorter time to assess a death sentence.

Now, after spending a third of his life on Death Row, Pres Morris looked childlike. Hair grew in patches on his head. All his skin was smooth as a baby's. His mouth opened in a coo and his eyes were wide, fascinated by the nothingness in his large hands.

"He doesn't even remember John," Chris answered the question.

"I expect you're right. Something sure set him off quick, though. He went for John like electricity going through a wire. Snapped his neck before any of the guards could take a step. Around this place you just can't tell. . . ."

Chris stood watching the killer. In John Tinnamon's prime he could have thrown off the Press Man, probably have hammered him into the ground. But in his last years on Death Row Tinnamon had been shedding flesh, willing himself unearthly even before his time came. At his death he had been a shadow of his former self—the violent self that had put him here.

No one could blame the simpering brute who crouched before Chris in the narrow cell. Morris was directionless, like a spark bouncing out of a fireplace, or like what Stillwell had called him, an errant blast of electricity.

Pres Morris lay beyond guilt, but someone else did not.

"I'd like to see another one of the inmates by myself," Chris said.

Stillwell glanced along the aisle. "Him?" Chris nodded. "He wasn't there," Stillwell said. "He was in his cell, he had nothing to do with it."

"Still . . ."

The guard captain considered. He spoke sternly. "I won't open his door for you."

"That's fine," Chris said quietly. "If you'd just go back down to near the entrance. Or even back to your office. I can ask the guards to let me back out when we're done."

Stillwell had looked at the murderer next to them nonjudgmentally. He gave Chris a more critical study. "I'll be down at the cage," he finally said.

"Thank you."

When Stillwell had climbed back down the ladder Chris turned slowly. Only a few steps took him to the next cell. Malachi Reese's cell lay close enough for him to have overheard everything Chris and the guard captain had said. But Reese didn't seem to be paying attention. He sat on his bunk, leaning back against the wall, his head nodding as if he were listening to good music, a cup of coffee or a highball glass at his elbow. But there was no music and no refreshment. Reese entertained himself in a nightclub of his mind.

Chris didn't know why, but he knew who had killed John Tinnamon. He refused to believe Tinnamon's death was a result of random violence, just as he'd refused to believe that about the drive-by shooting. Pres Morris, who had killed John Tinnamon, had had no known grudge against him; in fact Morris' mind was too shallow to hold a grievance for long.

Chris didn't know why Malachi Reese would want John Tinnamon dead either, but the two men were connected through Chris. It wasn't idle chance that death had followed Malachi Reese to Death Row.

"Tell me again you're not a murderer," Chris said.

Reese didn't pretend to be startled. He looked up with a smile of recognition. "You do have faith in my powers," he said. "I don't believe I've ever had a stauncher fan than you, Mr. District Attorney."

"John Tinnamon warned me someone was out to get me. He said he'd investigate further and get back to me. I ignored him because the captain told me John had no way of knowing anything. He didn't have any contact with anyone in the outside world. But you were here with him. And it's no coincidence that the man who killed John sits a few feet from you day and night. You played on that poor bastard's mind. You worked him until he thought he had some reason to kill John Tinnamon."

It must have taken a massive effort of will. Communication was hard enough between those cells. Chris stood listening to the constant low-level noise of the row, almost used to it already: clashing radios, the drone of the televisions, loud voices, an occasional shout from near or far. Just getting Pres Morris' attention would have been hard enough. Putting an idea across to him, one strong enough to make him leap on John Tinnamon and break his neck, must have taken days and nights of concentrated programming.

But Reese had nothing but time.

"It does sound like me," Reese said suddenly, still smiling. "Like the me you painted at trial. Able to reach out even from here. . . ." Reese stretched his long fingers toward Chris and laughed.

Chris unbuttoned his shirt further, baring his chest and abdomen. "I'm not wearing a wire," he said.

Reese barely glanced at him. "I know you're not, Chris. Stand-up guy like you, you wouldn't stoop to that." But Reese made no admission. He sat dreamily as if listening to another few bars of the unheard music. "But tell me," he said lazily. "Why would I do such a thing? If I'm so all-powerful as you think, why would I even need to talk to a loser like John Tinnamon? I'd just work my vast array of underworld contacts back in Gotham City. . . ." He laughed again.

"I know why," Chris said. Here in Reese's presence, he suddenly understood. Reese looked at him expectantly. "Because you come to this place, doomed and gone, and you feel your power fraying. You don't want to call on the people back home right away. You want to surprise them, show them you can still reach out and accomplish things even without their help. That makes it all the surer that they will help when you do call on them."

Reese didn't move. He stared across the cell as if abstractly considering the theory Chris had put forward.

"So you have to use the materials at hand, and there's not much. San Antonio's pretty under-represented here on the Row. And so many of them are half a step from psychotic; you couldn't trust them. John Tinnamon seemed like a reasonable man. At least approachable. He led you on, didn't he?"

Reese stirred. It seemed to be the silence that moved him, or some discordant note in what passed for silence on Death Row, rather than Chris's question. Reese glanced out through the bars, past Chris, then came and stood there, a yard from Chris, still not looking him in the face.

"You're right about one thing," Reese said amiably, shaking his head. "It's devilish hard to network here. Hardly anyone worth knowing. The men you meet——" He made a mildly disdainful face, as if over an underbaked dessert. "——haven't kept up their contacts. Most of them have pretty much forgotten the world outside, and let it forget them."

He was toying with Chris. Chris struck back.

"John Tinnamon played you along. Acted interested, drew

some plans out of you. That pissed you off, didn't it, when you realized he'd fooled you? That you'd revealed too much to somebody who didn't want any part of you?"

Particularly Reese wouldn't have wanted an African-American like John Tinnamon confirming Chris Sinclair's claim that Reese was still plotting, still organizing his revenge far behind the scenes. So Reese had done what he habitually did when someone proved too stubborn an obstacle for him to overcome with words.

"Besides," Chris added, "a friend of mine, rather an expert on the subject, thinks you're addicted to murder."

Even here Reese had found a way to feed that addiction; here in the one place where men felt most safe from sudden death.

They had been talking in tones of easy banter, but that very easeful manner of Malachi Reese's had convinced Chris as nothing since trial had that he stood in the presence of a man who'd never felt remorse. Who had killed John Tinnamon just because of his thin connection to Chris.

Finally Reese turned his head to look Chris in the eyes, and caught his angry stare. "And what are you going to do about it?" he asked.

He had a good question. What can you do to a man who's already on Death Row?

Reese oddly fit his surroundings now. He appeared as well-groomed as ever, but not as crisply. He stood relaxed in his gray prison coverall, casually close to the bars, undisturbed by the ceaseless noise of the Row. Even the shouts and conversation around Reese seemed orchestrated; he had become the master of Bedlam. His eyes still shone with self-contained intelligence. Chris looked into those eyes and saw rage. Fine lines showed in the brown irises. Those bulwarks containing the hungry void of Reese's pupils were crumbling.

Reese's closely trimmed black beard no longer looked Christlike. He fit the Row, where men were delivered because they couldn't control themselves. Reese's anger was more subtle, but just as constant. Here he had all the time in the world to plan and to brood, to grow bitter over what he considered his denied opportunities. Malachi Reese remained an extraordinary man. Chris wanted to strangle him but he also wanted to reach him.

"You could have been more than this. People responded to you. You could have been—"

"What? Mayor? President? Me? Could I really? Let's put my name on the ballot and see. *My* face wasn't made for billboards. Not in this free land."

Chris said stubbornly, "Yes, you could have been if you'd tried. Mayor? Hell yes. Like black men did in New York, Los Angeles, Chicago, Dallas. . . ."

"It doesn't mean anything. Mayor's just a front man, I knew that early on. Like that punk Win Phillips. I won't be that for anybody. I'm not going to do the grin and shuffle. I'm not going to carry anybody else's water. I'm going to be in charge of my own life."

Chris heard a note of envy. Did Reese ever think about the high road not taken? "You could have been something extraordinary," Chris said sincerely.

"Like what? A leader of my people?" Reese assumed, then dropped an oratorical tone. "Dr. King is dead, man. They're all dead. Somebody like you gets to all of us eventually."

"Because you are a murderer," Chris insisted.

"A natural response to my environment. Didn't you hear my punishment evidence?"

"I knew it," Chris answered, remembering Reese's fearful childhood.

"But do you know what it's like? To tremble at every sound of a door opening. To be so completely at the mercy of people who— No, of course you don't."

Chris stood there on Death Row at a loss for words. He wanted to say he was sorry, but that would have been so inadequate it would have made Reese rightly contemptuous. After a pause Chris skipped the consoling part, saying instead, "But other people have—"

"Responded in different ways, yes," Reese interrupted, again the cool sociologist. "I suppose that's what drew me to politics," he mused. "You can spend your life in fear or you can be the feared one. *You* understand."

That distasteful intimacy had grown between them again. Chris did understand. If he didn't feel that urge to dominate, why had he run for District Attorney? If he didn't want to give orders, he would cheerfully have remained an apolitical lawyer. Maybe Chris hadn't had a glimpse into Malachi Reese's mind during trial. Maybe it had been a dark recess of Chris's own.

He backed off from their confrontation. "You killed John Tinnamon for guessing about your plans. Why do you tell me?"

"Go ahead," Reese smiled. "Tell everyone I'm behind a conspiracy against you. They'll think you're even crazier."

He had a point. Reese had made sure that Chris was isolated. What had made the District Attorney's two best witnesses at trial so believable—one was dead and one was dying—now left Chris alone. Reese wouldn't allow him even a pitiful ally like John Tinnamon.

Chris wrapped his hands around the bars of Reese's cell, assuring himself of their reality. "I'll have to do what I can to speed up your appeals process."

Reese didn't betray a moment's uneasiness. "Flog that horse all you want. Even if what you did to me survives appeal, it won't survive politics. Some day a governor'll come along who'll be outraged over the way you convicted me. Not this one we got now, maybe not the next one. But the pendulum's always swinging. One of these years a governor with a social conscience will be elected, and she'll owe her election to the people who believe in me. I'll make sure she thinks so. I won't be forgotten."

So Reese didn't even believe in the eventuality of his execu-

tion. Given that belief, his ease on Death Row became under-
standable. It gave him a cell to himself, leisure to plan, and the
best platform an inmate could have. Reese was right that his trial
would be given closer scrutiny and any public pronouncements
he made would have added weight, because he lived under a
sentence of death. He had wanted that. He had asked for it from
his jury and been given it.

Again Reese studied him, paying Chris the compliment of
careful scrutiny. In everything he'd said Reese took Chris for
some stooge of the establishment. Reese painted the battle between them as a revolutionary versus Chris as the emissary of the
status quo. Reese's own ambition made Chris feel small. In his
mind his own words came back to him: *You could be more than this,*
Reese's eyes said.

Sounds had died down. The two of them stood on the mountaintop, viewing the offered world. Chris knew what was on the
table. Help free Malachi Reese, and anything the D.A. wanted he
could have. With Chris's lawful authority and Reese's real power,
the two of them could rule an empire.

Having Reese's respect would be part of the bargain. Reese
still watched him, sidelong but alertly, his expression familiar, as
if through a crowd he caught a glimpse of a friend. Chris felt
drawn toward that face, that could open into the warmest of
smiles.

"I'll stop you," Chris said.

Reese smiled. He stepped close to the bars. "How? You've already done your worst to me. Your arsenal is spent. Now sit back
and watch. I figure my life expectancy on the row is about twelve
years. Yours is a lot less."

Chris remembered the drive-by shooting. "You already tried
to have me killed and failed."

Reese shook his head with easy sincerity. "If I wanted you
dead, you'd be in the ground already. Hey Press Man, catch!"

Chris turned his head and took a step back, both bad mistakes.

He was leaning back, off-balance, when Reese's hands shot through the bars and hit Chris's chest with staggering force. Chris fell sideways, stumbling, trying to keep his balance but falling back a few steps, back toward the ladder, safe from Malachi, almost righting himself until an arm shot out of the cell next door and pulled him tight. The back of Chris's head hit the steel bars, stunning him. He began struggling upright, groggy, when the arms came around his throat.

It happened too fast for Chris even to suck in air. The thick arms banged his head against the bars again, then the arms slid across his neck like twin pythons and Pres Morris' hands had him by the throat. His thumbs exerted tremendous pressure against the sides, trying to find each other through the thin resistance of Chris's neck. His fingers dug in, trying to crush the D.A.'s windpipe. Chris's air passage shrank to nothing, he couldn't make a sound. He clawed at the hands but that had no effect, and he couldn't reach behind him to get at his attacker's eyes or groin. The killer was protected by the bars.

As Chris's vision closed down to a narrow tube he saw a reflection in the TV screen in front of him: Malachi Reese in the cell next door, watching his experiment like a scientist. No gleaming eyes, only detached observation. Chris started slipping down the bars, out of breath, feeling his mind dying.

Then Reese spoke. "Stop, Pres!"

The pressure on Chris's throat eased. A trickle of air made his lungs scream for more.

"That's right," Reese said gently. "Just a game, Press Man. Throw him back to me."

The hands fell away from Chris's throat. It may have been too late: his windpipe felt already crushed, at first his gasping brought no relief, but then he took a strangled breath. A hand pushed his shoulder, almost gently, and Chris fell forward onto his knees. His shirt open, he felt exposed. Drawing life again produced no gladness. He felt only fear that life could be snatched away in an instant. When he tried to see he feared his eyes had been damaged. The world was dim and red. Malachi Reese stood beside him, the blood-redness spreading out from him; a dark angel of death hovering over Chris.

Noise of shouting finally made itself heard. The inmates nearby screamed approval, but the cries had been taken up all over Death Row, so Chris's escort couldn't tell the source. Captain Stillwell came out of the guard cage down below but didn't come hurrying up the ladder yet.

Through the noise came Reese's voice, melodic, self-assured, easy: "No. That's not my plan for you. Not yet. First I'm going to strip you naked in public. I'm going to take your reputation and everything else you have and then I'm going to show everyone how powerless you really are."

Chris sat on the concrete barely able to move. No irony attended the spectacle of the man in the cell in the deepest hole in prison, waiting to die, sitting back casually and threatening the District Attorney. No bars separated them. Chris's life was in thrall to a man under sentence of death.

Reese smiled confidently. "In the meantime, who do you think for my first exclusive interview? Barbara Walters or Jane Pauley?"

No one had to speak to Chris twice during the next work week. He was focused. He couldn't tell what detail of a pending or new case might be a clue to the unfolding of Malachi Reese's plot against him. First, Reese had threatened, he would take the District Attorney's reputation. What was Chris's reputation? For sharpness, for being a tough prosecutor? He had promised in his victorious campaign to make the office more efficient, to give no case less than full attention. After his Death Row visit to Malachi Reese, Chris fulfilled that promise with a vengeance.

He came striding into the misdemeanor section on the fourth floor of the Justice Center. Misdemeanor took most of the fourth floor of the Justice Center, down one flight from the main hub of the D.A.'s office. Life there for beginning prosecutors beat at a hectic pace as they were thrown into the swirl of heavy case-loads, but at the same time their efforts were seldom subjected to much scrutiny from the press or the highest echelon of the administration. People who committed DWI and shoplifting weren't usually real criminals. Misdemeanor penalties reflected that reality.

So Chris's appearance produced an immediate tension. Young prosecutors who had been standing around the common area of the secretaries' desks on this winding down Thursday afternoon stood up, almost at attention. Others crept out of their offices.

The lone exception, Mike Martinez, El Rojo, remained sitting on a desk, swinging one leg. He watched his boss curiously. The thin, blonde young woman with whom Martinez had been hud-dling stood, though, and Rojo smiled at her intensity.

Chris approached her, holding out a file. The young prosecu-tor watched it as if it were an indictment against her.

"This case," Chris said without preamble. "It's on your docket for Monday, isn't it, Connie?"

The young woman looked at the name on the file. She prob-ably had more than forty cases on her next week's docket and hadn't had a chance to look at any of them yet, but she tried to look knowing. "I think so, sir. Is there a problem with it?"

"No, it might be an opportunity," Chris said. "I read the of-fense report and I think there may be more going on here. I'm going to talk to the arresting officers. Don't make any kind of offer until you clear it with me first."

El Rojo had taken the file and was glancing through it. "Mar-ijuana?" he said with slight incredulity.

"That's what they busted him for because that's all they could get," Chris explained. "But I think they were watching him for another reason. Look at the guy's record. And he was coming from a party when the police stopped him."

"Illegally, I'd say offhand," Martinez interjected, skimming the offense report describing the defendant's arrest. His young blonde friend shot him a look, clearly asking him to butt out.

"You see, they wanted him," Chris said without a loss of momentum. "All I'm saying is, let's look into it. Talk to his lawyer on Monday, Connie. Feel him out about an exchange of information. Who attended the party with him? What was it about?"

"What was the party 'about'?" she said hesitantly. She had rather a small face, which drew smaller in agitation.

"What did they talk about, that kind of thing. If he doesn't have a lawyer, even better. See what he'll tell us."

"Chris," Mike Martinez said, holding the file up by thumb and forefinger as if it had an odor. "This is a Class B possession of marijuana. There are probably certain of us in this room who've had that much in our pocket at one time. Long enough ago that the statute of limitations has run, of course."

"But we don't have this man's kind of record," Chris said insistently, staring at his recalcitrant assistant. Rojo remained unfazed.

"Another good point," Rojo said. "Here's a guy who's already done a five-year stretch for burglary, and we're gonna hold a sentence of, realistically, five days in county jail over his head? Whoooh." He feigned a shudder.

Chris did not lighten up. He looked more closely at Martinez. What was his hidden agenda? Why did he want to protect this suspect? "May I ask what your interest in the case is, Mr. Martinez?"

"I'm—kind of an advisor." Martinez tried to give Chris a clue with a significant sidelong glance at his pretty young friend.

Chris ignored it. "Well, I'm giving the advice in this case."

"Sure, sure."

"All right, Connie? Report back to me." He gave her the file and a hard, fast look.

"Yes, sir. Of course."

Chris turned and walked smartly away, but not fast enough to miss hearing Mike Martinez say, "I wish I could leave a woman quivering like that, just by looking at her. Must be satisfying."

Chris didn't turn back.

Chris remained on constant alert. His nights were much like his days. All night long he seemed to walk the Justice Center hallways and the streets of San Antonio. He woke in the mornings with his legs twitching.

He also bore the loneliness of vigilance. His first day back from Death Row he called Anne and said, "You were right." He described his encounter with Malachi Reese. He and Anne both took the things Reese had said as admissions of guilt.

But Chris didn't make plans to see Anne. He didn't want her to be seen with him. He felt very much a target, and didn't want her in the gunsights with him.

He stayed like that for a week. But the small confrontation with El Rojo in the misdemeanor section helped Chris, in the perspective of a day later, draw back and look at himself. If Reese were very smart—and he was—he would have given the District Attorney the warning that he had, then sit back and do nothing. Sit idle for weeks at least. Reese had nothing but time. His only plan might be to drive his adversary crazy with waiting, while Reese pinned his hopes on his appeal or eventual pardon from a receptive governor.

Chris was wasting his energy in constant worry, in trying to be everywhere at once. From far away, Malachi Reese must be laughing at him. Even if Reese were planning something, it would be a long time before it happened. Chris sat back in his chair, relaxing for the first time in a week.

He was wrong.

Chapter 10

"Chris—"

He sat up in the darkness, already moving toward the edge of the bed. He'd caught the phone on its first ring. She didn't identify herself and didn't have to. He recognized Anne's voice over the line. He also heard the urgency in her whisper.

"Someone's inside," she said very softly but distinctly, afraid Chris would still be groggy with sleep, and she'd have to repeat herself. She needn't have worried about that.

"Get out!" he said, inclined to whisper himself, but putting great emphasis on the words. He found himself standing, reaching for his pants on a chair beside the bed.

"I can't," came Anne's voice. "They're— Shh!" She stopped talking, then the line went dead.

Cursing, Chris grabbed his cellular phone and, without hesitation, the pistol from his bedside table. He always knew where the gun was these days. Could he let it do its job again, as it had done for someone else in the past—point it at someone and pull the trigger? He didn't know, but as he raced out his door he knew he could smash the heavy chunk of metal into someone's face.

Anne lived maybe ten miles away, a lifetime. Chris ran the two red lights before he got to an entrance ramp, and on the expressway he screamed past slower cars, weaving from lane to lane. As he drove he called both 911 and a police phone number he knew by heart.

When he exited and turned into Anne's neighborhood of Monte Vista it seemed strange that the streets remained so quiet and the houses locked up tight. Hadn't they heard him coming? He didn't try to sneak up on Anne's house. His car roared, his brakes screeched when he pulled to a stop at the house. No cop cars yet. The fear flashed through Chris's mind that they wouldn't respond, that this was all part of the conspiracy.

He left his headlights shining like beacons and ran up the front lawn, barefoot in the grass. The front door was locked. Chris pounded on it, picturing what might be happening just inside. He was about to break the window beside the door when he looked through it, through the unlighted living room, and saw a window already open on the side of the house.

Chris ran around the corner of the house, ignoring the gravel of the driveway cutting his feet, found the open window, and wriggled up through it. He fell onto the floor inside the house and scrambled up, making sure he had a firm grip on the gun. He held it close to his chest, pointing up, so that if it fired it would take his face off.

He had fallen into the dining alcove. The heavy old table stood unconcerned, the dishes in their place settings denying that anything bad had happened. Chris glided through the arch into the living room. That room lay empty, too, but someone had been there. The door to the spare bedroom Anne used as a home office stood open. The office had been ransacked. The filing cabinet stood open, papers spilled on the floor.

The silence told him he'd come too late. Whatever had happened was already done. He hurried toward Anne's bedroom, but dread tried to hold him back. It had been long, long minutes since she had called him, and he knew from experience that murder happens quickly.

This bedroom door was closed. Before Chris reached it he

heard a muffled thud, then two screams. Anne's scream carried his name. Chris threw the door open, burst into the bedroom and saw Anne in a T-shirt, standing, miraculously alive. She pointed. Beside her a masked burglar winced and clasped his own hand, that Anne had just bitten. Chris leaped at him. The two of them slammed back against the wall, the burglar losing his breath in a loud huff.

Chris forgot he had the gun until he brought up his hand to punch the man. Then he stepped back, resisting the urge to slash the gun across the burglar's face.

And a defensive lineman barreled into Chris, knocking him across the room. Anne had been pointing for a reason. She fell to her knees, scrabbling for Chris's dropped gun. The second burglar, a big man with a thick trunk, backhanded her almost casually and picked up the gun. He grabbed his partner, growled, "Let's go," and half-dragged the smaller man out of the room.

Chris scrambled up, but stopped to lift Anne to her feet. "Did they hurt you?"

She shook her head. "I was hiding. They just found me a minute or two before you came in."

He squeezed her hand and ran. The burglars had a head start but had wasted time heading for the open window, then veering aside when they saw police lights in front of the house. When Chris came out of the bedroom, police were knocking loudly on the front door, calling to be let in. Beneath the noise he barely heard the intruders going through the kitchen and being stopped a moment by the back door. He went quickly after them. The back door still swung from the burglars' passage as he went through it.

It was three o'clock in the morning, the dead of night. Anne didn't have a light in her back yard, and her trees made deep shadows out of moonlight. Chris barely saw two dim figures across the yard, going over the tall, wooden back fence. He hurried after them, shouting so the police would know where to follow.

He cracked his toe on a tree root, shouted in pain, and kept going. The fence made only a momentary obstacle. When he dropped on the other side of it, into a poorly maintained back yard where the grass stood taller than his ankles, he saw the two burglars already going over the side fence of this neighbor's yard. A big dog growled at their heels. As the burglars topped the fence the dog turned toward Chris.

So did the bigger of the two burglars. He paused atop the fence. Chris saw the flash before he heard the gunshot. The shot zinged by his head. He dropped to the ground. The burglar went over the fence. The dog came running toward Chris, growling.

"Easy, boy."

Chris rose to his feet, adrenaline making him shaky. First he had to get by the dog, then over the side fence, then guess which way the burglars had gone. If he did catch up to them, he'd be killed.

Reluctantly, but with his decision hastened by the dog, Chris went back over the fence into Anne's yard. The damned dog tried to take a chunk out of his calf as Chris retreated. The teeth grazed his leg.

Chris limped back toward Anne's house, where lights had come on and he could see blue-suited bodies moving. Chris hurried toward the front to alert one of the uniformed officers still in a car which direction the burglars had gone.

But it wouldn't do any good to catch them. They were common thugs, there were thousands like them in San Antonio. They wouldn't admit, maybe didn't even know, what they'd been after—to kill Anne, to scare her? Their break-in was the kind of message Malachi Reese sent. He might not have had anything specific in mind; just get word to the burglars that the psychiatrist kept money or drugs in the house, aim the thugs at Anne that way and let them go, just to see what happened.

Or they might have had worse intentions. *I'm going to take everything you have,* Malachi Reese had threatened. Starting with Anne?

Chris went into the house. There were cops milling through

it, but he immediately saw Anne standing in the living room, being questioned by a detective. Chris went to her and put his hands on her face. She gave him a strangely stern look, maybe because the cops were still there. "It's okay," she said. She felt his fingers tremble. Anne held his wrists firmly, letting him feel her alive. "They didn't hurt me."

Her eyes penetrated his, delivering a message kept secret from the cops roving through the house. She had a strong grip. Chris heard Anne's message. She wouldn't faint, ever again. She had passed beyond giving in to fear.

"Where'd you hide?" Chris asked.

"Under the bed." Anne shrugged. "No prize for originality, I know. I just wanted them to think nobody was home, and it worked for a while, until they started searching the room."

Chris grinned. A plainclothes detective stood patiently tapping his notepad against his hand, giving them a moment, aware something was going on even though neither Anne nor Chris said a word.

Chris wanted Anne to move out immediately and forever, preferably into charming quarters inside police headquarters or, as a compromise, the security area of Fort Sam Houston. Anne proposed matter-of-factly to spend the rest of the night of the burglary in her own bed. "Not under it," she said pointedly, and Chris saw again the firmness of her determination not to be a victim. Chris was furious at what had happened. Anne didn't rage; she displayed the steely character that had kept pioneer families on this frontier in spite of everything—and had gotten some of them scalped.

Anne let herself be talked into moving out for a few days while a security company reinforced the house with an alarm system, lights, and better locks. Chris invited her to stay with him, assuming she would, but Anne showed another sort of determination, not to be stampeded into letting their relationship grow artificially. "I'll be okay," she said. "I've got friends." She kissed Chris long and deep at the end of that frightening night, but she went to stay with one of those friends in the interim. Anne wouldn't let a dependency develop that she or Chris might think deeper than it was because of their predicament.

Chris thwarted that determination of hers a bit by thinking about her constantly, even more than he thought about Malachi Reese. After his confrontation with Reese on Death Row, Chris had thought he could keep Anne safe by staying away from her. Now he saw it was too late for that. Reese obviously knew about Anne, knew what she meant to Chris.

But Anne stayed on his mind for other reasons. The fear subsided gradually as nothing else happened. Still he wanted to know her whereabouts every moment, whether she was laughing without his being able to watch her, or being forced to listen to someone say something trite or idiotic, and Anne with no one handy with whom to exchange an ironic look.

The last night before she moved back into her house she did come and stay with him in his condo. They didn't go anywhere. They lingered much longer than any other gourmet would have over the chicken-and-pasta dinner Chris had cooked. After an hour they didn't mention the burglary or Malachi Reese again.

"What would you be doing if you were home right now?" Chris asked her later.

"I don't know, reading probably."

"On the treadmill."

She shrugged, watching him over the rim of her coffee cup. "And what do you do when I'm not here?"

Think about you, he thought automatically. He didn't say it, but Anne shot an even sharper look at him, as if she'd heard.

She smiled. "I'll tell you one thing, at home I'd be more comfortable." She had slipped off her shoes long ago, but still wore the suit in which she'd come from work.

"Spend a lot of time naked, do you?"

She kept smiling. "Let a girl have some secrets."

Chris said, "Why don't you go ahead and get comfortable?"

Anne rose leisurely and carried her cup to the kitchen. Chris heard her rinse it out and put it in the dishwasher. She trailed a hand lightly along his shoulders as she walked back past him and into the bedroom.

Anne's presence in his home refused to allow the evening to fall into commonplace, no matter how casual they were with each other. It almost startled Chris to see her there, at his table, crossing his carpet. She stood out in the minimalist setting of his white, barely furnished condo. He'd made his home very simple. Anne was continually complex.

He heard the rustle of clothes, then the bathroom door close. After a few minutes he followed her, blinking in the dark bedroom; the light that fell from the living room didn't penetrate far. When the bathroom door opened the harsh light almost blinded them both until Anne turned it off, then they found each other more by touch than sight. She had on her bedtime T-shirt that fell to her thighs. Chris pulled its loose collar aside and kissed the top of her shoulder. He brushed the spot with his fingertips, then kissed it again. Anne sighed deeply as he moved to her neck. For the moment, she had no comeback.

He pulled up the T-shirt's hem and found only her skin underneath. Chris didn't say anything either. Anne stepped close and pulled his mouth down to hers.

Later the bedroom didn't seem so dark. Chris could see across it to the chair beside the door.

"I like your clothes laying on my chair. Adds a little style to the place."

"Well, anything would," Anne laughed. She turned her back

on the sight of her clothes, putting her leg atop his. Her fingers stroked gently along his collarbone.

"The chair is yours," he said. "Whenever you need a place for your clothes."

"Thanks."

An eerie time passed. It couldn't be said that nothing happened. Chris resolved disputes in the office. Protestors still confronted Chris, but he spoke to as many community groups as would have him, and was often shouted down or just shouted at. City Councilman Win Phillips appeared at many of these functions, and he and Chris engaged in impromptu debates about the District Attorney's office's racial statistics. The name of Malachi Reese continued to be invoked, of course. Phillips spoke of Reese as if he hadn't been convicted, as if Reese had been thrown into a gulag without a trial. Once, in front of a crowd in a church fellowship hall, Phillips amazed Chris by saying to the audience, "Do you know that an inmate on Death Row was murdered a month ago? Not only is Malachi's life being wasted in that hellhole, he is in actual physical danger."

Chris stared at the city councilman, looking for irony but seeing none. Phillips' eyes shone with fervor. Like many elected figures he had a public persona and wouldn't deviate from it in public. Chris longed to question him alone, but the chance didn't come.

In the public settings where they did meet Chris was bound to lose their confrontations, but he won some respect for listening and for endurance. Sometimes he took another prosecutor or two along. When he invited Lynn Ransom to one such speaking engagement she asked, "For display?"

"For contrast," Chris said.

Anne delivered a paper at a conference in New Orleans. Chris resisted angling for an invitation to tag along, then wished he had. Anne wished he had too. Another weekend night she spent at the hospital bedside of one of her teenage patients who had attempted suicide. "In a very half-assed way," Anne confided soberly. "She'll do better next time."

Chris watched his back. He and Jack continued investigating Reese's connections. They found a great deal to reinforce their suspicions that Reese had been owed more political favors than anyone had suspected, but they couldn't connect him to the murder of Adolfo Rodriguez. Reese's killer seemed to have gone into hiding. "Maybe got arrested for something else," Jack said hopefully.

Chris got a call from Mayor Raeburn Foley, who had of course heard about the ongoing investigation. The subsequent meeting between Chris and the mayor lacked any pretense of cordiality. It would have ended in a shouting match except that Chris walked out. "I guess you politicians have to develop this knack for forming alliances," Jack Fine observed.

Chris looked for Malachi Reese's hand in every crime from murder to shoplifting and didn't find it anywhere. Life went on. The city simmered rather than burned. It needed only a gentle touch to tip it into violence again.

As Malachi Reese had predicted, within three months he was the subject of a nationally televised interview. Reese made the perfect newsmagazine story, one big enough for a nationwide audience, but obscure enough to make it appear the reporter had had to dig for it. Neither Barbara Walters nor Jane Pauley got the exclusive, the Reese story belonged to up-and-coming Priscilla Newcombe, who made up for her blonde good looks by being the toughest interviewer since Mike Wallace.

Chris and Anne watched the segment of the TV show from

Chris's couch, the room dimly lit, the television screen providing the only animation. "This woman interviewed you, alone in your office?" Anne asked, the first time she had even feigned jealousy.

"She has this knack of staying silent after you've finished your answer, just staring at you as if she knows better and is going to spring it on you if you don't come clean yourself."

"Maybe her earpiece had fallen out and she didn't know what to ask next," Anne said uncharitably.

But apparently Chris had been too dull or his answers too complex to make the screened version of the story. Newcombe looked very professional and like a seasoned investigative reporter as the tape opened with her stalking across the parking lot where Victor Fuentes had been murdered.

"This is where assistant city manager Victor Fuentes met his death, in an apparently random act of urban violence," the reporter said accusingly. "Police didn't arrest anyone. The case fell into the stack of unsolved murders. Then, months after the killing, they came up with a suspect.

"Malachi Reese," Priscilla Newcombe said dramatically, and did a one-minute summary of Reese's career as peacemaker, troublemaker, and community activist, illustrated by still photos and the taped footage of Reese seizing the Confederate flag from the protestor. The flag dissolved to a shot of the prison unit where Reese "now waits for his sentence to be carried out."

"They didn't let her onto Death Row, did they?" Anne asked.

Chris shook his head. But Newcombe's interview with Reese had been taped dramatically enough to form the centerpiece of the story. The camera shot Reese through the thick mesh of the visiting pen that made Reese look very much a prisoner locked away from the world. The visitor's side of the room must have been crammed with equipment, but the interview's deliberately minimal professionalism made it look as if Reese and Priscilla Newcombe were alone, kept apart by the same barriers that now separated Reese from all mankind.

"He got to her," Anne said as soon as Reese's face came on the screen.

Chris didn't answer. His breath came shallow with the mix of fear and anger and guilt the sight of his adversary inspired in him. Chris felt transported into the visitation room himself. Reese looked more haggard than the last time Chris had seen him—added age around his eyes—but his essential dignity remained intact. Reese leaned forward so his face captured the camera. He didn't fidget. The lighting was grainy, except around Malachi Reese.

"Surely they didn't arrange that halo effect on purpose," Anne said.

Newcombe asked about the murders, giving Reese his chance to make his denial, which he did simply and with a touch of weariness, as if his innocence were already a given.

Newcombe's questioning had been uncharacteristically gentle, but next she hit the prisoner with a harsh question about his pending execution. The camera held tight on Reese's face to catch any fleeting fright. It failed.

Reese's nostrils flared as he drew a long, contemplative breath. Then he spoke in a measured flow of words, his eyes first fast on the reporter's face, then moving to the camera.

"No one can be content to die—to let the world go on without you. But whether you die in honored old age surrounded by a loving family or on a table with poison running through your veins, the best you can hope for is that you've touched some lives. Your influence will live on. I have that satisfaction. I will live on.

"You heard Martin Luther King, Jr., say it as if he knew he was not long for this world: It's all right to die. I have been to the mountaintop."

Reese's face appeared saintly in its composure. He had known, better than Chris, that he could only influence this story when the camera was on him. Reese's eyes wouldn't let the camera go.

The rich store of life displayed in his face made his impending death seem even more of a tragedy.

"I think of John Adams on his deathbed saying, 'Thomas Jefferson still lives,' not knowing his longtime rival had preceded him into the afterlife that same day. But they both live still. Abraham Lincoln is dead. Ghandi is dead. The first person who realized we could use fire is long dead without anyone knowing who he was. But the world is better because they lived. I have that satisfaction too. They can kill me but they can't undo my accomplishments."

Reese stopped talking and let the camera have his face as long as it wanted. He had grown younger as he talked. He looked still full of vigor and unachieved good works. He faded.

Priscilla Newcombe closed with an endnote taped in the parking lot of the prison unit at night. Her piece had made Malachi Reese's execution sound imminent rather than prospective and years in the future. The camera took in not only her own gleaming face and long-legged build, but the stark prison building in the background, as if at any moment its lights might flicker.

"My God, is that a tear in her eye?" Anne asked, but quietly, her usual caustic commentary muted by Reese's speech.

Priscilla Newcombe showed obvious effects of her contact with Malachi Reese, but her voice emerged strongly, tinged with anger. She, too, stared straight into the camera, and spoke clearly into the microphone she held close to her chin. "In ancient Athens there was a philosopher the authorities thought had grown too influential. They did to him what the state of Texas plans to do to Malachi Reese: killed him with poison. But we have forgotten the names of those authorities, while they failed, finally, to silence Socrates."

"My God," Chris said. "I've killed Socrates."

But he and Anne couldn't find any occasion for jokiness after the interview. Malachi Reese knew what most people thrust into public view do not, that no deed exists except as it is portrayed. Doing something isn't enough; in fact it's nothing, after the cameras start turning. That's when reality can be shaped. Reese's appearance had been a performance. To his supporters it had been one of exquisite sincerity. Protests about his conviction would begin anew the next day. This time they would be nationwide.

To Chris, feeling very alone in his condominium even with Anne watching him, the speech had been a declaration of war. One pointed remark of Reese's had been aimed at Chris, he felt sure. Reese's John Adams–Thomas Jefferson vignette about outliving a rival had shot straight out of the picture tube into Chris's heart. It was okay to die, but not to be beaten. Malachi Reese had no intention of letting that happen. His works would continue.

"You talk about a criminal mastermind, you're talking fantasy, in my experience."

In other circumstances Chris might have smiled, because the speaker talking so authoritatively about his experience was all of twenty-eight years old. But Mike Martinez—El Rojo—had in spades the knowledgeable tone that is common among prosecutors.

A small group had gathered in the common area of the felony section of the D.A.'s office, the group growing larger as word filtered out that the District Attorney had joined them. The office looked very modern, with discreet fluorescent lighting, metal desks, computer screens, and dual plastic wastebins for trash and recyclable material. The secretaries in charge of answering the phones could pick up the receivers if they couldn't break that habit, or otherwise just speak into the tubes that circled their necks and ended just in front of their mouths. Then they could send the call to a person, to voicemail, or into the nether region of hold. A couple of large printers could spew out criminal records or replies to defense motions, or prosecution motions written more or less by computer, with only a few human amendments. The District Attorney's Office was the largest law firm in the city, twice the size of its largest civil competitor, and finally under Chris's administration it had begun to act the part. Prosecutors bustled professionally, very few strolled the halls. Few of the young prosecutors could remember the cameraderie of easygoing bull sessions about cases and people. That's why Chris had chosen to pass on his plan in this way—bit by bit, to small groups in different sections—rather than calling the whole staff together in a huge session like a pep rally.

Anne stood at the front of the group with him, striking the young prosecutors with the oddness and probable importance of the occasion. Chris wanted Anne to talk to them about what she'd observed about the way Malachi Reese's mind worked. Anne wore a suit, but a casual expression. She had worked with many of these prosecutors on child abuse cases. She gave out nods here and there, and small smiles.

Oddly, Chris, the source of most of the modernizing in the office, most missed the old days of spur-of-the-moment prosecuting. That was the main reason he tolerated the relative laxness and expansiveness of someone like El Rojo—that and that Martinez had a manner that would not be repressed, even by higher authority.

Martinez continued, "I mean, your average criminal is what?—seventeen, nineteen? A real mastermind to them is someone who comes up with a plan of throwing a towel over the video camera before they snatch the twelve-pack of beer. I mean, I spent two years in juvenile and I didn't come across one kid smart enough to tie his shoelaces. I'm talking people who can barely work Velcro."

"But they can all pull triggers," Chris said. He spoke quietly but his voice carried clearly in the silence that followed this remark, as they all remembered that their boss wasn't talking about

an impersonal conspiracy. They looked at him for signs of how
he'd been affected by the drive-by shooting. To these kids the
crimes that formed their daily workload had little reality. As Jack
Fine had said to Chris, they'd never seen a body still fresh on the
floor, leaking away its life's possibilities. By the time the assistant
D.A.s got a crime the victim either had passed on or had become
just a pain in the ass to deal with.

All prosecutors should have been shot at, Chris thought. *Or shot.
It should be a job requirement.*

Toward the back of the group Lynn Ransom leaned on a filing cabinet, watching Chris and the rest of her fellow prosecutors. She was the only person in the gathering who didn't look
fazed by Chris's remark about being shot at. Her large brown eyes
held a gleam of amusement at the thought that these tough prosecutors were shocked by the idea of shots being fired in *their* direction.

Chris went on, "I've asked Dr. Anne Greenwald to tell you a little about Malachi Reese. Some of you know Dr. Greenwald—"

"Oh, no, psychological insights," Mike Martinez groaned
quietly.

Before Chris could rebuke his assistant Anne strolled over to
him. Martinez smiled as she came toward him.

Anne said, "Mike and I have worked well together on several
cases, haven't we, Rojo?" She put her arm around his neck af-
fectionately. "Mike is very flexible about new ideas. He has any
number of ways of avoiding them."

Briefly she turned her hug into a headlock as widespread
snickering broke out. It wasn't often that anyone answered Mike
in kind.

Chris coughed to regain their attention. "I agree, Rojo, I
haven't seen too many criminal geniuses myself. That would
make criminals all the easier to manipulate, wouldn't it, if someone really had the will and the forcefulness to try it? And these
grunts don't have any scruples against anything."

Chris stood up straight. "Just look for connections, that's all I'm asking. Dig a little harder than you have before. Ask yourself if the motive in a burglary makes sense or if there might have been more to it. Cops don't look for these patterns. We can."

"In our spare time," someone muttered. Chris looked searchingly at the young faces.

"Talk to each other more about your cases. That's all. Think bigger than the people you prosecute do."

Lynn Ransom had come forward to join the group. Chris wanted to ask her if she'd seen Malachi Reese's interview, but he assumed that Lynn, like Chris himself, had grown tired of being asked questions with racial overtones.

He turned away from the group to speak to Anne for a moment, and conversation became more general, with Martinez again dominating it, returning to his original theme.

"And you see how none of 'em can buy pants that fit? Sorry, Lynn, don't mean to criticize, ah, cultural differences. That's what I mean, my people are imitating your people. And the white boys are copying both of us. Jeez, whatever happened to ambition? Upward mobility? Now the most they want is this ghetto chic that—"

"So to better yourself you have to turn white?" Lynn Ransom asked.

"Hey, I am white, honey. Check my census form. You, though, I'm afraid there's no hope for."

Chris whirled around, horrified that the city's racial antagonism had invaded his own team. But Lynn and El Rojo were grinning at each other. Martinez made a "gotcha" gesture with a pointing finger. Lynn smiled at him with the fondness of a fellow candor freak. Neither she nor Mike could ever say anything less than the truth.

Later Chris saw the pair in whispered conference as he passed them in a hallway. They stopped talking and looked at him blankly. Chris wanted to ask them if they thought the boss had fallen over the edge. They were the only two people in his administration with the nerve to say it, but they still might not say it to him. If a crazy person asks if he's acting crazy, how does one answer?

About four o'clock that afternoon Chris had to go from the Justice Center to the old courthouse across the street for a meeting of Commissioners Court. Instead of taking the tunnel he walked out into the September sunshine. Chris's shoulders no longer hunched when he stepped outside, though he remained watchful. Only one car passed in the street, a red Mustang convertible, even brighter than its driver's hair. El Rojo waved.

"Investigating a scene," he called.

It was the oldest and most feeble excuse for leaving work early. But Chris couldn't help smiling as he shook his head at Martinez's boldness. Chris crossed the street and the red Mustang rolled happily out of sight.

The next morning Chris came to work a little later than usual. His secretary, Irma Garcia, a short woman who had not been dainty when Chris had hired her, and had grown once in office, stood blocking his door. Irma's face still looked youthful and usually cheerful, but her hips befit a mother of four. She could have been designed for blocking doorways.

"Don't read the report," she said.

Her face was so solemn, with dried tears streaking her cheeks, that she looked gray.

"What's happened?" A hollowness began spreading from the pit of Chris's stomach.

Irma didn't answer. He had to push past her to open his door.

He had left his desk neat the night before. The only things on his blotter now were a couple of sheets of fax paper. Irma followed him as Chris hurried to the desk, dropping his briefcase.

The fax was a police offense report, the preliminary form, still in the detective's cramped handwriting, not yet typed. Chris looked at the top of the page, the box for the time the report had been written. Three o'clock that morning.

Then the box for the crime, where the detective had scrawled, "Murder." Odd. Usually they said "homicide," a more clinical term.

He started reading, a report of an anonymous call to an empty house before midnight, and the finding of a body. Then Chris flipped to the second page, which contained more information in boxes, including the names of witnesses and victims. The report listed no witnesses. It listed the victim's name as "M. Martinez."

Martinez is one of the most common names in San Antonio, but Chris knew immediately. "Mike?" he asked. "Our Mike Martinez?"

Irma started crying again. Chris skimmed to the bottom of the report, where a hastily scribbled sentence said, "Victim tentatively identified as Mike Martinez, an ass't D.A."

Irma snatched the pages from him, crushing them. "That's enough!" she shouted.

"Why? What don't you want me—?"

But Irma had passed beyond communication. Her shoulders shook. She lowered her face into the report. Chris ran past her, yelling, "Paul!"

His first assistant's office door stood open. Chris saw Paul Benavides on the phone, his face dark. Chris hurried toward him, past the horrified blurs of the other secretaries' faces.

Paul almost screamed into the phone. "I don't give a damn! Who told him he could leave? Well, call him back here! . . . I do, goddamn it, I do!"

He slammed down the phone. Chris had never seen his usu-

ally unflappable assistant so furious. "Patrolman who first made
the scene left for Las Vegas this morning. Had non-refundable
tickets. His supervisor told him he could go, told him we don't
need him right now."

"But—?" Chris asked.

"I want everybody here!" Paul screamed in his face. Chris put
a hand on his arm and Paul's face crumpled. He looked as if he
were about to start crying like Irma.

Chris's hollow feeling had now consumed his body. He didn't
seem to have a heart, or lungs, or blood. In the face of his first
assistant's obvious grief Chris knew he had to take charge, but the
responsibility just deepened the hollowness.

"*Do* we need him?"

The question brought Paul back to some sense of his job. He
sniffed, raised his head, but wouldn't look at Chris. "I don't know.
I just want to do something. They say not. They already have two
suspects in custody."

Suspects. The word made it real. A name scrawled in an information box was too abstract to make Chris believe in the death
of someone as vital as El Rojo. But suspects in custody—live
people under arrest for having committed murder—that brought
it home. Mike Martinez was dead.

"Jesus." Blood drained out of Chris's face, and his arms. If he
took a step he might fall.

Paul stared brokenly at him. He shook his head, unable to
offer solace; unable to help himself. The sound of renewed sobbing came from outside the office.

Chris steadied himself with a hand on Paul's desk. "What is it
Irma doesn't want me to know?" he asked.

The question stiffened Paul Benavides. He stood taller, but
his face still looked as if it might split apart. "The details," he said.
"He was—he was tortured, Chris. It was horrible."

Paul fell into his desk chair. "I made the ID. When they
couldn't reach you they called me."

No one, then or later, reproached Chris for not having been

home at three o'clock in the morning. But guilt abruptly poured into his hollowness. What had he been doing at the exact moment his assistant had been murdered?

"Thank God," Paul continued. "Thank God his parents didn't see him. I stayed at the medical examiner's office until they came. I wouldn't let them look. I told them it was him. I promised them. I couldn't let them remember him like that."

Paul's horrified expression said that he himself could never forget his last view of Mike Martinez.

And a different portion of Chris Sinclair's brain kicked in. Looking at his first assistant's stricken face, the thought came unbidden to Chris, *I wonder if he can duplicate that expression on the witness stand?*

The hollow feeling in his chest and his legs had turned cold. Cold was good. Ice would be strong enough to hold him up.

"These suspects," he said. "Where are they?"

Chapter 11

Chris walked the three or four blocks to the central police station. At one point he realized he had just passed the spot where he and Anne had been shot at, and he couldn't remember how he had gotten there. Had he walked down four flights of stairs in the Justice Center, or taken the elevator? Had anyone spoken to him on his way? Had he told his staff his destination? He couldn't remember.

He walked through a soundless world. Nothing had caught his attention inside the bustling Justice Center. Someone could shoot at him again and he wouldn't hear. Chris hovered bemused somewhere outside his body. If he let himself slip back into full consciousness he would be engulfed by guilt. Somewhere on that silent walk he had realized that Mike Martinez hadn't been killed by random violence. Malachi Reese had promised to strike at Chris and he had. Chris was certain of that.

Footsteps behind him, heels clicking fast on the pavement. Chris turned and Anne Greenwald ran into him. She wrapped her arms around him and clung, sobbing quietly and rocking. "I'm so sorry," she was saying.

Chris had been with her only a few hours earlier, but now he couldn't smell the scent of her hair and barely felt the pressure of her arms. It was as if Anne were a ghost, or he was. He or Anne could as easily be dead now—or should be.

Seeing Anne made him feel weak. He couldn't let that ice inside him crack. He would fall apart.

"What is it?" she said. "Have you gone into some prosecutor mode?" She studied Chris's face, turning analytical. He started to brush past her, she stopped him, and Chris shouted, "He wants to hurt me! Me. And to do that he has someone killed he doesn't even know."

Then he did walk past her. Anne hurried to keep up, not talking anymore. Chris tried to think ahead to what he should do next, but he wasn't thinking at all. Going up the shallow steps to the police station's front door he slipped and went down on one knee, and he stayed there. Anne knelt beside him, her arm around his back.

Chris choked, his voice full of guilt. "I haven't even looked at the photos yet. I should—"

"Don't."

"I have to. That's all that's left of—"

"No it's not. Don't think like that. There are your memories of him. All the people who remember him. That's what's important. Not this grisly funeral business."

Chris opened his eyes, expecting to see brown hair turning red in the sunlight. He remembered an image of Mike, the one time his assistant had convinced Chris to play basketball with his guys. El Rojo had assigned himself to cover his boss, so they went against each other all day. At one point they both scrambled for a loose ball. Mike had gotten to it first, close to the basket. Not even thinking of passing off, Rojo had gone straight up. Chris had gone up with him, stretching to block the shot, but Mike had jumped first. He sailed inches higher. Rojo's face had been wide with laughter as he stretched high and the ball lifted gently off his fingertips, arcing toward the basket. It didn't even matter if it went in. Mike Martinez's joy had been in the exertion, in beating someone to the ball, feeling his body work. Mike had been playing shirtless, his torso slick, and as they'd come down his sweat had rubbed off on Chris's T-shirt.

Chris knelt on the cement, stroking his shirt.

"Don't go in here now," Anne said. "Give yourself a break."

So Chris stood up and opened the door and led the way up-stairs to the homicide detectives' offices and the interrogation rooms.

Chris's theory that Malachi Reese was behind the murder took a blow when he saw the suspects. They were skinheads, young white men who hated anyone of a different tint. Chris paced in the dim hallway outside the two interrogation rooms into which detectives had separated the suspects. The expanse of skin above their foreheads made them hard to tell apart. One was slightly bulky, the other skinny. "What are they, seventeen?" Chris asked, angry that his adversaries didn't look more formidable.

The glowering homicide detective in the hallway with him said, "He is," pointing to the skinny one. "The other one's nine-teen. Both got juvenile records, minor stuff. Never been to TYC, just probation. Apparently they both got smarter about a year ago, because they haven't been arrested in that long."

TYC was the Texas Youth Commission, juvenile prison. Since neither of these had even been that far, they weren't remotely hardened criminals. They looked like boys, even down to their sullen postures. Mike Martinez could have handled these two.

At the thought of Mike Chris stiffened again. He studied the suspects more closely. In the interrogation room on the left Sergeant Mannie Esparza, the same detective who'd taken Chris's statement after the drive-by shooting, was browbeating the skinny one. In the other room the more muscular kid sat alone, the detectives letting him think. "I'll try this one," Chris said, turning that way.

"No," Anne said.

The detective in the hallway gave Chris another of those looks, the one that asked why the District Attorney had brought his girlfriend along. Chris didn't give him any kind of answer. He hurried to follow as Anne went into the interrogation room on the left.

Inside the bare room Sgt. Esparza looked up quickly. He frowned at Anne but didn't say anything as she quietly took a seat against the wall. Esparza didn't look much friendlily at Chris, but he expected the D.A. to play his part. "What'd the other one say?" he asked.

The suspect sat in a slat-backed wooden chair, solid once, now rickety with age. Chris stood in front of the kid and stared at his bald dome until the guy looked up at him, his eyes dark and defiant. "He said this guy did all the dirty work," Chris answered.

The skinhead didn't hesitate. "Bullshit. Me 'n Ray're family. He's not gonna rat me out. And I'm not gonna do him either, so you guys are wasting your time."

His voice sounded briskly confident. Chris tried not to show the discouragement he felt as he asked, "What's your name?"

The boy sneered so broadly his lip threatened his eye. "They call me Crackback."

"His name's Donny," Esparza said disparagingly. "Donny Sturns, but he probably picked the last name at random. Damn sure he doesn't know who his father is."

"Better than knowing your mother's a whore like yours," young Sturns responded wittily. Esparza stepped toward him, his sudden rage so convincing that Chris put out a hand to stop him.

Forced into the good-cop role, Chris sat down close to the suspect and said quietly, "Listen, Donny, you've been arrested before, but not for something like this. You know who you guys killed? He was one of my assistants. Most of these cops knew him and liked him. They're not going to let this one go. Ever."

Sturns shot a glance at Esparza, whose face must have confirmed what Chris had said. The suspect didn't have a response, but the movement of his eyes showed he was thinking.

"So here's what's going on," Chris continued quietly. "You and your friend Ray are in a race. You're not just racing each other, you're racing the cops who are still out investigating. We know there were more of you involved. Cops'll find them just like they found you. Then the only question will be whose life is over and who does the smart thing. Somebody's going to talk, Donny. You know that. The rest of you are going to go down for capital murder. Capital. That means even if you don't get death you get forty years. Forty years before they even talk to you about parole. That's your life, Donny. You go into prison and you spend your whole life there, and maybe you come out the other end a sixty-year-old man. Forty years. More than twice as long as you've been alive. Do you have enough brains to understand that?"

Sturns' tongue flickered at his dry lips. He glanced at Chris then past him, his eyes shooting around the small, ugly room.

The boy hunched his shoulders and leaned close to Chris. "Listen," he said, the gush with which confession always begins. Chris's breathing eased.

"Me 'n Ray weren't even there," the boy continued. "We were with your girlfriend here. Both of us. Me on—"

Without Chris's even willing it his foot shot out, hooked the front leg of the boy's chair and jerked forward and up. The chair went over backwards with Sturns in it. The back of the chair hit the concrete floor with a loud crack, but the back of the kid's head took some of the hit too. He got up holding it, and before he regained his grin he gave Chris a look like a child who's been punished unfairly, hurt and mad at the same time.

Chris stood glaring at him, fists clenched. Chris had just made himself useless to the confession process, he knew that. He could no longer talk reasonably to the kid, in that professional murmur that implies, *We're all pretty much the same down inside, aren't we, Donny?* Instead Chris estimated how much damage he could do to the little bastard before Esparza pulled him off.

"Did you jump when he screamed?"

Chris almost jumped himself. Anne's voice sounded eerie. She had spoken quietly but very distinctly, and in the small room, with acoustic tiles on the walls and the ceiling, her voice had a hollow reverberation as if it came from beyond the grave.

It startled the three men in the room. The kid looked at her uncertainly. Anne still sat against the wall, shoulders hunched and arms together as if she were cold, leaning forward with complete absorption, consumed by a need to understand. "He must have screamed some time, the way they hurt him. Did it scare you? Did it make you jump?"

Anne stood slowly and walked toward the skinhead. "A scream goes right through you, doesn't it? It's like the pain escaping and going into *you*. That's why everybody laughs after somebody screams in the movies, because for a second it hurts, and it scares you."

The kid had slipped back into his tough-guy pose. "I like to hear 'em scream," he said, staring at her.

Anne dismissed that. "Did he not scream at all? At first he took it, didn't he? He was strong, Mike was."

The kid licked his lips and glanced at the two men, calculating how much he could wise off without giving anything away. He made a very smart decision not to say anything, but that meant he kept it inside. His eyes went distant as Anne kept talking.

"Think about him in that place with all you strangers. He didn't even know what was going on. Did he ask you? 'Why are you doing this to me?' Think how scary that must have been. Not knowing how far they were going to go. But he took it for a long time, didn't he? Did you wonder if you'd do that well? At some point you wanted to say stop it, didn't you? Knock it off, let him go. But then they might have turned on you. It could have been you getting punched and kicked and cut, and crying in your own blood."

"I don't cry," the kid sneered, probably unaware that his bravado sounded a little pathetic and his eyes gave him away.

"No, robots don't, do they?" Anne stood close to him. She kept her voice low, but it encircled him. "That's for women, like your mother. She's probably crying now because you're in here. Like Mike Martinez's mother, crying because her son is dead."

The kid stared at the floor. Anne raised her voice for the first time as she lifted it at Chris and Esparza. "Could you two zombies get out of here, please?"

The men started as if they'd been caught intruding. The detective began to say something, then changed his mind and followed Chris out of the room. They stood shoulder to shoulder in the darkened hallway, hands in their pockets and silent as they stared through the one-way glass back into the interrogation room. Their exit made Donny momentarily bolder. He paced around Anne, who stood still. Her lips moved relentlessly. The boy snapped something at her and spat on the floor close to her feet. Once he even lifted his hand close to her face, and Chris was so caught up in the scene he didn't think of interfering. Anne didn't take her eyes off the boy's, and Donny stood immobile. He couldn't look into her eyes and he couldn't touch her. His hand went for an angry gesture instead.

That seemed to use up all his energy. He slumped into a chair and Anne sat close beside him. He said something softer, his prominent Adam's apple went up and down in his throat, and his eyes glistened. His hands stiffened helplessly.

Anne finally touched him, and Chris knew what she said. A speaker in the hallway carried voices from the room, but it was turned down too low to catch her murmur. Chris may have read her lips. Anne said, "You're too tough to rub where it hurts, aren't you? But I will."

She put her hand on the back of the boy's head where it had hit the floor when Chris had jerked his chair out from under him. She rubbed gently. The soft pressure brought the boy's head to her shoulder. She caught him and held him. Donny let himself be held, even turning his head to lay his cheek on her shoulder. Anne sat rocking him while the boy talked and cried.

"I've never hugged a suspect," Sergeant Esparza said.

Chris turned toward him quickly, ready to snap back, but Esparza wasn't being snide. He looked thoughtful, as if hugging were a technique worth exploring.

Chris watched Anne's lips move, watched her listen as the kid talked. She looked no more intense than he'd seen her at other times, but something in her focus told Chris he was seeing her life's work. Anne's eyes reflected the concern he had seen before in other contexts, she spoke in the concentrated way he knew, she drew the kid to her shoulder with the deep well of empathy that had called Chris as well. But she did all this without one of the qualities Chris loved best about her: irony. He understood, watching her, what mattered to Anne Greenwald, without reservation or deprecation.

Anne might not have passed on what Donny Sturns told her, but that didn't matter. A video camera in the interrogation room captured everything. Donny had been told that, but he'd forgotten the camera, as they often do. It didn't matter. Donny had grown willing to talk. After his session with Anne he gave a written statement, and he named the leader of his gang, who had initiated the attack on Mike Martinez and made sure it ended in death: Lee Griggs. The name sounded vaguely familiar to Chris, and it meant a lot to Esparza.

"I knew it," he said to Chris in his office after Donny had been thoroughly debriefed and sent to protective isolation. "Bad, bad piece of work," Sergeant Esparza said. "No wonder this boy was scared of him."

The case had begun. They had their first solid piece of it, thanks to Anne. Donny continued to be very cooperative. After that morning with Anne, he was their boy.

For a while.

———————

There was no question who would prosecute the case. Someone once mentioned the phrase "special prosecutor," but Chris dismissed that idea quickly. He wasn't related to Mike Martinez, no law said Chris had to recuse himself, and he didn't even consider the idea. Chris wanted to be on top of the case as it evolved. With the accomplice agreeing to testify, the murder case looked strong for the prosecution, but something would go wrong with it at some point, Chris felt certain of that.

He drew up an arrest warrant himself for the skinhead leader, Lee Griggs. Early one morning a homicide detective and two uniformed police officers served the warrant at Griggs' parents' house. Griggs, twenty-one years old and unemployed, still lived at home. The police officers timed the arrest nicely, after the parents had gone to work and while Griggs was still in bed. By the time the first period school bell rang for other kids, Lee Griggs sat in custody.

Chris went to see his new adversary at the police station immediately after the arrest. August burned the sky and the pavement; it was already sweltering by mid-morning. Stepping into any building was a relief. Chris re-donned his suit coat as he walked downstairs in the cool white police station. The walls were white, the floor scarred linoleum. The old building had a studied lack of personality. No one challenged Chris as he made his way to the booking area.

A small crowd of cops had gathered there, many more than were needed to fingerprint and photograph an arrestee. The only other civilian in the room, Lee Griggs, was the center of attention. The young suspect no longer had sleepy eyes. He looked just the way he wanted to look, like an American nightmare: a tattooed menace with a metal-studded wristband and a perpetual snarl. As a sergeant fingerprinted Griggs half a dozen cops stood around him. They fell silent when the District Attorney came in. Griggs paused in midstream of an obscene diatribe and turned to look.

Chris sighed. "Was that necessary?" he asked the room at large.

Because Lee Griggs had a bruise on his left temple, near his eye, and a smear of almost-dried blood at the corner of his mouth.

The homicide detective, the ubiquitous Sgt. Esparza, stepped forward and answered, "You tell me. Treviño?"

A young uniformed officer stepped out from behind another cop and came forward into the light. He looked much worse than Griggs. A gash across his cheek still dribbled blood. It would need stitches. The young officer's face also featured a black eye and a swollen lip.

"I'm sorry," Chris said. Inside, where the prosecutor in him dwelled, he felt relieved. Let the defense try to raise an issue that the arrest had been overly brutal. Chris would have Officer Treviño's face in response. "Take a picture of him, please," he said to Esparza, of Treviño.

Lee Griggs, sitting in a straight-backed wooden chair beside the booking desk, laughed loudly. "Yeah, record that for posterity. Why don't you take an X ray, too, try to find his balls that I kicked up inside his guts?"

Chris, dead-faced, just stared at the laughing skinhead, as he would have at an oil stain under his car. Griggs continued to laugh as Chris walked out of the booking office.

Sgt. Esparza followed him out into the hall to ask, "You want in on this?"

Chris shook his head. He stood very stiffly in the hallway. He kept his voice low, but it jerked out of him as if it hurt his throat. "I don't care if he talks or not. I don't care what he confesses to or who he's willing to give up. He's getting nothing in exchange. Don't make him any promises, because all he's going to get from me is a promise of a death sentence."

Esparza nodded, as if that had been understood. But saying it hadn't afforded Chris any relief at all. Whatever he could do to Lee Griggs wouldn't be bad enough.

Lee Griggs hadn't impressed anyone with his intelligence. But he quickly hired a smart, not-to-be-trusted defense lawyer who cleaned up his act fast. By the time of Griggs' arraignment, his first appearance in court, his tattoos were hidden beneath his navy blue suit, his light brown hair had grown out into a soft Caesar-style cut, and he gave Judge Lois Henricks a smile like a shy schoolboy. The judge didn't smile back. After ten-year stints as both a prosecutor and a defense lawyer, Judge Henrichs' susceptibility to boyish charm had dropped to nil. But jurors would probably look on young Griggs more favorably, especially as they wouldn't hear about his rap sheet until the punishment phase of trial, if it came. Lee Griggs turned his smile on the District Attorney and it gleamed more brightly.

Chris wouldn't rely entirely on Donny Sturns' testimony against his former leader. He assigned Jack Fine to investigate Mike's murder personally and set his best researcher, First Assistant Paul Benavides, to looking for the connection between Lee Griggs and Mike Martinez.

One day in Chris's office Paul dropped a stack of pages on the desk and said, "I can't find it."

The dark streaks under his eyes testified to how hard Paul had been working at the case. Mike Martinez had been Paul's protegé, and friend. "They met in that teen club, but I don't know where they knew each other from before that. Mike had some younger cousins still in high school, but he didn't know Griggs or any of his gang."

"Mike spent two years in juvenile—" Chris began to suggest.

Paul nodded wearily. "But he didn't run across any of these guys. Lee Griggs was already too old to be prosecuted as a juvenile when Mike was there. No. Griggs has a baby sister who got sent to TYC almost two years ago—"

"Did Mike—?"

Paul shook his head. "He never had anything to do with her case. He was gone from juvenile by the time she got sentenced."

Paul's knowledge of everyone's family background showed how far he had dug and found no connection. And Chris couldn't think how to even start looking for a link between Malachi Reese and the racist Lee Griggs.

"Listen, there's something else." Paul sat up with renewed energy. "You need a dark face beside you at trial. I'd like to do it."

Chris cleared his throat thoughtfully. Stern, authoritative Paul Benavides had a little secret: trials scared him. As a lawyer he had prepared his cases so thoroughly that he seldom had to go to trial. When he did he could get through the trial with rigid self-discipline, but his breath came shallow the whole time as he waited for disaster to strike. This was not an uncommon reaction among lawyers, some of whom managed to hide it as well as Paul did, but Chris had worked with him and knew his secret. He thought he saw relief in his first assistant's face when he said, "Thanks, Paul, but you need to run the office while I'm caught up in this.

"You're right, though, about the dark face."

With Lee Griggs beginning to look like a normal young man, it had grown harder to picture him as a vicious killer who had murdered Mike Martinez over the shade of his skin. Chris should have someone prosecuting the case with him whose very presence might goad the defendant into a racist outburst in court.

"It has to be someone very good," Chris said.

"Of course."

"Ask her to come see me, would you, Paul?"

They were thinking of the same person, Lynn Ransom. Not only one of the best prosecutors in the office, Lynn was one of the few African-American ones. In fact her appearance made her ancestry hard to pin down. The planes of her face showed as many traces of American Indian and the Caribbean as they did of Africa. Being American, she undoubtedly sprang from some vigorous combination platter of genes.

When Lynn came into his office Chris stood up from Lee Griggs' file. The record was scary in its commonness: juvenile shopliftings, truancy, finally car theft, then misdemeanor assaults, DWI, and an aggravated robbery that had been dropped when the victim left town and refused to return for trial. Then something had happened, Griggs had become the leader of this skinhead gang and it had seemed to come on him like a civic responsibility. A couple of times he had appeared at a school board or city council meeting as a sort of spokesman. No one took him seriously because of his appearance, but someone should have investigated how he made a living and what he did with his time. No one did because the petty arrests had stopped. When his criminal record had gone silent Lee Griggs had become most dangerous.

Lynn didn't say a word as Chris greeted her and led her to the social corner of his office, near the couch. Neither of them sat down. Lynn stood nearly six feet tall and didn't hide the fact by slouching or wearing low-heeled shoes. Her hair fell to her shoulders, tightly rippled like black water when a storm is impending.

Chris said, "I'm going to prosecute this Lee Griggs."

She nodded.

"Mike was a friend of yours," Chris went on. "Good friend?"

She shrugged, then nodded.

"I liked him too. Can we put that aside and hold our feelings in check?"

"Do I have to?" Lynn didn't fall for a second for that "we" line. The District Attorney would be trying the case no matter how he gave in to his feelings. She was the one who had to try out for the team.

"We have to be professional. You know this Griggs' lawyer, Gloria Files? Our case is pretty iffy, and if we don't pay attention she'll slide him right out from under us." Chris hadn't felt much eagerness from his assistant. "Do you *want* in?"

"Let me ask you a question," Lynn answered. "Are we going for death when it's a white boy who killed a minority?"

"What do you think?"

She studied him. Her manner toward her boss eased, her eyes came alive. "Oh yes," she said. "I want in."

Chris had something else to ask her. "I don't know what things are going to be like outside the building. Sitting with me might subject you to—hostility. Even danger. I wouldn't want you to—"

"To be on this trial?" Lynn said, her passion finally showing. "I'll risk it."

For the first time in what seemed a long time Chris felt less alone professionally. Lynn's edginess was well-known in the office, she wouldn't let anything pass without questioning, and she was considerably less than friendly toward her boss. But there could be no doubt she and Chris shared the same goal.

"All right," he said. "Let's get to it."

They were still working two hours later when Anne Greenwald walked into the office to keep a lunch date with Chris. Lynn stood halfway between the office door and the desk on which Chris was leaning, pointing her outstretched arm at him as if making a jury argument. When the door opened behind Lynn she whirled like a gunfighter, then slowly lowered her arm and smiled.

"Hello, Dr. Greenwald."

"You two know each other?" Chris asked.

Anne didn't answer. Lynn said, "Dr. Greenwald was my witness once."

"Oh, that's right, that was you, wasn't it?" Chris said, remembering the story, one that had helped establish both women's reputations in the D.A.'s Office. Anne, testifying in a sexual-assault-of-a-child case, had refused to answer a defense lawyer's question about something the young victim had told Anne in confidence. When the judge had informed Anne that there is no doctor-patient privilege in Texas and that jail was the only alternative to answering the question, Anne had answered, "I have my own standards to answer to."

But the defense lawyer had backed down from asking the question. "Rumor has it," Chris said to Lynn, "he withdrew the question because you told him you'd break his arm if he put your witness in jail."

"That's the Family Channel version of the story," Lynn said. "There's much better versions than that."

That afternoon Chris and Lynn were back at work on Mike Martinez's murder. Chris was determined to indict the case as capital murder, which meant he had to find another felony charge to add to the murder. "It must've been kidnapping," Chris said. "Why else would Mike have gone to that house with them? This abandoned house with a bunch of skinheads? Would you have done that?"

Lynn didn't answer directly. She was looking at the photographs Chris had spread on his desk: photos of the teen club where Mike Martinez had met his killers and of the house where he'd been murdered. "He probably didn't know it was a bunch of them," Lynn said. "Most of them were probably waiting at the house."

"Okay, so why would he have gone with one or two skinheads? No, they took him from that club. In the parking lot, maybe."

"What was he doing in some teenie club in the first place?" Lynn said.

This argument had a very serious consequence; deadly, in fact. The weakest part of their case was the capital element, the fact that promoted the crime to a death penalty case rather than simple murder. Murder in the course of committing one of a short list of other felonies is capital. Chris argued that Mike Martinez had been kidnapped and then murdered. That would serve. But Lynn picked that theory apart as tenaciously as the defense lawyer would.

"I don't know," Chris admitted, about why Mike Martinez had been in the teen club where witnesses had seen him the night of the killing. "Did he hang out in places like that? I hate to think it, but did he—like teenage girls?"

When Lynn saw that her boss seriously wanted an answer from her she grimaced. "We weren't that close. He didn't share his pickup techniques with me, but I have a hard time picturing it, don't you?"

They bent again in study over the pictures of the club and the house and the street map that showed how many miles the places were from each other, until in exasperation Lynn brushed it all aside.

"Screw pictures. Let's go look at the place."

The teen club lurked behind its parking lot on an obscure industrial street behind the airport, near Northeast Stadium. By daylight the building looked grim, a big cinderblock cube indistinguishable from the nearby warehouses. A neon scrawl over the metal front doors announced its name but, when turned off, the neon tubes looked rusty and disused. Chris and Lynn stood in the empty parking lot trying to picture the nondescript building as a hotbed of teeny hormones and festivity.

"Lighting probably makes it look better at night," Chris said doubtfully.

"Darkness," Lynn answered. "Darkness would help this place a lot."

They walked around the building, found a side door, a back alley with a Dumpster, but no clues unless one counted the District Attorney's lifting his foot in the alley to discover the tail end of a marijuana cigarette. "Do they still call these roaches?" he asked.

"I wouldn't know, sir."

Undoubtedly a lot of dope got smoked in the teen club's parking lot on Friday and Saturday nights, but inside the only stimulants were loud music and Pepsi. Chris could picture El Rojo swaggering through the place, smiling disdainfully on the children pretending to party, but he couldn't imagine Mike staying long or coming more than once.

"He must've been meeting someone for a reason. Or picking up some member of his family. Maybe he never even got inside the club. Maybe the skinheads were in the parking lot, and as soon as they saw him they . . ."

Lynn didn't help the theorizing along, and Chris's voice trailed off.

"Let's go see the damn place," Lynn said.

"I'll call Jack to meet us," Chris agreed. Clearly they needed an investigator.

In the car he and Lynn continued to guess at what had happened, but Lynn kept injecting facts. "We'll ask his family if they know why he was there, and we'll ask the medical examiner if he could have been knocked unconscious before—he was killed. But Mike's own car was at this other house, Chris. If they kidnapped him, how did that happen?"

"They took it too," Chris said, but so lamely Lynn didn't bother to answer.

Unconsciously Chris expected to see El Rojo's bright red Mustang convertible when he and Lynn pulled up in front of the house where Mike had been killed, but the street was empty. An empty quality suffused the whole neighborhood. The little street looked stunted, like the young trees that had been planted by the builder but hadn't developed. The subdivision, like the trees, had never quite caught hold. Chris saw three *For Sale* signs on this one block. The occupied houses looked as if renters lived in them. Their yards were patchy. The paint jobs didn't match, but there wasn't much to distinguish the houses from one another, either. They were small-frame three-bedrooms, somewhat less than fifteen hundred square feet each. The neighborhood, a few miles south of downtown, had been built in this location for no particular reason except that the developer had thought it could blossom into a middle-class enclave in a lower-middle working-class area. It looked as if he'd guessed wrong.

The August sun turned everything crispy: grass, the view to the horizon, tempers. Across the street a young boy bounced a ball against the front of his house. A voice yelled at him from inside to knock it off. The boy eyed Chris and Lynn and tossed the ball again.

"You sure this is it?" Chris asked, because the house where they'd stopped didn't stand out from those around it, except perhaps that its yard was even less tended.

Lynn nodded. As if in confirmation, a nondescript white Ford pulled into the one-car driveway and Jack Fine emerged. He didn't say anything, just held up a key.

When they approached the front door Chris saw tag-ends of yellow police tape that had once marked the place as a crime scene. Someone had torn the tape almost completely away. Maybe the police themselves, because they had finished investigating. Jack unlocked the door and preceded the prosecutors into the interior.

Inside, the house gave itself away immediately. The front door opened directly into a small living room. Two sagging armchairs sat side by side like the thrones of an impoverished kingdom. The thin carpet looked as if it had been chosen abstractly rather than by a family that had to live with it. But the room had no semblance of normality. The walls were covered with graffiti, swastikas being the most recognizable symbols. One wall had been smear-painted black, with slashes of red. The ceiling had also been slashed with paint, and was discolored from smoke.

Here and there Chris saw smudges of fingerprint powder, showing where police had been through the place. Usually the powder struck a jarring note in a family home, but here it looked natural. The house seemed built to be a crime scene. It was impossible to imagine that anyone had ever lived here.

Bags from hamburger places, cigarette butts, and other discards littered the floor. Chris's feet made a scuffling sound as he walked slowly toward the far doorway. When he reached it he looked back and saw that Lynn hadn't followed him. She stood a few feet inside the front door, immobile except for her eyes, which were surveying the small room. Lynn breathed very shallowly, as if afraid of what she might smell. The house had captured her. Very slowly she crossed the room, taking in its decorations in her peripheral vision. She looked straight ahead as if she might lose the pathway, until she passed Chris, heading into the house's interior. Jack came up to guide the tour.

A hallway to the left must have led back to bedrooms. Jack said, "Nothing much to see down there," and turned the other direction. Chris followed him through another doorway into a small kitchen with an electric range and a hole where a refrigerator should have been. Chris turned on one of the stovetop burners and felt slightly relieved when the concentric circles didn't grow warm. The house had no electricity.

"What did they do for lights?" he asked.

Jack had already been through the house with the cops. His

eyes moved from place to place like a man with no sense of nostalgia visiting his boyhood home. "They had big flashlights. But they seem to have favored candles."

He nodded toward the counter containing the kitchen sink. The wall behind the sink ended waist-high so that a person in the kitchen could look out into the next room, a dining area/den. Graffiti and symbols also covered the panelled walls of that room. A Formica table sat in the center of the room as if it had significance. Chris walked around the counter into the den and saw what Jack meant. There were candles everywhere: on the floor, on small tables, some tall enough to stand alone. Against the far wall, behind the table, stood a tall, tarnished silver holder for nine candles. Chris looked at Jack. Were these little would-be Nazis so ignorant they didn't know they were lighting their chamber with a menorah? Jack shrugged.

The room should have been bright, but a thick piece of burlap, nailed right into the wall, covered the one large window, making the room dim even in midafternoon.

"This is where he was killed?"

"Yes." With his eyes Jack indicated the table. Chris walked to it and didn't ask any more questions. Later he would, at the office, but here in the room the killing was too painfully apparent without asking for details: the table, the candles, skinheads wearing hoods, some grotesque ceremony.

"They shaved his head," Jack said. Chris winced. It seemed the cruelest detail. Jack knew it. He didn't say any more.

Chris stood by the metal-legged kitchen table, put his hand on it, and a shock went up his arm. It was the shock of vision: fear and pain still lived in the table. Chris tried to do what he'd come to this house to do, look for the telling details that would make the crime scene vivid for a jury. But the room struck him too forcefully for analysis. The nasty walls closed in on him. He heard sounds that might have been his own: the grunts of someone trying to hold it together through intolerable pain, the hissed breath of someone doing something he knows is horrible.

Chris's hand clenched. Unconsciously he brought it to his chest.

"Chris?"

"Yeah." He turned, thinking he'd composed himself, but when he saw Lynn standing in the doorway from the kitchen he knew he hadn't. Her face looked as tragic as Chris's. She sagged against the wall. Like Chris, she was sucking in the room's poison, making the pain part of her. Her wet eyes met Chris's. Neither of them said anything.

Chris turned his back on the room and walked to the back door of the house, turned its deadbolt and opened the door to the back yard. He felt grateful for the sunlight. The back yard had a little more grass than the front, but it was all stark yellow. The yard sloped down to a cyclone fence that separated it from the yard of the house behind. A woman stood hanging clothes on a line while a toddler circled her feet. She glanced at the strangers emerging from the skinhead house and didn't nod or wave.

"Is she our witness?" Chris asked. Someone had made a 911 call to complain about noise, that was how police had found Mike Martinez's body so shortly after he'd been murdered.

"No, the one next door," Jack said. "She wanted to be anonymous, she didn't realize 911 would record her phone number automatically."

Another innocent trapped by technology. But Donny Sturns and the other suspect had been captured by more routine police methods. After the killing they had gone back to the same teen club and unknowingly fallen into a common pattern of criminality: overstimulated by what they'd seen and done, and probably pharmaceutically as well, they'd gotten into a fight at the club. Police came in response, and witnesses told the officers that before the fight the two had been bragging about killing someone, one of the most common ways newborn murderers get themselves caught. Murder is a crime of passion, not of planning. If police find a body and no one near it, no one in the next room sobbing a confession, they know at once that they are dealing with a criminal of more than ordinary cunning. That had been Lee Griggs. He had had the sense to walk away. He had only been caught because he associated with nitwits.

"Did she see Lee Griggs? Can she identify him?" Talking made Chris's lungs work again. His face and the backs of his hands already felt burned by the sun. He welcomed the sensation.

"She says no," Jack reported, his opinion apparent in the words. "But look at her house. Kids' toys in the yard, but no kids playing outside. No clothes on the line. Weren't any yesterday, either. Housewife with young kids can't go two days without doing laundry."

Maybe she's got a dryer, Chris thought of saying. *Maybe she's not home.* But he knew his investigator would have checked out both possibilities. "She's scared," Jack said. "Calling in a complaint about noisy neighbors doesn't make you too scared to let your kids play outside. I think Lee Griggs came in this back way, cutting through the yard of that empty house next door to her. When he left the same way she looked out and saw him. She says that didn't happen, but I'm going to talk to her again."

"I will," Lynn said. She had followed them out into the sunshine. Jack Fine glanced at her, apparently wondering if Lynn thought she possessed some sympathetic influence over witnesses he lacked.

Chris understood the intensity with which Lynn stared at the witness's back yard. This damned house made him want to act. Do something. Do anything.

"The main thing I want to know right now is why was Mike here. What was his connection to these punks? Why did he meet them?"

Lynn and Jack looked back at Chris with equally bland expressions, just waiting for instructions, offering no speculations. For a moment it struck Chris as odd that two such quick thinkers had gone so suddenly silent.

They had all had enough of the house. Chris turned abruptly and went back inside, walking quickly through the murderous den with his head down. He moved so briskly that the sounds of his own footsteps might have obscured the other, smaller noises, except that once through the kitchen he stopped to wait for Lynn and Jack. In the sudden quiet Chris heard the shuffle from the hallway that led to the bedrooms.

His partners, catching up, saw the alarm on Chris's face. Jack jumped past him, ripping his pistol out from his belt and aiming it rigidly in front of him in the approved police academy style. He found no target down the hallway, but the first bedroom door stood ajar. Chris remembered its having been closed.

Chris pointed toward the door, but before he could whisper or signal he felt a flurry of motion beside him and in his peripheral vision a handgun appeared, coming toward his head. "Shit!" he said with a rush of panic, and scrambled down the hallway toward Jack. The gun followed him. Chris glanced back and saw Lynn holding the gun, a pistol she'd produced out of nowhere. She had it pointed at the ceiling, and her arm shook slightly from the stiffness of her posture.

"What the hell?" Chris said. No one answered him. Jack kicked the bedroom door and it flew back, but didn't hit the wall behind. Lynn leaped past Chris and pointed her gun into the room. Her eyes widened. "Goddamn it," she shouted, and ran into the room.

"No!" Jack screamed. He had thrown himself against the door, holding someone trapped behind it against the wall. Chris hurried to take over the post, pushing the door against someone struggling powerfully. "Okay," Jack said, Chris eased off, and Jack reached behind the door and dragged out a boy of twelve or thirteen who kept struggling until Jack showed him the pistol, close to the boy's nose. The boy went quite still then.

"Lynn!" Jack shouted, risking a glance back over his shoulder.

Chris went to help his assistant, but she didn't need him. She had grabbed another kid by the shoulder and was shaking him.

"What the hell's the matter with you?" she screamed. "What are you doing here?"

The boy, who like his friend looked pe-teenage and African-American, quivered in her grasp. "Nothin', nothin'," he stammered. "We just wanted to look around. We saw this place on the news."

The bedroom stood empty, a room absolutely devoid of personality. The boys must have come into the house through the front door that Jack had unlocked, followed softly behind the prosecutors, but been surprised when Chris had re-entered the house so quickly. He had heard their hurrying footsteps as they'd tried to hide in the bedroom.

"This ain't no damned tourist attraction," Lynn said loudly. She pushed the boy's thin chest. "Out!"

The boy scrambled to obey, brushing past Chris and out the door of the room. Jack and the other one had already vanished. Chris stared rather aghast at Lynn, whose chest heaved and eyes blazed. He understood her reaction. The house, the scene of Mike's murder, had stretched all their nerves already. Hearing the intruders had produced a rush of adrenaline that quickly translated into anger. The body wanted to kill someone. That reaction didn't go away just because the danger turned out to be nonexistent.

Lynn still gripped her pistol, luckily pointed at the floor. "Lynn," Chris said cautiously, but with as much authority as he could muster, "I trust you have a concealed handgun permit."

Lynn stared at him unflinchingly, replacing the gun in her purse while a beat or two of silence passed. "Of course I do," she finally said.

They went outside. Jack stood in the front yard, staring down the street. "They had a buddy waiting for them," he said, "but he took off when he saw me."

The two boys also stared gloomily down the street, where their friend's car had almost driven out of sight. The boys glanced over their shoulders at the prosecutors, then began walking briskly away.

"Those boys don't live in this neighborhood," Chris observed. "They look a little lost."

"Just kids," Lynn said dismissively.

"Yeah," Jack answered, still staring down the street, "but their friend's old enough to drive."

In other circumstances it would have been fun to watch Donny Sturns in a room with Lynn Ransom. Their informant's black hair had grown out into a shapeless burr that made him look even more boyish than his seventeen years. His arms and legs seemed too long for him to manage. Now that he'd thrown in his lot with the prosecution Donny seemed eager to please. Squirming in a chair, he looked comical, but Chris remembered him as a foul-mouthed skinhead dripping hateful remarks. Chris had found some skinhead pamphlets scattered around the abandoned house; vile stuff, racist drivel not even internally consistent. This boy had been part of the group that had formed around such mindless hatred of others. Abstractly he hated "niggers." But when he looked up at Lynn it seemed clearly to be the first time Donny had shared room space with an American of African descent.

Lynn spoke to him as to a child. Not her own child. A child for whom she felt no tenderness but one she'd been stuck caring for. Donny frowned with the concentration of following her. His eyes displayed a different confusion, the war between his racist indoctrination and the reality of Lynn Ransom in front of him. Since the battlefield of this war was Donny's mind, which wasn't large enough to contain such contradictions, he kept sliding back and forth between one perception and another. He'd be listening, trying to please Lynn with his attention, then he'd remember that, oh yeah, she was one of them. His lip would curl like in the old days with his friends, but before his mouth even assumed full sneer position he'd grow afraid that Lynn might read his thoughts and his face would go back to stage one, a blank stare.

Chris would have bet Lynn knew the effect she had on their witness. But she didn't care about educating Donny. She just wanted to get what she could from him as quickly as possible. Lynn didn't treat Donny as the key component of their case against Mike Martinez's killer. She only thought him a tiny puddle of information that might evaporate at any moment.

"You and your friends didn't just happen to bump into Mike Martinez at the teen club, did you? He was there to meet you, right?"

"Right. I think so."

"What do you mean you think? Look kid, don't try to tell me what you think I want to hear, 'cause you don't *know* what I want to hear. Just tell me what you really know, okay?"

"Well I don't know," Donny whined. "Lee set all that up. You know, I wasn't in on that."

"You must've heard something, though, about what they'd said to Mike."

"Sure," Donny said, but stopped to think while Lynn crossed her arms and almost tapped her foot in impatience.

Chris stood back and let her work. The trio were in his office. The prosecutors had had Donny brought over from the jail, thinking he might breathe more easily and therefore talk more freely away from the building that also housed Lee Griggs. The setting of Chris's office was also supposed to promote intimacy. The distasteful part of being a prosecutor is having to befriend one's witnesses. Sometimes they grow genuinely friendly toward each other, the criminals and the prosecutors. At some point before trial this little group had to bond into a team. So far there seemed no danger of that happening.

"I was at the house, waiting," Donny said. "With the others. Lee and Yvonne were meeting your friend at the club."

"Yvonne?" Lynn said.

"Lee's girlfriend. He liked to take her along at the start of deals. He said it'd make the guy relax. Think nothing was going on. Maybe Yvonne liked being in on it, too, I don't know."

Chris and Lynn looked at each other. Another name. Donny didn't seem to know he'd said anything significant.

"So was Yvonne at the house too?" Chris asked.

"No, she didn't come. I guess she stayed at the club."

Donny obviously preferred being questioned by the white district attorney. He leaned toward Chris, almost eager. Chris looked at Lynn to resume the questioning, but when she didn't he asked, "So what was the deal? What did they say to Mike Martinez to get him to the house?"

"We were buying something from him," Donny said indifferently.

Chris didn't follow that statement at all. He glanced at Lynn, who stared at their informant as if she didn't believe a word he said. "Buying what?" Chris asked Donny.

"I don't know. Can I stand up?" Donny stood and stretched, shuffled a couple of steps toward the windows of Chris's office. He was a tall boy, thin but with large hands. Probably mean in a fight, when the odds were all on his side. Donny turned and rubbed his hands together and gave Chris an odd look: embarrassment. Occasionally Donny would remember that he was describing how he and his friends had murdered Chris's friend, and then he would give the District Attorney this totally inadequate glance of apology: *Gosh, sorry about that.* The look made Chris want to beat the shit out of him. This time Donny saw that.

He wet his lips and said nervously, "Guns, I think. Lee had a new gun when he came in the house and he thought it was funny that he'd gotten it from—from your friend."

Chris went on with the interview in the approved way—casually, as if he already knew more than Donny about the whole transaction—but inside he was seething.

Chris took time to think about the interview with Donny, and then he remembered the way Jack and Lynn had fallen strangely silent in the skinhead house. Chris went looking for his partners and found them together. He stopped in the doorway of Lynn's small office and when Lynn and Jack looked up at him he said, "Is somebody going to let me in on what everybody seems to know about Mike, or are we going to wait and let me be surprised by it at trial?"

Lynn and Jack didn't glance at each other guiltily and they didn't make any feeble denials. After a moment Jack said, "I wasn't sure that's what'd been going on, but I thought maybe. Mike had this—sideline. Once in a while he'd check out confiscated stuff at the police impound. If he found something he liked he'd make an offer and likely as not—you know, everybody liked Mike—they'd let him buy it before it went to auction."

"Stuff like what?"

"Anything. Bicycles were good. Stolen stuff that never got reclaimed. Anything that could be resold."

Lynn said, "Mike's parents have a resale shop. He'd pass the stuff on to them, they'd sell it for a profit. It didn't seem to hurt anyone."

Chris hadn't known anything about Mike Martinez's parents. Lynn obviously had. She and others in the office had known about Mike's sideline business, too. Everyone—cops, prosecutors—had looked the other way because it had seemed harmless enough even though it was, technically, illegal. Those confiscated items should be sold to the highest bidder, the money going into the county or city treasury.

El Rojo had been meeting with the skinhead Lee Griggs in order to sell him something. Mike hadn't been confronting Griggs, he'd been making a business deal.

"Guns? He was going to sell confiscated weapons to a gang of skinheads?"

"He probably didn't know they were skinheads," Jack said, making excuses for his dead friend. "They were wearing caps when he met them at the club. All Mike had to sell were a couple of pistols, not automatic weapons or anything—stuff they could just as easily have bought at a pawnshop."

Chris found this a sad revelation. Mike had gone to meet his murderers with a profit motive in his heart. There's never a clean pitched battle between good and evil. Both sides spend too much time consorting with the enemy. Malachi Reese would unwind from murder and blackmail by carrying meals to shut-ins. Mike Martinez took an occasional break from prosecuting criminals to steal from the taxpayers.

"Makes the whole thing seem a little sordid, doesn't it?" Chris said sadly. He wondered if a jury would see it that way: as just a transaction between criminals that had gone awry, with El Rojo getting more or less what he'd deserved.

"So he wasn't pristine," Lynn said fiercely. She didn't spend time brooding over good and evil, and she wouldn't let this case dwindle away because her trial partner went philosophical. The look in her eyes almost blew Chris's hair back. "So he had this little sideline that didn't hurt anybody and these goddamned skinheads found out about it and used it to rob him and kill him. This wasn't some business deal gone bad. This was them luring Mike in because they wanted to murder him. Let them bring that up at trial. I'll rip them apart."

Chris believed her.

————

Preparation for the trial of Lee Griggs obsessed Chris, but he discovered that Anne didn't want to hear about it. She didn't say so directly, but he soon learned from the way she looked away, offered no comment, and changed the subject as soon as possible, that he needed to find other things to talk to Anne about during their frequent dinners and nights together. He didn't talk about her safety, either. Nothing else had happened to Anne since the burglary of her house. She seemed safe. Still, Chris preferred being with her after sundown, for all kinds of reasons.

Anne knew them all. One night as they walked through downtown San Antonio after dinner, from the crowded Riverwalk to emptier streets near where they'd parked, she felt the pressure of his gaze and she smiled and said, "We're not really this important to each other, you know. That's just an illusion, because we got thrown together during all this. . . ."

"But if you believe in the illusion it can become reality, can't it?" Chris asked.

Chris put his hand on her neck and felt her tension: the emotion that wanted to grip him, the control that kept her from it.

"What's the matter?"

"Nothing." Anne's eyes were shining. She reached for his hand and pulled him toward the parking lot where her car waited.

Apparently in Donny Sturns' sessions with Lynn and Chris the ex-skinhead discovered that he liked to talk. Chris woke the Tuesday after Labor Day, three weeks after Mike Martinez's murder, to discover that his prime witness had given a newspaper interview. In stark newsprint the few details Donny gave of the killing were horrifying. Then Donny talked about his former leader, and the interview turned more chilling. "Lee's bragged that he'll do other people when he gets out. He likes it. He won't stop."

Chris could sense the gentle pressure from the newspaper interviewer as Donny expanded. Lee Griggs idolized Adolf Hitler, Donny said. Mass murder was his ambition. Donny, his one-time disciple, made Griggs sound like the worst menace San Antonio had ever faced.

The last paragraph made Chris's mouth close tightly. The story concluded, as other news stories in the next few weeks would conclude, that luckily the prosecution's case against Lee Griggs appeared airtight, and was being handled personally by a District Attorney everyone in America knew to be a very resourceful trial lawyer.

Gloomy premonition settled on Chris.

Chapter 12

Summer ended, technically speaking. The heat didn't let go in any sense. Early autumn is warm in San Antonio, if not outright hot. The city's tension didn't break in a fall thunderstorm. No cold front cooled passions. El Rojo had been murdered in a hate-crime; the indictment Chris obtained called it that. Even one such well-publicized killing reinforced the fear that anyone could be murdered at any time by strangers for no good reason.

Through this atmosphere Chris Sinclair and Lynn Ransom pursued their investigation like two people who happened to arrive at the same party without having known the other would be there. They didn't have much to discuss about their case against Lee Griggs, which seemed very straightforward. Sometimes Lynn and Jack went out on their own to view evidence or question potential witnesses. Chris brooded alone. Lynn still studied him, gauging her boss's sincerity. Chris spent no energy trying to win her over. In a way he liked her watchfulness. It seemed like having the city at his elbow.

He and Lynn went together to find Yvonne, Lee Griggs' girl-friend. She worked at a Whataburger on the city's northwest side, the most heavily populated and fastest growing section of San Antonio, the main direction white flight had taken. The neighborhood where they found Yvonne looked like the most bulging corner of any big city: expressway, strip centers, traffic-clogged streets, franchise restaurants.

The prosecutors chose their time well, three o'clock in the afternoon, long after lunch, before the after-school crowd. The small dining area had been cleaned, the grill turned off. Chris and Lynn identified themselves to the manager, who said Yvonne could take a break. Was she in trouble?

"No. Just maybe a witness," Chris said reassuringly, wondering what the truth might be.

When Yvonne came slowly toward them Chris thought the manager must have made a mistake. The girl's skin looked smooth and firm—and brown. She was a pretty girl with big eyes and pouty lips and she seemed more than a touch, um, Hispanic. Her last name, Davis, didn't mean much by way of ethnic identity in San Antonio. If Lee Griggs dated this girl seriously, that made him more complicated than he seemed. Chris didn't like complexity in a defendant.

"Yvonne Davis?" Lynn said.

"Mmm huh."

"Your manager said you can take a break to talk to us, if that's okay with you."

Yvonne shrugged, which became an exaggerated glide as she slid into the plastic seat of a small booth. Chris and Lynn took the other side, squeezed together. Chris frankly studied the girl in her orange and white uniform, designed to be worn more perkily than Yvonne did today. She didn't appear sullen or glaring, but her posture made it clear she knew who they were and what they wanted and they had no chance of putting anything over on her.

Chris was just old enough that to his eye the important years between eighteen and twenty-two didn't display themselves on faces. Yvonne's age appeared to be somewhere in that range: old enough to vote and to be out of high school, too young to serve liquor.

Lynn began in a businesslike tone that left open the possibility of sympathy. "You know we're prosecuting Lee Griggs?"

"Yes."

"And he's your boyfriend." Lynn paused, the girl barely nodded, Lynn continued as if it hadn't been a question. "So of course you won't want to cooperate with us. You've probably talked to Lee's lawyer?"

Yvonne shook her head. "I want to stay out of it."

"I understand, but you're not out of it. You were there that night, the night of the murder."

"No," Yvonne said sharply.

"Not at the house, maybe, but at the club ahead of time. You met Mike Martinez. Don't lie, Yvonne, a lot of people saw you."

Yvonne sat up straighter. "Okay. I saw him at the club. But I didn't know what was going to happen."

A little paper hat confined Yvonne's long black hair to the top and sides of her head, but when she shook it a long tail fell down her back. She glanced at Chris, who hadn't spoken. He imagined her smiling, and imagined himself Mike Martinez, looking into her brown eyes and, as Lee Griggs had planned, relaxing his guard.

Not that Yvonne looked like a *femme fatale,* or even a teenaged flirt. She had a seriousness about her, as if fun had been extinguished early in her life. She seemed a little fragile, too, which might have appealed to the arrogance in Lee Griggs, and made Chris feel like a bully just sitting across the table from her.

"You're going to have to convince me of that," Lynn said. "If you did know what your boyfriend had planned, that makes you a party to murder. We've indicted everybody else we know was involved, and I will indict you too."

Yvonne's eyes blinked widely and she looked angry for the first time. "You don't threaten me."

"That's right, I don't. I just tell you what's going to happen. You just answer two or three simple questions for me and maybe you can stay mostly out of it."

"I can say no, can't I?" Yvonne asked. She glanced at Chris.

But Lynn wouldn't let her attention go. "You can here in the Whataburger. But then one of two things will happen, maybe both. We'll charge you with capital murder. Or we'll call you as a witness at trial and if you refuse to answer there we'll ask the judge to hold you in contempt and put you in jail."

Lynn had a natural talent for the bad-cop role. Even when threatening, her voice didn't sound angry, only very sure.

The three of them sat silent for a minute, then Lynn spoke again. The sympathy that had lurked in her voice throughout her questioning had come to the foreground. She extended her hand along the table toward Yvonne. "Listen, girl, you don't want to be in jail. Not now."

Chris didn't know what Lynn's emphasis on the last word meant. Yvonne did. Her cheeks reddened. She dropped her eyes.

"You seeing a doctor?" Lynn continued. "You have to, you know. You can't make that up later. You have to stay very healthy now." Yvonne looked up, her cheeks glowed brighter, and she didn't answer. Lynn took a pen and one of her cards from her purse. "I'm going to give you the name of a doctor. You go see her. You do, I'm going to check. If you need a ride, you call me."

Lynn held the card out. When Yvonne kept her hands under the table Lynn said, "Don't worry, she's white." Yvonne laughed a sort of gasping exhalation of relief and took the card. She tapped its edges against the tabletop.

"So now you're gonna be my friend?" Yvonne asked.

"I doubt that. There's just some times in life you especially have to take care of yourself. I just want your kid to be healthy and smart so I don't have to put him in jail fifteen or twenty years from now."

The pregnancy wasn't apparent to Chris. Yvonne's uniform top was rather loose, but certainly not tentlike. Her cheeks were rather plump. Maybe Lynn had seen something in her walk.

Maybe Lynn had a great familiarity with pregnant women. Who knew? She had certainly guessed right.

"I'm going to call you as a witness," Lynn said. "Here's what I'm going to ask. How did you and Lee meet Mike in the teen club? What did you talk about? Everybody saw the three of you together, I can prove that anyway. The conversation just tells me how much you were involved."

"I wasn't," Yvonne said quickly, then paused to let them know she wasn't going to let herself be manipulated. But she continued. "I thought Lee was maybe just going to cheat him. Mr. Martinez was going to sell him something, that's what we talked about, and I thought maybe Lee wasn't planning to pay him, that's all."

Chris asked his first question. "How did Lee know to contact Mike Martinez in the first place?"

"I don't know. Lee had a way of finding out things like that. I don't know. He liked to be mysterious, you know?"

"But you knew from the beginning it was some kind of scheme," Lynn said.

"No. A trick maybe. Like a joke. I didn't know it would be this. Not killing. I still don't think Lee could've—done—what they say he did. Somebody else in the gang, maybe."

She looked scared and close to tears and therefore very sincere. "I won't ask you about that," Lynn said gently. "Just about the meeting ahead of time. Okay?"

The girl nodded, shamefaced. As she looked down at the card in her hands, Lynn and Chris looked at each other for the first time since they'd entered the Whataburger. Let the girlfriend hold on to her illusions, if she could. They had another witness to say Mike's killing had been premeditated murder. All they needed from Yvonne was what she'd just agreed to give: the details of the trap the skinhead leader had used to lure Mike in. Chris and Lynn had just heard the sound of the last piece of their case clicking into place.

Chris stood at his desk in the late afternoon. He wore a suit, but his tie was pulled askew, and his hand in his pocket kept rattling his change, over and over, like a man losing count. Into the phone Chris said to Anne Greenwald, "But I thought I had a great case against Malachi Reese, too. Then something happened. I'm waiting for something to happen in this one, too. I've got Donny Sturns in protective custody; I don't think Reese can get to him. I can't think of any other important——"

"If you were my patient," Anne interrupted, "I'd be writing 'indications of paranoia' in your folder right now."

Chris smiled. His hand stopped jittering in his pocket. He pictured Anne at her own desk, in the clinic a few blocks away at Santa Rosa Hospital. She'd be leaning back. She would have slipped her shoes off and might be massaging one foot. Outside her office, someone would be waiting to see her.

"Do your patients call you like this," Chris asked, "looking for reassurance?"

"All the time," Anne answered, spacing out the words. "One way I know they're getting better is when they stop calling so much."

"I don't think that's going to happen in this case," Chris said. His shoulders had noticeably relaxed. He wondered how soon he could knock off work for the day and wander over in the direction of the Santa Rosa.

He didn't hear whatever Anne said next because his office door came open hard enough to hit the wall. Jack Fine hurried in, his arms full. "Chris!" he said sharply.

The investigator didn't call his boss by name very often. Chris didn't remember his ever saying it in this tone, as if a friend were in trouble. "I've got to go," Chris said into the phone. "I'll call you later."

"What is it?" Anne's voice sharpened too.

"Nothing bad. I'll call you.

"What?" he said as he hung up and Jack Fine came beside him and dumped his armful of things onto Chris's desk.

"Remember those kids?" the investigator said without preamble. "The ones who came wandering into the skinhead gang house like it was the wax museum open to the public?"

Yes, Chris vaguely remembered the intruders. Much sharper was his memory of Lynn pulling her pistol out of nowhere and cocking it right next to Chris's ear.

"I followed them outside and found a car waiting for them, remember?" Jack continued. "I got the license plate number. Guess who it's registered to?" Jack couldn't help pausing for emphasis. "Councilman Win Phillips."

Chris winced. "Oh God, Jack, please don't tell me—"

Jack quickly raised a hand. "I'm not implicating the city councilman. He was giving a speech that afternoon, somebody gave him a ride. Nobody knows where his own car was. Supposed to be back at his district office. But this guy drove the car sometimes."

Jack picked out of the pile on Chris's desk a photograph of a very young face, one that had a certain defiance in the tilt of his chin. Chris picked it up and stared into the boy's dark eyes, which seemed to look back at him. Something in that dark stare urged a memory on Chris. . . .

"Is this a mug shot?"

"Juvenile probation," Jack confirmed. "Two years ago when he was fourteen. But he's gone straight since then. Does volunteer work for Phillips, and the councilman points him out as an example of how a young man from a bad environment can turn his life around."

"Do you recognize him? Did you see him in the car outside the skinhead house that day?"

"That was him," Jack said without doubt. Jack Fine remembered faces. He'd been trained for it and he concentrated. Chris

Sinclair had never had to do that. The young man in the photo looked familiar to him, but why?

"He sat in the car outside the skinhead house that day and sent his two little friends inside to check out what we were doing, while he lurked in the background. Pretty smart for a kid."

Chris's shoulder blades tingled. He looked again into the face in the photograph.

"Now look," Jack continued, eagerness betraying itself in his voice. He unrolled a much larger photo, a group shot. A crowd of people stood in the sun, but they weren't posed for a formal picture. Then the faces began to look familiar.

"The crowd at the crack house demolition."

"Right," Jack said. "Just before you found Mr. Rodriguez inside. Look."

He stabbed one face in the crowd with his finger. Chris studied it. A young black man staring over the shoulders of two other spectators.

"God, Jack, I can't tell . . ."

"I can. Besides, I had it isolated and blown up." Jack found another photo in the pile of things he'd dropped on Chris's desk, a much better, bigger picture of the young face. Blowing up the face had robbed it of its edges, but made it easier to identify. Chris could read the young man's expression now. The face stared much more eagerly than the people around him. Chris saw expectancy in that stare. And a smile.

Why would anyone be smiling in that crowd? Had Mayor Foley just cracked a joke on the porch of the crack house? Unlikely, on that solemn occasion. No one else in the larger crowd picture looked remotely entertained. But this teenager watched happily. Chris held the photo a long time, until he would never forget it. In the boy's smile, as in his stare, he thought he recognized another face.

"My God," he finally said. "Is he Malachi Reese's son?"

"I wish I knew," Jack said. "Nobody seems to know who his

father was. The father's never been in the picture, at least in public. This young man's name is Malcolm."

"Malcolm?"

"Malcolm Turner. Same last name as his unwed mother." Jack's voice didn't accuse, just made observations. If the mother had never married, the father could be anyone. "He has that minor juvenile record, that's all. But—"

"You don't have to convince me," Chris said. He dropped the photo as if it had bugs crawling on it. "Pick him up. Have him arrested."

"For what?" Jack said. Now his own urgency had died. He walked around Chris's desk, shoulders slumped. "Hanging around in a crowd? Trespassing at the skinhead house?"

"How about unauthorized use of Phillips' car?"

"I strongly doubt the councilman would press those charges." Jack had obviously already considered the possibility and dismissed it.

"He's the one," Chris said. He didn't know where his certainty had come from, but it possessed him. "And I don't want him running around loose while I'm trying this case. Pick him up. I don't care if it turns out to be a bad arrest later on—"

"There's one thing we could have him arrested for," Jack said carefully. "If you recognize him as being one of the shooters who shot at you and Anne on Flores Street that day."

An awkward pause passed slowly. Chris looked at the face in the photos and tried to remember the dark interior of that evil Pontiac as gunfire poured out of it. He pictured a dark face wearing a headband.

"I think so," Chris finally said.

With extreme neutrality Jack asked, "Will you swear to it?"

To obtain an arrest warrant, they would need a sworn statement from a victim of a crime, swearing that this young man had done it. After another long pause, Chris said quietly, "Yes."

The word acted as a starting gun for Jack Fine. Suddenly he

was in a hurry again. Gathering up his materials, he said, "I'll bring you an affidavit. It's right, Chris, I'm sure of it. Maybe when I arrest him we'll find more evidence." In the doorway, just before he closed the door, he said, like a benedictory prayer, "Maybe if we get real real lucky he's still got the knife he used on Mr. Rodriguez."

Chris nodded. Amen. Jack left.

Chris stood picturing that smile, the one shared by Malcolm Turner and Malachi Reese. Soon, in a day or two, they'd have Malachi's henchman in custody. Chris could breathe a little easier knowing Reese's killer wouldn't be on the streets to try to ruin this trial as he'd tried to intervene in the last one. The prosecution team had made one more successful foray against Malachi Reese.

And so trial began.

The parking garage felt oppressive, as always, with its dimness, trapped air clogged with exhaust, and the rumble of engines vibrating the floor. But when Chris walked out into the October sunlight the morning Lee Griggs' trial would begin, he felt the first hint of fall in the air. Heat didn't blanket the city as thickly as it had for months.

He also approached his job more easily because there hadn't been protestors in front of the Justice Center in weeks. Maybe things were returning to normal.

But the first day of trial had brought out a small crowd. The sight of them made Chris feel weary, but then he approached the protestors curiously. What did they have to protest about this prosecution? Maybe Griggs had some skinhead supporters, but if the defendant was smart he would have asked his crowd to lay low. As for anyone else, Chris couldn't see where moral indignation had a place to stand in his prosecuting a white thug for killing one of Chris's own assistants.

Sure enough, the protestors didn't display a solid front. Chris saw two of them arguing, a large African-American man with a sign and an equally imposing black woman in a suit. No, she wasn't a protestor. She was, of course, Lynn Ransom. Not one to maintain a dignified silence and pass controversy quickly by, Lynn had stopped to answer back to the man who had yelled at her. Chris came abreast of them just as the discussion reached its peak.

"Just stay out of it, bitch! Let the whites and browns all kill each other."

"They can!" Lynn shouted back. "Except nobody touches my friends."

Chris took her arm and kept moving, and Lynn let herself be pulled away. They went through the front doors of the Justice Center and around the short line of people waiting to pass through the metal detectors. Prosecutors and judges were exempt from the electronic searches. Going up the wide stairs, Chris said, "I'm sorry. I told you it might be hard on you. If you——"

Lynn laughed out loud. "If that was your idea of a scary encounter, you've led a sheltered life."

"I guess I have," Chris said. "Up until recently."

Another crowded courtroom. This one seemed more abuzz with curiosity than with hostility. Chris didn't feel he had to watch his back as he strode to the front of the room with Lynn.

The defendant and his lawyer were already in place; Lee Griggs was sitting at the defense table wearing a cheap black suit. Cheap was probably good. He could have decided to dress so well he looked too smooth, too fastidious to have been involved in something as messy as this case. But a smooth appearance wouldn't engender jury sympathy. The cheap suit made Griggs look like one of them, a working class boy the prosecution was trying to squeeze into a murderer's role that fit him as poorly as his suit did. Calculation had gone into the defendant's clothing. His lawyer was on the job.

The defense lawyer straightened from talking with her client. She looked rather slight, and not very sure of herself. She was a shark in pantyhose.

Chris almost didn't recognize Gloria Files. The last time he'd seen her she'd been blond. Today she had medium length dark hair and a good tan. Goodness, had she become Hispanic? *Whatever works* could have been Gloria Files' motto. She smiled at the district attorney and said, "Good morning, Chris."

"Ms. Files." She was one of the very few criminal lawyers in town with whom Chris didn't want to be on a first-name basis. There is usually an easygoing camaraderie in the criminal law world, even between adversaries. There's no money at stake, no reason to go for one another's throats. But Gloria Files came out of a different tradition. She had been an up-and-coming young associate at a good civil firm when she'd done something so underhanded in a products liability case that when it was discovered the judge had sanctioned the firm, which had in turn dismissed Gloria. A civil firm's firing a lawyer for being too devious is akin to Satan kicking one of his demons out of Hell for excessive cruelty to the customers, but Gloria Files had managed it. Soon after that she had surprised people by opening her own office and specializing in criminal law. She had decided quite deliberately that the smartest lawyers generally weren't to be found practicing in the criminal world, and a tough, aggressive lawyer could make a quick name for herself there. She had been right. In only a year or so she'd become prominent enough to attract a high-profile client like Lee Griggs.

Gloria Files was short, and wore very high heels that sometimes made her walk a little awkwardly. They also made her legs appear long, so that her figure seemed to bunch up at her bust and hips. Some lawyers had suggested that she appeared a bit

gawky in a deliberate attempt to endear herself to judges and ju-
ries. Whatever worked.

In the weeks of investigation that had turned up no certain
link between Mike Martinez's murder and Malachi Reese, Chris
had lost his certainty that Reese had somehow engineered the
killing. But with Gloria Files for the defense he remained wary
that the case would take an unexpected twist.

Chris and Lynn walked around the State's table, so their backs
were to the judge's bench and the jury box. They looked at the
audience, where potential jurors would sit to be instructed on the
law and questioned. This position also gave Chris a chance to get
a good look at Lee Griggs. In his white shirt and narrow tie the
defendant looked dressed up for his high school graduation,
much younger than his twenty-one years. His hair had grown out
nicely, still short as a military school cadet's. He kept his head
down. When his eyes came up they glanced shyly at Chris. Chris
stared at him, remembering Mike. Griggs grew a little smile, as
if he could read the district attorney's mind and they shared a
pleasant memory.

Chris wanted to tell Griggs not to think himself such a mastermind. In fact he had acted only as a puppet for a mind much
more far-reaching. Chris would almost have made a deal with the
skinhead in exchange for a chance to question him freely, to ex-
plore the connection through which Malachi Reese had somehow pointed Griggs in Mike Martinez's direction.

But however cunning or stupid Lee Griggs might be, he was
what Sergeant Esparza had called him, a bad, bad piece of work.
He worked at being as evil as he was capable of being. No deal
would be offered. Chris planned to prosecute Griggs to the fullest
extent he could. He stared at the young man with the soft smile.
Chris thought of him in that room with Mike, smoke be-
smirching the air and a pack of young fools grinning and baying.
Something seemed to slither behind Lee Griggs' eyes.

Either Griggs gave up on trying to charm the district attorney, or he didn't have his true nature as carefully controlled as his appearance implied, because just before the jury panel entered the room the defendant leaned close to the prosecution table and, looking straight at Lynn, said to Chris, "I see you're recruiting out of Dumpsters these days."

Chris put out a hand to restrain Lynn, but it wasn't necessary. She sat watching Griggs with quiet but unrelenting hatred. "If they offered me a billion dollars," she said, "I wouldn't be your white ass for one day after you get to prison."

Griggs grinned.

Jury selection required delicate maneuvering. Chris wanted to question potential jurors about their racial attitudes, but that might not be a part of the trial at all. The defense would probably deny that Lee Griggs had killed Mike at all, not contesting whether the murder had been a hate-crime. Besides, what good would such questioning do? People won't admit to their prejudices. So after the ritualistic questioning, when Chris and Lynn sat alone in a small court conference room to make their peremptory strikes, they were thrown back on their own prejudices. The obvious strategies were for the defense to try to load the jury with Anglos like the defendant, the prosecution to fill the jury box with minorities who would be more likely to sympathize with Mike Martinez. So Chris and Lynn went down the jury list making minimal comments, tossing white people off the jury, until Chris balked at one.

"Damn it, this guy would make a good juror for us. Worked at the same job for twenty-five years, raised four children, never been in trouble. . . ."

Lynn interrupted, "Chris, if Mike was here, this guy wouldn't be able to stand him. He thinks people should stay in their places, they shouldn't—"

"But he's not going to see Mike Martinez strutting around the courtroom. He's going to see this."

Chris pulled one of the autopsy photos out of a file folder. "You think she's going to try to justify *this*? Appeal to some racial intolerance to say Mike had this coming because he was too cocky or some damned thing?"

Lynn didn't flinch from the photo. But she said relentlessly, "You don't understand." It seemed to Chris he'd been told that a lot lately.

Lynn kept her voice down, but richness began to fill it, making the words bloated with feeling. "People don't say these things out loud. They don't even think them in sentences. But there's this little infestation, it crawls into your skull right back here and says you've got to keep these people in their places. Even with decent people, there's this subliminal message that, yeah, they should have equal schools and nice houses, but not in my neighborhood. Not with my children."

She fell silent, seeing Chris staring at her. There was no point in his answering. Impossible to deny receiving subliminal messages.

"That's not true of everybody," he said. But he took his marker and drew a thick black line through the white juror's name.

So a very mixed group of twelve citizens finally took their seats in the jury box and looked expectantly at Judge Lois Henrichs. The judge in turn handed over the show to the prosecutors. "Call your first witness."

Chris and Lynn had decided to present their case a little unusually. The common prosecutorial wisdom is to call the second most vivid witness first, saving the strongest until last. The first witness should set the scene of the crime for the jury. Instead

Chris and Lynn had decided to smack them in the faces with the horror of the crime.

"Dr. Parmenter, your Honor."

The medical examiner came briskly up the aisle and took the witness oath matter-of-factly, then sat and looked directly at Chris. Dr. Hal Parmenter wore a blue shirt and a diagonally striped tie, but no jacket, as if he'd come straight out of his office and just doffed his lab coat along the way, which was probably true. A thin, serious man, the medical examiner also had an amazingly goofy grin that sometimes broke through in the most peculiar settings, but that wouldn't happen today.

Chris said, "Dr. Parmenter, would you please tell us what qualifies you to be the medical examiner for Bexar County?"

Gloria Files stood and said, as if extending a professional courtesy, "We'll stipulate to Dr. Parmenter's credentials."

"Thank you, but I'd like the jury to hear them," Chris answered. So Dr. Parmenter went through the list of his medical degrees, residencies, specialized training, and autopsies performed, well over a thousand in his eight years in the medical examiner's office.

"I guess with all your experience you can learn a lot from examining a body," Chris said in a folksy tone that sometimes crept over him during trial.

"Yes, an amazing amount of information," the doctor agreed. "But sometimes with surprising omissions. And always that essential mystery remains."

"What do you mean?"

Looking at his hands, Dr. Parmenter said slowly, "You can take a car that's smashed into pieces and a good mechanic can work on it, restore it, and when it's done he can drive it to California. But I see a body that's relatively undamaged, I can fix what's wrong with it quite easily, but he's gone. I could put the body in perfect working order again, but it wouldn't do a bit of good. The animating force is gone. What became of it?"

Chris sat surprised. He and his witness hadn't planned this. Dr.

Parmenter had come to court in a strange mood. Gloria Files was caught off guard too, so she hadn't objected. She stared at Chris, waiting for him to try to spring the punch line to this philosophical testimony, but all Chris could do was return to the mundane.

"Dr. Parmenter, on August third of this year did you conduct an autopsy on a person named Miguel Martinez, known as Mike?"

"I did."

"How was he identified to you?"

"I knew him personally," the doctor said, looking down.

"Was that an unusual circumstance for you?"

"Very. It was only the second time I've performed an autopsy on someone I knew when he was alive."

Perhaps that accounted for Dr. Parmenter's reflective mood this afternoon. Chris resisted the urge to delve into his witness's feelings. "Could you describe for us Mr. Martinez's condition?"

"A healthy adult male in his late twenties," the doctor said by rote, barely glancing at his report. "Approximately sixty-nine inches tall, weighing approximately a hundred and fifty-two pounds. That's—after the loss of a great deal of blood. No sign of disease or other disability."

"Injuries?"

"Oh yes. Extensive injuries. I've seldom seen a body so traumatized, even in a major car wreck."

"What type of injuries, Doctor?" Chris felt Lynn stiffen beside him. He, too, had tightened up, his throat wanting to close and choke off his voice. Chris groped for and failed to find the clinical detachment he'd always been able to achieve during trials.

"There were a lot of cuts, the kind made by a knife blade. Almost all of them were superficial, but there were many. Long cuts down the fronts of both thighs. To the arms. On his face here, here, and a fairly deep one on the forehead." Dr. Parmenter made a diagram of his own face, leaving red lines with his fingernails that slowly went away as he continued talking. "Most of the cuts were on his chest and abdomen. I've indicated on the graph here—"

"Are you referring to a written report, Doctor?"

"Yes, the autopsy report that I made at the time."

"Was that report made during the normal course of business by a person who had personal knowledge—"

"No objection," Gloria Files said peremptorily. She sat tight-lipped, angry at the emotional nature of Dr. Parmenter's testimony, to which there was no good way for her to object.

Judge Henrichs ruled with a trace of irony, "If you're offering the report into evidence, it will be admitted."

"Thank you, your Honor. That's State's Exhibit One. Doctor, you were saying?"

"On page two of the report there's a diagram of a human body where I've drawn in many of the cuts. On Mike's chest it looked as if someone had tried to cut a crude design, that would have dripped blood rather extensively."

Chris didn't ask questions about the design. Jurors could puzzle over it to their own satisfaction. It was angular, could have been a swastika, could have been a hexagram. It had been bloody with Mike's blood, that was what mattered.

"Doctor, you characterized these cuts as superficial. Do you have an opinion about whether they would have been painful?"

"I'm sure they were. A paper cut hurts like hell. But you can chop off your arm in a thresher and you get that endorphin rush so fast you don't feel anything. It's the more minor cuts that hurt the most."

The prosecution had called the medical examiner as a hammer with which Chris could pound pain into the jury, but instead Chris was the one being hurt. He kept flashing back to that room in that awful house, the table that had hurt his hand. Dr. Parmenter's testimony put Mike there so that Chris kept seeing him. He didn't realize how long he'd paused until Lynn laid her hand on his arm.

"Besides cuts, were there other types of injuries, Doctor?"

"Bruises," Dr. Parmenter said quickly. "Again on the face, the top of his head, a large one on his right arm. Contusions, several of those."

"Which means what, Doctor?"

"A contusion is a scrape, basically. The worst of those were on his neck. All around the neck, but particularly across the front."

"What does that mean to you, Doctor?"

"A ligature. Something tied around his neck, tight enough to choke him. He must have been held down or held back, so that when he tried to get up or move forward the rope scraped the front of his neck. I know it was a rope because we found hemp fibers in the scrapes."

Chris spoke quietly, wanting to be nothing more than an off-stage voice. The jurors' attention was riveted on the medical examiner. "What killed Mike, Doctor?"

"I could say any number of things. Overall shock to the system. Bleeding. He would have gone unconscious, maybe more than once, from the choking. On his face around his nose and eyes were broken blood vessels that indicate straining for air. That kind of struggle can lead to heart attack. But I think what killed him is the one deep stab wound just beneath his ribs on his left side. There were also cuts on his hands, what we call defensive wounds, meaning he tried to block the knife or grab it. You can follow a line of one of those cuts, all along the inside of his arm, then into the wound in his abdomen. As if he lunged forward and tried to grab the knife and his attacker stabbed him. It was a deep cut and it cut an artery. Mike Martinez would have bled to death very quickly after that."

This conclusion offered some perverse relief. His friends could believe Mike had fought back and his killer had stabbed him sooner and deeper than he'd intended, cutting short Mike's pain as well as his life.

"I pass the witness," Chris said, and turned to his assistant to see if he'd forgotten anything. There were a couple of notes on

Lynn's legal pad from early in Dr. Parmenter's testimony, then her note-taking had stopped.

Meanwhile Gloria Files was saying thoughtfully, "Doctor, your description sounds like a man who was in a knife fight."

"I'd say it was a man who was tortured," Dr. Parmenter said sharply. Usually he was bland and easy with defense lawyers.

"Well, that's one interpretation," Files said reasonably, "but those slashes on his arms and chest could have been made by an opponent trying to make Mr. Martinez back away from him, couldn't they?"

"But that doesn't account for the other injuries."

"I'll get to them. Would you answer my question, please, Doctor?"

"Yes," the medical examiner said almost sullenly.

"Yes, he could have sustained those cuts during a fight?"

"Yes."

"Thank you, Doctor. And the bruises and the contusions you described, you've seen similar injuries on someone who's been in a fight, right?"

"Yes, similar."

"Even what you characterized as the fatal wound, that could have been inflicted by someone who was trying to protect himself, couldn't it?"

Glaring at her, Dr. Parmenter said, "I can't read the mind of somebody I haven't examined."

"Well, exactly."

"But your explanation leaves out the rope burns and the main fact, that his head was shaved."

"You didn't mention that before, Doctor. Mr. Martinez's head was shaved?"

"Yes, it's in my report."

"That couldn't be called an injury, could it, Doctor? A shaved head is rather fashionable these days. Many athletes—"

"This one was inflicted on him," the doctor said emphatically.

"He was nicked and cut in the process, scraped. There were tufts of hair left, as if someone did it hurriedly and with the victim resisting."

"Or as if Mr. Martinez had done it himself and wasn't yet used to shaving his head," the defense lawyer said smoothly. Before Parmenter could answer she said, "Tell me, Doctor, in this altercation you've described, don't you think the other person involved would have been injured as well?"

"I have no way of knowing."

"Well, the extensive cuts, the bruising, as if maybe this started as a fistfight before knives were pulled, the way you described Mr. Martinez having fought back against his attacker, doesn't it seem reasonable that the attacker would have gotten cut or injured himself during all this?"

Dr. Parmenter stared at her, not wanting to answer. Now his partisanship was playing against him, because the jurors saw what the true answer must be, and why the medical examiner didn't want to give it. "Possibly," he finally said tightly.

"Very likely, wouldn't you say, Dr. Parmenter?"

The doctor knew he'd lost his professional detachment. Trying to regain it, he said, "I'd say probably, yes, the attacker would have suffered at least some minor trauma. But not necessarily."

Gloria Files ended her questioning, satisfied. Beside her, her client looked too smug, even raising his unmarked hands off the table. As effective as Dr. Parmenter's testimony had been, the medical testimony was supposed to appear to come from an impartial professional. Files had lifted Parmenter's emotional involvement even higher, thus undermining his conclusions. During the defense lawyer's questioning Parmenter had sounded more like Mike Martinez's friend than like an objective, reliable observer. The doctor gave Chris a small apologetic shrug as he walked away from the witness stand. But Chris didn't worry. Gloria Files had done what she could to lessen the impact of the testimony, but it had still been brutal. Now came the time for one of the prosecution's most difficult effects: from killing Mike Martinez before the jury's eyes to bringing him back alive.

"The State calls Hortencia Martinez," Lynn announced.

A bailiff went into the hallway to call the witness and Lynn stood at the gate in the railing to wait for Mrs. Martinez, Mike's mother. After a minute the lady came slowly up the central aisle. She looked up only when the gate opened for her, then she smiled briefly at Lynn and patted her arm.

Mrs. Martinez was a heavy woman. After she took the oath and sat in the witness stand her body settled in the chair. She had a broad, light brown face with thin lips and a generous nose. Mrs. Martinez had the slump of defeated old age in every line of her body, but her face bore few wrinkles and her curly hair remained mostly dark brown. Three months ago she hadn't been old.

Chris didn't remember ever having met Mrs. Martinez. Lynn had. Lynn had asked to be the one to question her.

"Mrs. Martinez, where do you live?"

"Here in San Antonio. All my life."

"Are you married?"

"Yes, for thirty-five years. My husband Gustavo is in the hall."

"Do you and your husband have any children?"

As abruptly as that Mrs. Martinez's dejected expression turned to active grief. Tears sprang into her eyes. Her mouth and then her voice trembled. "We had one son, Miguelito."

Mrs. Martinez's pain wasn't remotely fake. It was obvious she was trying to hold it in, which made it all the more difficult to watch her.

Lynn's voice was perfect kindness. "He also called himself Mike?"

"Sí. Yes."

"How old was your son, Mrs. Martinez?"

"He was twenty-eight. I had him late in life. For years Gustavo and I didn't think we could have a child. Then Miguel was like a miracle baby—"

Gloria Files stood and tried to sound compassionate, too, when she said, "Your Honor, I have to object. This is unresponsive and irrelevant."

"Yes," said Judge Henrichs, also kindly. "Sustained."

"I'm sorry," Mrs. Martinez said, which sounded even more pitiful. "It's all right," Files said as she took her seat again. She smiled at the mother of her client's victim.

Lynn hesitated to do what she had to do next. She had rehearsed Mrs. Martinez's testimony with her, and she had also just sat and listened to her. She understood how much Mrs. Martinez had doted on her son, and she had expected an emotional display on the witness stand. That was, after all, why the prosecution would call the victim's mother as a witness. But now it seemed unnecessarily cruel, in front of all these strangers. The jurors watched Mrs. Martinez sympathetically. The courtroom had grown hushed. Lynn drew an eight-by-ten photograph from a file folder and walked to the witness stand.

"Mrs. Martinez, this is marked State's Exhibit Number Two. Can you tell me what this is?"

The photo had come off a table in Mrs. Martinez's living room. Mrs. Martinez had taken the picture herself at Mike's law school graduation, then had it blown up. Mike had just been turning toward the camera, neck stretched, smile bright, his mortarboard falling off. He stood, full of confidence and mischief, looking not like a brand-new lawyer, but like a boy delighted to find himself in a man's body.

Mrs. Martinez's studied the photograph silently. The tears welled out of her eyes and spilled down her cheeks. She tried to speak and failed, then with a little gasp said, "This is my son Miguel. Mike. Mike," she repeated, her voice breaking as she lifted her eyes to the courtroom's ceiling.

Lynn laid her hand on the old woman's shoulder as she said, "We'll offer this, your Honor."

Gloria Files just nodded. "That will be admitted," said Judge Henrichs. Lynn handed the photograph to the jurors to pass among themselves. There he was, their victim. The prosecution's case. They couldn't let Mike be just a name in an autopsy report to the jury, an item of evidence at a crime scene. This exhibition had been necessary to make Mike real.

Lynn slowly took her seat and asked a question she hadn't been sure she would have to ask. "Mrs. Martinez, what feature of your son's was he most proud of?"

"Objection," the defense lawyer said quickly, sounding genuinely puzzled. "Relevance?"

"Ms. Files raised this herself," Lynn said, an ambiguous answer, but Judge Henrichs trusted the prosecutor enough to say, "Overruled."

It looked, though, as if Lynn's legal victory would be in vain, because Mrs. Martinez appeared puzzled. "Feature? You mean like— Oh, you mean his hair. His hair, yes. Mike was so proud of that. Where he got it I don't know. No red hair in my family." She smiled. "But it was true when he was outside his hair looked red. So he called himself that crazy name sometimes. El Rojo."

"Was that important to him?" Lynn asked gently.

Mrs. Martinez nodded brightly. For the moment her son had come alive for her again. "It was something that made him different, and Miguel loved being different. He always wore his hair long so he could show it off." Mrs. Martinez shook her own head, and though her tight curls hardly moved, for the first time Chris saw Mike's resemblance to her. His smile had been hers, but bolder, ratcheted up a few notches.

"Did Mike ever talk about maybe shaving his head?"

"Never. He would never have done that." Mrs. Martinez suddenly pointed fiercely at the defendant. *"He—"*

Gloria Files spoke very quickly. "Objection, your Honor. I think this would be hearsay. At any rate it's unresponsive."

"Sustained," the judge said neutrally.

Mrs. Martinez looked up at her. She didn't apologize this time.

Judge Henrichs looked back at her, wanting to convey her sympathy but clinging to her impartial role. Mrs. Martinez said to the judge, "Can I say something?"

"No, ma'am, I'm afraid not. Only when you're asked a question."

And Lynn had no more questions. She and Chris had decided not to ask Mrs. Martinez about her son's occasionally supplying items for his parents' resale shop. That was a very slender connection to Mike's meeting with Lee Griggs, and they had other witnesses to establish that more soundly. "Thank you, Mrs. Martinez. I pass the witness."

The defense lawyer hesitated only a second before saying, "No questions." Get this woman out of here.

Mrs. Martinez didn't want to leave. "Can't I say something else?" she asked again. She opened her arms wide. Lynn shook her head, so did the judge. Mrs. Martinez looked longingly at the jury. It was her one chance to talk to them about her son. She couldn't let the chance pass.

But Lynn walked to the witness stand and held out her hand. After a moment Mrs. Martinez took it. She had already done her part, whether she knew it or not. She had brought Mike Martinez alive and showed that jury that at least one life was forever devastated by his murder.

Mrs. Martinez walked quickly out of the courtroom, a returned vigor in her step, as if she had someone young and eager to keep up with.

The trial was going pretty smoothly from the prosecution's point of view. They hadn't gotten to the hard part yet, but both their first two witnesses had given them more than the prosecutors could have expected. The jurors looked both solemn and anxious. They stared at Lee Griggs, who mostly kept his eyes down and shook his head. Gloria Files put her hand on his arm and stayed close to him, demonstrating that her client was nothing to fear.

Then came the first little bump in the smooth road. When Lynn announced as the State's next witness Yvonne Davis, Chris heard a stir and turned and saw Griggs' young girlfriend rising from her seat in the audience. It had been a month since Chris and Lynn had first interviewed her, and the girl had become more visibly pregnant. She came forward dutifully in response to her name, but Lynn frowned at her and Gloria Files stood quickly, shaking her head.

"Your Honor, this witness has been in the audience. Letting her testify would violate the rule, which we invoked at the beginning of trial."

Judge Henrichs remembered. The rule that kept all witnesses outside the courtroom, so they couldn't hear one another's testimony, was nearly always invoked by the defense, and this trial had been no exception. "Young lady," the judge asked sternly, "have you been in the courtroom since the beginning of this trial?"

"Yes, ma'am," Yvonne said meekly.

"Then you can't testify. Didn't anyone tell you you had to wait outside?"

"No, ma'am."

Chris had heard Lynn tell the girl exactly that, that she wouldn't be allowed to sit through other testimony, but there was no point in contradicting what Yvonne had just told the judge. No matter what she'd been told, Yvonne had violated the rule. Maybe they hadn't made court procedure clear enough to her. Judge Henrichs looked at Chris and Lynn as if they were amateurs, and told them, "Call another witness."

Yvonne shrugged at the prosecutors apologetically. Gloria Files, back to the jury, was smiling. Lee Griggs winked at his girlfriend, wearing a grin that matched his lawyer's. Lynn stared at them both from the railing.

"It's okay," Chris whispered to her. "We didn't need her much."

"I just hate to let these two jerks think they got away with something," Lynn answered in a voice not as quiet as Chris's.

"Counselors?" the judge asked in that patient tone which meant she was running out of patience.

"We'll have to call a couple of those kids who saw them together in the teen club," Chris whispered to Lynn, and as Lynn walked quickly out of the courtroom he turned to the judge and said, "Your Honor, we had anticipated Ms. Davis' testimony taking the rest of the afternoon. Since she's unavailable to us we need to ask the court's indulgence for a short recess in order to bring our next witnesses—"

"All right, I'll give this jury a break." The judge emphasized this was a favor for the jurors, not the prosecution. "But tomorrow, Mr. Sinclair—"

"Yes, your Honor. We'll have everything in place."

Chris and Lois Henrichs had worked together and had also opposed each other, and this was not the first time he'd appeared in her court. Outside the courtroom they were very friendly toward each other. Henrichs, who had been a good trial lawyer herself, respected Chris's abilities and knew he wasn't deliberately delaying the trial. But the judge also knew she would not be doing the prosecutor a favor by appearing to be on his side. One or two of the jurors looked at the District Attorney sympathetically as he appeared chastened.

"We'll begin again at nine-thirty tomorrow morning," Judge Henrichs announced firmly.

As soon as the jurors were out of the room Gloria Files began intently conferring with her client. Lee Griggs didn't pay much attention, instead he grinned and obviously congratulated her. The prosecution's first two witnesses had gotten the jury's attention firmly, but then the defense lawyer had denied them Yvonne Davis, not a crucial witness but one who would have helped the

State's case. Gloria Files glanced up at Chris with a serious look of inquiry, no longer smiling triumphantly.

Chris stared at her happy client. Lee Griggs thought things were going well. Trial is a funny business. Even as the lawyers strive to make the events come alive for the jury, everyone is safely removed from them. That seemed to have happened even to Griggs, who had been in that room, who had seen Mike's pain up close, who had watched him die. Hadn't the medical examiner's testimony put Griggs back in that room, as it had Chris? Hadn't Mrs. Martinez given him even a moment of remorse?

Apparently not. Griggs felt the D.A.'s regard and turned and grinned at him again. *I'm beating you,* Griggs' smile said, but Chris didn't engage him in the duel. He just stared, as at a specimen.

Griggs didn't compare with Chris's last trial opponent.

Chris remembered those few moments during Malachi Reese's trial when everyone except him and Reese had become unreal. Chris had understood a sociopath's mind; he had slipped into it himself. He could again. The way he felt made trial seem a frail ritual. This was personal.

Somehow the District Attorney's thoughts or at least his mood came through in his stare. Lee Griggs blinked and stopped smiling. "Hey," he said in slight alarm, as if Chris were advancing on him.

Anne Greenwald was waiting in Chris's office. He only had time to give her a quick hug.

Lynn stood waiting by the desk. She said, "This probably means we'll get to Donny-boy's testimony tomorrow. You want to bring him over from the jail, go over what he's going to say again? We've got some extra time."

Chris shook his head. "I don't want him to sound over-rehearsed. Let's just look at his statement."

The written statement Donny Sturns had given police, describing the murder, wouldn't be admitted in evidence, unless the defense chose to offer it. That was very unlikely, since the statement laid all the blame for the killing on the defendant. Donny hadn't accepted any responsibility himself, but just the fact that he'd been present to see what he described implicated him.

"Why does somebody do something like this?" Lynn asked. "Take part in a murder, join right in with everybody else, then a few hours later describe it all to the cops? Why do they always do that?"

"Ask Anne," Chris said. "Why ask me psychological questions when we've got an expert here?"

Anne didn't react to the mention of her name. She paced at the far side of the office as if trying to disassociate herself from the prosecutors. But she couldn't ignore Lynn's speculative eyes on her.

"That's right. We have you to thank for our best witness, Dr. Greenwald. I've been wondering about that, wondering if the defense would bring up some weird defense that cops coerced this confession by bringing a psychiatrist in to work on poor Donny. I know you weren't there working for the cops. So why did you do it? Why'd you question Donny?"

Chris started to answer, to try to describe that room, that awful day, when Mike had only been dead a few hours and there'd been an urgency about finding his killers. Anne had felt that urgency too. As if it were something they could still do for Mike. In an odd way, too, she'd been defending Donny Sturns from Chris and Sergeant Esparza, who'd both been ready to kill him.

But Lynn asked a good question. Questioning Donny in front of the police video camera hadn't been very professional for a psychiatrist who shouldn't have been on anybody's side in that

interrogation room. And it hadn't been very in character for
Anne, either, whose sympathies in spite of everything had been
with Donny Sturns.

For a moment after Lynn asked the question Anne looked almost frightened. She'd been caught. Then she looked very weary,
and resigned. She didn't make an easy denial.

"The room was so full of pain," she said quietly. "I just started
talking. It's what I do, you know? Try to make people understand
their pain. Donny Sturns wasn't my patient. Maybe I shouldn't
have talked to him, but I . . ."

In the context of that morning what Anne had done had
made perfect sense. Chris had never since asked her about it.
But now he understood her not wanting to talk about the trial
in the weeks since that morning in the interrogation room. Anne
felt guilty. She'd stepped in where she had no business and she'd
drawn the boy's awful story out of him, when he'd had no reason to trust her and probably shouldn't have.

Anne's eyes met Chris's across the expanse of the office. The
room had been full of pain, she'd said. But not Donny's pain. He
had been nonchalant and hostile. Chris had been the one hurt-
ing in that room, stricken by guilt as well as grief. Anne had
seen Chris in pain and she'd done what she could to help. She
had questioned Donny Sturns because it was the only thing
she could do at that moment to help Chris. She'd done it
for him.

"I've got to go," Anne said suddenly. Chris walked toward her
but she quickly shouldered her purse strap, muttered good-bye,
and went out the door. What Anne had said had been a declaration of love, embarrassing in front of a spectator, whether Lynn
understood or not.

Maybe Lynn did. "Sorry," she shrugged to Chris.

Chris sat at his desk and looked at the photographs arrayed
there. Most of the photos might become exhibits for this trial.
But Chris's Malachi Reese folder, never far from his hand, also

lay on the desk, and pictures from it had spilled into the ones of
Mike Martinez.

Lynn said, "After Donny testifies tomorrow we'll have Griggs.
The little bastard's too stupid to realize it, but his day's almost
over."

In one photo El Rojo grinned, leaning back against the hood
of a car. "That Mustang," Chris said. "It was redder than his hair.
That was one of the things he'd bought from the cops."

"One of his better deals," Lynn agreed. After a moment she
said, "It won't be enough, will it?"

Chris shook his head. Lynn meant that convicting Mike's murderer wouldn't go far toward assuaging anyone's pain. It wouldn't
do a damned thing to restore the animating force Dr. Parmenter
had mentioned. Mike would still be in the ground.

But Chris meant something else. He still gave more thought
to Malachi Reese than he did to the current defendant. *I'm going
to show everyone how helpless you are,* Reese had threatened. Having one of Chris's own assistants killed certainly fulfilled that
threat. Reese had engineered Mike's murder, Chris felt certain of
that. The young man—Malcolm Turner—showing up at both the
crack house and the scene of Mike's murder convinced Chris of
Reese's involvement. They had young Malcolm in jail now. Jack
Fine had seen to his arrest. They'd taken one of Reese's killers out
of circulation, and Chris was trying to put the other one on
Death Row.

But Chris wanted more than that. He had hoped to prove definitively Reese's connection to Mike's murder, evidence good
enough to take to a trial, or at least to the press. He wanted public blame.

"No, it won't be enough," Chris said.

After a moment, staring into space, he slightly changed the
subject. "I'd like to put video monitors on Death Row. Take away
their TVs. I want videotapes running, home movies. I want those

murderers to see their victims when they were alive. See the years they took. . . ."

Tension filled the silence that lasted for a minute after Chris stopped talking. Maybe Lynn saw his vision. But she cleared her throat and said, "Courts would probably call that cruel and un-usual."

"Cruel? To make them live with what they've done? Yeah, you're probably right."

Lynn stood over his shoulder, looking at a photo in front of Chris, a picture of Malachi Reese smiling in the midst of a group of prominent friends. "What's your grudge against him?" she asked softly.

"Not grudge, fear. If I told you everything I think he's be-hind—" He exhaled, giving up. "—you'd think I was an obses-sive crazoid like everyone else does."

Lynn sifted through the pictures. Chris knew she hadn't ap-proved of his going for the death sentence against Reese. So few other people were as convinced as Chris of the extent of Reese's crimes. He didn't feel like trying to make a convert, especially out of Lynn.

He and she worked together well in trial. They hardly had to talk about which witnesses each would question. It seemed nat-ural. And he certainly didn't have to worry about Lynn losing focus. Chris was the one who seemed to have too much in mind. He stared out the window at the darkening silhouette of the city until Lynn said, "See you in the morning. Get a good night's sleep."

He laughed appreciatively at the joke.

With Anne and then Lynn gone the office seemed very empty. The outer office staff had gone home. Chris felt the silence of the whole Justice Center beneath him. Public buildings, designed for crowds, seem especially vacant at night.

He went to turn off his desk light, then instead sat and looked through his photos again. Malachi Reese receiving a plaque. An old picture of Reese on a dais, applauding the speaker. Chris had identified everyone in all the photos, groped through them a hundred times for connections, but there were too many possibilities. Hell, he could find three different chiefs of police standing smiling with Reese at different times. City Council members, the mayor, national politicians. Where should he start, where stop? Lou Briones had tried directing him, but Lou was gone.

Some of the photos seemed part of Chris's life by now, others had lost their familiarity. He came across one he didn't remember, of Malachi Reese at the wheel of a convertible, waving to the photographer. A woman in the passenger seat leaned forward to say something. Both were laughing, a social occasion.

Suddenly Chris stared at the photo. The whole car Reese sat in didn't show in the picture, but enough of it did for identification. The black vinyl seats that would sizzle in the summer. The classic lines of the car. The convertible gleamed with red paint, bright and shiny as freshly spilled blood.

El Rojo had bought the car from the police after it had been confiscated from Malachi Reese.

Chris caught a 7:00 P.M. flight to Houston. His stomach rumbled on the plane, he hadn't taken time to eat anything. He urged the plane forward. He couldn't get there fast enough. Back on the ground, in his rental car, he broke the speed limit all the way to Huntsville.

Night had fallen, visiting hours on Death Row long over by the time Chris arrived. Soon it would be time for lights out, which came early on the Row. But Captain Stillwell remained on duty. He seemed almost glad to admit Chris to the prison unit. As they walked down the wide central corridor the guard captain said to Chris, "Something's buzzing around this place. Ever since they saw Reese on TV, there's a very weird atmosphere. We got protestors outside having fistfights with each other. Inside— I don't know. There's something in the air. There's always little conspiracies here, you know. I usually hear about them before all the inmates do. But this time I can't get a clue. There's a sense of—"

"Solidarity," Chris said.

"Yeah. Maybe that's it. The Row always pulses, you know. But now—there's even, like, a celebration going on. These guys are passing around a rumor that the death penalty's going to be abolished."

"Yeah, right." Anti–death-penalty sentiment wasn't very strong anywhere in America. In Texas opposition to executions had been reduced to a lunatic fringe.

But Malachi Reese could have convinced his fellow condemned of his power to make changes, in the legislature or in the public mind.

"I know, I know," Stillwell said. "But something's happened. Or gonna happen. I can't find out what."

After Chris's flight from San Antonio and drive to Huntsville, landing on Death Row completed his sense of dislocation. He could have been on a moon colony. This place was its own world. And as Stillwell had said, it buzzed constantly. This is where Chris should have come for information.

"You know of a gang called White Lightning?" he asked, naming the gang Lee Griggs had headed in San Antonio.

"Sure," Stillwell said. "Little local outfit, but aggressive. A comer." He analyzed it like a sales representative assessing a new rival.

"You have any of them here?"

"Couple of affiliates maybe," Stillwell said.

"I suppose you have to keep them separate from the African-American inmates."

"You'd be surprised," Stillwell answered easily. "These guys can work real well together when they want to. Word comes through the grapevine, Can you do me a favor on the outside? If the offer's good, even a mean-mouthed racist doesn't ask where the request's coming from. Things are different here."

Yes, things were different. And with Malachi Reese they'd be more different still. Reese had found a way to network after all.

Chris and Stillwell walked as they talked. They came to a guard cage and a guard opened the door for them, admitting Chris and Stilwell to one of the branches of Death Row, one of the three-tiered cellblocks. Stillwell gestured Chris through. "You know the way."

The captain hung back near the door and let Chris climb alone the ladder to the second level, then walk down the corridor past the cages. Night on Death Row: it had taken Chris two and a half hours to get from his office to Houston Intercontinental Airport, another hour to get out of the airport, rent a car, and drive to Huntsville. It seemed late on the Row. The place felt densely populated but unusually quiet. From some radio a song about Jesus played so softly it could have been playing only in memory. The air itself held a breathing watchfulness.

Chris walked slowly but not cautiously. His neck had grown so stiff he could hardly turn his head. For an hour after he'd seen the photo of Malachi Reese sitting in the red convertible Chris's heart had raced, adrenaline urging him to kill. The trip to Huntsville had settled him down but not eased his tension. It had been pressed down within him, waiting to be released.

He stood alone outside Malachi Reese's cell. Chris's feeling of being watched increased and became localized: he could see Reese's eyes, darker than the perpetual dusk of Death Row. Reese was awake, waiting for him.

"El Rojo had your car," Chris said flatly.

Reese smiled slightly. He lay back on his metal shelf of a bunk. "I loved that car," he said reminiscently. "I bought it new and kept it. I'm not a car man, but that one— It was part of me, like a room of my home."

Reese's voice frowned as he sat up. "I loaned it to friends sometimes, and one of them got busted in it. Cops knew it was my car, they could've released it to me. They confiscated it just to spite me. I could have gotten it back, but by that time I was busy with you. Then your little friend stole it from me."

Reese stood slowly. Chris's hands wanted Reese to walk close to the bars. Reese knew it and obliged. Chris stared at him. Chris had put Reese behind these bars, waiting his turn in line for the execution chamber. But Chris didn't want the State doing that job for him.

"I hate to think of that car all alone," Reese said sadly. "Lying there on the street abandoned."

Reese's concern for metal was chilling. "You had a man killed over a car?" Chris asked unbelievingly.

Suddenly Reese stood coiled right in front of him, inches away, his eyes dangerous. "No. Don't you get it yet? I did it to get at you. To show you can't even protect your own."

Chris's rage drained away in the face of Reese's less rational fury. Chris realized he hadn't saved anyone from anything. Instead he had released something monstrous on the world.

He thought of what Dr. Parmenter had said about animating force, that dies out when the body does and can't be brought back. Malachi Reese stood on Death Row full of the force of life, seeming taller than the walls. What was *his* motivating force? Would it live on after the State stopped Reese's heart?

"Don't you understand he was alive? He wasn't some game piece. On his best day Mike Martinez had more life than you'll ever feel. He—"

"Does it hurt, Chris?"

Reese asked the question with curious intensity, as if he really wanted to know the answer. His hands gripped the bars. His eyes gleamed. "Now you gonna put that stupid little skinhead right here beside me? Great joke, isn't it?"

Suddenly Chris felt a great hurry to get home. It had been senseless to come here. Reese had told him exactly what Chris wanted to know, and it didn't do any good at all.

Without a word Chris turned and walked away, going faster as the sound of his shoes pursued him.

"Only the beginning," Reese's voice called. "Just wait. . . ."

Chapter 13

When court convened the next morning at 9:30 Chris sat at the State's table. Lynn came into the courtroom with the thick file, took her seat beside him, then frowned and said, "Did you sleep?"

He had a little, in a chair in the Houston airport, waiting for the first flight back to San Antonio at 6:00 A.M.

"You look like death warmed over," Lynn said.

But Chris felt as alert as a squirrel that's just heard a twig snap. This would be the crucial day of trial, when the jury heard from the accomplice witness Donny Sturns, when the prosecution case would be wrapped up in excruciating detail. They had Malachi Reese's henchman in custody, but that no longer eased Chris's fears. *Just wait*, Reese had said on Death Row. Chris waited—for Malachi Reese's hand to reveal itself.

When trial began the prosecutors re-entered the evidence slowly, by calling two kids and the adult assistant manager who had seen Lee Griggs talking to Mike Martinez at the teen club earlier in the evening, the night of Mike's death.

"Did you see them leave together?" Lynn asked a thin boy with a shadowed complexion and ears too big for his head.

"No ma'am, I didn't notice. There were a lot of people there."

They couldn't blame the boy for that omission. Yvonne Davis had been supposed to supply that information for the jury.

"Do you know Yvonne Davis?" Lynn asked.

"Yes, ma'am."

"A young pregnant woman who was supposed to testify for the State yesterday?"

"I guess she was, yes, ma'am."

Yvonne hadn't come to the courtroom today. Lynn would have pointed her out for identification if she had been in the room. "What's her relationship with this defendant, if you know?"

The boy glanced at Lee Griggs as if for permission to talk about something personal. Griggs gave him a benign look. Chris and Lynn must have talked to more than a dozen regular patrons of the teen club, and they were all scared of Griggs. They'd only gotten two to agree to testify by promising to ask them only innocuous questions. The kids didn't have any more significant information, anyway. They hadn't seen anything important that had happened that night.

"Yvonne is Lee's girlfriend, I think," the boy said hesitantly.

"Was she there at the club that night too?"

"Yes, ma'am. I saw her talking to Mr. Martinez too."

"Did she leave when Lee Griggs did?"

The boy frowned as if in thought, though he had already given Lynn this answer a few minutes earlier in the court's conference room. "No, she didn't. I remember looking around later on and seeing Yvonne still there, but Lee was gone."

"As if Lee Griggs had business?"

Gloria Files stood and spread her hands and said, as if she'd indulged the prosecution long enough, "Objection. Calls for speculation."

"Sustained," Judge Henrichs agreed.

Lynn gave the defense lawyer a look much more baleful than accounted for by the mild exchange. Lynn had been off-track anyway. She wanted the jury to be able to figure out that Yvonne Davis would do what she was told, it had been the defense's idea to keep her off the witness stand. Gloria Files looked innocent as she took her seat again.

The witness, a boy named Jimmy, hadn't been worth much. The defense lawyer hardly cross-examined him. After Lynn said, "No more questions," and stood to announce the assistant manager as the State's next witness, Chris whispered to her, "I'm going to go check Donny out while you wrap this up." Lynn nodded, unperturbed at being left alone at the State's table.

Chris walked as unobtrusively as he could to the side of the courtroom opposite the jury box, to an unmarked door behind the bailiff's desk. Chris nodded to the bailiff, who unlocked the door with a key on his large, round key chain, looking around the courtroom all the while. The bailiff stuck his head through the doorway, then waved Chris in. After Chris went through the door it closed behind him and he heard it lock. He'd had a lot of that lately, being locked in.

This room beside the courtroom wasn't nearly as spacious as Death Row. Between every pair of courtrooms in the Justice Center lay a small holding area such as this one. Straight ahead a short passageway led to a door to the courtroom next door. The hidden T-shaped area had arms leading to courtrooms. The trunk of the T held a small elevator that could only be operated with another key, and three small holding cells.

In the old days prisoners had been brought from the jail in leg chains and handcuffs, then herded through the public hallways of the old courthouse to the various courts where they were bound. The architects of the much newer Justice Center had arranged for more decorum. Prisoners still arrived in vans, but the vans disappeared through large overhead doors on the ground floor. From that parking area a metal staircase led up to a half-floor hidden between the first and second floors of the Justice Center. The floor, called One-point-five, housed a miniature jail. Passageways from One-point-five led to elevators through which prisoners could be distributed to the various courtrooms without ever disturbing the public halls, passing through the Justice Center walls like mice.

Each of the small holding cells provided to the individual

courtrooms was basically a large toilet stall. It held prisoners waiting to plead or be sentenced. Lee Griggs had been in here before
trial started, sitting anomalously as a prisoner in a cell, but wearing a suit and looking displaced.

Donny Sturns had been brought up separately, after Griggs
went safely into the courtroom. Chris had made sure the two
would never be together. Griggs had been Donny's leader, in-
spiring loyalty out of fear. That fear could only have grown after
Donny saw Lee kill a man. Chris didn't want Donny to think
Griggs could get close enough to Donny to give him so much
as a dirty look.

So now Donny sat alone in the holding cell. The door stood
ajar, Chris looked in and saw his prime witness in the classic
prisoner's posture, feet spread, elbows on his knees, head slumped.
Donny didn't move. Chris stopped moving himself, suddenly
afraid.

"Donny?"

Slowly, slowly the boy lifted his head. Chris looked for blood.
Then Donny smiled. He had a small smile, not much of a facial
movement at all, but it gave some life to his pale face. His eyes
remained strangely lifeless.

"Hello, sir."

"Are you all right?" Chris went to sit beside him on the narrow metal bench.

"Oh yes. Just resting."

Donny wore a white shirt, gray slacks, and a blue blazer. Chris
had bought the clothes for him after Donny's mother had said he
didn't have anything nice enough to wear to court. Donny's
wrists came thin and bony out of the sleeves.

Chris spoke earnestly, trying to animate his witness. "We've
been over this and over it, Donny, but this time it's going to be
different because you're going to be in the same room with
him. Don't be afraid of Lee, look right back at him. If he's staring at you while you testify and you look down at the floor, or

can't meet his eyes, you'll look like a liar. You don't want that, do you?"

"I'll be all right," Donny said, but his voice sounded limp.

"Look at me. Are you going to tell this story? All of it?"

Donny nodded. His hands clenched together. Staring into his pale eyes, Chris saw some flint there. Somewhere inside Donny's paleness and thinness he had a strange strength.

"Don't worry. Don't be afraid of Lee, he can't get to you." Chris stood up, waited for Donny to rise beside him, and added, "But I can."

Donny smiled as if hoping that was a joke.

When Donny took the stand Chris relaxed a little, because Donny did just what he'd been instructed to do: he looked at Lee Griggs, and he didn't flinch from the eye contact. Griggs looked searchingly at his former colleague. Chris liked the contrast between them. Whether Griggs testified or not, the jury would have to decide between these two. Gloria Files would undoubtedly argue that Donny testified the way he did just to save himself, because of his own guilt. The jurors would look at these two and decide which had been the murderer and which a more-or-less innocent bystander. Chris liked his guy. Donny looked like a born follower. He looked like a boy, not yet grown into his body. Lee Griggs was twenty-three, a man. He would have looked credible on a football field. He had broad shoulders and his hands, which his defense lawyer kept having to pat to remind him not to clench them into fists, looked strong. His hair crept an inch or two down his forehead, making him look like a Roman soldier. Not a good look under the circumstances. The prosecution's witness, Donny, still had a look of innocence. By contrast, Lee Griggs didn't.

Donny was Chris's witness. As Chris began questioning him,

he remembered asking Donny questions in the interrogation room of the police station. A long time seemed to have
passed since that day, but Chris's sense of urgency hadn't diminished.

"Please state your name."

"Donny Sturns."

"How old are you, Donny?"

"Seventeen." Donny sat up straight, as if someone had reminded him.

"Are you in high school?"

"I was, until all this. This should be my senior year, but—I've
been in jail."

Chris turned. The defendant sat close to him across the narrow space between the prosecution and defense tables. Chris
reached out, almost touching Griggs' shoulder.

"Donny, do you know this man I'm pointing to?"

"Yes sir. It's Lee Griggs."

"How do you know him?"

"He's a friend of mine. We used to hang together."

"Used to?" Chris asked.

"Well, not since I've been in jail." Donny shrugged, apologiz-
ing if anybody thought he had made a joke.

Chris stood and walked to the witness stand, carrying the
eight-by-ten picture of Mike Martinez. Mike smiling, full of life.
Chris handed the picture to Donny, who studied it obligingly. He
didn't show any remorse as Chris had hoped. The boy didn't
have the capacity to bring the past to life.

"Now I'm showing you a photograph, State's Exhibit Number Two. Can you identify the person in that picture?"

Donny kept staring at the picture. "I know who it is."

"Who?"

"He's the man who was killed," Donny said. Chris frowned.
They had talked about this. No passive voice in testifying: not
"the man who was killed"; it should be "the man Lee killed."

Then Donny handed the photo back to Chris and said, "I remember seeing his picture in the paper."

Chris stood less than three feet in front of Donny, staring at him, damning him, insisting that he say it right. "When did you see Mike Martinez alive, Donny?"

Donny put his hands together and looked up at Chris. "Never, sir."

Everything dropped out of Chris. From inside his hollow chest a thin shrieking sound, unheard by anyone else, began to fill his ears. He knew if he turned his head he'd see Lee Griggs smiling and Gloria Files covering her mouth with her hand. But Chris kept staring at his witness. Donny still had that innocent look. Chris wanted to slap it off his face.

"The night of August third of this year, you were inside a house at Three-fourteen Pine Meadows."

Chris didn't even say it as a question, but Donny shook his head. "I don't know that street. I've never heard of it."

Chris turned away from that innocent expression. He walked slowly back to his seat, ignoring the defense table. Lynn's fingers were flying through the State's file. She found the statement Donny had given to police and pushed it in front of Chris.

"Were you with Lee Griggs that night?" Chris asked, desperately hoping that Donny was just confused, that he'd answer truthfully if Chris found the right question.

"I don't think so," Donny said, frowning as if in remembrance. "If it's the night I'm thinking of—"

"The night you got arrested."

"Yes, sir, that's what I thought. I was at the teen club that night, but I was with some other guys. Lee wasn't there. He didn't get arrested that night, did he?"

He turned that damned questioning look on Chris. They both knew that Lee Griggs hadn't been at the teen club when Donny was arrested the night of Mike's murder. Griggs hadn't been arrested until the next day, until Donny had fingered him.

Donny's innocent expression, which Chris had been so glad to have on his side a few minutes earlier, now looked like an evil parody. Pretense had fallen away. Chris was at war with his witness. His case against Lee Griggs had just disappeared.

He looked down at the statement Lynn had put under his hand. Chris could use this statement to impeach Donny's testimony. In that way he could at least get to the jury the true story, the one Donny had given to police.

But Donny had given this statement after Anne had questioned him in the interrogation room. When Chris tried to introduce it into evidence Gloria Files would challenge it on that basis. Chris knew that for a certainty. Donny would lie about what had happened in the interrogation room. The defense would put Anne on the witness stand and question her professionalism, her integrity—damned Gloria Files would lay out Anne's relationship with Chris in leering detail. The prosecution could argue the personal relationship was irrelevant, but it would all come out. Anything to distract from the real issue of the case. To put different suspects before the jury. Whatever worked.

Chris pushed the statement aside. As Judge Henrichs asked his name and he replied, "One moment, please, your Honor," he started going through the voluminous file himself. Lynn understood what he wanted. Her hands brushed his, passing quickly through the white papers to the darker newspaper clippings.

Chris stood and spoke directly to the judge. "Your Honor, this witness's testimony is a surprise to me. It's a change from what he's told me before."

"Objection!" Gloria Files almost shouted, coming up from her seat. "He's testifying to the jury."

Mildly, Judge Henrichs instructed Files in the law. "It's what the prosecutor has to claim in order to be allowed to impeach his own witness. Is that what you're asking to do, Mr. Sinclair?"

"Yes, your Honor."

The judge nodded. Lynn put a newspaper clipping in Chris's hand. Chris walked toward Donny, holding out the article. Chris's

-yes locked on his witness's. Donny looked back at him passively, hat strange dead look coating his eyes. He could keep up the taring contest indefinitely, because he wasn't there.

"Take a look at this newspaper clipping from last month, Donny. Do you recognize it?"

"Yes, sir. It's Miles McKinley's column."

"Mr. McKinley interviewed you?"

"Yes, sir."

"You talked to him about the murder, didn't you? You told him a somewhat different story than what you've just testified in this court?"

Barely bothered, Donny admitted, "Yes, I did."

"I'll offer this as a State's exhibit, your Honor."

The defense lawyer objected even before Chris could hand her the article to examine. "This is just a shameful attempt to make his case a different way, your Honor, with hearsay from outside court."

"That's overruled," the judge said, not bothering to explain that she let the statement into evidence to impeach the witness, not for its intrinsic truth. Judge Henrichs was not the nervous kind of judge who tries to explain things for the appellate record.

"May I read portions of this to the jury, your Honor?"

The judge nodded. Chris quickly scanned the column. The paper kept folding over his hand flimsily. "Question: 'Who killed Mike Martinez?' Answer, from Donny Sturns." Chris pointed at his witness. " 'Lee did. Lee Griggs. I didn't even know what was going to happen. It scared the hell out of me. Lee did it all. Even up to the end I didn't know what he was going to do. I thought he was just going to cut the guy up some. We were all in on that. But it was Lee who stabbed him.' You said that, Donny?"

"Yes, sir, that's what I told Mr. McKinley."

"That was the truth, wasn't it?" Chris asked, hopelessly willing the truth out of his witness. But Donny was shaking his head all through the question.

"No, that was all a lie. I didn't see anything like that. I just said that because the police officer who arrested me said Lee had already been arrested and he was blaming everything on me. So I thought I'd get back at him. But the policeman was lying to me. Lee hadn't even been arrested before I had. Everybody lied to me. I just lied back."

"You knew the details of the killing pretty well, didn't you?"

Again Donny shook his head. "Only because the police told me. And that part about me helping to cut him, that was just silly boasting, sir. I'm in jail, I need to sound tough."

Donny smiled innocently, shrugging an apology. Chris stared at him contemptuously, which had no effect. Donny didn't even seem to see the District Attorney.

Chris handed the newspaper column to the jurors to pass among themselves. Turning back toward his seat, he saw Lee Griggs openly grinning at him, an ugly sight. Chris stopped, which prompted Griggs to smile even more broadly. Chris hoped the jurors were watching him. Chris would have voted guilty based solely on the defendant's face. It was almost all he had left.

He took his seat. "Lee Griggs has also been in jail, hasn't he, Donny? How many times have you talked to him since you were both arrested?"

"Not any. You told me not to."

"Then how did you know he hadn't told the police you were involved in Mike Martinez's murder?"

Donny blinked. It was the first time his story hadn't flowed smoothly. Chris watched him. Donny looked toward the defense table and finally said, "My lawyer. My lawyer checked the State's file and said they didn't have any statement from Lee to use against me."

Chris kept his voice steady and unoffended. "You wanted to talk to Lee, didn't you, Donny? If he's your friend like you say?"

"Ye-es," Donny said slowly. "But I was afraid of what would happen to me if I did."

"It's easy to get messages to people inside the jail, isn't it, Donny?"

The boy in the witness stand hesitated, then licked his lips and said, "I wouldn't know, sir."

"You mean Lee didn't get any messages to you? Your friend? He didn't try to talk to you?"

Donny shook his head. To Chris he looked unbelievable. Feeling himself on shaky ground, Donny suddenly blurted out, "I just couldn't lie about Lee anymore! That's why I'm telling the truth now."

"That's good, Donny," Chris said, the friendliness in his voice now a sarcastic parody. "Is that the big punch line Lee told you to come out with?"

"It's just the truth," Donny said humbly.

Bearing down, Chris said, "You saw Lee Griggs kill Mike Martinez, didn't you?"

"No."

"Did you ever see him kill anyone else?"

"No." Donny tried to sound shocked at the suggestion.

"Beat someone up? Hit someone with a chain? A baseball bat?"

"No sir, nothing like that. Lee's not like that."

"You and him and the rest of the guys ever burn a cross in somebody's front yard?"

"Burn a cross? That would be sacrilegious."

"You're not like that, are you, Donny? You're just some guys, hang out at the Boys' Club, shoot some hoops, right?"

"Well, sometimes." Donny sounded genuinely confused. He dropped back into his prepared text. "We weren't a gang. Just friends. We just hung out together."

Lynn's fingers had been going through the file again. She handed Chris a photograph. He put out his hand again and she handed him another. Carrying both, he walked back toward Donny, who looked a little more apprehensive this time as the

District Attorney approached him. Chris showed him one of the photographs. "Recognize this, Donny?"

"Yes, it's me."

"The way you looked the night you were arrested, the night Mike Martinez was murdered?"

"Yes, but—"

Chris thrust the photo in the jury's direction. It was Donny's mug shot. In the picture he looked more scared than scary, but he was a far cry from the innocent boy in the witness stand. His head was shaved, his eyes sunken. In the picture he at least looked like someone who *wanted* to be a menace.

"Just some pals who hung out together?" Chris said to the jury, while Gloria Files shouted, "Objection! He's displaying something not in evidence. This isn't relevant, this is just an attempt—"

"Let me fix that," Chris said. He showed the other picture to Donny Sturns and said, "Who is this?"

Again Donny hesitated, but he obviously recognized the face in the other picture. "That's Lee."

"The way he used to look, before he got himself cleaned up for trial?"

"Well, sometimes—"

"I'll offer these as State's exhibits, your Honor."

Gloria Files made a futile objection. After Judge Henrichs overruled it Chris handed both photographs to the jury. The jurors passed them around, glancing from the pictures to the defendant and the witness. The photos showed young thugs trying to sneer into the police lenses, not the clean-cut young boys in court today.

This hollow victory was the best Chris could do for now. "Pass the witness," he said.

Mind spinning, Chris watched the jurors passing the newspaper column among themselves, reading it carefully. Chris had put a small one over on Gloria Files, who didn't have the crimnal law experience to have asked that the parts of the article not specifically dealing with the murder be blacked out before the jury saw it. The column had other things to say about Lee Griggs: his plans to murder again, his admiration for Adolf Hitler. With that and the photograph of the defendant in full skinhead mode, Chris had probably managed to prove to the jurors' satisfaction that Griggs was despicable. But Chris could no longer prove him a murderer.

He understood now why Donny had given that interview. It had been a further part of Malachi Reese's plan: portray Lee Griggs as a horrible menace, let every reader in San Antonio know how dangerous he was—then show that the District Attorney couldn't convict him, even with a supposedly lay-down case. As things stood now, Donny's change in testimony meant Griggs would walk out the courtroom doors, maybe before the case could even go to the jury. The prosecution had had only Donny to provide the testimony of what had happened inside the skinhead house. Now they didn't have that. Without sufficient proof, an honest judge would grant a defense motion for acquittal without even letting the jury decide—and Chris knew Lois Henrichs to be strictly honest, no matter how much she might sympathize with the prosecution.

Gloria Files asked her first question in cross-examination. She was prepared, not at all taken by surprise by Donny's testimony. "Why did you lie and say Lee murdered Mike Martinez, Donny?"

She had led Donny back into the prepared script. Quickly he said, "Because the police said if I didn't they were going to charge me with it. And the District Attorney said he'd get me if I didn't say what he wanted."

Instantly Chris's hands shot to the arms of his chair, his mouth open as he started to jump up. But then he quickly remembered Malachi Reese's trial, and an outraged Reese screaming, "That's a lie!" In his mind Chris saw Reese grinning at the thought of having put his adversary in the same position.

Chris listened coldly as Gloria Files had Donny repeat that he and the defendant had been nowhere near the abandoned house where Mike Martinez had been murdered. Chris's eyes were burning a hole in Donny's face. The boy didn't notice.

"Go round up those kids," Chris whispered to Lynn. "The ones who heard Donny bragging about the murder." Lynn was up and moving before he finished speaking.

When the defense lawyer passed Donny back, Chris sat and stared at him. Chris felt self-satisfaction emanating from the defense table. Donny didn't project that, though. He played his part well, sitting there quietly, hands folded.

Finally, still slumped in his chair, Chris said, "There's not much point in my asking you any more questions, is there, Donny?"

"Objection," the defense lawyer said quickly. "Improper question."

"Sustained."

It had been rhetorical anyway. Chris went on, "No matter what I ask, you're going to stick to what Lee Griggs programmed you to say, aren't you?"

Files rose again. Her objection clashed with Donny's answer. Judge Henrichs sustained her again.

"Are you afraid of Lee?" Chris asked.

Donny looked at the defendant, who smiled encouragingly at him.

"No, sir. He's my friend."

"So you'll do what you can to help him, won't you?"

Donny shook his head. "I won't lie."

"Your whole life is a lie," Chris said, drawing a final objection.

When Donny was released he stood uncertainly, until the bailiff waved him over to his desk. Judge Henrichs said, "Call your next witness."

Chris stood. "I'm not sure who that will be, your Honor. This last witness's change in testimony has disrupted the State's case. I need time—"

Gloria Files quickly answered, gesturing to her client, who did his best to look innocent. "I object. This man has had this false accusation hanging over him long enough. He deserves a speedy trial."

Judge Henrichs gave the matter brief thought and said, "I'll grant a continuance for the rest of the day. We're in recess." As she rose she added, "This case has been full of surprises for you, hasn't it, Mr. Sinclair?"

Chris could only nod. As the last juror exited the courtroom Chris heard a whoop, almost in his ear, and turned to see Lee Griggs raising his arms in triumph like a boxer. He leered at the prosecutor, then dropped his arms around his defense lawyer and kissed her full on the mouth. Gloria Files pushed him away, but did not look displeased as she glanced at Chris. She saw the case shaping up into a major triumph for her. Nothing else mattered. Files was the perfect lawyer. Nothing outside the courtroom was real for her.

The small prosecution team gathered in Chris's office, bringing the shreds of their case. Lynn said, "Jimmy remembers hearing Donny bragging about killing somebody before the fight started at the teen club. He'll testify to that."

"Killing 'somebody,' " Chris said. Lynn shrugged. She knew the problem.

"Goddamned little Donny probably never even knew Mike's name," she said.

Chris turned to his investigator, Jack Fine. "What about your lady, Jack? The neighbor who saw Lee Griggs running out of the skinhead house that night."

The investigator said carefully, "That's what she saw. But I promised her we wouldn't call her as a witness." Lynn gave him a look and Jack said, "Okay, so I lied to her. But if you can't prove the case even with her——"

"All right, Jack. I won't burn her unless it would help. So

what've we got?" Chris asked. "We can put Griggs with Mike shortly before the murder, we can show him leaving the house soon after—"

"Along with a herd of other assholes," Lynn pointed out.

"Yeah." Chris had been pacing, activity giving the illusion of accomplishment. He stopped and leaned back against his desk. "But that's a long way from putting the knife in his hand. Only Donny could do that for us."

"What about some of those other skinheads?" Jack suggested. "Aren't at least a couple of them still in custody? Make them an offer, get one of them to testify."

"After what happened in court today?" Lynn said. "Trust me, word's gone out. If they all keep their mouths shut they're all gonna walk."

"We've made offers to them all along and gotten nothing," Chris added. "They're not going to talk now."

They stood in various slumps, heads bowed toward one another. Jack's hands were in his pockets. Lynn looked elegant in a gray pinstriped suit, but her hands gripped behind her back made her shoulders strain the suit's seams. Their voices held no hope, even Jack's when he said, "At least you got the newspaper column to the jury. That says enough to convict him."

Yes, all their pieces together were enough to demonstrate convincingly to any reasonable person that Lee Griggs was a murderer. But the law required more.

"Not if Gloria Files does her job," Chris said quietly. "She's entitled to a limiting instruction telling the jurors they can't consider the statement as evidence of guilt, only for impeachment of Donny. If she gets that, we still don't have any evidence that Lee Griggs murdered Mike."

"I think we can trust Gloria to know that much law," Lynn said. None of them had ever before heard anyone suggest trusting Gloria Files, but in this context they all agreed.

Lynn lifted her head, her face ready for battle. "I say we go for it. Put on everything we have and let's see what happens."

No one joined her in her sudden enthusiasm. "Yeah, we'll go for it," Chris said. "But will the judge?"

"I'll tell you one thing," Lynn vowed. "That bastard's not going to get away with this."

Chris didn't ask her what she meant.

When they came out of Chris's office Irma Garcia, his secretary, said, "Dr. Greenwald called from downstairs."

"Where is she?" Chris looked around the spare, functional outer office.

"She didn't want to come up. She asked for you to meet her on the third floor."

The trial courtroom was on the third floor, but court had been recessed half an hour earlier. No one should be left. Chris walked through the maze of the D.A.'s offices, wondering if Anne had grown so intent on distancing herself from his professional life that she wouldn't come in the office anymore. But that would be silly, and Anne Greenwald didn't do silly things. Chris walked faster, hurrying down the stairs. Lynn followed.

Anne waited at the bottom of the stairs on the third floor. She put out a hand to halt their rapid descent.

"What is it?" Chris said.

Anne only inclined her head. Chris looked where she indicated, down the length of the empty hallway. At the far end the public hall ended at a smaller corridor that circled around to the judges' chambers. There at the junction of the public and private hallways sat a wooden bench that gave a semblance of privacy. A girl sat on the bench, her head down. She didn't seem to be waiting for anyone, she had just found a quiet refuge to be alone.

"Who—?"

Anne said, "Sometimes there's more action in the hall than in the courtroom."

Chris had always suspected that. But the hallway offered no

spectacle now. Only a girl sitting alone. Chris recognized her as Yvonne Davis, Lee Griggs' girlfriend. The former State's witness who had put the first glitch in the prosecution's case by sitting in the trial audience so she couldn't be called as a witness. That tiny event seemed long ago.

"What's bothering her?" Lynn asked.

"The skinhead troop, the ones who aren't in jail, went romping off to celebrate and nobody invited her along," Anne said, but she wasn't answering Lynn's question.

Chris started walking toward her then turned and motioned Anne to join him. She shook her head.

"This time you're on your own. I'll give you a hint, though. After Mrs. Martinez testified, after Yvonne left the courtroom, Yvonne followed Mrs. Martinez out. She spoke to her. It wasn't a long conversation."

Chris frowned, hungry for information and for strategy. "Maybe we should get Mrs. Martinez back here."

Lynn brushed by him and walked down the hallway. Chris hurried to catch up. Behind them Anne sat on the stairs and looked at her hands.

Lynn knew that her height could be intimidating. Sometimes she used it, sometimes she diminished it. When Yvonne looked up at the sound of footsteps Lynn quickly bent to sit on the bench. Not right next to Yvonne, but close. Chris remained standing.

"Yvonne?" he said. "You know what happened in the trial?"

Lynn made a small gesture that stopped him talking. Yvonne looked frightened for a moment at being surrounded by the prosecutors. Lynn bent her head low as if in supplication or comfort.

"You talked to Mrs. Martinez, didn't you? She's a nice lady. I've had supper at their house." Lynn smiled. Her eyes were wet. "You should see that place. Pictures of Mike. . . . The old lady's face still lit up when he walked in the room. When he'd say he had to leave she'd hug him and straighten his coat like he was going off to his first day of school. What did she say to you? Did she tell you about Mike?"

Yvonne rubbed the mound of her pregnancy. She sniffed. "I told her I was sorry. She didn't know who I was. She patted my stomach and told me to—take care of—"

Tears broke from Yvonne's eyes and fled down her cheeks. Lynn moved closer and put a tentative hand on the girl's stomach. Yvonne held the contact.

"He was her only child, girl. She would have given her own life for him. In a second, without thinking about it. You can understand that, can't you?"

They were both crying. Lynn almost whispered the next words. "You so sure you want Lee to go free? He killed that mama's baby, Yvonne, over nothing, for no reason at all. You think he'll be a good father?" Lynn put her hand on Yvonne's cheek and forced the girl to look at her. "He hurts people and likes it. Has he hurt you?" Yvonne didn't answer, but a moment of silent communication passed between them. Lynn's face, so broad and brown, looked very young for a moment. Her eyes were a frightened child's. Then she became a strong woman again. "I know he has. I know what that means. You know it, too, don't you? You gonna put this baby in his hands?"

Yvonne didn't answer. After a moment the two women noticed that the District Attorney wasn't participating in the conversation. They saw Chris standing apart, his face white as he stared out into the empty public hallway.

"What is it?" Lynn asked.

"He haunts this place," Chris answered in a hollow voice. "I can see that courtroom door opening and Mike coming out. Whistling or snapping his fingers, and you wouldn't know if his case was going well or falling apart. You just knew he was in trial and he was—crackling." Chris's fingers suddenly spread as if electricity had shot through him. "God. I've never known anybody who loved life so much. You saw him in the club," he suddenly said to Yvonne. Tears still streaked her face. "Did you see him laugh? He must have, in that place. Mike's laugh could change the whole tone of a room. Like a fresh coat of paint on the walls. No matter what other people were talking about. Did you see him laugh?"

Yvonne's face crumpled, her hand going to her mouth so the prosecutors weren't sure they heard correctly what she muttered next: "I have his blood on me."

"What?"

Yvonne straightened up. "Lee should never have made me listen to that testimony," she said. "That poor woman . . . He didn't care. . . ."

Lynn held her, rocking back and forth. Chris turned suddenly. He thought he'd heard the heavy courtroom door open. But the hallway remained empty except at its far end where Anne still sat quietly. Chris's shoulders tingled. Lynn Ransom stared up at him as if she saw the ghost in Chris's face.

The girl sobbed quietly.

The next morning the trial players reassembled. At the State's table Chris and Lynn sat very subdued, not talking, and looking as glum as two people who've decided their ship is going down and the lifeboats are worm-eaten. Beside them Lee Griggs still bubbled, as much with the pleasure of triumph as in anticipation of his release. Gloria Files sat more subdued, but her eyes sparkled. The prosecution had had eighteen hours to patch together a case, but the defense lawyer felt prepared for whatever the State might offer.

Everyone rose when Judge Henrichs entered, and when seats were resumed Chris was the only person on his feet. Before the judge could signal to the bailiff to bring in the jury Chris said,

"Your Honor, the State's next witness is going to be Yvonne Davis."

Like a re-enactment, Yvonne stood up from the audience, her face blank and pale. This time Lee Griggs and his lawyer were surprised to see her there. "Your Honor, this witness has already been disqualified," Files said.

"I think we can take care of that in two or three questions, your Honor."

"All right. Young lady?" Judge Henrichs gestured and Yvonne came slowly forward.

"Yvonne?" the defendant said. As his girlfriend passed him without answering Griggs said more harshly, "What are you doing, Yvonne?"

Judge Henrichs paused in the act of swearing in the witness to point at Griggs. "If you want to testify you'll get your chance. Until then you keep your mouth shut. You shout out again and I'll have you gagged faster than a slap in the face. And I don't mean a gag order. You got me?"

Griggs didn't answer. His glare became more general. It took in the whole courtroom.

Lynn did the questioning. "Yvonne, you were in the courtroom yesterday to hear the testimony of two of the State's witnesses?"

"Yes," Yvonne almost mumbled.

"Hadn't I told you to wait outside until it was your turn to testify?"

"Yes."

"Why did you sit in the audience instead?"

"Lee told me to," Yvonne said, looking at him for the first time.

Lynn transferred her attention to the judge. "Your Honor, this witness only heard from two witnesses who didn't testify to the facts of the murder. Her testimony can't have been influenced by—"

"Just a minute. Let me get this straight," Judge Henrichs interrupted. She turned to Yvonne. "The defendant told you to sit in the courtroom during other witnesses' testimony?"

"Yes ma'am."

"Did his attorney speak to you?" Judge Henrichs looked at Gloria Files as she asked the question, and Files made circular, self-absolving motions with her hands.

"No ma'am," Yvonne said solemnly.

"All right. Since the violation of the rule was at the instigation of the defendant, he can hardly call on the rule for protection now. I'll let the witness testify. Bring in the jury."

Lynn feared she would lose Yvonne again as the jurors filed into their box. Lee Griggs stared at his girlfriend intently, no longer hostilely. His eyes implored. Yvonne had lowered her head. Lynn knew that when Yvonne looked up and caught Griggs's expression Yvonne would falter.

They were all, spectators included, silent in the courtroom. For a moment the shuffling of the jurors' feet made the only sound. The presence of the jury returned animation to the others, as if a black and white scene were being slowly colorized. Lynn drew a breath and said, "May I approach the witness?"

"You may."

"Tell us your name, please."

When Yvonne looked up she didn't see Lee Griggs, she saw Lynn walking toward her, intercepting Yvonne's line of sight with the photograph Lynn held.

"How do you know Lee Griggs, Yvonne?"

"We're engaged," Yvonne said softly. She stared at the eight-by-ten photograph of Mike Martinez as it approached her.

"Did you and Lee meet this man the night of August third?"

"Yes."

"Do you know his name, Yvonne?"

Yvonne nodded. "He said his name was Mike Martinez."

Lynn placed the photograph in her witness's hand. Yvonne

was reluctant to take it. When she did she stared into Mike's face and her thumb compulsively rubbed the photo as if she could feel the texture of his shirt. Maybe some residue lingered from Mrs. Martinez's holding the picture to identify her dead son.

Lynn resumed her seat. "What did Lee Griggs tell Mike Martinez that night at the teen club, Yvonne?"

Gloria Files stood quickly. "Objection. Hearsay."

Lynn answered, "It's not offered for the truth, your Honor. Just what this witness heard."

"Overruled."

Gloria Files remained on her feet for a moment after the judge's ruling. She put her hand on her client's shoulder. The gesture did its work. Yvonne turned to look at her boyfriend at the defense table. Griggs's eyes held hers.

Lynn said quickly, "What did Lee say to him, Yvonne?"

"He said he wanted to buy some things Mr. Martinez had to sell," Yvonne said vacantly.

"Did they negotiate that night?"

"A little bit. They made plans to meet later."

"Did they leave the club together?"

"Yes."

"Did you go with them?"

"No. My part of the thing was over."

Lynn's voice strengthened. "What did you think, Yvonne, when they walked out of the club together? Did you know what was going to happen? Had Lee told you?"

"Objection!" the defense lawyer almost shouted. "Hearsay. Speculation. And besides that it's irrelevant what this witness thought."

No, it was the most relevant question Lynn had asked so far. It didn't matter that Judge Henrichs sustained the defense objection. Lynn saw Yvonne answering the question in her own mind. The girl's gaze turned inward as she relived what was for her the last moment of Mike Martinez's life. *Had* she known? She had at least guessed. Yvonne's eyes dropped from her boyfriend's face to the picture in her hand.

"What was the last thing Mike Martinez said to you?" Lynn asked.

"He said it had been nice to meet me." Yvonne stared at the picture, then put it facedown on the railing of the witness stand.

"Did you see Lee Griggs again that night?" Lynn asked, with her distinctive blend of sympathy and insistence. Lynn felt for her witness, but she insisted on having this story told or there'd be hell to pay.

"Yes. Lee called me later and I met him at his house."

"What kind of state was he in?"

"He was wild," Yvonne recalled. Her gaze returned to her boyfriend. His eyes implored her to stop. "Manic. He was jumping around, he had loud music on, he couldn't stop himself from moving."

"Did he tell you what had happened with Mike Martinez?"

"Objection, hearsay," Gloria Files said quickly. She added her questioning stare to her client's. Yvonne didn't glance at her.

"This is going to be an admission against interest, your Honor," Lynn explained. Judge Henrichs nodded. An exception to the hearsay rule is when someone has admitted committing a crime or something equally bad, the justification being that someone would only say such a thing about himself if it was true.

"Yes, he did," Yvonne said. She looked at her boyfriend with changed eyes. Rather deadened. Her voice came out flatly. Lee Griggs looked surprised, as if she were possessed.

"Lee said he took Mr. Martinez to this house they had, where the gang met. There were other guys waiting there. He called it a surprise party."

"What happened there, Yvonne?"

"He didn't tell me much of it. But he wanted to celebrate. I could see what had happened. Lee had blood on him. He hadn't even changed his clothes. He was covered in it. I knew a person couldn't lose that much blood and still be alive." Yvonne was crying. Her hand fell on the photo in front of her. Her voice twisted as she said, "Lee's pants were stiff with blood. He loved it. He wanted me to feel it. He made me dance with him. He held me tight against him. He laughed and laughed. . . ."

Griggs stood up suddenly at the defense table, the cords in his neck standing out. His mouth clamped in a tight line, but he slammed his fist down on the table, demanding attention. His fist dominated the scene. The table shook. Griggs's eyes were maddened. After a moment the bailiffs leaped toward him, his lawyer laid her inadequate-looking hand on his arm, and Griggs subsided. But for that moment he stood in the courtroom like a statue of rage. He glared at his girlfriend, demanding she shut up, insisting on control.

Yvonne looked straight at him. She continued to cry, but not out of fear of her boyfriend's rage. Everyone in the courtroom looked at Yvonne and saw that Griggs' fury was a familiar quality to her. Yvonne's arms slumped at her sides, as if she offered herself for a target. She had no shock in her expression, only woeful comprehension. She knew what he was. She had always known.

Gloria Files tugged on her client's arm, but when that had no effect she turned away from him. When bailiffs rushed in to force the defendant back down into his chair, the defense lawyer scooted her chair away from him. Files shook her head in disgust.

She didn't have much more to offer when final arguments began. The nice-boy image Files had so carefully constructed for her client lay hopelessly shattered. The defense lawyer argued that only Lee Griggs' righteous indignation over a lying witness had brought him out of his chair, but looking at the jurors' faces she cut that argument short.

It took the jury half an hour to find Lee Griggs guilty of El Rojo's murder.

Chapter 14

The punishment phase of Lee Griggs' trial went quickly, and so did the jury's deliberations afterwards. After the jurors read their verdict in court and were dismissed, Chris Sinclair didn't have to "give" a press conference. He just had to slow down and the press took a conference from him. Chris had never gone the "no comment" route. Sometimes he enjoyed talking to reporters. This was not one of those times, but he knew that the microphones and cameras and notepads represented everyone in San Antonio interested in what had just happened in the courtroom, and he had no right to withhold explanation. He stood in the hallway outside the courtroom and patiently waited for the questions.

"Are you disappointed in the verdict?" shouted the most persistent voice.

"How can I be disappointed in the maximum sentence?" Chris asked reasonably. "Life plus a ten-thousand-dollar fine. That'll put Lee Griggs out of circulation for a long time."

"But you lost the death sentence," said the pretty brunette from Channel Four. "The capital murder conviction you were seeking."

"I can't blame the jury for that. Our capital element was kidnapping. But once we lost our witness who'd been inside the house, our only evidence was that Mike Martinez went willingly to that house, even though he was tricked into going there. You can't blame the jury for finding Lee Griggs guilty just of murder. Even that took some imagination. Then at punishment they gave him everything they could."

"Never blame the jury," came a sly echo from Miles McKinley, the columnist who'd been the last reporter to leave Lou Briones' last press conference, as well as the one to interview Donny Sturns.

"Well, not this time," Chris said.

"What about you, Ms. Ransom? Are you satisfied with the verdict?"

Lynn stood tall and silent beside Chris for a long few seconds. The reporters oddly let the silence last, watching Lynn's brooding face, where anger was giving way to other emotions. "Whatever the verdict was," she finally said surprisingly softly, "it won't matter to Mike Martinez. But Lee Griggs won't be eligible for parole for thirty years. I hope that's some comfort to Mike's family. And I don't honestly know which is worse: to draw a death sentence or to go to prison at the age of twenty-one knowing you're going to spend your whole youth and most of your adulthood there. He'll have a long time for regrets."

The reporters let that be the strong last word. Chris felt Lynn's insistent grip on his elbow, and they walked away alone, down the Justice Center hallway. "Besides," Lynn added to Chris in an undertone, "young Griggs is going to have an interesting life in the general prison population, once they know what he is. He would've been safer on Death Row. He wanted a race war? I know some guys inside who're going to make him very happy."

Chris took her vindictiveness in stride, since he shared it. On the stairs he turned to her and said earnestly, "Lynn, you know you were on this case partly for a reason."

"A visual reason," she said humorously, but with no trace of a smile.

Chris nodded. "But I wouldn't have had you with me if I

didn't know how good you are. You did great work here. I couldn't have gotten a conviction without you. The way you talked to Yvonne—"

Lynn's gaze moved up the stairs, toward nothing. "We weren't just handling her, were we, Chris?" It was strange how no one walked past them on the stairs. Even the sounds of the Justice Center were muted. "Does he still haunt this place?" Lynn asked.

Chris stopped to feel for Mike's presence. "I think he always will," he said. "He owns this place, like those dead guys own the Alamo."

"Senseless," Lynn muttered, a tear forming.

Chris shook his head. "It was brutal and it was evil, but it wasn't random. Murdering Mike was part of a plan."

They stood silent on the stairs, being haunted.

That November day the weather turned very Novemberish. When Chris walked out of the Justice Center about four that afternoon the gray sky hung so low that the turrets of the old courthouse next door seemed likely to pierce it. The world felt small. The clouds were layered and thick and more interesting than the colorless landscape.

Chris sauntered, no place really to go. He had tried calling Anne and couldn't reach her at any of her numbers. But as he came down the Justice Center steps empty-handed he saw her at the end of the sidewalk, sitting at the wheel of her car, parked illegally. She got out, gave him a small wave, and waited.

He felt so glad to see her. Suddenly they seemed to have been transported miles away. Anne had her arms crossed, looking seriously purposeful, but a smile beginning.

"How did you know I was coming out?"

She held up a cellular phone. "I have a mole somewhere among your enormous staff."

Irma Garcia had urged Chris to go home, insisting he had no

other work that couldn't wait. She hadn't let him take a briefcase, either.

He put his arms around Anne. She wasn't dressed for work, she wore jeans and a plaid shirt, which made her look nothing like a lumberjack. Chris wished he had jeans waiting in his own car, that he could drop his suit on the sidewalk. "Got plans for tonight?" he breathed into her ear.

"Big plans. Get in."

That was when he saw the suitcases in the back seat of her Volvo. One of them was his.

They slid into the car and Anne took off, driving smoothly, watching the sparse Thursday traffic and smiling because she knew Chris's eyes were on her.

"You are a wonderful woman," he said, beginning to relax for the first time in days. Weeks.

"Don't start the compliments yet. Leave yourself room to build." She put her hand on his leg. He felt her individual fingers through the thin fabric of his suit. She slid her hand a few inches, curving her fingernails around his thigh.

One thin beam of sunlight sliced the clouds, so that just in front of them a tree suddenly burst into flaming red.

Chris dropped his tie and his suit coat into the back seat and loosened his collar. He didn't even ask where they were going. When Anne climbed onto Interstate 10 West it became clear she was heading out of town, but the suitcases had already been a major clue to that.

She explained without being asked. "At your place the phone would be ringing constantly, the news would be on. And God forbid they should track you to my house."

"I have to be available," Chris said idly.

"In case there's an emergency and someone has to be prosecuted in the middle of the night?"

He smiled. "What about you, you're the one with crises."

"Let 'em be crazy for a couple of extra days."

Anne watched the road through their conversation. Chris watched her. He followed the muscle that curved around the side of her neck and up into her jaw. He put his hand there, nestling under her hair. Anne smiled. When she did the skin beside her eye formed tiny ridges. Chris caressed them with his thumb. Anne took a deep breath.

He actually felt his shoulders loosen when they crossed the county line, out of his jurisdiction. Maybe it wasn't escaping his responsibilities, maybe the view of the land eased his tension. They were still on the modern divided Interstate but out of the city. The land rose steadily as they edged into the hill country. Anne turned on the heater in the car, very low. Outside, grass and stunted oaks and mesquites sparsely covered the long sloping land. But after they turned off the Interstate a long stretch of color appeared, all the more vivid for the passages of gray-green they'd traversed. The day as it closed turned drizzly, perfect weather for the hill country. They imagined they could hear the droplets plinking from the bare branches.

They came rather abruptly into Fredericksburg, a tiny farm town that had been founded a hundred and fifty years earlier by tough German settlers who had never imagined that their descendants would turn the place into a tourist attraction. Main Street, the five or six blocks of it that comprised the heart of the commercial district, was professionally quaint, lined mostly with antique shops, art galleries, and restaurants. Anne parked at one end and left Chris in the car while she ran into a small office and returned with a key and a map. The sign on the office's window said "Bed and Breakfast" in old-fashioned curlicued letters.

Chris read the map, but Anne knew pretty well where to go. She drove only three or four miles out of town, but that was enough to isolate them on back roads and farmland. They drove across a cattle guard through a log-and-wire gate and Anne parked in front of a cabin that looked as if it had been built by one of those first settlers—or carefully reproduced by Disney craftsmen a week ago. It was made of cedar logs with the bark still peeling off in places, stones holding up the plank porch and composing the chimney.

"Rustic," Chris said.

"Yeah, it might not even have a VCR." Anne jumped up onto the porch and went through the door ahead of him. Inside, the cabin proved to be almost a miniature. A small front room served for all the waking living space: living room, tiny kitchen, dwarf dining table. The antique furniture looked spindly, but closeness made the room comfortable, everything inclined toward the fireplace.

Anne had already gone through into the back room. "You can build a fire, can't you, boy scout?" she called.

"You kidding? Of course. Fires are my specialty. Where do you think they keep the gasoline?"

The cabin had firewood and firestarter blocks and newspaper. Chris managed to start a pretty good blaze, then made a couple of trips outside for more wood and to bring in the suitcases. He felt a little grimy in his day-old white shirt and limp suit pants, so he opened his small bag with more than a little curiosity about what Anne had picked out for him. Inside were socks and underwear, a pair of jeans, tennis shoes and one colorful shirt.

"You didn't bring me much choice in the way of clothes," he called.

He heard her in the doorway and turned. Anne had taken off her jeans and unbuttoned the plaid shirt, which hung only to the tops of her thighs. Her hair was tousled, falling to her shoulders. She had washed her face so that it shone. Her gray eyes glinted greenly, set off by her dark hair and the red shirt. She posed ironically, one hip cocked so that her legs were lithe and lovely.

"It's not a dress-up weekend," she said.

Chris got a quick look at the bedroom, which was also old-fashioned but of a different period and place than the rustic front room: the bed had a brass headboard, a thick flowered comforter, and fluffy white pillows.

But Anne led him into the bathroom, which turned out to be large and very modern. A whirlpool tub on a sort of stone altar dominated the room. Anne had filled it with water and bubble bath. She left him alone in the bathroom for a few minutes and when she returned Chris was almost dozing in the tub, sinking in the warm water under the glow of the ceiling heater. But the sound of her shirt hitting the floor raised one of his eyelids, and when she lowered herself into the tub opposite him his interest stirred. The water rose more than waist-high, with bubbles rising in mounds and valleys above. Bubbles bearded Anne's breasts, one nipple like Santa's bright red nose peeking through. The ends of her hair made jagged wet points against her skin.

"It's not really big enough for two," Chris said.

"No, we'll have to huddle together." Anne turned on the whirlpool jets. They just lay in the wonderfully vibrating water for long minutes, until her legs slid atop his and he used her legs to pull her toward him, her smile widening until it engulfed him.

When the tub became too small indeed they emerged and dried hastily, still pleasantly moist when they burrowed into the Victorian fantasy bed.

The night grew cold by their south Texas standards, but they had no food in the cabin so a couple of hours later they bundled into their jeans and jackets and drove back into town, to the Gallery restaurant, which offered a nice range of choices, coat and tie elegance upstairs in the Blue Room, German food and kitchen tables in the front room, tablecloths and Italian in the back. Chris and Anne chose the back, sitting at a small table close by a window that looked out on a courtyard where rain dripped off wrought-iron furniture. It looked like the courtyard of an abandoned castle under an evil spell. But inside the restaurant was warm and cozy, decorated in a Gay Nineties style. Anne and Chris still held their own warmth, not shared with anyone else.

When they were settled behind red wine and potato-skin appetizers Chris said, "What's ironic is the way Gloria Files screwed us around at the very beginning but that turned out—Sorry." He looked out at the drippy rain.

"You can talk about it," Anne said. "I didn't bring you away to pretend none of it happened. Tell me."

Anne had been around during the aftermath of Mike's murder and the trial, but she hadn't been in the courtroom and there'd never been much time for Chris to talk to her. He had shared more with Lynn.

"What's ironic is how Gloria Files pulled her little trick at the beginning, keeping Yvonne Davis in the courtroom so she wouldn't be allowed to testify for us. She didn't think about what Yvonne would hear while she was sitting there: that horrible medical testimony and watching Mrs. Martinez. That's what changed Yvonne. We would have lost otherwise."

"Lawyers do tend to neglect the human element, don't they?" Anne said.

Chris took her hand and held it to his lips. "Not me, though, right?"

She smiled. "You're showing definite signs of improvement."

His heart clenched as if some tragedy were impending. He wanted to hold her tighter. He wanted to stay out here forever, away from their lives. "Anne—"

She leaned toward him. "You can start the compliments now."

"I love you."

His voice had come out unexpectedly heartfelt. He said it without embellishment. He saw Anne start to make a joke, then frown worriedly, because she'd heard his sincerity. Her eyes softened. Her grip on his hand tightened. She touched her tongue to her lips as she tried to come up with a reply, but her eyes held on Chris's and that was answer enough.

Then Anne sighed with sudden recognition.

"Is that the waitress standing behind me, waiting for me to let go of your hand so she can plop food down in front of us?"

"Yes it is," Chris smiled.

"Could you ask her if we can get it to go?"

Their lives awaited them in San Antonio. The first thing Chris did upon his return was to go see Lee Griggs in the jail. A sort of exit interview. Soon Griggs would be on his way to the state prison system.

A captain of the guards let the District Attorney see the prisoner in one of the offices at the jail. Security around Griggs had loosened. He no longer had a capital murder indictment pending, he had become just a murderer with a life sentence, not all that rare a creature in the Bexar County Jail. In his orange coverall he looked painfully ordinary. Chris looked at him and thought, *People feared this kid. They did horrible things because they were scared of what Lee Griggs would do to them if they didn't.* Now Griggs looked like a boy on the first day of school. Chris thought about the reception Lynn had promised would be waiting for Griggs in prison.

If this were an official interrogation Griggs' lawyer should have been present. But it wasn't that formal. Chris didn't care if Griggs confessed. They were done with that. Chris only wanted confirmation of what he believed, that somehow Malachi Reese had gotten to Griggs, put the thought in his head of murdering Mike. How could someone arrange that?

Griggs still smoldered. He had grown madder than ever. His lip curled when he saw the District Attorney sitting on the corner of a metal desk waiting for him.

"Your pal got what was coming to him," he snarled.

So Griggs had given up playing it coy. Chris held his temper. "How do you figure that?"

"He prosecuted my sister," Griggs snapped. "Got her sent to TYC."

"She had a bad time of it there—" Chris began.

"She got raped by a guard!" Griggs screamed. He came close to Chris. Griggs' spittle sprayed Chris's suit. Chris didn't move.

"I don't think so," he answered quietly.

Being contradicted made Griggs even more furious. "She had a baby, goddamn it!" His voice grew softer, but his eyes turned even meaner. "A little brown baby. Shit. But I got 'em back, I guess." He grinned, but his grin wasn't very good. It didn't look happy.

"You are an idiot," Chris said.

Griggs' hands came up. Chris stood up and pushed him back. Before Griggs could move again Chris said, "Were you in juvenile court the day your sister was sentenced?"

"I was busy that day."

"That's what I figured. Did you check the records? No. Mike Martinez was a juvenile prosecutor all right, but he didn't have anything to do with your sister's case."

Griggs looked uncertain. "Who told you he did?" Chris asked.

Griggs licked his lips. "This should've been my defense. If that stupid bitch—"

So he no longer loved his defense lawyer. A guilty verdict often has that effect. The other odd but common post-trial effect was that Griggs felt a sort of comradeship with the man who'd prosecuted him. They'd shared the experience. And since Griggs had become mad at his own lawyer, by contrast he'd grown willing to share with Chris. He wanted to talk, and the District Attorney was handy. Chris had had this kind of revealing chat with other defendants after other guilty verdicts.

"Who told you?" Chris insisted.

Lee Griggs looked down at the floor. "A voice on the phone," he mumbled. "A guy who said, 'The prosecutor who got your sister knocked up likes to sell things on the side. You could arrange to meet him. His name's Mike Martinez.'"

Chris could almost hear the voice, soft and authoritative. Not Malachi Reese's voice—he would have been on Death Row at the time—but the words were Malachi's. Quietly brutal words, making perfect sense to the brutal clod Malachi had chosen as his instrument of revenge.

"He lied to you," Chris said.

Griggs shook his head. He sneered again. *"You're* the one lying. I know why you'd lie to me. Why would he? Somebody wouldn't call me up just to tell me a lie."

"To get you to do a job for him. He picked you out, Lee, because he figured you were dumb enough to do exactly what he wanted with just a little push."

Griggs was still mad as hell, but he looked confused as well. The conversation, with only a slight elevation, had gone over his head. "Who?" he growled.

Chris pulled a photograph of Malachi Reese out of his breast pocket. He'd chosen the photo carefully for this meeting: Malachi in a dark suit, looking very handsome, very African.

"Him," Chris said.

Griggs stared at the picture. "You lying bastard."

"You did a dirty job for him, Lee, and your reward is life in prison. Maybe you'll run into him there. He's at the Ellis Unit, on Death Row. His name's Malachi Reese. Be sure to tell him he owes you one."

He thrust the photo into Lee Griggs' hands and walked out of the little office.

"An anonymous call," Chris kept saying that evening at Anne's house. "That's all it took."

"Killers aren't very smart," Anne said. "It takes a really dumb guy to think murdering someone will improve things."

But explanations didn't help. After a while she just put her arms around him and held him. Chris couldn't let go of the case, though.

"It leaves me nothing," he said. "I wanted to find Reese's trail, and this is just nothing. An anonymous call."

"Forget it," Anne murmured. "What more could you do to him anyway?"

She stroked his temple. Chris didn't forget, of course. He never would, but gradually the problem receded to the back of his mind.

Some things did change, their lives improved in the wake of the Griggs trial and the trip to Fredericksburg. Chris no longer had a big case pending, he had time to show up at Anne's office and take her to lunch, to spend weekends together. Danger seemed to have retreated from them for the time being. Chris remained rather constantly tense waiting for Malachi Reese to strike again, but that gave Anne good reason to rub his shoulders and lie full-length atop him. Their voices were softer than in the past; they understood each other's murmurs. Once in a while Chris put his hand on his phone just before it rang with Anne calling.

In the weeks after the trial Chris's public reputation grew unsettled. Now he had done his best to put a white man on Death Row, too, and he'd done it with the help of an African-American woman. Of course the politically correct party line still said he'd done all that just for show, but not as many people subscribed to the party line anymore.

One Saturday afternoon Chris went to the Robert Dawson Community Center on the near east side, where the grounds had been set up like a carnival, with food booths and games for kids, but instead of clowns they had a platform for speakers. The organizers billed the occasion as a rally for peace and justice, though some of the speakers were militant in their insistence that justice was impossible. Chris walked through the crowd in an open-collared shirt and khakis, sipping a soft drink and turning with an open, questioning expression when he heard his name muttered. He stood below the platform listening to one speaker who more and more directed his anger at the District Attorney, until one of the event organizers came to Chris and said reluctantly but politely, "Wouldn't you like a turn?"

Chris allowed himself to be led on to the platform. Laughter died across the grounds. Five hundred people turned watchfully toward him, including two cops leaning against their patrol car out on the street. Chris stared into individual faces for a long moment, seeing anger and curiosity and hope, and said, "My name is Chris Sinclair. I'm the District Attorney of Bexar County, so some brands of justice are my responsibility. And I am all for peace. But I didn't come to speak to you. I came to listen."

And he walked down again. At the foot of the steps Win Phillips, the city councilman for this district, stood waiting. Phillips frowned at him—if someone happened to snap a photo it would not show the councilman and the District Attorney in friendly conversation—but Phillips looked at Chris more directly than he had during their other meetings. He spoke thoughtfully. "I don't know what to think about you," he said.

"Well that's an improvement," Chris answered.

"You had Malcolm Turner arrested," Phillips said accusingly.

"He fired shots at me, Mr. Phillips. And I suspect him of much—"

"I know what you suspect." Phillips still watched Chris closely. The councilman had light brown eyes. They projected curiosity, not anger. "At first I thought you were starting some kind of vendetta."

"If I had a political agenda I would have had you investigated," Chris answered softly, "because you let him use your car."

"That's what I expected."

"But I told my investigator I knew you couldn't have been involved. I told Jack not to pursue that."

Phillips didn't offer thanks. He remained a study in thoughtfulness as Chris turned and walked into the crowd. After his short speech people at the rally talked to him. Some wanted to tell him about the mistreatment of a relative by the justice system, some wanted to report crimes that should be prosecuted. The complaint-to-compliment ratio ran about a dozen to one. But Chris listened receptively and at least they talked. "Come see me," he said to more than one.

But even while his image improved slightly, no taint of Mike Martinez's murder fell on Malachi Reese. Chris made public the pictures and records showing that El Rojo had been driving Reese's car. No one thought the pictures were faked: too many of Reese's friends remembered him in the car. But the link could easily be dismissed as coincidence. Chris's "explanation" of how Reese had manipulated Lee Griggs into killing Mike was no more than a hunch. Chris wouldn't share that publicly. Of course if he did, the skinhead, from prison, would deny the idea vehemently, outraged at the suggestion that a black man had pulled his strings.

Christmas passed, and the first dreary weeks of January. There were already spring-like days when Chris said in his office one day, "We've had that kid Malcolm Turner in jail for too long. I have him charged with murder but I can't prove it."

Jack Fine answered, "Nobody got killed during your Griggs trial. You and Anne haven't been bothered while we've had Turner in custody. Doesn't that prove something?"

Chris shook his head. "Not to a legal certainty. He's been denied bail twice now, but if we can't prove his connection to Malachi Reese I'm going to have to cut him loose, before a judge does it for me. Then what?"

Jack shrugged. "Have to catch him at something else."

"*After*," Chris said vehemently. "After he hurts somebody else. I'm sick of waiting for after."

Jack touched Chris's arm, a very light touch, but coming from the investigator it was a very tender gesture. He said gently, "I understand that, Chris."

"Besides," Chris continued more quietly, "I doubt Malachi only had one guy on the outside willing to do what he wants. If he did, he's damned sure working on new connections now. He got to Lee Griggs with an anonymous phone call. Who made it for him? Where's his pipeline to the outside world?"

Jack frowned. "But you've already taken your best shot at Malachi. What more can you do to him? Legally what can you—"

Chris laughed harshly. "I'm not talking legally."

The next morning he knocked on a pebbled glass door on the fifteenth floor of the Tower Life Building, a sort of gothic spire one block from the courthouse, festooned with gargoyle faces and law offices, including that of Leo Pedraza, one-time District Attorney and currently attorney for Malachi Reese. The secretary who opened the door looked startled, first when she recognized Chris, then at the sight of the two investigators and three uniformed police officers crowding the hall behind him.

"Hello, ma'am, we have a search warrant," Chris said politely, as he brushed past her and the other searchers entered the office more brusquely.

"Wait," the secretary said ineffectually. "Let me tell Mr. Pedraza—"

The outer office was rather large, furnished with the secretary's desk, client chairs, and three large filing cabinets, which one investigator immediately started opening. Two short wings off the outer office led to three more offices. Chris went through the middle door and found Leo Pedraza standing, startled, behind his large old-fashioned wooden desk. Files and papers covered the desk, and from the doorway Chris saw two more stacks of papers on the floor. The search would not be fun.

"Hello, Mr. Pedraza. I imagine you'll want to read this."

Pedraza took the warrant with fingers that shook slightly, but not from fear. His face grew dark behind his famous thick moustache. "I knew you were crazy, but what judge is equally insane?" He started skimming the search warrant, then looked up in renewed surprise. "Malachi? There's no case pending against Malachi Reese."

"What makes you think not?"

"You're going to prosecute him again?"

"Stranger things have happened," Chris said, beginning to shift files on the lawyer's desk. He hoped to see Pedraza glance toward a drawer or move to prevent Chris from studying any particular stack of papers.

Pedraza didn't give him the satisfaction. He began to recover himself nicely, his bluster warming up. "You are wildly overplaying your hand, my friend. Have you heard of attorney–client privilege?"

"Yes I have, including the exceptions to it. The privilege doesn't apply to evidence of a crime or planning of a crime."

Pedraza glared. "You're accusing me of conspiracy."

Chris walked over to the wall, knelt and started looking through the files stacked there. Pedraza came and put his foot on the stack, demanding an answer. Chris stood up next to him. "Reese is giving orders. But prison officials read all his mail except his legal correspondence. There's only one person who can be passing on his instructions, Leo."

They stood nose to nose, the former District Attorney and the current one. Pedraza looked furious. Chris waited to receive his threats or his punch. When neither came Chris realized that Pedraza's fury was hollow.

The search continued. Pedraza went off to court—after the contents of his briefcase were carefully inspected—and returned an hour later to find his office still crowded and cluttered. Chris would have kept the search quiet, but since Pedraza had been to the courthouse—Rumor Central—news of the unprecedented search would be filling the outside world by now. Pedraza immediately saw that the searchers had found nothing. "You bastard," he said triumphantly to Chris. "When I file suit do you think I should call this libel, slander, or just invasion of privacy?"

"We found your Reese files," Chris said, holding up three conspicuously thin file folders. "But there're hardly any letters from your client here. I know he's written you more than this. He's written to you at least once a week for the nine months he's been in prison. Where are they?"

Pedraza sneered. "I don't save every scrap of paper that comes into this office."

Chris looked ironically around the outer office, portions of which were nearly knee-deep in paper. He didn't even have to say *Bullshit*.

"What have you done with his letters? Have you destroyed the incriminating ones, or do you have a secret file someplace?" Pedraza still looked contemptuous. So did Chris. "Why're you taking so long to answer, Leo? Don't you have a good lie ready?"

"I'm still counting the reasons why I don't have to answer anything you ask."

This snit fight wasn't doing anyone any good. Chris turned to the secretary's desk, dialled a phone number, and said, "Go ahead, Jack." Hanging up the phone, he said, "That's the search starting at your house. And your storage unit. We know about that too."

Chris was sorry to see Pedraza smile briefly, before resuming his tirade. The defense lawyer remained furious about the searches, but they didn't frighten him. *Damn*. This had been Chris's only idea, the only connection he could guess in Malachi Reese's pipeline to the outside world.

They were still searching, but listlessly, half an hour later, while Leo Pedraza sat in one of the client chairs looking more and more smug, when a shadow loomed in the pebbled glass of the outer door. Chris's heart leapt hopefully. Another confrontation would beat the hell out of this paper-shuffling. But the visitor didn't enter. The shadow stooped and a rubber-banded stack of mail plopped through the mail slot.

Pedraza glanced at the envelopes nervously. Chris pounced on them and sorted through them quickly. He went through them again more dispiritedly and handed them to the waiting secretary. "Your phone bill says Second Notice."

Chris realized too late that he should have intercepted Pedraza's mail secretly until he caught something good. He couldn't do that now. Pedraza and Reese were warned.

Idly he watched the secretary sort through the mail, leave three of the envelopes on her own desk, and carry the rest through the open doorway into her boss's office. Since a few minutes after Chris had come in, the secretary had done her best to pretend the searchers weren't there. She carried on with her typing and phone calls and when one of the searchers got in her way she would just stop as if she'd suddenly decided not to go that way after all. Chris watched her leave the mail in the top of a wooden box on Leo Pedraza's desk, and shook his head in disgust with himself. "Anybody check the in and out boxes on his desk?"

Nobody answered. Still shaking his head, Chris walked into the inner office, quickly followed by its occupant, who began blustering anew.

The in and out trays for mail were nice, boxes made of varnished dark wood rather than wire baskets. First Chris sorted through the mail on top, that he had already seen, then went deeper into the pile. Like most lawyers, Leo Pedraza took too long to get around to answering his mail. One letter bore a postmark two months old.

Chris's fingers stopped, and he sighed. He had come to a small manila envelope, six inches by nine, which carried a handwritten return address that said, "M. Reese." The address was the Ellis Unit of the state prison, a unit Chris had come to know well since Reese's incarceration on Death Row there.

Chris held up the envelope between two fingers, smiling. Leo Pedraza said sullenly, "Of course I get mail from him."

The manila envelope was less than a week old. It had been slit. Chris opened it and took out a thin sheet of lined paper that said only, "Dear Leo, please pass on the enclosed as per past instructions. Salutations."

Only a smaller envelope remained, unaddressed. Chris opened the smaller envelope to find a Hallmark card. Chris frowned. "Early for Easter."

The front of the card displayed a drawing of the risen Christ in all his glory, obviously beyond his earthbound incarnation. The printed message inside came from the New Testament: "This is my beloved Son, in whom I am well pleased." Below it Malachi had written, "I, too, shall rise again."

That was all. But the printed message held Chris's attention: "My beloved son."

He had found evidence of the source of Reese's continuing power to accomplish things in San Antonio: he'd left in place a lieutenant who owed him the loyalty of blood.

Chris held up the card, his eyes hot. "Who do you deliver these to?"

Pedraza, of course, didn't answer. As he'd pointed out in his legalistic way, there were so many good reasons why he wouldn't say a word.

The card proved, at least to Chris's satisfaction, that Malachi Reese had a son in San Antonio. It confirmed his suspicion about Malcolm Turner, the sixteen-year-old he suspected of murdering Chris's witness during Reese's trial.

But the certainty brought no satisfaction, and soon gave way to other doubts. He had Turner in custody. Why would Reese send him a card? That connection didn't do him any good anymore. Why send a congratulatory card from prison to jail? Un-

less Reese, too, realized that the boy would soon have to be released for lack of evidence.

Chris soon thought of another possibility. Malachi Reese had
another child still at large in the outside world.

Chris's two triumphs in court felt ephemeral, leaves pulped under
a Cadillac's tires. Law didn't matter to Malachi Reese. Chris
couldn't sleep waiting for him to strike again. During those sleep-
less nights he worried about Anne, if she weren't with him. Both
Anne and Malachi Reese were constantly in his thoughts. Later
he wondered why it had taken him so long to put them together.

Anne arrived at Chris's condo on a Friday evening, late but
laughing as she came in, using her own key. She wore a workday
dress but had put on a weekend face, a happy, expectant expression with just the trace of a wicked thought crossing her mind.

Chris had gotten only half-undressed, tie and suit coat dis-
carded, white shirt unbuttoned, feet bare. He sat on one of his
chrome-legged dining table chairs that he had pulled over near
the patio doors, staring out into the dark night, shot with headlights passing on Broadway.

"What's the matter?" Anne called lightheartedly. She hurried
to throw herself on him, but she stopped when he turned to her.

Chris looked at her abstractly, studying the changes in her
face. "Someone shot at us," he finally said. "Shot at me, I thought,
but Reese denied trying to have me killed, and I believe him. I
don't think he's lied to me yet. He doesn't want me dead, not yet.
But he could kill you."

Anne didn't appear startled by the idea. She just watched him.

Chris set down a cup of very cool tea and stood up. "Did you
lose a patient shortly after that drive-by shooting? Did someone
stop seeing you professionally?"

"Chris, you know I can't say anything. God, I wish I could. I've prayed to think of a way to tell you——"

So he had guessed right. Even Anne had lied to him. He couldn't take anyone at face value, or trust any appearance.

"Don't stare at me like that," she said. "I'm not some stranger."

"I thought about you while I was having Leo Pedraza's office and home searched. That's what happened to you. Somebody broke into your office and your house looking for a file. They thought you might have some inside information. So do I. You were always so positive of Reese's guilt. You knew more about him than I did. They shot at you once, but then the attacks stopped. Because the drive-by was a warning, but not aimed at you. It did its work, it told your patient to stay away from you. The one who'd told you about Malachi Reese. You were treating his son, weren't you?"

Reluctantly, as if she were breaking a covenant, but so slowly he didn't believe her, Anne shook her head.

"Lives are at stake, Anne, and I don't have any other way to get to him. Give me some hint."

"I just did," she said. "I'll tell you something else. My patient was in deep pain, suffering the terror of beginning to question fundamental lifelong beliefs."

"Reese's teachings?"

She nodded again. "You might have an ally there. But you have to be very careful."

"How can I be, Anne, when I'm groping in the dark?"

She came and held him for a long time, but she wouldn't tell him any more. Anne wouldn't violate a trust, no matter what. She did what else she could to help him, including listening while he spun theories. When Anne talked, even in her small offhand remarks, she heard Chris listening for clues in everything she said. She smiled sadly and stroked his forehead.

Chapter 15

Then Judge Phil Pressman, who had presided over Malachi Reese's trial, took action, deciding to return Reese to San Antonio. Not only that, he planned to make a show of the occasion.

On the appointed day, a small crowd filled the courtroom. A smaller and more sullen crowd of juvenile prisoners sat chained two by two in the jury box. Judge Pressman had grown, if anything, more sure of his own eccentric judgment since the trial. He looked over the courtroom as if the audience had come to receive his royal favors.

"Judge, this is crazy," Chris said. "You shouldn't have anyone in here. Certainly not other prisoners."

Judge Pressman preened. "It's an excellent idea. The death penalty is supposed to be a deterrent, isn't it? What better use of it than to let these juvenile offenders, just starting out on the wrong path, see what the end of that road is?"

The carefully worded speech made Chris look around for a microphone. Judge Pressman sat up straight behind the bench, his robe freshly pressed. The outer doors of the courtroom were locked, but a television cameraman just outside one of the glass panels pointed his camera in the judge's direction. Judge Pressman lifted one of his long, freckled hands but decided not to risk looking vain by checking his hair. Instead he smoothed one sandy eyebrow, as if in thought. Chris saw the uselessness of talking to him. The judge wouldn't even look at him.

It was early spring, almost a year since Reese's trial. Judge Pressman had grown irritable and impatient waiting for the state Court of Criminal Appeals to issue an opinion in the appeal. Spring had ushered in an election season, Judge Pressman craved media attention, and he had decided to bring Malachi Reese back to town to set his first execution date. This would be purely ceremonial—execution would be stayed for years, until Reese's lawyers exhausted his appeals—but Judge Pressman didn't mind presiding over a ceremonial occasion.

The day's event should have been an austere affair, with the courtroom full of bailiffs and no spectators. Instead the spectator seats of the courtroom were half-filled, and worst of all, ten young prisoners sat in the jury box. Judge Pressman had had them brought in their jail coveralls and thongs to receive an object lesson. The young offenders averaged about fifteen years of age, but the crimes they were charged with ranged from aggravated assault to murder. Judge Pressman had fallen prey to some sugary Andy Hardy past if he thought these young thugs to be still impressionable enough to be deterred. Instead they probably idolized Malachi Reese, if they knew his secret reputation.

Malcolm Turner sat in the front row of the jury box, the sixteen-year-old accused of murdering Adolfo Rodriguez during Reese's trial. Chris tried to catch the young man's eye, but Turner looked downcast to the point of looking drugged. Jail had apparently not been good to him. The juvenile judge had released Turner on bail while Chris tried to build a murder case against him, but two days earlier Turner had gotten arrested again after being found in violation of the terms of his release. In a search of his school locker, a gun had been found.

"This boy in the front is charged with capital murder," Chris said to the judge. "It's dangerous to—"

"Which you can't prove," Judge Pressman said mildly. "Everyone knows that. Let's throw a little fear of the Lord into him before you have to let him go."

Chris seethed quietly. Unfortunately, judges are in charge of their courtrooms.

Outside the Justice Center, protestors had re-emerged in full force. They clashed with one another while awaiting the arrival of the heroic prisoner. Judge Pressman couldn't be blamed for them, or for the crush of reporters outside the courtroom, including at least a couple of national correspondents. Reese himself would have announced his second coming to the press and his supporters. But Pressman had even let some of those supporters into the courtroom. Reese's supporters represented a substantial segment of voters, and the judge vowed to be inclusive. Some half a dozen Reese backers, supposedly the more rational faction, sat quietly in the spectator seats, glancing around, waiting for the main event or at least an opening act. Judge Pressman waved to them.

The most prominent person in this contingent, Win Phillips, the city councilman from the east side, sat with his arms folded, looking severe. He seemed to be a judge himself there in the center of the courtroom. Judge Pressman beckoned to the councilman, offering a seat inside the bar, but Phillips ignored him. In no way would he offer his stamp of approval on these proceedings.

A tap at the back door of the courtroom, the door that led behind the courtroom to the court offices and jury rooms, drew the attention of the nearest person. A young bailiff named Jaime Sanchez, the thinnest uniformed man in the room, opened the door at a nod from the judge, peeked out, and admitted the two last visitors, ushering them in hurriedly so he could lock the door behind them.

Anne Greenwald and Lynn Ransom entered together, surprising Chris. Anne hadn't told him she planned to be here. Her appearance raised his tension level several notches. He crossed to her and said quietly, "What are you doing here?"

"I asked Lynn to get me in," Anne replied just as softly. "I wanted to be here. I want to see him."

"Malachi?" Chris remembered Anne's unusual interest in this defendant. He wondered if her former patient were here. Chris's eyes swept the young prisoners in the jury box. Several of them looked at Anne closely all right, but not in recognition. Chris wanted to stand between Anne and the lost boys, or better yet have her out of the building.

Anne withdrew quietly. Things hadn't gone askew between her and Chris, but her secret remained a constant presence in his thoughts of her. He hadn't been able to prove a family connection between Reese and Malcolm Turner, and Anne hadn't offered him any help.

Lynn didn't acknowledge her boss. She looked severe in a suit and unadorned white blouse. Lynn's thick hair was swept back from her face. She had the profile of a warrior. Chris remembered Lynn's criticism of his going after the death sentence against Reese. It was just like her, harboring those feelings, to come watch the sentence being imposed.

Lynn went close to the jury box, looking down at Malcolm Turner with a fierce frown. But she didn't confine her anger to the boy in the jury box. She glanced around the courtroom and walked away, behind Chris.

Chris could only be grateful that the judge hadn't allowed a TV camera to set up on a tripod right in the courtroom. But that one just outside the locked doors shot continuously. They were all performing a pantomime for a TV audience. Suddenly the camera turned. Judge Pressman caught the motion and turned too, because Malachi Reese had just entered the courtroom.

Those protestors out on the building's front lawn waiting to see Reese carried up the Justice Center steps in manacles were going to be disappointed. He had been brought into the building in an anonymous van, then hustled upstairs through the Justice Center's hidden passageways. Malachi Reese made a quiet entrance through the side door and entered the courtroom before anyone realized. He stood unaccompanied for a moment as his guard stopped to relock the side door of the courtroom.

Then the first spectators saw him, and gasped. Even Judge Pressman looked taken aback. To those who remembered Reese as a businessman in tailored suits his appearance was shocking. He had grown almost gaunt in prison. In his orange coverall, hands handcuffed in front of him, he looked like a torture victim. The shortsleeved coverall hung baggily on Reese, revealing a triangle of his chest and his long arms, as if Reese had been dragged out of bed and brought to court in his pajamas. More startling to those who knew him was the way Reese fit this prisoner's uniform. He had aged much more than a year since he'd left San Antonio. He had a haggard look and a dead stare. Reese looked more like the Count of Monte Cristo near the end of his long captivity than like a man in his prime who'd last been seen in this courtroom less than a year earlier.

Chris Sinclair, the only person in the courtroom who had seen Reese inside his prison cell, knew that Malachi Reese had *not* turned into this pathetic stick figure. Imprisonment hadn't beaten Reese down. Nor had the loss of his wardrobe.

But Reese's shuffling manner relaxed the bailiffs, who recognized that institutionalized look. "Watch out," Chris said, but if anyone heard him no one reacted. There were two bailiffs close beside Reese, another who took up a post at the corner of the jury box, and four more scattered throughout the courtroom. They had plenty of manpower for one shackled prisoner, more than enough.

His primary guard brought Reese directly before Judge Pressman's bench, where the prisoner straightened with respect. "Good morning, your Honor. I hope I haven't kept the Court waiting."

Now Chris's neck prickled like mad. This kowtowing zombie wasn't Malachi Reese. Chris moved closer, a few feet from the

prisoner, but Reese wouldn't look at him. He kept his obse-
quious stare on the judge, which obviously gratified Pressman.

"Mr. Reese, I have a sad duty to perform today. I've brought
these young men to observe, hoping it will be instructive for
them. Gentlemen—" Pressman turned toward the juveniles.
"This is Mr. Malachi Reese, who was once one of the most respected men in this community. But now here he is, because he
made mistakes of exactly the kind some of you have made."

Reese seemed to notice the prisoners for the first time. His
sad gaze encompassed them. "How very wise, your Honor.
May I—?"

Judge Pressman waved him toward the jury box. In his ankle
chains and with his hands handcuffed in front of him Reese
shuffled toward the boys, who watched him attentively. Reese's
guards stayed right at his elbows. Chris stood close too, trying to
read Reese's face. He felt no communion with him. Reese's prisoner disguise was complete.

Lynn stood off to the side, half-turned away from the group
in the front of the courtroom, divorcing herself from the spectacle. Anne watched Reese with intense fascination.

The prisoners were young, but most of them had spent more
time on studying sullen, hard looks than they had on algebra. But
they paid Malachi Reese closer attention than they ever had a
teacher. Some of them watched him with awe. Looking at them,
Chris felt certain they knew Reese's underworld reputation.
Reese's chains didn't faze them. The boys saw the handcuffs as
only a temporary disguise, or the setup for a magic trick. Chris
thought so too. And he thought he saw something else in two or
three of the young faces that made the hair stand up on the back
of his neck: anticipation.

Reese stood in front of the jury box, leaning toward the juvenile prisoners like a missionary playing to a crowd of the un-
saved. His voice rang with solemn earnestness. "The judge is
absolutely right, young men. I pray to God you never see what
I see every day. I see men around me on Death Row who wanted

the best out of life but weren't willing to work for it, and now they have no lives at all. *Death* Row. That's all they've earned. Some of them are barely older than you. Let me tell you . . ."

Reese drew everyone's attention. Pressman leaned over his bench toward the prisoner. Reese's opening remarks almost sounded like the beginning of a confession. His supporters watched from the spectator seats, waiting for the Reese they knew to re-emerge.

"People once admired me——" Reese continued quietly.

"We still do!" a voice rang out. But the sound quickly died and Reese talked over it, with a slight smile. "——for my ability to get things done. For my attempts at justice for the weak and the beaten. But I took an alternate route, young men. I made my own way, and I made enemies. That doesn't have to be your way. I had to fight the system, but you don't have to. Things are more open now. The system will embrace you if you let it. Isn't that right, Mr. Sinclair?"

Being drawn into Reese's monologue startled Chris. Reese beckoned to him but Chris stood still, putting his hands in his pockets. "Yes," he said noncommittally, and had to clear his throat.

"*This* should be your role model," Reese said. "Not me." He paused a moment as the young prisoners stared hostilely at the District Attorney. "Yes, it's hard to picture, isn't it?" Reese said with a smile. "But it could be you. You have that opportunity. Look at her."

Lynn stood over close to the railing, across the courtroom from Reese. She too scowled at being held up to the audience. "*She* could serve as your role model. There she is, a prosecutor. Working within the system. With opportunities for life such as you've never dreamed of. Miss, won't you——?"

Lynn shook her head. She began walking, aiming to pass behind Reese and maybe out the side door of the courtroom. Chris knew her expression, the one of having heard enough.

But as Lynn passed close to the bailiff Malachi Reese shot out his long handcuffed arms and gripped her shoulder. Lynn looked up, startled.

"Won't you give them one break?" Reese asked pleadingly. "One piece of your heart?"

"Sir," said one of the bailiffs warningly, grabbing Reese's forearm. Lynn shrugged angrily, freeing herself. But she turned toward the young prisoners in the jury box as if she had to respond. She would never back down from a challenge.

Even Chris, standing close to the action, didn't see what happened next. There were too many people knotted together, Lynn in front of Reese, his guards behind him, one guard's arm still extended toward Lynn, Lynn unexpectedly close to the jury box.

Suddenly the front row of prisoners rose as one. They all wore ankle chains, but that didn't slow them as they came over the short wall in front of them. Lynn stumbled toward them.

"No!" Reese shouted, jumping back so that he entangled the two bailiffs behind him. And now the second row of prisoners were moving, swarming over the bailiff who stood beside their jury box. The prisoners on the front row had engulfed Lynn Ransom. One skinny brown arm went inside her jacket and came out with her pistol.

The spectators in the audience rose as one, shouting. They tried to see, they tried to help. Malachi Reese had fallen to the ground, and at least one shot had cracked through the courtroom.

The spectators cut off the bailiffs back by the courtroom's front doors. The guards screamed for the spectators to get down, but their shouts were lost. The bailiffs scrambled forward, knocking people aside, but their progress was much too slow.

Because by then Malcolm Turner had Lynn's gun. He fired at the bailiffs on the ground with Malachi Reese. Behind him, another kid had the other bailiff's gun.

Chris had jumped back reflexively, then spun and went for Anne. He tried to push her toward the back door of the courtroom, the door being guarded by the young bailiff Jaime Sanchez.

"Move!" Sanchez shouted. He pushed Chris and Anne hard out of his line of fire then went for his sidearm, but the delay had cost him. The kid in the jury box, on his feet now, saw Sanchez as the most immediate threat. The prisoner aimed and fired. Sanchez screamed. Blood sprayed from his neck, splattering the side door of the courtroom.

The prisoners moved quickly as a tangle of snakes. In seconds they had spread from the jury box. One boy vaulted over the side, landing on the closest bailiff. The leg chains didn't slow him down. The handcuffs served as weapons as he hammered his clenched fists down again and again.

Others swarmed over the two bailiffs Malachi Reese had brought down. One prisoner dropped sickeningly with his knee on an exposed neck.

His partner grabbed up the guard's gun and moved forward. Chris flung himself across the sad splayed form of Jaime Sanchez. He got his fingers on Jaime's pistol, but just as he did he heard a loud cranking click and looked up to see the prisoner three feet from Anne, pointing a cocked Glock at her chest. The boy looked at Chris with a small smile. Chris had no chance. He lifted his hand away from the gun on the floor, raising his hands palms outward.

Anne's face had gone white. Her eyes darted, but found no place good to look. The courtroom swarmed with orange coveralls. Several spectators had gone for the hall doors, but those doors were locked, so the would-be escapees piled up there, crushing a bailiff posted by the door. When he managed to push free, a kid scrambling in that direction shot him. The bailiff grunted, clutched his chest, and sat down hard against the doors. Over his shoulder the wide eye of the TV camera outside the doors took everything in. Tape rolled as the horrified cameraman stared into the courtroom.

There could be no doubt the attack had been organized. After the first kid had moved none of the others had hesitated. Only one bailiff had managed to get off a shot, and he had been swarmed over a moment later. Two boys were still kicking him. A minute into the assault, they were already in the aftermath. One kid was at the side door, the one through which they'd been brought in, frantically trying to fit a key into its lock. The ringleader, Malcolm Turner, carrying a pistol, first shouted at him then went over and slapped him. "Not yet!" he screamed. The one trying to escape left off, whimpering.

The snapping of locks and the clank of dropped chains rattled throughout the courtroom as the prisoners found keys and freed themselves. Two of the boys removed Malachi Reese's leg chains, over his feeble protests. That completed the turnabout. The prisoners were free. Six of them had guns—no, seven, one had Lynn's pistol too—but Malcolm Turner remained obviously in charge. His black eyes shone with fierce happiness. "All right!" he raised a cheer.

Then he turned to the palest person in the courtroom, having to lift his eyes. "Come down and join us, Judge," he said softly.

Judge Pressman hadn't moved. Nor did he do so when the kid ordered him. Pressman's mouth opened as if he were about to issue an instruction, but his eyes just gaped.

Then came a voice everyone knew: Malachi Reese's. He stood in the middle of the front of the courtroom and lifted his arms. He spoke calmingly to the spectators. "Folks, everyone get down, please. Down, out of harm's way, under the seats. That's right, thank you. Let me try to defuse the situation—"

Win Phillips stayed on his feet as if he might take charge, but seeing the armed and wild-eyed boys he sat down again.

"Who died and made you king?" one scraggly boy said to Reese. Reese turned toward him but kept his voice general.

"Boys, listen to me. This is a bad, bad idea. But it can still be all right as long as you don't hurt anybody else. Let's be calm now."

His voice had a soothing effect, even in the chaos. The fifteen or twenty spectators in the courtroom did as he asked. As they went down, first to their knees, then down on their faces under the pews, their last sight was of Malachi Reese standing benevolently, his face radiating confidence. This was the Reese everyone remembered. The savior of crisis. He seemed to glow slightly, as he always had in the lights.

Judge Pressman followed Reese's instructions, too, ducking down under his bench. With the spectators out of the way the boys took charge, ushering the bailiffs together and sitting them, whole and injured alike, against the wall opposite the now-empty jury box. As the juveniles did so, waving pistols and making threats, Malachi Reese talked to them gently, reaching out toward various of the boys.

The TV camera would show him silently pleading for the safety of the hostages.

Chris saw that line of sight between Reese and the camera. And he saw that when Reese turned his back on the camera his face changed. Reese's eyes grew fierce, his stare more pointed. He looked across the courtroom at Chris Sinclair and Reese's eyes smiled.

Chris knew then who had organized this takeover. Worse yet, Reese had let him see. Reese wanted Chris to know exactly what was happening, and who was in charge.

The only civilians still on their feet were Chris and Anne and, over by the jury box, Lynn Ransom. Lynn licked her lips and didn't say a word. Her eyes were going in all directions, but they never lit on Chris. Gently Chris pushed Anne down, telling her without words to join the anonymous mass of hostages on the floor. Anne went down, but kept her face upturned, watching.

One of the boys with a pistol sauntered toward Chris. "This one's the District Attorney. Let's take him. They'll deal over him."

Some of the steel returned to Malachi Reese's voice. "No." Reese had a handcuff dangling from his left wrist. He snapped the other cuff around the District Attorney's right wrist. Chris stared at the steel links. He and Reese were bound together. "You'll have to kill me too," Reese said.

He locked eyes with the young gunman, and after a moment the boy looked away first. Malcolm Turner had dropped out of the leadership role; he stood guarding the bailiffs, obviously awaiting orders. This other gangly teenager had stepped forward, ready to assume command. Chris searched the young prisoner's face for a resemblance to Reese, but couldn't see one.

"Her then," the kid said, pointing to Lynn. "No," Reese said again. The boys who were spread around the courtroom, half of them holding pistols at their sides or raised in the air, watched Reese closely. At the outside doors faces pressed against the glass. Probably a crowd filled the narrow hallway outside the back door of the courtroom, too. They were on the third floor of the Justice Center, a building full of armed sheriff's deputies. The juveniles had no idea what to do next. They looked at Malachi Reese, waiting for instructions.

Reese stood out from everyone. He wore the same orange coverall but had decades of seniority over the boys. His sharp beard made his eyes look brighter. His eyes gave orders. Chris stood right next to him, handcuffed to him, and saw every slight move of Reese's face. Out of the corner of his eye, Reese still smiled at the District Attorney. Chris scanned the courtroom for an ally or a way out and saw nothing. The spectators kept their heads resolutely down. The bailiffs were pushed facedown against the wall. If one's head twitched it drew a kick.

The would-be leader of the boys looked uncertainly at Reese. Chris felt Reese's slight head movement. The boy with the gun looked toward the bailiff's desk, under which Anne Greenwald lay, then back to Reese for confirmation. This time Chris looked directly at Reese when Reese nodded, only with his eyes.

Reese stood with his back to the courtroom audience and the glass-paneled doors. The television camera wouldn't have caught his signals. Its footage would show Reese negotiating with the captors, pleading for the hostages. Chris, standing beside him, understood clearly that Reese had planned all this orchestrated chaos and remained in charge of it, but no one would be able to corroborate Chris's belief. The bailiffs, judge, and spectators lay facedown against the wall or under the seats. They couldn't see Reese giving the orders.

"What do you want?" Chris said loudly, walking forward so that he dragged Reese a step or two. "All right, you've done it, now do you want to get out or do you just want to die here? The central police station's three blocks away, and the sheriff's office isn't much farther. You gonna stand around here 'til the place is surrounded by cops with rifles? Look through those doors if you think news of this isn't travelling."

The boys watched him. Two or three of them licked their lips. Their eyes darted, hitting blank walls in every direction. "Come on!" Chris shouted. "The only way out is the way you came in. Open the door, let's go. There's cars down in the garage. Take me, I'll go. Move!"

He started marching. At least half the boys moved with him. The one who'd tried the side door earlier jumped toward it again.

Chris's right arm jerked back behind him. He almost went down, staggering.

Malachi Reese stood like a statue. The boys who had been moving toward the side door shrank from his glare. The boys' leader said, "We need to make sure we got transport out of here. We need to impress 'em."

Reese nodded almost imperceptibly, approvingly. He did it again when two of the boys dragged Anne out from under the desk. Out of the mass of faceless hostages where Chris had tried to leave her. Anne's head snapped as they jerked her forward. But her eyes were alert. "Listen——" she began.

Once they had pulled her out into the open Anne became a witness. Chris remembered what Reese had done to the last witnesses against him. Anne stared at Reese. What did she know about him, what had his child told her? Reese must have wondered the same thing. It was a Reese-like masterstroke to have Anne here. Killing her offered him both revenge and safety.

One of the boys held her in front of the judge's bench, ten feet in front of Chris, who had juvenile guards beside and behind him and his right arm handcuffed to Reese. Chris couldn't move, and he knew what was about to happen. "Please, wait," he begged, but that only made Reese's smile broader.

"Pick up that phone," the head boy snapped to one of his unarmed minions, pointing at the bailiff's desk. "Just punch any buttons, they'll answer. Tell them we're serious. Unless that side door opens in two minutes and there's a van—no, two vans—waiting for us downstairs, we start killing people, starting with her."

He put his gun to Anne's head. Outside, the TV camera watched. Malachi Reese lifted his hands in supplication, dragging Chris's hand up with him. But Reese's eyes told the boy he was doing exactly the right thing.

"Don't you see this man's plan?" Anne said loudly. "You don't have a prayer of getting out of here, he knows that. He's using you. He's going to trade all of you for the chance to be a hero, to get out from under his own death sentence. He's got nothing to lose. He certainly doesn't give a damn about any of you. Why would he? Is he your daddy? Look at him."

Reese's head jerked minutely. Malcolm Turner came forward and put his gun's barrel across Anne's lips, like a bit in a horse's mouth. He leaned into her ear and said harshly, "One more word—"

"Put down your guns!" Reese said loudly to the juveniles, playing his role of peacemaker. "Stand behind me. I'll get one of these good people to unlock those front doors and I'll stand with you so no one shoots at you. I'll find you good lawyers, you can be safe from this."

"It was a lawyer got me here in the first place," one boy sneered, and others snickered.

Reese turned his back on the TV camera again, facing Anne and her captor, and leaned down toward Chris. Chris saw the ghost of Reese's old familiar smile. Anne saw it too. She knew. "Watch very closely," Reese said lovingly to Chris.

Standing, he looked at the young gunman. "I believe the time is up," Reese said softly.

The boy's eyes narrowed. He nodded. He tried to smile like Reese. It just made him look squinty. He cocked his pistol.

"Make him do it," Anne said quickly, gesturing at Reese. "Are you such a stooge you're going to commit his murder for him while a TV camera records it? Are you really as stupid as he thinks you are?"

"Shut up," the boy said. He clipped her lightly with the pistol barrel. Chris lunged forward but was held in place not only by Reese but by the two other young thugs behind him.

Finally, from her post beside the jury box, Lynn Ransom started forward. "Stop this. Get away, all of you."

Another kid with a pistol was standing in her path. He pushed Lynn back and almost earned himself a slap in the face. Lynn's hand came up and so did the boy's pistol.

"No!" said the commanding voice beside Chris.

Everyone stopped. Just with his eyes, Reese directed the boys' attention back to Anne. They took his silent orders. The two holding Anne forced her up straighter. Anne was talking, steadily and softly. Chris heard her say, no fear in her voice, "Look at me. Look at my eyes." But the boy with the gun was watching only Malachi Reese. He held the gun barrel firmly against Anne's temple.

Again, Reese's eyes nodded assent.

"Malachi!" Lynn said sharply, angrily. But she was as helpless as Chris. As anyone was against the angel of death.

As Reese had said, he wanted Chris Sinclair to live, to be publicly humiliated. But he also wanted gradually to strip Chris's life from him, as Chris had taken Reese's life. He knew what Anne meant to Chris. Reese wanted Chris to watch her die.

Reese spoke inside Chris's head. *I'll get her before you get me,* Chris heard him say.

Boys held Chris solidly in place on every side. Anne stood too far away, too closely guarded. Hopelessness unmanned Chris. *"Oohhh,"* he moaned, and slumped forward in a faint.

"Wait!" Reese snapped out.

The order, delivered in Reese's familiar, commanding tone, rang strangely: not "stop," but "wait." Out under the pews, a black minister raised his head curiously. He and Win Phillips exchanged matching frowns.

What Chris had prayed for turned out to be true. Murdering Anne and getting away with it wasn't enough for Reese. It had to happen before the District Attorney's eyes. "Drag him up," Reese ordered. Too loudly. Across the courtroom, the spectators-turned-hostages heard and tried to understand.

The boys around the courtroom were getting very restless. They cared more about all those stares on them through the glass-paneled doors than they did about the drama at the front of the courtroom. They wanted out; time tugged fiercely at them. The boys drifted closer to one another, jerking their chins up, asking questions with their eyes. "Man, let's——" one of them began.

Up at the front, the fallen Chris lay as dead weight under the hands of his captors. The two boys tugged at him ineffectually, each awkwardly trying to lift the District Attorney with only one hand. One boy stuck his pistol in his pocket and reached with both hands for Chris's free left arm. The other boy leaned down for a better grip.

Suddenly Chris came up backwards, fast. The back of his head hit the reaching boy in the nose. The boy screamed and dropped his gun, grabbing for his gushing nose. Instead of trying to pick up the gun, Chris slammed his elbow back into the other kid's stomach. The boy oofed and bent over. His gun clattered from his pocket.

But Malachi Reese grabbed the gun first. He pointed it at the kids holding Anne and said loudly, "Let her go." But his face said something different. Silently he mouthed *Now.* His expression fiercely ordered them on. The one boy still had his gun pressed to Anne's head. His finger tightened on the trigger.

Several things happened at once. Chris screamed and leaped, pulling Reese with him, but coming up far short of Anne and her captors. This struggle, though, served as the last straw for the most frightened of the conspirators, the young, unarmed boy who'd hovered near the side door of the courtroom, the door that led to the holding cells and the elevator out. The boy screamed, "Let's get out of here!" and leaped for the door. This time he turned the key in the lock. As he scrabbled at the handle, the door came open forcefully.

And Lynn Ransom launched herself, over the witness stand, one foot pushing off the judge's bench, through the air like a high hurdler, aimed at Anne and her captor.

There were cries and shouts and thuds and a gunshot that rang over it all. Chris screamed louder than anyone as he struggled to his feet. In the next instant his vision blurred out of focus, as if he had plunged back into that shadow world he had once entered in this courtroom. But it wasn't a vision that obscured his sight, it was water. The side door had slammed open, knocking the scared kid back, and three bailiffs entered with a firehose that they trained indiscriminately across the courtroom, knocking everyone back or down. The front doors of the courtroom also burst open and a second powerful stream of water blasted from that direction. Wet bodies slithered and slipped everywhere. The uninjured captured bailiffs came off the wall, grabbing at kids and scrambling for guns.

Chris tried to jump, slipped, fell, then felt himself dragged forward. He skidded to a stop face-to-face with Malachi Reese.

Reese's eyes blazed. The earthwork circles that had once contained the fury in his black pupils were crumbled away to nothing. He glowed with insanity. "I'm trying to save your life!" Reese screamed, putting his arm around Chris's neck.

Reese stuck to his pose, just as he had planned. He'd never intended to escape, only to create a crisis, then emerge as its hero— though there would be a few tragic losses such as Dr. Anne Greenwald. But the situation would provide the final step in the rehabilitating of Reese's public image: saving the life of the man who had killed him.

But Reese still had unfinished business. His arm fast around Chris's neck, Reese appeared to be trying to pull the D.A. to safety. But Reese's eyes also searched through the melee, until he saw Anne's pale face amid the knot of dripping people. It wasn't just that Reese insisted on his vengeance. Anne had seen too much. She had seen him giving orders to the wayward boys. He couldn't let her live. Reese took aim with the pistol he still held, under the cover of bodies and water.

But he'd had to release his choke hold on Chris. Chris pushed Reese's arm aside. The pistol cracked and someone moaned. Then Chris again stood face-to-face with Reese, their wrists locked together. Reese grinned at him. Chris couldn't take him by surprise. Reese could read Chris's mind as well as Chris could his, and Reese acted more instinctively. Chris tried to butt him, but Reese easily shrugged that aside. As Chris drew back Reese brought his knee up.

Chris spun aside to avoid being kneed and then kept spinning. His arms outflung, he whirled like Zorba the Greek. Centrifugal force caught his mismatched twin. Reese spun in the opposite direction, his hand flung outward too. Chris pulled hard with his handcuffed arm and kept turning, until he and Reese were spinning across the courtroom like children holding hands on a playground. Either would have slipped and fallen except for the force that gripped them both, twirling.

The courtroom spun around them. Water still gushed. Some spectators stayed under the pews, but not all were that wise. Most of the throng were on the floor, and anyone who jumped or staggered up gained the immediate attention of the better-organized bailiffs. The boys in orange coveralls made good targets. Some still had guns, but few got the chance to fire.

Chris and Reese's momentum only stopped when Reese slammed into one of the counsel tables. Chris leaped atop him.

A small army of bailiffs poured through every door of the courtroom. They mopped up, almost literally, stepping on hands that held guns, smashing through strugglers, knocking everyone in their path to the floor. They acted on a lesser version of the grand philosophy of war, kill 'em all and let God sort them out.

When the deputies reached Malachi Reese and pulled him roughly away from the District Attorney, they almost jerked Chris's arm out of its socket.

"Thank God I was able to save so many lives," Reese gasped out before he was taken away. Microphones picked up the words. Microphones weren't needed to hear the District Attorney screaming, "Get it off me, get off, unlock it, where's the damned key?" When a deputy finally got the handcuff unlocked Chris whirled and ran back into the courtroom. Most of the boys were gone, jammed back into the holdover cells. The spectators were struggling to their feet. Stretchers moved through the drenched, overturned courtroom. Chris pushed and leaped his way to the front, calling her name.

Faintly, he heard her answer. Anne was close to where he had left her, up by the judge's bench. She was kneeling, head bent. Choking, trying to breathe?

"Here," she called a little more strongly, reaching one hand back for Chris. She turned just for a moment, and he saw her face streaked with blood. He grabbed her hand and tried to pull her to him, but Anne resisted.

He saw that she was kneeling over one of the lost boys. Anne had pulled his orange coverall down over his shoulders so she could reach his chest wound. She held the improvised bandage of her blouse on the wound, pressing down hard to stop the bleeding. The boy gasped, sucking in breaths with a tortured rattle. Water made his face shiny. He looked twelve years old. Lynn Ransom knelt at his head. "Hold on," she urged him softly. "Hold on. She's a doctor."

Two paramedics arrived with a stretcher. "Just hold it in place, ma'am. Right, that's right. Let me—" The emergency technician put his hand next to Anne's, sliding hers out of the way. Blood surged around the corner of the bandage for an instant, until the paramedic slapped a larger bandage over the whole thing.

Chris put his jacket around Anne's shoulders. She stood with her hand out, looking at Chris with a lost expression. Her hand was covered with the boy's blood. Then she put her arm around Chris's neck and hugged him so hard it seemed they would merge. They stood soaked in blood and water and the miraculous feeling of drawing breath.

Chris closed his eyes for a long thankful moment. When he opened them he was looking into the face of Lynn Ransom.

Two days later Winston Phillips, city councilman, stood in a place unfamiliar to him, the District Attorney's private office, and said, slowly but distinctly, "It may be that I owe you an apology."

For once Chris didn't know what to say. The sight and sound of Win Phillips standing there stiff with the effort not to be stiff struck him so oddly. Phillips hadn't offered his hand, but he didn't have his arms folded in his characteristic judgmental stance, either.

The councilman had already done better than apologize. The day before he had held a press conference to say what he had seen in the courtroom. "I saw Malachi Reese directing that operation, as surely as if he were issuing orders through a bullhorn," that day's *Express* quoted him as saying.

Anne had given a much more detailed interview convincingly describing the way she'd seen Reese order her murder. Her account might have been dismissed if it hadn't been corroborated by several of the spectators, foremost among them the man who now stood in Chris's office.

"I'd like to see the evidence you have against Malachi," Phillips went on. "All of it, not just what you presented in court."

"A lot of it's just speculation."

"You're lucky to have that much, with Malachi." Phillips realized this was the first time he'd even implied criticism of Reese. He and Chris gave each other a long look.

"I appreciate that. I'll bring what I've got to your office," Chris promised. "Now, I'm sorry, but there's someone else I have to see."

"Somebody important?" Phillips said, hostility flaring again.

"Very."

They went side by side to the outer office, where Chris asked Irma Garcia, "Is Lynn in her office?"

As Irma nodded, Phillips turned to Chris. "Lynn Ransom?" His manner thawed. "Listen, if she's going to need a job, tell her— Ask her to come see me, will you?"

"Thank you," Chris said sincerely. "I'll say that for her, because I don't think you'll hear it from Lynn."

And then Win Phillips offered Chris another first-time sight: he grinned. He had a winning smile, completely open and easy.

"I know the type," he said.

Chris found Lynn in her small office. She had begun packing, but half-filling two boxes had exhausted her energy. She stood staring out her narrow slit of a window. Chris watched her from the doorway, aware that she knew he was there.

"Got a dollar?" he asked.

Lynn looked at him strangely. Chris glanced at her purse lying on the desk. Lynn opened it and held up a dollar, which Chris plucked from her fingers. "You just hired me," he said. "Now whatever you say to me is a privileged communication.

"Probably a conflict of interest there."

"We'll let somebody else worry about that. Anyway, my only advice is not to say anything. There'll be a special prosecutor appointed to investigate what happened in the courtroom. Don't tell him anything. Or me, or anybody else. Just ride it out."

Lynn watched him closely, her face impossible to read. Late afternoon sun slanted through her narrow window on this day after the battle in the courtroom.

"It was your gun that started it all, Lynn. But looking at it as a prosecutor, it'd be hard to prove anything in the way of intent. Malachi Reese pushed you toward those boys. Don't say anything else. That won't be enough even to indict you—unless you give them ammunition by talking."

"Funny, you don't sound like a prosecutor." When Chris didn't answer Lynn asked, "How's Anne?"

"She's okay. She'll be all right." Chris glanced at the phone, wondering exactly where Anne was. "You ever been shot at? Leaves you weird for a long time afterwards. You get these adrenaline rushes and nowhere for them to go."

"And equally low lows," Lynn said knowingly.

Lynn hadn't spoken to anyone from the press. It would have been nice if she had confirmed Anne's account, but Chris would never ask her for that. Lynn was already torn badly enough without Chris's pressuring her to testify against Malachi Reese.

"There's no reason for anybody to think you helped plan it," Chris said earnestly. "That kid Malcolm knew you carried a gun. You pulled it on his friends that day in the skinhead house." He paused. "So of course Malachi would have known it too."

Lynn looked up quickly, her eyes wet. "Chris—"

"Don't say it!" Chris stepped close to her and said more quietly, "You don't have to anyway, Lynn. I know. I'd be willing to bet you weren't trying to help him escape. It was just Malachi's chance at redemption. Talk the kid out of the gun, look heroic, maybe get a commutation of his sentence. That's probably what he told you."

"He never meant—"

"Listen to your lawyer," Chris said sharply. His hands were close to Lynn's but not quite touching. "Don't talk. Don't try to justify anything. Don't give them motive. For God's sake don't let on to anybody that Malachi Reese is your father."

The words reverberated, as if they had sounded through the whole building. But only Chris and Lynn had heard. Lynn closed her eyes. She drew away again. "Did Anne tell you?"

Chris almost laughed. "You know better than that. She wouldn't give you away. It just kind of dawned on me gradually. Particularly after the way you said his name in the courtroom. 'Malachi!' You sounded furious at him personally. He was breaking a promise to you. But still—"

"What was I supposed to do?" Lynn asked with a trace of her old fierceness. "Leave him on Death Row if I had a chance to do something about it?"

Chris nodded. "I know you weren't the one carrying out his orders."

"How do you know that?"

"Because I know—I *know*—" he emphasized; Lynn stared at him. "I know you didn't have anything to do with Mike Martinez's murder. I know that."

Lynn's eyes glistened. Anguish forced its way up her throat, out her eyes. "He was my friend, Chris. He was. I had no idea. Maybe it was my fault, though. Killing El Rojo was a message to me: don't get too close to anyone on the other side."

Chris put his arms around her. They still had Mike as a connection. He and Lynn would always have that between them.

He drew back and tried to sound businesslike, pulling a paper from his pocket. "By the way, this letter of resignation of yours, somehow it never reached me." He put the letter down on the desk and leaned toward her again. He spoke softly and urgently. "Don't even take a leave of absence, Lynn. Just go on with your job. I don't know who they'll appoint as a special prosecutor. I certainly won't be able to influence that investigation. But you just work right through it, okay, like nothing happened. I need you here. All right?"

"You sound like such a conspirator." Lynn smiled tightly. "Is this a Vito Corleone thing?"

Chris knew what she meant. The Godfather had advised his son to keep his friends close but his enemies closer.

"I am your friend, Lynn. At least I want to be."

The city still seemed to be aswirl, not with activity but with speculation, conversation. A few people who would always be convinced of Malachi Reese's innocence thought him the hero of the courtroom crisis. But the number of Reese's supporters dwindled rapidly, as did their certainty.

The tide of the media had turned. The columnist Miles McKinley wrote, "Bad things do seem to keep happening in Malachi Reese's vicinity." That was the tone: speculative, confused. Reese quickly began losing his official support. No one planned trips to Death Row to interview him again. His voice would shrink to the sound of absence. Soon he would be just another forgotten inmate, the worst fate Malachi Reese could suffer.

But these changes left Chris with nothing to do. After he returned to his own office from Lynn's he looked around and couldn't think of any good reason to be there. He called Anne's office but didn't catch her in, of course. So he drove home slowly, taking the long way down Broadway instead of the expressway, passing the expanse of Brackenridge Park, drawing contentment from one of those perfect spring days that San Antonio regularly produces. The bright but still gentle sunlight picked out new buds on young spindly trees. At his condo complex Chris walked around. The water in the pool had grown cloudy from lack of tending, but he caught the last of that air that had a crystalline quality that made a viewer think not only that he could see for miles but could see things in the air that hadn't been there a day before.

The sun sat just above the horizon when he began trying to call Anne again and finally got her on her cellular phone in her car. "Where are you headed?"

"Home." Anne sounded weary. "Maybe later a pizza. That's about all I'm up for."

Chris said, "Well, you can relax your guard, at least. Lynn confessed."

A long silence made him think he'd lost the connection, then Anne said cautiously, "I strongly doubt Lynn 'confessed' to anything. And other than that I don't know what you're talking about."

No, he hadn't expected Anne to fall for that. But her pause had told him he was right. "It was that card that threw me off," Chris said, as if she'd agreed. " 'My beloved son.' I guess they don't make any that mention a daughter."

"I tried to tell you," Anne said quietly, realizing he did know the truth.

"I understand that now. When I asked if you'd been the doctor for Reese's son you said no, even though I knew you had treated his child."

"God, Chris, I wanted to tell you. Because you didn't know the stakes. During the Lee Griggs trial, you were duelling with Reese in more ways than you knew. He had hammered into Lynn that you were the enemy, you were evil. But when she worked with you she didn't see that. You started winning her over."

Chris stared out his big patio doors where the light was dying.

"That's why she tried to give me a clue," he said. It had been after Lynn's visit to his office that he had found the photograph o Reese in the car that had gotten El Rojo murdered.

Chris and Paul Benavides had talked it over and decided they couldn't figure out how Lynn had planted the idea that sh should be Chris's second chair in that trial. It had just seemed obvious to both of them. Lynn must also have given Judge Pressman the idea of filling his jury box with juvenile offenders wher he had Reese brought into court, but that would be impossibl to trace to her too. By this time Pressman had embraced the ide as his own. Lynn had her father's gift for manipulation.

"Can we not talk about it anymore?" Chris asked the phone "It seems like I've been sitting inside buildings speculating for about a decade. You know what a beautiful day we missed today In my neighborhood there are so many oak trees, live oak trees that lose their leaves in the spring. On windy days the leaves are just falling like snow, so it looks like fall again. It looks like Fred-ericksburg, and Fredericksburg makes me think of you. Then the sun shines, and it looks like summer, and that makes me think how your hair lightens a little in the summer and how your skin gets just a little color so your eyes look greener. I wonder how your eyes would look with the Gulf water behind them. They're almost the same color, except that your eyes are so much brighter, they look like when the sun sparkles on the waves. And I picture your arms and your legs in the water, moving, and me beside you. Floating together or just lying on the sand. Thinking about turning toward you and just as I do I know you're turning too. . . . You know it's been almost a year now that we've known each other and we haven't been to the beach together? I have to just picture it. Picture you . . ."

He paused. "You're not keeping up your end of the conversation," Chris said.

When her voice came it had changed. She no longer sounded tired. "Some things shouldn't be said over a cellular phone," she said. He could hear her sudden urgency.

"Like what?" Chris said, but the phone had gone dead in his hands. Slowly he went about changing clothes, wondering when he would hear from her. Barely ten minutes later his door burst open and Anne said, "My God, how you can talk. You were destined to be a lawyer!"

She was smiling. She no longer sounded weary at all.

"So what couldn't you say on the phone?" Chris asked, but by that time she was holding onto him. Chris held on too. This was what couldn't be said on the phone: holding each other, touching, the miracle that they were both still alive, lips meeting, laughing very seriously, arms and legs entwining.

Eventually, they did get around to saying it.